It's a rare case. It's personal. For the first time in her career, Detective Eva Naslund knows the victim….

Naslund felt sure Thom was dead. Her friend wouldn't simply walk out of the bay, laughing off the northwesterly…

She eyed the skiff again. If the blood was human, they'd need a full forensic team.

World-renowned painter Thom Tyler is murdered in Georgian Bay, Canada. The consensus is that Tyler had no enemies. Why would anyone murder him?

Detective Sergeant Eva Naslund goes to work with a homicide team from OPP Central. They find no useful blood, print, or DNA evidence. They turn to financial forensics and criminal psychology. Tyler's paintings are worth millions, yet he's deeply in debt to banks and his art agent. Just as the investigation opens a new lead, courtesy of Tyler's friend, J.J. MacKenzie, MacKenzie is murdered. The team is back to ground zero—with two murders to solve.

KUDOS for *Bay of Blood*

"Potter has written the quintessential Canadian murder mystery with a literary flourish and all the elements of a riveting read." ~ Lesley Choyce, author of *The Republic of Nothing, Sea of Tranquility, The Book of Michael,* among others

"There are many clever details in Potter's Bay of Blood with close parallels to Tom Thomson's life and death (1917). However, Potter takes his readers on a fascinating 21st-century chase, with bells and whistles never dreamt of one hundred years ago: cell phones, female detectives, Russian operatives, and shady Toronto art dealers." ~ Sherrill Grace, University Killam Professor Emerita, University of British Columbia, author of *Landscapes of War and Memory* and *Inventing Tom Thomson*

"A genuine page-turner! Detective Eva Naslund grapples with few clues and many suspects, all of whom seem guilty of the murder of her friend, an internationally famous painter. Page after page, Potter reveals captivating character twists and Naslund's creative forensic skills." ~ Bertrum MacDonald, Information Management Professor, Dalhousie University

"This elegant, insightful murder mystery is a credit to its genre. The mystery unfolds with an homage to the magnificent landscapes that inspired Canada's legendary Group of Seven. Clearly the work of a seasoned writer, this expertly-crafted novel is the first to be published from journalist and foreign news correspondent A.M. Potter. Fortunately, he has more up his sleeve." ~ Suzanne Barcza. Litbrowser.com, Author of *Likely Stories*

"A modern detective story set in the timelessness of a small town. Layered like paint, the details and characters create a complex picture. This candid vista of human nature is laid bare against the Canadian landscape." ~ S.M. Collins. Author of *To Be Human Again*

"In Eva Naslund, we discover a sleuth who is sympathetic, vulnerable, and smart. Bay of Blood is an exciting new entry in the world of detective fiction. I look forward to volume two." ~ Ken Haigh. Author of *Under The Holy Lake*

"*Bay of Blood* is a whodunit with soul. Detective Eva Naslund is a gem. She's both logical and intuitive, both tough and approachable." ~ Patrick Tilley, retired RCMP Detective.

"Balancing captivating descriptions of a close-knit, waterside community full of eccentric characters with blow-by-blow scenes of violence, grief and careful police work, Potter keeps us in the story right to the end with his excellent writing and research skills. If you love feeling the danger of murder lurking behind every page, *Bay of Blood* will keep you reading well into the night." ~ James White. Author of *Cisco*

"A highly recommended, satisfying read. Each new deviation in this multiple-murder story gradually reveals the character of the original victim, leading to a clever, well-rounded and totally plausible solution. I look forward to more revelations in the future." ~ Jane Bwye. Author of *Breath of Africa*

Bay of Blood

A. M. Potter

A Black Opal Books Publication

GENRE: MYSTERY-DETECTIVE/WOMEN SLEUTHS

This is a work of fiction. Names, places, characters and incidents are either the product of the author's imagination or are used fictitiously, and any resemblance to any actual persons, living or dead, businesses, organizations, events or locales is entirely coincidental. All trademarks, service marks, registered trademarks, and registered service marks are the property of their respective owners and are used herein for identification purposes only. The publisher does not have any control over or assume any responsibility for author or third-party websites or their contents.

DEDICATION

To Stan & Em. They gave me the tools.

Ars longa, vita brevis.
Art is long, life is short.

Chapter 1

Colpoys Bay, Georgian Bay, Ontario, July 8th:

Predawn stars salted the sky. Thom Tyler pushed his skiff off the dock, paddled hard to point her nose into the wind, and immediately raised the sail. Off he tore, skimming across the water toward White Cloud Island.

To the east, the sky shed its blackness. A pale red flush crept across the bay. He settled in the cockpit. A few moments later, his neck-hairs bristled. He sensed hostile eyes burning into his head. Shifting nonchalantly, he leaned portside to inspect the shore. All quiet. Just the inky outline of Mallory Beach. Still, he was sure someone was there.

A car engine started. Very strange, he thought. There were never any cars about at this hour. He saw no lights. The slowly revving engine headed north. Was someone tracking him?

Forget it, he told himself and faced forward.

He turned his mind to sailing, easing out the mainsheet to spill some speed. Still, he flew over the water. He could smell the north: the clean sharpness of boreal forests. However, in the back of his mind, he felt uneasy. He sensed something out there waiting for him. His neck twitched. The strange car fueled his anxiety. Something was waiting for him.

Chapter 2

Wiarton, Bruce Peninsula. Ontario Provincial Police (OPP) Station, July 8th:

Got a little run for you, Naslund."

Detective Sergeant Eva Naslund looked up to see the detachment chief standing at her desk. Ted Bickell's pants were perfectly pressed. The creases looked like they could slice someone's throat.

"A boat just washed up near Cape Commodore," Bickell said. "Caller reported blood. Lots of it." He paused. "But I'm sure you can handle it."

Naslund nodded. Fair point. She'd had nothing but B&Es for the past two months.

Bickell handed her a slip of paper. *Donnie Rathbone. HW 1, 100220.*

"Not an emergency," he said. "No speeding."

She shrugged. On a day like today, she'd drive anywhere in the Bruce, fast or slow, the farther from Staff Sergeant Bickell, the better. As she drove east, the morning sun tinted Colpoys Bay a deep golden red. The limestone cliffs above Mallory Beach not only reflected the sun, they shimmered like suns themselves. A convoy of high white clouds raced across the sky.

Fifteen minutes later, she pulled off Highway One at a weathered blue bungalow with an unobstructed view of Georgian Bay. A run-down barn flanked the house. Across the highway, parched-looking Christmas trees stretched inland as far as she could see. It'd been a hot, dry summer. As she stepped out of her unmarked car, the wind whipped her pants around her legs. Georgian Bay was running high, churned by a powerful northwesterly. The Georgian was usually restless. It was essentially an inland sea. On calm days there was often a sea roll, even if only long and slow. Today there was a wave train. Line after line of breakers roared ashore.

She knocked on the front door. The man who answered was tall and fit, bearded, about fifty years old.

"Donnie Rathbone?" she asked.

The man nodded.

"Detective Sergeant Naslund, OPP."

"Detective Sergeant, eh? Sent out a top dog, did they?"

She chuckled and covertly pressed the recording button on her duty phone. "No, sir. They had no choice. I'm the only detective in Wiarton."

"Come on in then. Place is a bit of a mess. Wife's away."

"When the cat's away," Naslund said.

Rathbone grinned and led her to the kitchen. Passing the stove, she noticed a pan of congealed bacon. It was almost full. He pointed out the window. "There it is."

She followed his finger and saw a boat seemingly hauled up on the shore. "When did you spot her?"

"About seven. I got up a bit late, at six, went right to the barn, fed my pigs, and came back for breakfast. I noticed it then. So I walked down." Rathbone paused. "That's when I saw the blood. A helluva lot of blood. I came right back and called nine-one-one."

"Did you touch the boat?"

"No."

"Did you touch anything aboard it?"

"No. I watch them CSI programs, you know."

"All right. So, you noticed the boat about seven?"

"Right. Like I said, I was running late. Got up and went straight to my pigs."

Rathbone sounded a bit nervous. In any case, the boat could have been there well before 0700 hours. "Did you happen to look out to your shore last night?"

"Nothing there last night, not when I went to bed. At ten-thirty that was."

"Did you see or hear anyone on your property this morning?"

"No."

"Notice anyone in the bay? Boats? Swimmers?"

"Didn't see any."

"Did you see anything strange on the highway?"

"No."

"No one walking or running? No unusual vehicles?"

"No."

"Thank you."

ᙉᙎᙉᙎ

Given the apparently large amount of blood, Naslund drew a hooded clean-suit from her trunk and stepped into it. Instantly she felt constricted, yet twice as big. She pulled on shoe covers and gloves and walked carefully down the path to the shore, examining the ground. One set of boot prints going, one coming back. Rathbone, if the man was telling the truth. She'd impound his boots on the way out.

As she reached the fine-graveled shore, she eyed the boat. A skiff, about six meters long. The bow faced southeast. The stern was still in the water, but the boat wasn't moving. She'd settled into the gravel, as if she'd been there for days. Naslund figured the wind had driven her hard into shore. The mast and boom were intact, the sail torn to shreds. The hull was wooden, dove-gray with white trim.

That dove-gray hull. It looked like her friend Thom Tyler's skiff. She stepped to the side and read the boat's name: *West Wind.* Christ, it *was* Thom's skiff. Had he been forced to abandon ship?

Digging inside her clean-suit, she fished out her duty phone and called Thom's cottage. His other half answered. "Morning, Carrie. Eva here. Is Thom there?"

"No. He's out fishing."

"When did he leave?"

"About five."

Naslund glanced at the time—0738. "Did he go out alone?"

"As far as I know. I was in bed when he left. Anything wrong?"

Naslund ducked the question. "Are you sure he went out this morning?"

"Yes."

"Okay. Call me when he gets home." Naslund gave Carrie her OPP cell number, telling herself Thom would show. He'd abandoned ship and swam to shore, or a passing boat took him aboard.

Knowing that Thom always wore a blue life vest, Naslund pulled a pair of binoculars from her CS kitbag. Focusing the binoculars, she turned her head slowly, scanning the bay in sweeps.

No sign of a blue life vest, no floating bodies.

Follow the wind, she told herself. The northwesterly will drive anyone southeast. She stepped to the edge of the bay and scanned again and again.

Nothing.

Let it ride, she thought. Thom would show. He was the strongest swimmer she knew.

She walked up to the skiff and immediately saw a lot of blood, most of it inside the hull. She knew there'd been even more. The wave train would have washed some away. She paced the starboard side. At midship, two large splatter patterns spread from the gunwale down to the bilge, both about half-a-meter in width and a meter in length. She leaned closer. The main pattern presented wide-angle spray consistent with blows from a blunt force weapon. A lead pipe, she thought, maybe a crowbar. The other pattern resembled the spurting caused by a stab wound. Near them were two lines of fat circular drops, indicating blood falling at a fast rate, exiting large wounds. From the vector of the lines, she knew the source fell forward, toward the gunwale. Or was pushed.

She started down the port side. Halfway along it, she found the centerboard keel sticking out from the hull, almost completely detached, like a broken limb. No surprise. The skiff had grounded. She kept walking, finding no blood on the port side and none on the mast, sail, or mainsheet. However, there was blood on the starboard side of the boom. Had it hit Thom and knocked him overboard? Maybe. She re-evaluated the scene. No sharp protrusions on the boom. Two splatter patterns. If the boom had hit Thom, there would likely only be one—consistent with blunt force blood, not spurting blood. She filed the thought away.

Returning to the stains, she bent down on one knee. Her clean-suit felt even more constricting. She sniffed. The stains didn't smell fishy or gamey. She looked for scales or animal hair. Nothing. She stood and surveyed the blood again. It couldn't be from a small animal, like a dog or cat—there was too much of it. Could be from a deer, she reasoned, or a cow. Or a pig. Rathbone? Could be. But there were no other signs of animals present. The blood was likely human.

Seeing no signs of activity near the skiff—no prints or scuffs, no evidence of a struggle—she assumed the shore wasn't a crime scene. But the blood splatter suggested the skiff was. She had a blood kit in her car, but decided to call the white coats. Pulling out her duty phone, she called Central.

"Serology. Gerard LaFlamme."

Hot Doc, she thought, not that LaFlamme appreciated the nickname. He'd filed a complaint against two female detectives. They'd admitted wrongdoing then relabeled him THD, Très Hot Doc. "Morning, LaFlamme. Detective Naslund, Bruce Peninsula."

"Naslund, what gives?"

"Got some blood on a wooden boat. Suspicion of assault. I'd run it myself but I need a foolproof ID."

"Okay. Where are you?"

She gave him the location and hung up. Starting at the bow, she paced twenty steps inland, away from the skiff. Head down, eyes focused on the ground, she searched a grid about 200 meters square. No boot or foot indentations in the loose gravel, no prints on harder ground, no wheel or tire tracks leading away from the skiff. No butts, bottles, or cans. No wrappers. Nothing.

She walked back to the skiff and deliberately paced the starboard side from the waterline to the bow, this time with a magnifying glass. No hairs or fibers. Four partial fingerprints, wet and faint. Difficult to lift. Best left to a white coat. She paced down the port side to the waterline, but found nothing. Yet she sensed something was wrong.

She stood still and surveyed the whole boat, her eyes finally returning to the bow. That was it. No anchor rode-line tied to the bow. And no anchor. Why would

Thom go out without an anchor? He'd just added a new rode-line. She'd watched him do it at the marina three mornings ago...

&oso

"Good afternoon," Naslund had said, as she always did first thing in the morning. She gauged a person's mood by how they responded.

"Good evening," Thom replied.

Naslund grinned. As usual, Thom liked to be kidded. He wore old shorts and a sleeveless T-shirt. His tanned arms had the appearance of weathered leather. With his outdoorsman's face and long black hair, he looked like a Great Lakes voyageur. He moored his bigger sailboat at the marina, but was working on the skiff from his cottage boathouse.

She surveyed the skiff, a Mackinaw whose boom was raised so that a six-footer could easily slide under it.

"Want a muffin?" he asked and pointed to a paper bag. "Go on, have one. You need to eat more."

She did, but didn't want to show it. Since she'd split up with her husband Pete, she wasn't eating much. Although life had returned to normal, her appetite hadn't.

"You're always on the go," Thom said.

"Me?" she deadpanned.

"Yep, you." He chuckled. "Curiosity killed the cop."

"But luck brought her back." She reached for a muffin. As she ate it, Thom tied a new anchor rode to the bow with a solid knot, a tight bowline.

&oso

Now, eying the scene, Naslund took two steps back and dropped to her haunches. The clean-suit protested, slowing her movement. From hip-level, she studied the skiff. Something about it told her that Thom was dead. In her sixteen years on the force, she'd seen plenty of dead bodies. They'd all seemed vacant, abandoned by life. The skiff looked like them. Abandoned forever.

Naslund grimaced. Hoping for the best, she called in a Search & Rescue and then notified Bickell by radiophone. Although she normally used her duty cell, old-boy Bickell preferred radio-comm. He'd order his daily fish & chips by radio if he could. Afterward, she stood and faced the bay, trying to muster her optimism. Maybe they'd find Thom alive. Maybe he'd show up.

Turning her back to the wind, she called Carrie, who answered immediately.

"Eva here. I found Thom's boat, but not him. I called the Coast Guard for a search."

"What? A search? Why?"

"No need to worry. Thom probably swam into shore. He'll show up soon." Naslund stopped. She didn't feel like lying. Besides, Carrie had one of the sharpest minds she knew.

"Then why search for him?"

She had no good answer. She held back the information about the blood. "His skiff came ashore near Cape Commodore. Now we need to find him."

"Find him then. Find him!"

"We will."

"I want to help. Where are you?"

"You can't come here." Naslund knew the Coast Guard would call in the OPP Marine Unit from Wiarton. "Phone the station," she told her. "They'll be organizing search teams."

"Okay." Carrie hung up.

Naslund sighed. As much as she wanted to, she couldn't join the search. She had an investigation to run.

Worse still, she felt sure Thom was dead. Her friend wouldn't simply walk out of the bay, laughing off the northwesterly.

She inhaled deeply, held her breath for three seconds, exhaled slowly, and repeated the cycle five times—a trick she'd learned from Pete, a sports-therapist. It stilled her mind.

She eyed the skiff again. If the blood was human, they'd need a full forensic team. In the meantime, she needed one constable to secure the site and another to canvass the neighborhood to the east. After they arrived she'd revisit Rathbone then take the west. She glanced up at Rathbone's kitchen window. The man was watching her. She called the station. The dispatcher answered.

Naslund identified herself and gave the address. "Got a CS. Send two PCs."

Chapter 3

Naslund poured a coffee, slid her porch door open, and walked out into a humid morning with a sagging sky. The sun hadn't appeared. Colpoys Bay lay flat and sullen, darkened by leaden clouds. LaFlamme had identified the blood on Tyler's boat. It was human, Type O+, the same as Tyler's. When his DNA was available, the lab would determine if the blood was a match. Four white coats—a team lead, a CS video-photographer, and two forensic scientists—had arrived at the scene yesterday afternoon. They'd set up a MU, a mobile unit, next to Rathbone's barn.

Naslund dropped into a Muskoka chair and eyed the bay. Almost twenty-four hours had passed since she'd called in the Coast Guard. Hundreds of people had joined the search. From what she'd heard, Carrie had been tireless; she hadn't stopped all day. A PC had sent her home at 0400. No one had found any sign of Thom, or of his body.

Yesterday, Naslund had interviewed Rathbone again and cleared him of any suspicion.

The farmer had a "double" alibi. He hadn't been in bed with one supposed girlfriend; he'd been in bed with two. The two hookers independently corroborated his story.

Naslund had also interviewed dozens of residents along Highway One. No one had seen or heard anything. Unlike in Toronto, there were no CCTV or surveillance cameras near Commodore. She was starting her investigation blind and deaf. She sipped her coffee and swallowed hard. She'd been working the case in her mind all night. Due to the powerful northwesterly, there was only one direction a body could have traveled. Southeast toward a shore that had been searched and re-searched. Three times. She hated to admit it, but it seemed that the time had almost come. The time to switch to a recovery mission. Thom Tyler was likely at the bottom of the bay.

Naslund was familiar with recovery missions. A dead body normally sank to the bottom unless stopped by an obstruction like a net. If there were no currents, it settled close to where it went under. It was usually found within a radius equal to the depth of the water. In her view, Thom had probably been concentrating on his fishing, which made him susceptible to being knocked overboard by the boom or, as appeared likely, assaulted.

Assuming Thom reached his usual fishing spot, off White Cloud Island, she pulled up the local marine chart on her phone and drew a mental line from the northeast corner of White Cloud to the place where Thom's skiff grounded. The depth along the line ranged from a maximum of seventy-two meters to three meters close to shore. Thom's body likely lay anywhere from three to seventy-two meters on each side of the line.

She noted the geographic co-ords of Thom's fishing spot and the skiff's grounding spot. The distance between the two co-ords was 5.2 kilometers. She fed three numbers into her phone's calculator: 5.2 * .072 * 2. Result: .7488, about .75 square-kilometers. Well, she thought, a large search area, but a lot smaller than the mouth of Colpoys Bay extending into Georgian Bay proper, over twenty square-kilometers. The OPP handled recovery missions, not the Coast Guard. She rechecked the co-ords and called the chief of the Underwater Search and Recovery Unit.

"Morning, Superintendent Coulson. Detective Sergeant Naslund, Bruce Peninsula."

"Yes, Sergeant?"

"I'm calling about the Thom Tyler search. I don't mean to interfere, but I have a thought."

"Go ahead."

"I suspect Mr. Tyler is at the bottom of Georgian Bay."

There was a pause. "Quite possibly."

"If the mission gets turned over to you, I might be able to save you some time. I know where the skiff likely drifted from and where it ended." She supplied the geographic co-ords. "The maximum depth between the two co-ords is seventy-two meters. I think the body will likely be closer to the first co-ord, near the island." Enough said. Coulson's team could do the math.

"Might be," Coulson replied. "In any case, thank you. I'll keep you in the loop."

"Thank you, Superintendent."

Naslund downed her coffee, went inside, and got dressed: dark green slacks and blue-and-green short-sleeve shirt. Eight years ago, as an undercover narc in Toronto, she'd worn only black. Standing in front of the bathroom mirror, she brushed her auburn hair off her forehead. Two unruly locks fell back down. On the way out the door, she grabbed a stale Danish and left for Rathbone's property.

As she headed up Highway One, the sky darkened. Passing through Oxenden, population 162, she sensed every soul was asleep. When she parked next to the MU, the team lead, Forensic Sergeant Lance Chu, was opening the door. For someone who'd spent all night at a CS, he looked good. But he always did. She stepped out of her car.

"Morning, Chu. How goes the battle?"

"Howdy, Naslund." He shrugged. "Sometimes you get lucky. Most times you don't. We're on the don't side."

She followed him inside. It was one of the new units, with a brightly-lit workroom, whiz-bang kitchenette, compost toilet, and two supposedly tastefully decorated bedrooms, each with an upper and lower bunk. It reminded her of an up-scale house trailer. Not that it smelled like one. Instead of air freshener, she smelled cyanoacrylate, a compound used to help process FPs—fingerprints. It seemed Chu's team had worked some prints.

"Any matches?" she asked.

"Not yet. Got five FPs. All partial. Plus two hairs. Long strands, black. No follicles."

She nodded. Probably Thom's hairs, but they couldn't be conclusively linked to him. Only hairs with follicles, which held nuclear DNA, yielded individualization.

"Found them in the blood pool in the bottom of the boat, the…"

"Bilge," she said.

After videotaping the skiff and going over it with a proverbial fine-tooth comb yesterday, the team called in a mobile crane to haul it out of the bay. Now it sat on blocks well above the shoreline, protected by a CS tent, cordoned off by police tape.

"And the blood, of course," Chu said. "Gina Domani is on it."

"Good." Domani was the OPP's best blood-splatter analyst.

"Domani's completing her measurements. Will probably take her a few more hours."

"Do you mind if I go down to the boat?"

"All right, but don't get in her way. I know you, Naslund." He smiled. "Don't hound Domani."

"I won't."

He pointed a warning finger at her. "Hold your questions for later."

She nodded. Chu and company were painstakingly brilliant. It was the painstaking part that sometimes frustrated her.

Three hours later, she left the scene, no closer to knowing what had happened, but partially mollified. Except for the hairs and one FP, she'd detected everything the white coats had found. But she needed to know more. While they delivered dots—facts and details—her job was to connect them. Although she suspected murder, the evidence didn't yet support it. She was working a possible assault, not a homicide.

Thinking of Thom's size, she drove toward Owen Sound. Thom was a powerful man. She'd met him at a sailing regatta, where he'd single-handed a CS 33. He'd beaten everyone, including her and Pete, and they'd been a helluva team. On the water. She turned her mind back to Thom. It would take a strong person to assault him. Very strong. Then again, he might have been accidently knocked overboard by the boom. She re-thought both scenarios. Besides the blood splatter evidence pointing to two weapons, a blunt instrument and a sharp one, the boom had a high clearance. Five-and-a-half feet. She'd just measured it. Thom was used to maneuvering under it. Which pointed to an assault, not an accident.

Naslund concentrated on the road. She needed to set her mind free, to give herself a break. The traffic was light; the air, muggy yet clean. Southern Ontario smog rarely reached the Bruce. As the kilometers passed, the day brightened. Early afternoon sunlight bounced off the bay.

She attempted to stay focused on the day but her mind wouldn't let her. It returned to the case. She envisioned someone attacking Thom. One attacker didn't seem likely. What if there were two? That's more like it, she reasoned. That made an assault possible.

Having entered Owen Sound, she pulled into her favorite Chinese takeout. After eating chicken Kung Pao next to the harbor, she decided to return to Cape Commodore and systematically re-visit yesterday's interviewees. Surely someone would remember something new they'd seen or heard, some tiny detail that might begin to connect the dots.

By 1900, Naslund gave up. No dots, tiny or otherwise. No connections. She headed toward Wiarton.

Ten minutes along Highway One she received a call. She switched her cell to hands-free. "Sergeant Naslund, OPP."

"Superintendent Coulson, USRU. We found your man."

She didn't know what to say. "Good," she eventually replied.

"I understand you knew Mr. Tyler?"

"I did."

"My condolences."

"Thank you."

"By the way, he was near the island. About a hundred meters offshore. Looks like a suspicious death. They're bringing the body into Wiarton Marina."

"I'll be there," she said.

"A coroner's been called. A Dr. Kapanen. He'll join you there. One more thing. Good work, Sergeant."

"Thank you."

Naslund ended the call, feeling absolutely numb. She pulled off the highway and hung her head. She'd sensed Thom was gone, and yet now she couldn't believe it. It seemed impossible, Thom Tyler dead at the age of thirty-nine, the same age as her. He'd been larger-than-life. He was famous, and not only locally. He was a world-renowned painter. She'd once watched him paint the sky in less time than it took to dream it. Two sweeps of cobalt blue, a few dabs of cadmium red, finished with quick strokes of thalo blue—and he was done.

Now, looking up, she saw a car in her side mirror approaching very quickly. As the car zipped by, Sergeant Lance Chu waved at her. She retook the road and followed him. In Wiarton, he turned right on Claude Street and headed to the marina.

Naslund parked next to Chu's car and caught up with him on foot.

"Hey, fast car," she said as they walked to the OPP jetty.

He grinned. "Yep. By the way, who's the coroner?"

"Rudi Kapanen."

"Huh. I heard he's friendly with Finnish vodka."

"How can you say that?" she protested. "He's not friendly, he's enamored."

Chu chuckled. "Another pickled coroner."

"Exactly."

Reaching the jetty, Naslund spotted an officer from her station, Constable Chandler of the Marine Unit, plus a USRU sergeant and two USRU divers. She took control, motioning for the USRU team to wait and assigning Chandler to block off the jetty. Journalists were already gathering at the marina clubhouse, hovering like vultures. There was no sign of Kapanen.

She and Chu boarded the OPP boat. Thom's body lay on its back in the cockpit. Forcing herself to concentrate, she bent down on one knee and studied the corpse. Thom's arms and legs were pinkish-white, the color of trout flesh.

He looked like a wrinkled version of himself. His auto-inflatable vest hadn't inflated.

Purposefully bypassing Thom's head, she scanned the body. No evidence of trauma. Her eyes settled on the right ankle. There was a line wrapped around it. Even after hours in the lake, it was unmistakable. It was the new anchor rode. The anchor lay at Thom's feet, attached to the end of the rode not around his ankle. She did a double-take. The anchor was attached to him. Christ, he'd been dragged down by his own anchor. Not even the best swimmer could fight the pull of an anchor. She bent closer to the anchorless end of the rode. It hadn't been cut. Maybe the knot tied to the skiff's bow worked itself free? She dismissed that idea. She'd seen Thom tie the knot. Perhaps someone untied it and he hadn't noticed? Not likely. To add oats to a bubbling porridge pot, there was the malfunctioning life vest, which appeared equally suspicious.

Taking a deep breath, she turned to Thom's head. His mouth was open. His tongue had disappeared. His upper face was a bruised, swollen mess. His right eye could've been hit by the boom. But not the left one. She shook her head. It seemed to have been punctured with what looked to be a rapier, a thin one. She looked away. From what she'd seen, her friend wasn't only dead, he'd been murdered.

She felt momentarily lost. Almost immediately, her training kicked in. She turned away from the body and called Bickell. No radiophone this time. She didn't want civilians listening in.

"Naslund here. They found Tyler's body. I can vouch for that. We don't need anyone to ID it."

"All right."

"Looks like a murder. Pending the coroner's findings."

"I see."

"I have to attend the coroner's exam now, but I'll inform Carrie MacLean later."

"I'll do it, Naslund. And visit his parents as well."

"I should do it, sir. I knew him."

"You can't be everywhere, Detective."

Occasionally, Bickell surprised her. He was a good man at heart. "Ah, sir?"

"Yes?"

"Don't mention the murder angle."

Chapter 4

Naslund stepped aside as Forensic Constable Noreen Ross, the MU video-photographer, boarded the boat and snapped dozens of shots. Thom's face was completely in the shadows. In the dwindling light, his body looked one-dimensional, more an outline than a person. Eventually, Ross edged back and took a series of wide-angle shots. Job done, she signaled to Naslund and left.

Naslund turned to the USRU sergeant and asked for a summary of his findings.

"The body was recovered sixty-point-two meters down," the sergeant reported and then referred to his notes. "Latitude forty-four degrees, fifty-one minutes, twenty-one seconds north. Longitude eighty degrees, fifty-seven minutes, forty-two seconds west. Which translates to one-hundred-one-point-four meters southeast of the first co-ord you gave us."

She nodded. "Water temperature?"

"Six Celsius."

"Thank you. We appreciate your work."

"And yours, Detective."

The USRU team took their gear and headed to land. With the area cleared, Naslund and Chu waited for

Kapanen. The sun dipped below the western horizon. In the cedars ashore, doves cooed wistfully, marking the end of the day. She felt wistful as well. Chu seemed to know her frame-of-mind. He spoke quietly about the FPs. There were three different sets.

The coroner huffed up to the boat a few minutes later. His face was red, his nose, redder. As usual, regardless of the weather and his weight, he wore a tight three-piece suit. "I was just starting dinner," he complained. "Detective Naslund, are you in charge?"

"Of the case," she said. "FID Sergeant Chu is in charge of the presumed crime scene, the victim's boat."

"I didn't ask about the CS, did I?"

"No, sir."

"Don't call me sir."

"Sorry, Doctor."

She didn't smell any alcohol on Kapanen's breath or body. But that didn't mean he was dry. It often took hours for alcohol to be emitted through one's pores.

Kapanen and Chu boarded the boat. The coroner seemed steady on his feet. Naslund followed, switched on the boat's twin searchlights, and pointed them aft. The deck was instantly lit in stark white light. Kapanen blinked and then blinked again. Giving himself a shake, he pulled on a pair of gloves and knelt beside the body.

"Looks like a wet drowning," he soon said. "Note: I said, *looks like*. We need an autopsy to confirm that. Most drownings are wet. Eighty-five percent." He eyed Naslund. "Do you know the difference between a wet drowning and a dry drowning?"

"Yes, sir. I mean, yes Doctor." She often felt like a schoolgirl around Kapanen. She didn't mind occasionally joking about him but also wanted to impress him. "In a dry drowning, fatal cerebral hypoxia, or oxygen deprivation, does not result from water blocking the airway, but from throat spasms. Water never enters the lungs."

"Very good. You're learning." Kapanen pointed at Thom's mouth. "See that foam?" Naslund and Chu nodded in unison. "It contains blood and mucus, which usually signifies a wet drowning."

"What about the head wounds?" Naslund asked.

"What about them?"

"Maybe Mr. Tyler was dead before he entered the water."

"Oh? Why do you say that? Regard the foam, Detective. Foam," Kapanen pronounced, "often oozes from the mouth and/or nose of victims of wet drownings. Its presence indicates the victim became immersed while still breathing."

She nodded.

"Furthermore, the foam you see contains blood. The force of inrushing water causes the lungs of a living individual to bleed. A dead individual's lungs do not bleed. However, the evidence you see is not conclusive." Kapanen shook his head. "The autopsy will determine if the lungs contain microscopic lake algae. If they do, we have a wet drowning."

"Yes, Doctor."

"It's a good thing that the divers found the body. It might have taken weeks for it to refloat." Kapanen stood and scrutinized the two detectives. "Why?"

Naslund and Chu said nothing.

Kapanen rolled his eyes. "The human body weighs slightly more than fresh water. When a person suffers a wet drowning, they sink. As a body sinks, water pressure compresses gases in the abdomen and chest. As a result, the body displaces less water and, therefore, becomes less buoyant the farther it sinks. And if it does not sink?" The question was rhetorical. "You detectives should suspect another cause of death." Kapanen raised a finger. "So, what about taking weeks to refloat? What factors can affect the length of time it takes for a body to refloat?"

"A weight," Naslund said. "Like an anchor attached to the body."

"Well, yes. I hadn't thought of that. You people, always looking on the dark side."

"We have to."

"Indeed," Kapanen allowed. "Now, let's return to medical science. Think food consumption preceding death. Plus water temperature and depth. Foods high in carbohydrates, such as beer or potatoes—"

Or vodka, Naslund thought.

"—feed bacteria that elicit a quick refloat. In warm water, gases form rapidly, resulting in a possible refloat within days. In deep, cold water, bacterial action takes place slowly, and a corpse might take weeks to refloat. As you're aware, Detective Naslund—" Kapanen turned to face her. "—in the summer months, Georgian Bay has thermoclines, different layers of water temperature. While the surface temperature can be fifteen to twenty Celsius, the temperature a hundred meters down might be three or four. Do you know the depth and temperature where the body was recovered?"

She nodded. "Sixty-point-two meters down. Six Celsius."

"That would certainly retard the re-flotation process."

She figured that she and Chu had had enough schooling. She pointed to Thom's head. "What caused the damage?"

Kapanen turned back to the body. A few minutes later, he looked up. "Consider the right eye socket and orbital bones. I detect two or three blows by a blunt force instrument with a rounded impact surface. About six centimeters wide. Most likely metal. I don't see any wood splinters, although they may have been washed away by the lake. As for the left eye," Kapanen paused, "it seems to have been pierced with a pointed instrument. Metal. Again, no wood splinters. Perhaps a thin blade. I can't tell. We'll know more after the autopsy."

"Okay," she said. "What about time of death, post-mortem interval?"

"You expect me to tell you PMI?"

"An estimate, Doctor, of course."

Kapanen appeared to be appeased. "Well, we'll have to adjust the usual hat trick."

She nodded. The *hat trick*, she knew, was lividity, algor mortis, and rigor mortis. Lividity, or blood pooling, turned a body purple and pink. Algor referred to a body turning cold. With no blood flowing, body temperature dropped by about one Celsius each hour, until it matched air temperature. In this case, she realized, it had likely dropped by double that amount, until it reached water temperature. Rigor mortis, or body stiffening, generally started within two hours and became fully established in twelve.

"Considering the water temperature," Kapanen cautioned, "I can't be very precise. As for lividity, when the body is undressed we'll know more. For now, I see traces of blood pooling in the throat area, which is what I'd expect in the case of a drowning. A drowning victim normally assumes a position of face down and buttocks up. Of course, the traces could be bruises. As for algor, when a body has undergone submersion in cold water, algor is unreliable."

Nonetheless, Kapanen drew a liver thermometer from his medical bag and pierced Thom's right side. "Six Celsius," he read. "Given that thirty-seven Celsius is the norm, the victim died well over fifteen hours ago. That's the best I can do with algor. Now, rigor." Kapanen shook his head. "Again, the submersion complicates matters. I can't tell you with certainty when he died. However, I can tell you one thing."

"Please," she said.

"The victim died in the water. He was not killed on land and then moved. Note the semi-fetal position. The arms and legs are slightly bent at the elbows and knees. Although he is lying on his back, the spine is curved and the chin is tilted down. When someone dies on land, the head is typically rotated to one side, a position almost never found in a drowning victim."

"Good to know."

"Try to remember that," Kapanen said brusquely. "Now, consider the victim's hands. They are turned toward his face, with the fingers clenched inward. Victims often try to cover their mouths to prevent drowning. Rigor reflects that. All right, back to PMI. When does rigor normally set in?"

Naslund glanced at Chu. *Class still in.* She turned back to the coroner. "After twelve hours."

"How and when does it diminish?"

"Gradually, after twenty-four to thirty-six hours."

"Correct, Detective. Very good. Extensive physical exertion before death may speed it up or even trigger instant onset. However, I don't see evidence of that. There are no signs of cadaveric spasm. On the other hand, we have an obvious temperature effect. Cold retards rigor. Given the cold water—six Celsius—the length of the submersion, and the victim's size, I'd estimate full rigor took much longer than normal, roughly twenty-two to twenty-four hours." He eyed the corpse. "The victim still exhibits signs of rigor, with the exception of the face and hands. Considering the obvious loss of rigor in the facial muscles, for example, in the labial region—" Kapanen pointed to Thom's lips. "—and the hands, but not in the largest muscles, such as the quadriceps, we can deduce the body is currently losing rigor. I'd say rigor has been diminishing for fourteen to sixteen hours."

"Which means?" she asked.

Kapanen glared at her. "Which means the victim has been dead for approximately thirty-six to forty hours."

"Thank you."

"Approximately, Detective."

Naslund knew that, in itself, PMI was just a number. However, she always pressed coroners for it. With a PMI estimate, she could narrow down an investigation. If she could place a suspect at a crime scene during the PMI window, she could drill down. She had opportunity; she could probe for motive. "Your final findings, Doctor?"

Kapanen didn't skip a beat. "The victim suffered severe head trauma, but was alive when he entered Georgian Bay. He then drowned. The wounds he sustained were not self-inflicted. He was attacked. Cause of death: Drowning. Means: Homicide." Kapanen jutted out his chin. "Any more questions?"

She shook her head.

"I'll have my report delivered by midnight."

She had no problem with Kapanen's work ethic. His empathy was another matter. After he left, she waited on the jetty for the morgue transport. A full-moon rose above Colpoys Bay, its face redder than Kapanen's. It reminded her of a death mask. Up it climbed, dominating the sky.

Chapter 5

In Naslund's eyes, Carrie MacLean was incredibly gorgeous. Over the past year, Naslund had eaten dinner with her and Thom at least ten times. She supposed Carrie was a friend. And yet, in her experience, certain people often tried to take advantage—among them, not surprisingly, the beautiful. Carrie had already squirmed out of a 1030 interview. She'd seemed very controlled when Naslund had called her at 0900 that morning, as if she were hiding something. Bickell had said she'd been antagonistic when he visited her the previous evening, to the point of outright belligerence.

Now Naslund sat in her desk chair and leaned closer to the speakerphone. "Eva again. We need to see you this morning."

"This morning?" Carrie asked.

"The investigation began yesterday," Naslund reminded her. "It's just a routine chat. How's eleven-thirty?"

"Let's say tomorrow...." Her voice trailed off. "I'm sorry, Eva, I'm just not myself."

"I understand, but we need to see you today."

"Tomorrow. Okay?"

Naslund fought to contain her exasperation. "It has to be today. Eleven-thirty. We can meet at your cottage or you can come to the station." Carrie didn't reply. She wasn't a known suspect who'd be read her rights, but if she wanted to start off with a lawyer that was her prerogative. "You can arrange for a lawyer," Naslund said.

"Oh, no. I don't need a lawyer."

"Home or station?"

"I'll come to the station."

"Fine. Eleven-thirty."

Naslund hung up and turned her attention to the Tyler case file. An hour ago, Central had informed her that they were assigning a Detective Inspector to run the case. DI Lewis Moore was due at eleven. After the MacLean interview, Moore and Naslund had to hustle to Orillia for Tyler's autopsy. In the meantime, she was saddled with her least favorite task: completing case notes.

შოთ

Naslund observed Carrie MacLean enter the station via a security-camera feed running on her laptop. Carrie wore a loose-fitting pantsuit, not one of her usual body-hugging outfits. Although she normally let her strawberry-blonde hair down, it was piled on top of her head and knotted. Her cat-like green eyes seemed a few shades lighter. She looked strained, almost fragile—not herself at all, which, upon reflection, seemed appropriate. She *was* different now, a POI, a person-of-interest: Carolyn Cornelia MacLean, 414 Mallory Beach Road, Ontario D/L P6790-00530-53412, DOB 8/18/75, owner of Blue Bay Catering. She had no previous record: no arrests, no traffic infractions, no citations or complaints against. At the same time, she was on the wrong side of a murder line.

Inspector Moore had insisted on questioning her alone. After hearing about her delaying tactics, he'd informed Naslund that he intended to show MacLean her place. A POI couldn't be coddled, especially an evasive or belligerent one. Naslund hadn't replied. Besides, there was nothing she could say. Moore owned the case. Now she called him, a tall, thin man who moved with surprising quickness.

She pegged him at sixty. His shirt and suit were gray, his short hair grayer. He had the eyes of someone who'd seen it all a thousand times. "She's here, Inspector."

"Very good," he replied.

Naslund watched him materialize beside Carrie MacLean as if by magic. The POI almost jumped out of her chair. With Moore's height and bony face, he looked otherworldly, like a skeleton on stilts. MacLean stood and shook his outstretched hand. Naslund saw discomfort in her eyes then displeasure. *I'm not here to see you.* She switched camera feeds to watch as he led MacLean to the interview room.

No chit-chat, Naslund saw, no friendly gestures. Moore was all business. The two FID men who'd arrived with him had already departed for Tyler's cottage.

As soon as the door closed, Naslund left her office and took up her position in the shadow room. On the console screen, the interview room looked long and narrow. The ceiling hosted two sets of glaring fluorescent lights hiding high-tech cameras and microphones. Three flimsy wooden chairs flanked a small metal table bolted to the floor. The suspect's chair, known as the Slider, had a heavily waxed seat. Its front legs were a centimeter shorter than the back ones. The incline wasn't visibly evident, but anyone who sat in the chair slid slowly forward, right into the face of their interrogator.

Moore offered MacLean the Slider and sat across

from her in front of a stack of papers. "I'm sorry to bring you in so soon after the event," he began.

She stared at him. Naslund was sure she could read MacLean's face. *Event? How dare you?*

Moore smiled evenly. "Mr. Tyler's murder." He paused. "Miss MacLean, you seem annoyed by my word choice." He looked down his nose. "The word *murder*, I mean. You see, Mr. Tyler was murdered, we're sure of that."

"I am too."

"Why is that?"

"He was far too good a sailor to drown."

"But he did drown. The coroner's report conclud-ed—" Moore stopped to pull some crisp pages from the pile on the desk, fished a pair of half-moon glasses from a pocket and put them on. "—that Mr. Tyler, and I quote, 'suffered traumatic head wounds but died from water in-halation when he entered Georgian Bay.'"

The inspector dropped the report and eyed MacLean through the half-moons, his gray orbs eerily magnified. With his glasses on, he looked more unearthly. "When a man inhales water into his lungs, Miss MacLean, he ex-periences severe chest pain. He suffers simultaneous cir-culatory and respiratory failure. The victim usually suc-cumbs within four to eight minutes. Four to eight minutes of hell."

She flinched.

He jotted down a note. "Let's continue, shall we?"

She didn't reply.

"The coroner concluded that when the victim 'fell' into the lake he was alive. If a man were dead when he went overboard, he wouldn't draw water into his lungs the way the victim did." Moore leaned forward. "Dead men do not respire." His words hung in the air. "Miss MacLean?"

Her eyes seemed to say *enough*.

Moore kept going. "The coroner found foam in the nose and mouth containing blood and mucus. The force of inrushing water causes the lungs of a living individual to bleed. A dead individual's lungs do not bleed."

She turned her head away. *No more.*

"The victim's auto-inflatable life vest failed." Moore eyed her silently. "If it hadn't, he might have sur-vived—*even* though there was an anchor line attached to his right ankle. You see, if the life vest hadn't failed, he might have had time to unwind that line or cut it." Moore shook his head. "First, the victim's life vest fails and then somehow an anchor line, pardon me, a rode," he corrected himself, "gets wrapped around his ankle." He stopped. "Any idea how that happened?"

"No." She pulled herself back in the Slider.

Moore pretended not to hear her. "I repeat, do you know how that happened?"

"No."

He shrugged as if to say *you'll tell me eventually.*

Naslund wondered about the inspector's angle. He was breaking the usual rules of a first interview: make the POI feel comfortable, get them to open up by being pleasant. Apparently, it had served him well. Moore was a top gun. She'd heard that he had an eighty-six percent solve rate.

Moore leafed through the papers piled in front of him again, pulled out a thick booklet, and opened it. "This is a forensic report, Miss MacLean. Among other things, it details what is known about the victim's life vest. Our analysts found that the CO-Two gas cartridge failed to inflate the vest's buoyancy chambers due to a blocked valve. Vests of that make and manufacture rarely fail. They have—" He donned his specs and glanced down. "—a one in five million failure rate. Miniscule."

She nodded guardedly.

Naslund sensed her retreating into defense-mode, trying to decipher where Moore was going.

The inspector removed his glasses. "The vest showed virtually no signs of wear and tear. Apparently, it was almost new. So, a new vest, a first-class new vest, if I may say, failed."

She said nothing.

"Do you know when Mr. Tyler bought the vest?"

"No. Thom and I didn't shop together for boating things."

Moore scribbled a note. "Do you know where he bought it?"

"In Owen Sound, I think. I'm not sure." She shook her head. "I'm sorry. I'm not myself. My mind isn't working."

"What do you know about the vest?"

"It was blue," she said. "Dark blue."

Moore seemed about to lash out. He appeared to think she was stringing him along. However, he pursed his lips and sat back. "Given the blocked valve, the vest did not inflate automatically. However, the wearer could still have inflated it manually, with the mouth blow-tube. The report indicates Mr. Tyler tried to do so. His bite marks were found on the tube. Repeated marks, the bite of someone frantic, someone desperate."

Enough! her eyes seemed to say.

"Speaking of the report," Moore continued, "it states the anchor got released. Any idea how that happened?"

"No. I apologize, I rarely went aboard Thom's skiff."

"What about his bigger boat?"

"I liked it more, if that's what you're asking."

"Did you go aboard it?"

"Yes."

"So you know how to sail?"

"Yes, well enough."

"Then you know mooring lines, mainsheets, and jib sheets."

"Yes."

"And anchor rodes."

"Yes, of course." She seemed more at ease. "Whenever we dropped anchor, Thom would stay at the helm. I'd always go forward to handle the hook."

"Very nice. The *hook*." Moore smiled with insincere respect. "You're not a novice sailor, are you?"

"Oh, no. I've been sailing for over a decade."

"Is there anything you'd like to tell me about the skiff?"

"Tell you?" She looked confused.

"Why don't you tell me about the last time you were aboard?"

She appeared to scan her memory. "It was over a month ago, more like five weeks." She forced herself up in the Slider. Her face showed obvious exasperation. "Just at the dock."

Moore made a note. "What did you do, Miss Mac-Lean?"

"Do? Nothing. Thom and I sat in the cockpit and had a beer."

"A beer?"

"Two beers, Inspector, to be exact. One each."

"I'll take your word for it. Very well, let's step ahead, to the question of how Mr. Tyler ended up in the lake. Rumor has it," Moore began then shook his head dismissively, as if to say *groundless gossip*, "that he fell overboard while taking a leak, or while setting his fishing lines, or hauling them in. The usual tropes." He eyed the POI with apparent respect. "What do you think happened? Miss MacLean?"

Naslund saw that the *Miss* salutation was beginning to irritate MacLean. It was an old-school technique, designed to unsettle a female POI. Both confuse and anger her. At times, Moore sounded respectful, at others, contemptuous, his tone saying *you're a disgrace to your gender.*

"*Miss* MacLean," Moore repeated, "what do you think happened?"

"I don't know."

"Care to make a guess?"

She shook her head.

"A small guess?" he pressed. "Come, you must think something."

Think? her eyes said. *I can't think.*

He scrutinized her then continued. "I assume you know the victim's body was submerged for many hours."

She nodded.

"Well, you might not know this. DNA evidence is not affected by immersion in water. Fingerprints often survive as well. They did in this case." He paused to observe her reaction.

She nodded again.

"Given that the body was immersed in deep cold water, we have excellent prints. We fingerprinted Mr. Tyler's skiff as well and scanned it for DNA. The whole boat." Moore leaned forward and studied her. "We'll soon know if anyone interfered with it." He leaned closer. "In any way."

She said nothing.

Naslund watched the inspector lean back. He'd used the "lean in/out" method. It was subliminal. You leaned in, you invaded the half-meter the POI thought they owned, and then you leaned back when you had what you wanted. The inspector had what he wanted. Naslund assumed he took MacLean's silence as an implication of unease, if not guilt. Naslund did.

MacLean stared at her hands then looked up. "I know

you have to question me, but it's horrible." Her lips quivered. She seemed about to cry.

"Would you like to take a break?" Moore asked.

She shook her head.

"Coffee or tea?"

"No thank you." She straightened her shoulders. "I'm fine."

"Well, Miss MacLean, as I mentioned, Mr. Tyler's skiff has been combed for evidence. It is being treated as a crime scene. As of half an hour ago, so too is the boathouse and dock at your Mallory Beach cottage. That area is now off-limits to everyone, including you. An investigation team is working the scene as we speak." Moore stopped and studied the POI.

She didn't seem disturbed or defensive.

He jotted down a note. "When did you last speak to Mr. Tyler?"

She slumped in her chair. "Sunday night, when he went to bed. About nine-thirty."

"When did you go to bed?"

"Around eleven." She pushed herself back in the Slider.

"What did you do between nine-thirty and eleven?"

"Nothing."

"Nothing?"

"Well, what I usually do on a Sunday night. I relaxed, I watched TV."

"Anything else?"

"I read a while, for about half an hour I'd say. Before bed, I went down to our dock to cool off. I swam out from the boathouse for a few minutes and back. I always do that before bed."

"Was Mr. Tyler's skiff moored at the boathouse?"

"Yes."

"Did you go aboard?" Moore asked.

"No."

"Did everything look normal on the skiff?"

"Yes."

He made a note. "Where were you on Sunday until nine-thirty p.m.?"

"I worked a brunch function from seven in the morning until four. In Owen Sound."

"And after that?"

"I was at home."

"Meaning your cottage, Four-Fourteen Mallory Beach Road?"

"Yes."

"What were you doing?"

"Cooking, until around six-thirty. Then Thom and I ate dinner."

"It took you over two hours to cook dinner?"

"No. I also made meals for the coming week. They're in the freezer."

Moore studied her before speaking. "Was anyone else with you Sunday evening, other than Mr. Tyler?"

"No."

"Do you have any idea who might have been aboard the skiff recently? I mean, did Mr. Tyler sail with anyone else?"

"Yes, some of his friends."

"Who?"

She eyed the ceiling, apparently going back through her memory. "J.J. MacKenzie...Ward Larmer."

Moore recorded the names. "To the best of your recollection, when did they sail with Mr. Tyler?"

"Ward went out with Thom last week, at least three times. J.J. hasn't been out with him for months."

"Just to confirm, by Ward you mean Ward Larmer?"

She nodded.

"Would you say this Mr. Larmer knows the skiff well?"

"Yes."

"Would you say he knew Mr. Tyler well?"

"Yes. He's known him for years. Almost fifteen. Not that they were best of friends."

"Oh?"

"Ward's a painter, a friend, yes, but also a competitor."

"How so?"

Naslund sensed that Moore was being deliberately thick-headed.

"Artists, Inspector," she replied, "they're often in competition."

"I'll take your word for it. All right then, how *competitive* were Mr. Tyler and Mr. Larmer?"

"Very. Ward was always asking Thom how much he got for his work. And always envious when he heard the answer."

"How do you know he was envious?"

"I've known Ward for fourteen years, Inspector. I lived with him for two."

"And?"

"I can read him."

"I see. Well, Miss MacLean, on the subject of art, just so you're aware, the investigation team will be cataloguing all the sketches and paintings in Mr. Tyler's studio. I trust you'll cooperate fully."

"Of course."

"Two team members will be there well into the night. The studio contents are salient to a crime. *Murder.*" Moore stopped to emphasize the word. "Like the boathouse and dock," he went on, "the studio has been cordoned off with police tape. Do not enter it. Do not remove or alter anything, even things you think you own." He paused to let his words sink in. "Is that clear?"

She nodded.

"I'd like to ask you a personal question." He sounded solicitous.

"Yes?"

"What's your favorite Thom Tyler work?"

She didn't hesitate. "A painting he never finished. He considered it too realistic, but…"

"But," Moore prompted.

"Well."

"Go on, Miss MacLean."

"Well, I thought it was perfect." She seemed to be seeing the painting in her mind's eye. "It was a portrait of our cottage, from out on the bay. Thom sketched it from his sailboat. Looking at it, you felt drawn in to shore. The bay seemed to vanish. You were drawn to the cottage. You felt that it contained the whole world."

"Go on."

"I loved that feeling. I loved seeing our cottage nestled amongst blue-green pines, bounded by a beautiful blue sky."

"Sounds lovely."

"It was. When he was there."

"Ah. But he was never there."

"Well."

"Please, continue. It seems Mr. Tyler was rarely home."

"I…I suppose that's true." She straightened herself in the Slider. "Yes, I hardly saw him this past year. Anyone can tell you that. I work long hours at times, I admit, but only at times. On the other hand, Thom was always painting or getting a boat ready for a painting trip."

"Ah."

"He was a workaholic. No, worse. He was obsessive. He had no time for anyone."

Wrong, Naslund said to herself. Even when Thom was busy, he found a few minutes to talk to her. People often mistook them for brother and sister.

"What about you, Miss MacLean? Did he have time for you?"

"Well."

"Did he?"

"Yes, but not often."

"I'm sorry to hear that," the inspector said. However, his eyes were ablaze, as if he'd discovered a hidden treasure. Almost immediately, he doused the fire. "We'll be in touch. We may need to ask you more about Mr. Larmer."

"Certainly."

"And yourself."

"Certainly," she repeated, her eyes saying *sorry, I can't think very well.*

Bull, Naslund thought. Behind MacLean's eyes, she sensed her mind whirling. Carrie MacLean was on guard. While most of her words were straightforward, some of them were double-hinged.

Naslund felt confused. From what she knew of her, MacLean was always direct. Prickly at times, but direct. However, Naslund sensed she was withholding information. If so, what? She'd opted to come to the station. Was she hiding something at home?

Naslund shook her head. She was doing what she always did under pressure, trying to consider every angle. Relax, she told herself. Let the investigation unfold. Remember your father's advice.

Her recently-departed father, a former Metro Toronto superintendent, had taught her that to work efficiently, you often had to slow down.

"One more thing," Moore said. "We don't want to confuse your bio matter with anyone else's. We'd like to take a DNA swab and fingerprint you."

"Of course."

No hesitation, Naslund saw. Almost too cooperative.

Chapter 6

Orillia, OPP Central, Forensic Morgue. July 10th:

Every time Naslund walked into Central's forensic department, it felt like she was stepping into the future. The section was ultra-high-tech: a realm of whirring machines and stainless steel. As she approached the autopsy lab, she reflected again that in her society, in the twenty-first century, no expense was spared to solve murders. Murderers had to be found and prosecuted. The department always renewed her confidence that they would be.

Naslund followed Moore into the lab and nodded to the forensic pathologist, Dr. DeVeon Leonard. In many respects, Leonard was the opposite of Kapanen: humble and affable. Under his lab coat, he wore an open-necked blue shirt and jeans.

"Good afternoon, Detectives."

"Good afternoon," Moore and Naslund replied.

"Let's get right to it," Leonard said. "You two aren't rookies." He smiled. "We're audio- and videotaping this." He pointed to two cameras. "But please stop me if you miss something or have any questions."

The two detectives nodded. As Naslund knew,

Leonard was usually able to tell what had happened to a victim and in what sequence. Corpses generally divulged crucial evidence.

"First," Leonard said, "Dr. Kapanen's report was very thorough. I concur with his findings. In fact, I have relatively little to add."

"Good," Moore said.

"As you know, Detectives, logically, an autopsy proceeds from the outside in." The pathologist beckoned them forward.

In death, Thom looked smaller than Naslund remembered. The long autopsy table emphasized his diminishment.

"We'll begin with the head," Leonard said. "Dr. Kapanen reported the right eye and orbital region were impacted by a blunt force instrument with a rounded surface. I've concluded the instrument was a metal ball-peen hammer. The hammer head had a fifteen-centimeter circumference and was painted gunmetal gray. It deposited two paint chips of that color." Leonard stopped. "Don't worry. Besides the tape, my written report will include all the details. See here?" He pointed to deep circular indentations near the right eye. "There are three overlapping wounds. The orbital bones were crushed." He slowly traced the indentations with his pointer, careful not to touch them. "Lengthy immersion in water leaches blood from wounds. They may look like bloodless postmortem injuries, but they are antemortem. The heart was pumping when they occurred. If you look closely, I think you can see three different wounds."

Moore put on his glasses, bent closer, and nodded.

Naslund looked and nodded as well. "Doctor, could the victim have fought back after those blows?"

"Possibly. Everyone reacts differently to head blows. But given the depth of the imprints and the shattered bones, the blows may have disabled the victim."

"Would they have knocked him unconscious?" Moore asked.

"I don't think so. I see evidence of defensive wounds, which I'll point out later. An unconscious person cannot defend themselves. Furthermore, the victim had a thicker-than-average skull, about nine millimeters. The blows struck the orbital region, and thus didn't impact the brain directly."

"But surely they impacted it," Moore said.

"Certainly, Inspector, but not, for example, like three blows to the crown of the head. One thing is certain, he would have lost a lot of blood. Head wounds bleed a tremendous amount. A human body contains about six liters of blood. It's possible the victim lost half of it."

"I suspect he knew his assailant," Moore said. "Or wasn't worried. To bash him like that, someone had to get very close to him without raising suspicion."

"Valid point," Leonard acknowledged. "I didn't think of it. I can't think the way you detectives think. I know—" He smiled. "—I wouldn't want to." He winked conspiratorially at Naslund and then refocused on the corpse. "Consider the left eye. As Dr. Kapanen noted, it was punctured with a pointed instrument. That instrument was a metal screwdriver. The tip was eleven millimeters wide and had a star-like bit consistent with a Phillips design. There were no other identifying characteristics. In conclusion, a ball-peen hammer crushed the victim's right eye and orbital bones. A Phillips screwdriver pierced the left eye."

Naslund grimaced.

"It appears the assailant was right-handed," Leonard said. "The victim's left eye was attacked with the screwdriver, which suggests it was held in the assailant's right hand. You need more motor control to target an eye with a screwdriver than to bash an eye with a hammer, so it is likely that the assailant's dominant arm was the right one. As to the sequence of blows, we might make another assumption. The assailant likely delivered a few, or possibly all of the hammer blows first, to disorient or disable the victim, and then pierced the left eye. Any questions?"

The detectives shook their heads.

Leonard pointed at the victim's forehead. "The vector angles of the blows range from twelve to twenty-two degrees. Which suggests the assailant was taller than the victim or came at him from above." Leonard raised a cautionary hand. "I can't be certain which. In the stormy conditions prevalent, if the assailant were on a different boat, a wave could have raised the assailant above the victim. But three times? That again complicates certainty."

Exactly, Naslund thought.

"As I alluded to previously," the doctor continued, "there is evidence of defensive wounds. Look at the victim's right forearm. It appears he tried to protect himself by deflecting two blows. You can see indentations and bruising consistent with ball-peen hammer blows, there—" Leonard directed his pointer halfway up the radius. "—and there, on the wrist. Sorry to muddy the waters again, but I said *it appears*. It is possible that the wounds I just pointed out were not defensive, but targeted arm attacks."

"How possible?" Moore asked.

"I can't say. I apologize, I can't be more definitive." Leonard gestured diffidently. "Let's move on. There is another site to consider." He pointed to the corpse's right shoulder. "Consider the abrasion and the bruising. It appears the victim fell or was pushed onto a hard surface. The abrasion is seven-point-eight centimeters long. I reviewed the crime scene report. The Mackinaw gunwale is eight-point-two centimeters wide. I'd conjecture the victim landed on the boat's starboard gunwale with his right shoulder. I'd also conjecture his head remained inboard, which led to the blood pool in the bilge."

Naslund nodded. The man had read the case notes, *and* he knew boats.

Leonard walked down the table and stopped at the right ankle. "Now, let's unravel this. Not the actual line." He smiled. "My assistant will handle that later. Having attacked the victim and severely impacted his eyesight, I suspect the assailant wrapped the line around his ankle and pushed him overboard. Given that the other end of the line was attached to an anchor, it's not surprising that he drowned. Of course, I can't tell you how the assailant did that. And my suspicion is only a supposition." He paused. "Any questions?"

Moore held his fire, as did Naslund. It wasn't the pathologist's job to establish how the rode ended up around the ankle. It was theirs.

"All right, to the drowning. Dr. Kapanen suspected a wet drowning. His observations were precise and, I think, correct."

Leonard applied a scalpel and made a deft Y-incision in Thom's chest. The skin, which had puckered and whitened due to Thom's extended immersion, peeled off instantly. Naslund gagged. The room suddenly smelled like rancid liver. Her stomach churned, as it always did, regardless of how well she'd prepared herself. The doctor handed out safety glasses—when the corpse was sawn open, there'd be airborne bone slivers—and sawed through the rib-cage, removed the chest plate, and then extracted the inner organs and placed them on a side table.

After dissecting the lungs, Leonard called the detectives over. "Note the appearance. The victim's lungs are distended and brick-red. That indicates a substantial ingress of water. Which supports the conclusion of a wet drowning. Regardless, we'll analyze the lung tissues. I expect we'll find microscopic algae consistent with Lake Huron." Leonard turned to the heart and exposed the right ventricle. "Again," he announced, "we find water. A wet drowning victim often pulls water into their circulatory system." His eyes looked sorrowful. "Drowning's an awful way to go. A victim struggles fiercely, but succumbs in minutes. It's a horrible death."

Naslund silently agreed.

"Dr. Kapanen surmised the victim was alive when he entered the water and not placed there already dead. I concur with him."

Moore nodded.

"I also concur with his PMI estimate. The victim likely died somewhere between four a.m. and eight a.m. on Monday July eighth."

Moore nodded again.

"We'll be running a full toxicology screen," Leonard said. "The results will be back in three to four days. I'll release the body at six p.m. this evening, after we get toxicology specimens."

"Thank you," Moore said. "I'll inform the funeral home."

"By the way, I'm ordering burial rather than crema-tion, just in case we need to exhume. Any questions?"

Moore shook his head.

Naslund had one. She'd been thinking about Thom's assault. It was easier to attack someone on land than in a skiff in heavy seas. MacLean could be lying. She could have said that Thom left the cottage dock but attacked him near it. *Not likely*, an inner voice said. *She's not strong enough*. Maybe not, Naslund thought. However, if not her, someone else. An assailant could have attacked Thom on land, put him in the skiff, sailed out to White Cloud, and then pushed him overboard. In which case, the team would need to look for an assault scene on land. "Doctor, I understand the victim didn't die on land, but is it possible he was attacked on land, disabled, and then moved to the boat?"

"Possible," Leonard said. "In that scenario, we'd expect to see evidence of him being dragged or carried. Possibly bound first, in case he began to struggle." Leonard examined Tyler's ankles and legs. "Other than the anchor line, I see no evidence of ligatures." He moved slowly up the corpse to the head. "I see no ligature marks around the torso or arms and no abrasions consistent with dragging. And no evidence of a mouth gag. As to carrying, I see no bruises which indicate he was roughly handled or carried for any distance." Leonard carefully turned the body over. "Again," he eventually said, "I see no ligature marks, no abrasions consistent with dragging, and no bruises consistent with lengthy carrying or rough handling."

Naslund nodded. Maybe she was getting carried away. Her land-attack idea was complicated. Likely too complicated. The truth was usually simpler.

֍֎֍

Having stopped to eat dinner, the two detectives drove toward Wiarton after sundown. They didn't talk much. Naslund sensed Moore thinking and remained silent. She tried to let her mind rest. For the first time since being called to Rathbone's farm, she succeeded. The stillness helped. Dusk drew a cloak over the land. Other than in Owen Sound and a few built-up areas, they passed through the evening like a ghost, guarded by phalanxes of cedar and spruce and pine.

When they entered Wiarton station, the only person

present was Constable Kraft, the duty officer. Chu and company were at the MU. Moore's two FID men, Mitchell and Wolfe, were still at Tyler's cottage. It was too late to bring the team together.

Naslund followed Moore into the boardroom, a crowded chamber which was now the murder room. A few chairs had been shunted to the back wall. The boardroom table dominated the front of the room. Three computer hutches lined one side wall, desks for Mitchell, Wolfe, and Naslund. She'd willingly given her office to Moore, believing that a lead investigator needed their own space. Thinking room. A pair of hutches hugged the opposite wall, for two detective constables who were joining the team tomorrow, Conrad and Lowrie.

Earlier that day, Bickell had complained about losing his boardroom until Moore verbally drove him off. Naslund had enjoyed the show. It'd been like watching rams spar. Constable Chandler had enjoyed it as well. He winked at her as the bosses locked horns. Afterward, he pulled her aside.

"Did you hear what's new?" He grinned comically. "Bacon beer."

"You men," she said, "you have it all."

"Yep."

"What about us girls? There's chardonnay with oak chips. How about chardonnay with chocolate chips?"

"You could be on to something. Wine and chocolate. The wife would love that."

So would she, Naslund thought, and right now. Instead, she opened a bottle of water and sat at the boardroom table. Moore was just getting the full machinery of the investigation humming. To date, he'd assigned actions to four station PCs. Constables Chandler and Derlago were charged with questioning all fourteen cottage owners on White Cloud Island, Constables Singh and Weber, with canvassing the Mallory Beach area as well as the east side of Colpoys Bay. Any suspicious results would be turned over to Naslund and the two DCs arriving from Central. She welcomed the help. The DCs would also interview Tyler's family members and local acquaintances. She and Moore would handle all POIs.

Moore joined her at the table. He looked tired. "Well," he said, "the real work begins tomorrow. I suppose we could round up all the usual suspects," He grinned. "But I'm guessing there're none up here."

Naslund smiled. So the inspector had a funny bone. "Pretty law-abiding up here," she said. "Mostly B-and-Es. Plus a string of pot growers, and a few ex-pedophiles, returned to the community. We can talk to all of them. See what they might have heard."

"Right. Any ex-murderers?"

"Two down in Owen Sound, totally reformed from what we know."

He nodded. "It'll likely be someone close to Tyler. It usually is. Someone who knows him well, like a family member or a friend."

"Or knew him well years ago."

"Exactly. Could be a local, or could be someone from Toronto. He had a condo there, right?"

"Yes."

"I'll talk to one of my contacts at Metro. He should be able to do some legwork for us. I'm sure he can get Metro detectives to interview Tyler's city contacts when we have a list." Moore eyed her. "Any problem with that?"

"None at all." She hated cop turf wars: old boy posturing. Good news, Moore seemed to agree with her. She sighed inwardly. You never knew with old boys. "I'll make a list. Might take a day."

"Fine." Moore stretched then stood. "Let's leave it at that. Good night, Sergeant."

"Good night, sir."

As Moore left, she glanced at the clock on the wall: 2310. Another seventeen-hour day.

Outside, she stood beside her car and gazed heavenward for a long time. The sky was salted with stars. Constellations spun through the heavens, rotating earthward, seemingly falling from the sky. It felt like they would fall forever, until the sky was dark.

Chapter 7

Wiarton, July 11th

Naslund rolled over and read her watch: 0704. *Get up, you dozy head.*

After breakfast—porridge with dried cranberries (considered strange in Wiarton, but she had some big-city tastes)—she walked to her front door and picked up the town paper. Thom Tyler's picture dominated the front page. Underneath it was a color copy of his most iconic local painting, a depiction of Wiarton from Colpoys Bay. The sky came alive with his signature blues. The harbor buildings were exaggerated-white, making a town located just below forty-five degrees North look more Mediterranean than Canadian, like an archetypal Greek port.

She flipped the small paper open. There it was, a tribute on the third page.

Much-loved Painter Remembered
Visitation Today: 10:00 a.m. ~ 4:00 p.m. & 6:00 p.m. ~ 9:00 p.m.

Local friends and family, as well as art circles in Toronto and as far afield as London and Tokyo, were shocked by the news that Thomas Norton Tyler was found dead in Colpoys Bay on Tuesday, July 9th. A visitation will be held today at Bartlett's Funeral Home, 232 Berford St, Wiarton, 10:00 a.m. ~ 4:00 p.m. & 6:00 p.m. ~ 9:00 p.m.

Mr. Tyler's small sailboat ran aground on Monday, July 8th. There was a strong wind prevailing, but Mr. Tyler was an excellent sailor and swimmer. His body was recovered the following day, a hundred meters from White Cloud Island. Foul play is suspected.

Mr. Tyler, one of Canada's most celebrated painters, was especially fond of nature. He traversed the Great Lakes for months at a time in a sailboat outfitted with an artist's studio, in search of what he called the lost soul of Canada. He first won acclaim for his work over a decade ago...

Naslund dropped the paper. She could guess what was next: a glowing account of Thom Tyler's success, the world-wide appetite for his work. She shook her head. The Thom she knew didn't care about money or success. She pulled out her phone and called Moore.

"Detective Inspector Moore, OPP."

"Morning, Inspector, Naslund here. If it's okay, I want to attend Tyler's visitation."

The inspector didn't reply.

"I'll get a bead on his family and some of his acquaintances. Sort out who the new DCs should interview first."

Still no reply.

"I'll work from home until then," she added.

"When's the visitation?"

"Starts at ten hundred."

"Make it in by eleven hundred. I called a team meeting."

"Okay."

She signed off and strode to her dining room table. Mind focused on the case, she adjusted her laptop screen, navigated to Moore's interview of Carrie MacLean, and hit the play button. Forty minutes later, after frequently rewinding the video, she was still unsure about MacLean. She retrieved an apple from the fridge and ate it slowly. Savoring the simple taste, she tried to weigh the evidence.

Step back, she told herself. Consider the details. All her life, she'd remembered small details, like dates and times and things people said. She couldn't help herself; she was born that way. Now, rerunning MacLean's interview in her mind, she focused on the little things MacLean had said and done.

MacLean hesitated more often than Naslund had originally thought. MacLean admitted to knowing about anchors and rodes. She admitted to being aboard the skiff. She seemed defensive at times. She seemed to be overstating her mental fog. *Seemed*, Naslund reflected. That was the problem. *Seemed* didn't translate to guilt. Nonetheless, Naslund had no intention of going easy on her. She didn't owe Carrie MacLean anything.

Navigating to her inbox, Naslund found a new forensic report, an update on Tyler's skiff. The MU team had processed the skiff's anchor roller. They hadn't uncovered any FPs or DNA carriers, but the clasp was missing. She sat back and envisioned the anchor roller. You had to open the clasp to release the anchor. Perhaps someone pulled the clasp off? Someone impatient, she thought, or someone unfamiliar with the skiff. The report next noted that the skiff's adjustable centerboard was damaged. No surprise there. Two screws had popped out from the centerboard housing inside the hull. Seeing no evidence of tampering, the report concluded they were forced out by the heavy seas and/or the grounding. Naslund wasn't so sure. The grounding would have snapped off the center-

board, but housing screws rarely popped out. Had someone loosened them or removed them?

Shifting gears, she began a list of Thom's city contacts. A Toronto art maven had christened Thom and seven
other painters the "Gang of Eight," a tribute to Canada's
exalted Group of Seven. Over the last few years, Naslund
had met five of the eight at Thom's cottage. Four of them
lived in Toronto. She found their particulars on the web
and added them to a spreadsheet. She recalled that Thom
had been vice-president of a Toronto artists union. She
looked up the union president, phoned him, and convinced
him to email a members list. By 1000, she had the full
particulars of twenty-nine more names.

Shutting down her laptop, she walked to her bedroom
closet, found her best navy suit, and selected a dark blue
blouse. She had dozens of colorful blouses—all of them
"preposterous," according to Pete—but she couldn't wear
one today, not to a Baptist visitation.

Hair brushed back, she left her house and drove
downhill. Other than a car coming uphill, William Street
was empty. Maples lined the street, their leaves filtering
the morning sun. After years of working Toronto's un-
derbelly, she loved being stationed in Wiarton. The town
was low-key yet confident, an easygoing amalgam of past
and present. It was home to about 5,000 residents, a mix-
ture of limestone and tinted glass, of working boats and
pleasure yachts. Not long ago, it demarcated the outer
reaches of cottage country but now urbanites flocked to
the Bruce, flooding the area with city money, which, as
Naslund knew, wasn't all good news. The more money,
the more B&Es, fraud, sham bankruptcies, and arson, not
to mention Bickell's peeves: speeding and DUIs.

Although just opened, Bartlett's Funeral Home was
packed. The low ceiling reminded Naslund of a dungeon.
She made her way toward the casket to pay her respects.

Most people she passed bent her ear, claiming Thom Tyler had no enemies. She recognized the faces. As a cop, it was her business to know them. Half way to the casket, she got boxed out by a gaggle of church ladies. Why did they always set up shop in the aisle? Damned if she knew. When she'd gone to church as a girl—forced there by her mother—no one halted for a huddle in the middle of the aisle. Bit like parking your car on the Gardiner Express.

Slipping through the gaggle, she nodded to John R and John L then to another John, Johnny Mac, and yet another, Big John B. No surprise, she thought, in a town loaded with Johns. As her father had jokingly warned her, "The more Johns you find in that town, the more Baptist it'll be."

With her nods delivered, she fell into line and eventually reached the casket. Given Thom's injuries, the lid was closed. She bowed her head. She didn't fear her own end, but she hated seeing the end of others. Right hand on her heart, she inwardly said her goodbyes.

You were a fine man, Thom Tyler. You were a fine painter too, but I didn't tell you that. Many others did, enough for you to know your worth.

There is one painting I can't get out of my mind: The Tamaracks. *It is almost too beautiful. To me, those trees will always be Tomaracks, with their strong silhouettes and golden hue. Enough.*

Anyway, you didn't take your worth from painting. You took it from your life. You laughed easily. You always saw the glass half full.

Giving Thom a final inner salute, she turned and walked down the aisle.

In the main reception area, she signed the Register Book. Thom's parents stood nearby. John Tyler looked devastated. His snow-white hair, once jet-black like Thom's, hung limply on his forehead. The enormous dark bands around his eyes reminded her of a dejected raccoon. John's wife Deirdre seemed to be holding up better. She looked her usual self, with her still-youthful black hair piled on top of her head.

Deirdre was younger, true, but she also had more experience of death. Her side of the family, the Kellys, had lost more men to the Great Lakes than anyone in Wiarton, for they'd been schooner hands. Even today, many were laker crewmen.

Thom's siblings were scattered about the room, two from John's first wife Fiona Mitchell, who'd died in childbirth, and four from Deirdre. Fiona's oldest, Gordon, viewed the gathering like a captain surveying his crew. Being a successful accountant, he considered himself a big man about town. Naslund studied his face. He looked sad, but inconvenienced too. His sister Gillian looked even more inconvenienced. You never knew with half-siblings, Naslund thought.

She decided to put Gordon and Gillian at the top of the family list and continued her survey.

Thom's younger siblings and extended family appeared to be in shock, the whole dark-swathed clan of them hanging their long-necked heads, looking like bereaved black swans. Bottom of the list, Naslund decided.

She walked up to John and Deirdre Tyler. "I'm sorry for your loss," she said. The word wasn't adequate. *Desolation* came closer.

John managed a muted "Thank you."

Deirdre held Naslund's eyes. "Find out who did it."

She nodded. "We will."

Deirdre clasped her hands. "Get to the bottom of this."

"We will," she repeated.

Deirdre's plea intensified her sense of obligation. According to die-hard Baptists, people were put on earth to pray and obey, not to probe. But she didn't go to church, and she loved to probe. At the station, they joked that she salted her porridge with curiosity.

As Deirdre turned away, Naslund heard a commotion at the front door then a loud angry voice.

J.J. MacKenzie, she thought, and almost immediately John James MacKenzie, Thom's best friend, a local marine mechanic, burst into the reception room. His face was livid red. "I'm furious!" he roared.

The Baptist Sea parted.

"Damn right I am! You should be too!"

No one disagreed, at least not verbally.

John Tyler inched forward, approaching J.J. from the side. "Would you like a coffee, J.J.?"

J.J. stared at him then took in the gathering and bellowed, "He's not dead, you know! He was murdered."

Again, no one disagreed. And, despite the Baptist predilection for arguments, no one pointed out that a murdered man was, in fact, a dead man.

J.J. stormed out of the room.

Naslund made a move to follow him but Carrie MacLean was headed her way, dressed to kill. Loaded metaphor, Naslund thought, but true. In her sleek black dress, MacLean looked ravishing. She'd always been an exotic in Wiarton but today she appeared even more striking.

Rushing up to Naslund, she hugged her. It was the hug of a woman who didn't give a damn what anyone thought. She kept hugging Naslund. She was crying now. "Why, Eva?" Another gust of sobs. "*Why*?"

Naslund guided her toward a chair. Finally she had her seated, shoulders back, head upright. "Can I get you something?" she asked.

MacLean shook her head.

"Sit tight," Naslund cooed. "I'll get you a sandwich."

MacLean forced a smile.

When Naslund returned, the chair was empty. She walked toward the door. There MacLean was, down at the end of the hallway. Standing next to her was Ward Larmer. Although he'd rented a summer cottage in nearby Hope Bay, he looked like he'd just flown in from Manhattan. His thick red hair was swept-back and the lively cast of his eyes spoke of easy camaraderie. He needed a shave. But he always needed a shave. His burly torso was packaged in a tight blue suit framing a too-crisp white shirt and shiny blue tie. The clothes seemed more appropriate for a wedding than a funeral.

Naslund knew never to rush a judgement yet Larmer was an obvious POI. Arranging a friendly look on her face, she approached MacLean and Larmer. Coming closer, she heard MacLean say, "Not now, Ward, later."

Naslund slowed her step.

"Now," Larmer insisted.

"Later!" MacLean hissed.

"Later? Christ, now!"

MacLean tore off in a huff. Her heels beat a furious tattoo.

Larmer turned to Naslund and shook his head. "Look at her. Thinks she's starring in her own movie."

Naslund nodded agreeably. She was in work mode: everyone's friend, everyone's confidant. "Sandwich?" she offered Larmer.

"Why the hell not? Got to fly."

"Where are you off to?" she casually asked.

"My cottage. Getting things ready for some of the Gang."

She nodded. Other than Thom, Larmer was the most famous member of the Gang.

"They're staying with me," he explained. "For the funeral and all."

"That's good of you." Or suspicious, she thought. His

hospitality could be a cover-up, the kind of gesture a murderer might make.

Chomping the sandwich, Larmer made for the door.

Naslund stepped back to study the crowd, to observe without being observed. Her eyes swept the room. There was Louise Hennigan, Thom's previous agent, black from head to foot, from dyed hair to pointy-toed shoes, looking like a voracious crow. The crow flew past Naslund, chasing a rich Torontonian.

Inching farther back, Naslund melted into the wall. Someone had attacked Thom Tyler. Ward Larmer came to mind. Another man did as well: Thom's current agent, Jock MacTavish. Thom had once said that although MacTavish was a good salesman, he was probably cheating him. Naslund hadn't been surprised. She knew MacTavish. Her mother Elaine had once been "friendly" with him. MacTavish was money-hungry. Perhaps Thom had caught him red-handed, and MacTavish had to silence Thom? It was a stretch, Naslund knew, but sometimes you had to stretch.

Having recently spotted MacTavish and guessing that he'd head to the refreshments table, she stood near it. Keeping watch, she ate a peach tart.

No MacTavish.

She considered heading off to "bump into" him, but instead ate another tart.

No MacTavish.

Persistence, she ordered herself. Wait.

Ten minutes later, she called off her mini-stakeout. As she veered toward the table to deposit her empty plate, she saw MacTavish coming her way.

The agent looked ready to impress a bevy of heiresses. Although he was over sixty, very few people knew it. He was muscular and tanned. His blond-white hair was moussed and tousled. He seemed more a collection of expensive items—ring, suit, shoes—than a person. Despite the mourning venue, he wore a light pink shirt and a cyan-blue Harry Rosen suit, the lapels as narrow as his cream-colored tie.

"Eva, my dear, terrible news."

"Horrible," she commiserated.

He pulled her aside. "I hear rumors of suicide."

"Suicide?"

"Some say Thom killed himself. Attached an anchor to his leg and jumped overboard." MacTavish shook his head. "I'm going to quash that rumor. Bad for business. An untimely death, au contraire, is good news: dwindling supply, growing demand. The value of his work will skyrocket. Don't get me wrong," he hastily added, "I'd rather Thom was alive. He had brilliant years ahead of him. Absolutely brilliant."

"He did."

"Speaking of supply," MacTavish effusively said, "I have a wonderful selection. Why don't you tell Elaine to come down to my gallery? I'll give her first dibs."

Ignore the man's greed, Naslund told herself. Show a friendly facade. "I will. Thank you."

He smiled, unleashing a crocodile grin. "By the by, how is Elaine? I haven't seen her in months."

Me either, Naslund thought. Elaine was playing with another new man. "She's fine. Did you just arrive, Jock?"

"Half-an-hour ago. Traffic was awful near the city."

"Always is," Naslund lamented. "Been up much this summer?"

He shook his head.

"Too bad. I know how much you love sailing." MacTavish had a thirty-eight-foot Dufour at the marina. "When was the last time you got out?"

"Mid-June. Too long ago."

She nodded. She'd check that.

"Don't forget. First dibs."

"Thanks, Jock."

Naslund eyed MacTavish as he sauntered away. Had he attacked Thom? He had a boat. He was strong enough. She shook her head. *Enough speculation. You need some dots.* Slipping away from the funeral parlor, she drove to the station.

Chapter 8

Wiarton, OPP Station. July 11th:

Naslund strode into the station at exactly 1059 and headed straight to the murder room. She already knew that Moore prized punctuality.

The double doors were open. The room was packed. The MU team had taken one side of the ten-person boardroom table: Sergeant Lance Chu; Constable Noreen Ross, the video-photographer, who was now working Tyler's cottage with Mitchell and Wolfe; and the two forensic scientists, Constable Jamil Chahoud and Sergeant Gina Domani. On the other side were FID Constables Dan Mitchell and John Wolfe and two new men. Naslund assumed they were the DCs from Central, Stu Conrad and Rob Lowrie. The local PCs assigned to the case sat toward the back: Senior PC Elmore Chandler plus PCs Warren Kraft, Vik Singh, Tom Derlago, and Rosie Weber. Even Bickell was present. The staff sergeant had taken the chair at the opposite end of the table, facing Moore. Naslund sat at her hutch.

Moore called the meeting to order. He wore the same suit as yesterday. It looked grayer. After introductions, he asked if all present had read the Tyler Case summary notes.

Everyone nodded. Moore then asked Chu to update the room. He rose, walked to the whiteboard, and wrote three words: *BLOOD, PRINTS, DNA.*

"Well," he said and faced the room, "we have good news and bad news. The good news? We're further ahead than two days ago. The bad news? We're not very far ahead."

There were a few chuckles.

Naslund glanced at Moore. He didn't look amused.

"Let's start with what we know," Chu said. "Blood. By that I mean the victim's blood and ancillary blood. As the summary states, the victim suffered severe head trauma. He bled profusely. We know what weapons caused the bleeding: a ball-peen hammer and a Phillips screwdriver. And we know their characteristics."

Moore raised a hand to stop Chu. "Pardon the interruption." He addressed the gathering. "As it stands, the two weapons are missing. They are invaluable to our investigation. Absolutely vital. We need to find them." He scanned the room. "If you're tasked with questioning witnesses or POIs, don't ask about the weapons directly. Circle around to them." He turned to Chu. "Back to you."

Chu nodded. "Central has processed the victim's DNA and matched the blood at the primary scene, the boat, to the victim. The blood at that scene is all his. There is no trace of anyone else's blood. So we have zero ancillary blood. Which suggests the victim did not inflict any wounds on his assailant."

Or assailants, Naslund thought, but didn't interrupt Chu.

"Regarding the victim's blood, I want to point out an apparent anomaly. His blood was found near the end of the boat's boom on the starboard side, starting two-point-four meters from the mast, extending to two-point-eleven meters. However, according to the autopsy, there is no indication the boom hit the victim. Our blood splatter expert—" Chu stopped and gestured toward Domani. "—determined the blood was placed there with a cloth. Whoever did so staged the scene. They attempted to make it appear the blood came from a blunt force wound. Whoever did so didn't reckon with Sergeant Domani." He smiled. "She established the blood was placed on the boom with three swipes of the cloth. The cloth was a tight cotton-weave. The lab traced the material. It was imported from Bangladesh. Did that help us?" He shook his head theatrically. "Where does sixty-four percent of the cotton cloth in this country come from?"

"Plants?" Chandler said with a grin.

Naslund glanced at Moore again. Not impressed with Chandler's humor.

Chu chuckled. "And the other thirty-six percent?"

"More plants," Chandler said, "as in more factories."

"I can't say you're wrong." Chu smiled then caught a glimpse of Moore's face. The sergeant's mirth immediately disappeared. "In any case," he continued, "the full specifications are in the notes. As Inspector Moore stated, the assault weapons are vital pieces of evidence. So too is this cloth. It may contain trace material than can lead us to the perp." He stopped, took a swig of coffee, and continued. "Regarding the secondary scene—the boathouse, dock, and studio—we found no blood there." He took another swig of coffee. "Any questions about blood?"

There were none.

"All right," he said and pointed to his second word, "on to Prints. Unfortunately, we only have FPs, fingerprints. No bootprints, no footprints, no tire prints. The primary scene yielded three sets of FPs. The secondary scene was a minefield, riddled with cross-contamination. It yielded no clean prints."

Bad news, Naslund thought. But at least they had prints from the skiff.

"One set of FPs belonged to the victim, Thom Tyler, and one to his partner, Carolyn MacLean. The other is as yet unidentified. As to MacLean, we matched FPs on the boat's bow mooring line to her. Her FPs were likely deposited on the line sometime during the previous thirty days. Which is conflicting evidence. In an interview yesterday, MacLean said she hadn't touched the boat in five weeks."

Moore raised a hand. "We'll bring her back in a few days." He eyed the room. "That doesn't mean she's a second-tier POI. It means we need to gather more evidence. Remember this: every POI is guilty until proven innocent. Absolutely *every* POI." He waved Chu on.

Naslund realized the thirty-day FP estimate might not stand up in court. Any good defense lawyer could undermine FP evidence. However, she kept quiet, assuming Moore knew how fickle FPs were.

"Let's move to the final category," Chu said. "DNA. You've probably heard the old saw that the first rule of a CS is that anyone who's been there leaves something behind and takes something away. They might leave behind DNA, in a carrier like hair. And they might take away fibers, perhaps from a piece of clothing. Leave. Take. That's a pretty good rule. However, in this case, nobody left anything—other than the victim, that is. Our boat sweep yielded DNA carriers in the form of his blood, mucus, and skin. But we have nothing on the assailant, the perp. Or perps. We can't rule out multiple perps."

Right, Naslund said to herself.

"The perps didn't leave anything, other than traces of the cotton cloth. No personal blood, no prints, no DNA. They weren't likely greenhorns."

Naslund wasn't sure about that. She'd run it by Chu later. They could be lucky greenhorns. Georgian Bay could have washed away their DNA, even though it didn't erase other bio matter, such as Tyler's FPs and blood. Hair and skin weren't as sticky as prints and blood.

"Regarding take-aways," Chu continued, "at this point, we don't know who took anything away, or what they took. We have to find them first, or their cars or homes. Then we'll get their take-aways." He nodded to Moore and sat down.

Moore stood. "Thank you, Sergeant." He surveyed the room deliberately, paying particular attention to the non-detectives. "It should go without saying that no one on this team—no one other than me, that is—is authorized to talk to the media. That means no communication with reporters or journalists, local, regional, or national, web-based or otherwise. And no web posts. No Facebook, no Twitter, none of that. Is that clear?"

Everyone nodded.

"On another note, I don't abide by lone wolves. We're in this together, so we work together. Make sure everybody on this team knows what you're doing and what you're thinking. How can you ensure that? Always update your case notes. Always! Understood?"

More nods.

"As Sergeant Chu stated, we know how the victim was assaulted and with what weapons. But we don't know much more. Yet. That's where you all come in. Everyone in this room can help, whether actively, or in a support role." Moore stopped and eyed Bickell. "*Everyone* can help us find those take-aways." He paused. "Mr. Tyler was murdered Monday. We're already three days out. They say a case goes cold after forty-eight hours." His index finger stabbed the air. "This one won't! Dig into everything and presume nothing! All right, let's get to work. I've drawn up a list of actions. See the corkboard next to the door. Attend to your actions." He dismissed the meeting.

It was almost lunch time. Naslund let everyone file out of the room ahead of her. As she left, Moore called out. "I want to run something by you, Sergeant."

How about over coffee, she thought.

Moore had other ideas. He led Naslund to her former office. "Have a seat," he said.

She sat in the spare chair.

"Conrad and Lowrie are currently reading the complete case notes. They'll join us at fourteen-thirty. In the meantime, I want to explore a new avenue."

"Okay."

"As I said earlier, we're not done with MacLean." Moore pursed his lips. "We'll bring her in again. But I was thinking of bringing Ward Larmer in first."

From what Naslund had seen, although Moore liked to appear collegial, he did what he wanted. Regardless, she agreed with his plan. MacLean could wait. Given Larmer's words and actions at the visitation, he was an obvious POI.

"Incidentally," Moore continued, "Larmer will probably shed some light on her. This morning I went over the list of calls in and out of her cell number. Guess who phoned her three times yesterday?"

The answer seemed clear. "Ward Larmer?"

Moore nodded. "As it happens, he's got a raft of unpaid parking tickets in the city. A brace of speeders too. Seems to be the me-first sort. You knew Tyler. Do you know Larmer?"

"A bit," she said. "I socialized with him a few times at Tyler's place. From what I know, he's very self-confident. Self-centered too. Your me-first label fits."

"Good. We can't corroborate everything MacLean said, but I don't think she's lying about Larmer. According to what she reported, he was envious of Tyler." Moore smiled. "I know, she could be overstating things. Let's say half-envious. Let's call it potential motive."

"Okay."

"Larmer might have had another motive: Revenge. Remember what you told me about MacLean yesterday, on the way to the autopsy? Tyler stole her from Larmer."

"Not exactly. It was before I was posted here, but the way I heard it, she left Larmer for Tyler."

"Adds up to the same thing. I don't think Larmer would forget that. Losing a looker like her."

Looker, Naslund thought. Some men's labels for women were so predictable. From what she'd seen so far, Moore wasn't a full-blown chauvinist, yet he'd scored high on what she and fellow female officers called the CP—Chauvinist Pig—Scale, with *Pig* referring to *cop,* not *man.* After all, as her female friends joked, all men were pigs at one time or another. "That was ten years ago," she said.

"I know," Moore replied, "a long time to wait for revenge. But, as the crime psychologists at Central keep telling me, killings often arise from repressed emotions—desire, envy, love—the kind of sentiments that ferment for a long time. Ten years is not unusual. Despite what Larmer says, I wouldn't be surprised if he and MacLean were still lovers."

Really? Naslund thought. From what she knew, MacLean had eyes for Thom and no one else.

"As for opportunity," Moore continued, "having frequently sailed with Tyler, Larmer had access to the skiff on multiple occasions." He paused. "Potential motive and opportunity. A reasonable starting point."

Naslund agreed. Even with no apparent motive, Larmer was suspicious.

"I took a little drive this morning, out to Hope Bay. Nice spot."

She nodded.

"Our tip line got a call from one of Larmer's neighbors, a Mrs. Carson, an elderly lady who thinks he's suspicious. I went to see her. She saw Thom Tyler at Larmer's place five times last month. She said they were often arguing, sometimes even yelling at each other."

"Sounds plausible," Naslund said. "Larmer's a hothead."

"Beyond that, she doesn't like Larmer—'too sharply-dressed'—or his accent—'snooty Englishman.'" Moore paused. "I'd like to take a run at him today, right after lunch."

"Sure. Let me call him." She looked up Larmer's local number and called it for the inspector.

Moore switched on the speakerphone.

"Hello," a suave British voice answered.

"Mr. Larmer?" Moore said.

"Yes."

"Detective Inspector Moore, OPP."

"What can I do you for, Inspector?"

Do you for? Naslund thought. Did Larmer think this was a neighborly chat?

"We want to speak with you about Thom Tyler," Moore said. "I understand you're at Hope Bay."

"Correct."

"Good, you're close. We'll see you at one o'clock."

"This afternoon?"

"Yes," Moore said.

"Well."

The line went quiet. More delaying tactics, Naslund thought, the same as with MacLean.

"As you may know," Larmer finally said, "many of

Thom's friends are staying with me. How about tomorrow?"

"Today, Mr. Larmer. We'll be at your place in an hour."

"I have guests. That's not convenient."

"All right. Be at the station at one o'clock. Sharp."

"Pardon?"

"Sharp, Mr. Larmer."

"Oh, yes. Fine."

"Do you know where the station is?"

Larmer didn't reply.

"I'll arrange for a police cruiser to transport you. There's one near the end of your lane." It was bull, but a car could be there in less than fifteen minutes.

Naslund heard a screen door slide open. She sensed Larmer stepping outside to verify Moore's words and finding no proof one way or the other. "I know where the station is," Larmer eventually replied.

"Excellent. You are entitled to a lawyer. Bring one if you like."

"What for?"

"Please yourself."

As the inspector hung up, he shook his head. "Another ditherer. Can you interview him? I want to observe him from the shadow room."

"Of course."

Naslund returned to the murder room, booted up her laptop, and read the transcript of the inspector's Hope Bay interview. It was an understatement to say that Mrs. Carson didn't like Larmer. She detested him.

Chapter 9

At 1310, Naslund ushered Ward Larmer into the interview room. The POI had no lawyer in tow. He smelled of stale armpits.

"Have a seat," she said and pointed to the Slider.

"No 'have a seat, old friend,'" Larmer said. "No sandwiches?"

She ignored him and pointed to the Slider. He appeared to have aged a few months in a matter of hours. There were dark blotches under his eyes. He wore a tailored pinstripe suit and an open-necked shirt. Despite the change of clothes, he reeked. The confines of the room intensified his smell. It seemed he was nervous. Then again, it was a hot, humid day. "Mr. Larmer, I'm sure you know that Thom Tyler died in suspicious circumstances."

"Is that right?"

"Very suspicious." Naslund didn't like his voice. It gave the impression that anything he didn't know didn't count. "Where were you between seven p.m. on Sunday July seventh and seven a.m. on Monday July eighth?"

"At my Hope Bay cottage."

Larmer was using his legs to keep his back tight to the chair. He appeared to have prior experience with the Slider. They'd have to check his rap sheet again. She decided to needle him. "Address?" she barked.

He recited it.

She made no move to jot it down. She had his background details. "Occupation?"

"Artist."

"You claimed you were at Two-Twelve Hope Bay Road during the time period indicated. Do you have proof?"

"I phoned La Toya, my girlfriend, from there around eleven p.m."

"What's her full name and phone number?"

Larmer told her.

She wrote on a legal pad. "Did you use a cellphone or a land line?"

"Cellphone."

"As you may know, we can subpoena your exact geographical location." It was bull. They could get a close hit, but not the exact coordinates. All phone carriers were obliged to respond to a warranted location request. Using cell-tower triangulation, they could usually pinpoint latitude and longitude to within thirty meters.

"I have nothing to hide," Larmer asserted.

"Good. What other calls did you make during that period?"

"Which period?"

"The one just mentioned, Mr. Larmer. Between seven p.m. on July seventh and seven a.m. on July eighth."

The POI raised a finger to his lips. "Let me think. Okay, I know. I phoned La Toya again around midnight, then at seven a.m."

"Three times in eight hours?"

He nodded aggressively. "I love her, Sergeant."

Huh, a lover-boy. "Who else did you phone?"

"No one," he curtly stated and glared at her.

Naslund made another note. If lover-boy had been nervous, he no longer was. In fact, he was combative. "What about yesterday? Who did you phone yesterday?"

"Yesterday? Too many people to remember. I was helping organize the visitation and the funeral. As you know, many of Thom's friends are staying with me."

"Did you make any arrangements with Carolyn MacLean?"

"Arrangements?"

Naslund controlled herself. "Did you phone her, Mr. Larmer?"

The POI appeared to be scouring his memory. "Yes, I did. Three times, in fact."

She pretended to write that down.

He grinned. "You seem to like taking notes. I don't know why. I know you're recording me."

She eyed him disdainfully. "Let's go over things again, Mr. Larmer." She paused. "Just in case you 'forgot' something."

He shot her a look that said *Do-what-you-want, you fuckers always do*.

Naslund nodded sharply. *In your case, we certainly will*. "Do you have any proof of your whereabouts on July seventh, from seven p.m. onwards?" She smiled contemptuously. "Anyone who can verify your location? Other than you."

He shook his head. "I was inside."

"How about when you drove in from Toronto on Sunday? Perhaps someone saw your car?" She knew that Mrs. Carson saw him drive in on Saturday, not Sunday.

"I didn't arrive in Hope Bay Sunday. I'd been there since Saturday afternoon."

"What time Saturday?"

"Just after three. Three-oh-five, to be precise. I looked at the kitchen clock."

"Very good," she said. Bull, she thought, that's too precise. She changed topics to keep him off-kilter. "How long have you known Thom Tyler?"

He didn't hesitate. "Thirteen years."

"So, you're old friends?"

"Yes. Best friends."

"How long have you known Carolyn MacLean?"

"Fourteen years."

"Are you best friends?"

"No."

"Good friends?"

"No. We're ex-lovers."

"And that bars you from being good friends?"

"In this case, it does."

That seemed right, Naslund thought. She'd sensed as much with MacLean. "Did you visit Mr. Tyler and Ms. MacLean on Saturday or Sunday?"

"No. Thom and I were supposed to go painting on Tuesday."

"Just you and Thom? No Carolyn."

"Correct. Carrie, or Carolyn, if you prefer." Larmer paused and gave her an ever-so-polite smile. "Carrie never joined us on our painting trips. She isn't what you'd call a camping type."

"How do you know that?"

"Because," he slowly enunciated, "she said it."

"It seems strange that you didn't visit them. Mallory Beach is so close to Hope Bay. How far would you say it is on foot?"

"*On foot*?"

"Yes. Walking or hiking."

"I don't hike."

"How many minutes by car?"

The POI took a sip of water then another. He examined the ceiling. Naslund eyed him. Did he want to waste time? She'd gladly toss him in a cell and come back next week.

The POI kept studying the ceiling, adopting a thousand-meter stare for a five-meter room.

She waited, carefully scrutinizing his face. Some POIs could crease or un-crease their foreheads at will. Their eyes shifted depending on the light. However, people couldn't manipulate their mouths for a prolonged period. Mouths didn't lie. From the set of Larmer's lips, he was at ease.

Enough, she decided. "I said, 'How many minutes by car?'"

"Ten minutes. As you know. Allow me to clarify something, Constable Naslund—pardon me, Sergeant. The last time I saw Thom was on Wednesday, July third at sunset, that is, just after nine p.m. We'd sailed his Mackinaw all evening, and the evening before, and the evening before that as well. I'll be happy to make a formal statement."

Naslund sat back. Larmer was slippery. Everything he said seemed right, but small bits seemed too right. He was too confident.

As she examined his mouth, her scrutiny was interrupted by a knock on the door. Striding to the door, she looked through its small window. Inspector Moore.

The man motioned for Naslund to let him in.

Huh, she thought, what's this? She opened the door.

Within seconds, Moore invited her to take a seat and turned to the POI. "Detective Inspector Moore," he said and thrust out his badge. "Homicide. But I'm sure you guessed that."

Larmer shot him a look that said *piss off.*

Moore grinned then stood directly across from

Larmer, head tilted back, as if to say *now the real interview begins*. "I'm curious, Mr. Larmer. I wonder if you can enlighten me. How do you think Mr. Tyler ended up in the lake?"

"I don't know. I wasn't there, was I?"

"No? Well then, let me recreate the scene for you. It's unlikely that Mr. Tyler was taking a leak, as the saying goes. The recovery team found his pants zipper up. As to getting caught in fishing lines, he had none set. Now, the boom could have knocked him overboard but that too is unlikely. The boom on Mr. Tyler's skiff was attached to the mast at a height of..." Moore donned his specs and pulled some notes from a pocket. "One-point-six-seven meters." He looked up and studied Larmer through the half-moons. "That's five-and-a-half feet. Plenty of clearance, even for a six-footer like Mr. Tyler. Nevertheless, he ended up in the lake." Moore approached the table. "How?"

"I don't know."

"Is that right?" Moore shook his head and then sat and slowly shuffled his notes then shuffled them again and again—a tactic often used to set a POI on edge. Eventually, he removed his specs and carefully pocketed them, holding his words, trying to ratchet up Larmer's anxiety.

Larmer studied the ceiling.

Moore kept eying him, hoping to unnerve him with silence.

Larmer's gaze didn't waiver.

Naslund wasn't surprised by the standoff. Larmer and Moore might be physical opposites, but they were two of a kind: pit bulls. She wasn't surprised by Moore's sudden entry either. He was obviously the "takeover-when-I-want" type. Old boys often were. She got along well with most male colleagues. She wondered how things would evolve with Moore.

The inspector broke the silence. "I like interviewees who answer promptly. Don't you, Sergeant?"

"I certainly do," she said.

"Not to mention, cooperate." Moore eyed Larmer. "So far, I'd say you're failing on both counts."

The POI shrugged.

Moore pursed his lips. "Mr. Larmer, I understand you're a sailor."

"Yes?"

"Well then, you must know what makes a good sailor." Moore had a smile on his face yet none in his voice.

The suspect shrugged.

"Let me suggest an answer. A person comfortable with complexity. All those pulleys and ropes. An organized person. Beyond that, a practical person. Someone who can splice ropes or, let's say, adjust an anchor clasp." Moore let a few heartbeats pass. "When did you last change a car tire?"

"A what?"

"A car tire, Mr. Larmer."

"I don't change my tires."

"Oh? I assume a person who drives like you has quite a few flats. What happens when you get a flat?"

"I call CAA."

"Good for you." Moore abruptly stood, planted his hands on the table, and leaned closer. "However, I'm sure you're capable of changing a tire. You look strong. Do you lift weights?"

"Sometimes."

"Box?"

"No."

"Enjoy inflicting pain?"

Larmer's eyes narrowed, his face hardened.

Moore harrumphed. *I know you do*, his expression

said. "Why do you think we're interested in your strength?"

Larmer didn't reply.

"Let me tell you." Moore assumed his tallest height. "Someone pushed Mr. Tyler overboard. He was a big man, which suggests his assailant was a strong person."

Larmer said nothing.

Moore didn't mention the hammer blows. As Naslund knew, he wouldn't reveal everything they had, not yet.

"I'd say you're very strong." Moore smiled menacingly. "Very capable."

The suspect glared at him. "Of what?"

Naslund stood and took a step toward Larmer.

Moore slowly circled the table, his methodical footsteps echoing off the cement floor. When he reached Larmer, he stopped.

A few moments later, he brought his bony chin to within an inch of Larmer's ear, as if he were going to speak. But he said nothing. He continued pacing until he stood behind Larmer again. "You are free to go." He paused. "For the time being."

The suspect seemed unmoved.

Smug snot. Naslund wanted to cuff him in the ear. Better yet, kick him in the crotch.

Moore walked away and stood across from the suspect. "We'd like to request your cooperation."

"What for?"

"We'd like to fingerprint and DNA you."

"I know my rights."

"We can arrest you."

Larmer shrugged.

"I'll have a warrant by three," Moore said. "Tomorrow. Meanwhile, you can enjoy our hospitality."

Naslund knew it was a bluff. Moore couldn't detain Larmer without arresting him and they had nothing on him. Moore spoke into an intercom. "Constable Chandler?"

"Yes, Inspector," a deep voice growled—Chandler putting on his hard-ass act. He was a big man, the size of a linebacker. His voice was even bigger.

"We need a cell for Mr. Larmer." Moore eventually glanced at the suspect.

"All right," Larmer said as if he didn't care. "Process me."

Moore nodded. "Fingerprint and DNA the *detainee*," he said into the intercom. He smiled malevolently. "The interviewee, I mean."

"You want him released?" Chandler grunted.

"For now."

Moore eyed the man. "You are not permitted to leave the province."

Larmer didn't acknowledge him.

"Did you hear me?"

The suspect waited then nodded insolently.

ᥱᥣᥱᥣ

Sitting in Moore's office after the interview, Naslund gulped down a mouthful of cold coffee. On the one hand, she resented Moore's interruption—a seven, she figured, on the CP Scale. On the other hand, she accepted it. Top guns weren't known for their diffidence. They didn't care about stepping on toes. As it happened, her father had warned her about cops like Moore. He'd advised her to ignore them. Naslund agreed with him. Besides, it made sense to railroad Larmer.

Across the room, the inspector was pursing his lips. He leaned forward in his chair. "Larmer's a snake. No doubt about it."

"Agreed."

"If he's our perp, I'd say there's a good chance he left his cottage very early on Monday morning, before Tyler left his boathouse dock."

"Possible."

"Mitchell and Wolfe came with me when I visited Mrs. Carson this morning. They're ninjas, those two. They melted into the bush and searched for DNA carriers and prints behind Larmer's cottage, back to the Bruce Trail, which could take him to Tyler's place on foot. But they didn't find anything." Moore shrugged. "However, he could have walked down his driveway, crossed the road, and got in a boat. Mitchell and Wolfe found a jumble of prints across the road. Good cover."

She nodded.

"The man doesn't own a boat, but he may have 'borrowed' one. I spoke with Chandler. A small boat with an outboard would get Larmer up Hope Bay, around Cape Croker, and into Colpoys Bay in a few hours. Let's say he left around oh-three-hundred on the eighth, he'd arrive in Colpoys Bay in plenty of time to intercept Tyler's skiff and attack him."

She shrugged. "An outboard? I read your report on Mrs. Carson. She didn't mention hearing any outboard that night and she said she never sleeps."

"Right, but she might have dozed off."

"Okay."

"I'll re-visit her. I think Larmer used a water route. If he didn't use a motorboat, he could have sailed."

"True." It was a long shot, but worth pursuing. Naslund told herself to step back, to give Moore the benefit of the doubt. The inspector was a top gun. He had years of experience.

"I read the marine reports," he continued. "There was an eight-knot wind that night, steady all night, until it picked up near dawn. I checked with Chandler again. It would have taken about four hours to sail to Colpoys Bay in a small boat. I've asked Chandler to look into reports of stolen boats, plus all recent boat rentals on the Bruce, in any name. Larmer may have rented."

"Right," she said.

"Now we need some hard evidence. At this point, we're running on speculation. However, I'm sure of one thing. He lied to us."

She nodded. Lying was expected. Most people lied to them. Perps always lied.

"But I'm not sure what he lied *about*. His movements? His phone calls? His sailing routine with Tyler? By the way, Larmer could have other motives besides envy and revenge. There's always the old standby. Money. Other cultures murder for honor but North Americans usually do it for money. Let's examine the ownership of Tyler's paintings. Determine who inherits what. Ditto for his other assets." Moore raced on. "Let me take that up. I'll get a solid financial picture of who might have benefited from his death. I suspect Larmer did. If so, it'll give us ammo to probe his connection to Tyler."

"Right."

"We'll bring him back tomorrow, immediately after the funeral."

"Okay."

Moore stood. "I'll get Conrad and Lowrie."

Naslund nodded. After reading the Hope Bay transcript, she'd looked up the two DCs on the staff intranet. They were newbie detectives but not raw rookies, early-thirties, from what she could tell. Conrad was a former OPP PC, Lowrie, an ex-RCMP corporal.

Moore quickly returned with the DCs. Introductions complete, he pointedly asked the two if they had any questions about the case notes.

They had none.

"Nothing?" he asked again.

They shook their heads. Naslund sympathized with them. She probably wouldn't have asked anything either.

Moore summarized the recent interview with Larmer, and then opened the floor to suggestions.

Conrad remained silent. He appeared to be cowed by Moore.

"Might be good to look into Larmer's sailing ability," Lowrie said. "Does he own a boat?"

Moore shook his head.

"Does he swim?"

"Good question," Moore said. "I'll leave that to you to find out."

"Yes, sir. Do you know if he belongs to a gym?"

"Again, over to you." Moore sat back. "All right, Constables, we'll leave it at that. Sergeant Naslund, do you have a list of Mr. Tyler's family members and local acquaintances?"

"Almost complete. I'll email it to the DCs in fifteen minutes."

"CC me as well. DCs, I expect you to start your interviews tomorrow at oh-nine-hundred sharp. Get your schedules solidified this afternoon."

The DCs nodded and left.

A rush of annoyance surged through Naslund. The inspector didn't have to micromanage them.

"I'm going to visit Mrs. Carson," Moore said and shut down his computer.

Naslund watched him tighten his tie and assume his public face, his earnest, insistent face. The man seemed to have one gear only: full-speed ahead. Well, she decided, better follow Graysuit's lead. Back at her desk, she quickly completed the Tyler family and acquaintances list then strode to her car. It was time to talk to J.J. MacKenzie.

Chapter 10

Naslund had a good idea where to find J.J. Mac-Kenzie. At this time of day, the mechanic was usually taking a coffee break. She drove downtown, surveying the streets as she went. All quiet—as usual. The afternoon sun burned through a thin layer of clouds. The town seemed to be in siesta mode.

Up ahead, she spotted MacKenzie striding toward the Berford Coffee Shop. She parked and started walking. Although a tall heavy man, MacKenzie moved like a mountain lion, all power and dignity. He surged forward chin first, showcasing a big, bushy beard. She quickened her pace. The traffic light turned red at William Street and the mountain lion stopped.

She called out. "Mr. MacKenzie."

The mechanic looked over his shoulder then turned around. "Sergeant Naslund." He feigned alarm. "You here to arrest me?"

"Might be," she said.

"Didn't do it, Sergeant. He was my best friend. But I know you have to ask. And I have an alibi."

"Good. Tell me, for the record." For someone so angry at the morning visitation, MacKenzie now had a calm look on his face.

"I was in Hamilton for an Independents meeting. Left here Friday at four p.m., got back Monday at noon. You can ask my wife Marie. Plus about four hundred other mechanics."

"That's a lot of mechanics."

"Plenty more out there. We're going to put the Walmarts of the world out of business."

"Sounds good to me."

"Demographics, Sarge. More and more folks like the local touch." MacKenzie grinned then raised a hand in peace. "But we'll let the Marters die on their own."

"Good." Naslund nodded. "I'd like to talk about Thom. We were close this last year or so."

"He often mentioned you."

That was nice to know. "How about a coffee?"

"Sure."

დაება

"You're right," J.J. said as he stirred his coffee. "Thom loved being out on the water. He had a good life. A great life," he corrected himself. "And to think he was taken by the bay. That's almost the worst part of it."

"It's an awful irony," Naslund said.

J.J. nodded.

She took a quick look around. The place was empty. "Can I ask you something?"

"Go ahead."

"Why the irate act in the funeral parlor? You don't seem angry now."

"You're right. It was an act. I want people to talk about the enraged mechanic, that crazy man from Colpoys."

"They will."

"Good." He smiled. "Most locals are too taciturn. Too Scottish."

"Aye." Naslund mimicked her aunt. Growing up, she'd heard plenty of Scots burr. Her father was Swedish, but her mother's side was Scottish. "Hang on, I have more to say. Nae, I canna say more."

J.J. chuckled. "It's long odds, I know, but if people talk, it might uncover the truth about Thom's death. Gossip has wings. As my wife says, it flits around like a blue jay. Word will get back to me."

"Sounds good." Thom had once said that J.J. MacKenzie knew more about boats than anyone in Wiarton. With their canoe sterns and sharp prows, Mackinaws cut through the water like a porpoise, yet she figured they had a downside. "Can I get your opinion on something?"

"Any time."

"Personally, I find Mackinaw centerboards narrow and a bit weak. What about you?"

"I'll give you narrow," he replied, "but not weak. Thom's Mackinaw rode out dozens of heavy squalls. The centerboard was solid."

"Would you be willing to give testimony in court? You know, for the police?"

"Me? For the police?"

"Yep."

He eyed her without moving a muscle. "Maybe," he eventually said. "I'll be happy to give you an opinion at any time, but I'm not sure I'll testify. History, Sarge."

Naslund nodded. She knew that MacKenzie's father had been jailed for labor unrest in the mid-80s and had died in prison.

She hesitated. "What I'm going to mention now is supposition. Pure supposition."

"Understood. You never said it."

"Exactly. I think two screws popped out from the centerboard housing and I think they got forced out by heavy seas or grounding. Does that sound right to you?"

"No."

"Why not?"

"If she grounded, the centerboard itself would be damaged, but not likely the inner housing. Centerboard screws don't usually pop out—grounding, high seas or whatever—not in my experience. They're Phillips screws, not flatheads. You can sink them in deep. Plus they're inside the hull and behind a set of ribs. Pretty well protected."

"Thanks."

J.J. took a sip of coffee then looked up. "I've been doing a little investigating myself."

"Yes?"

"I have a bead on what might have happened to Thom."

"I'm all ears."

J.J. grinned. "I'd say you're more than ears."

"Was that a compliment?"

He grinned again.

"All right." She smiled. "Let's keep on track."

"No harm meant. I'm happily married. Would you consider my news an anonymous tip?"

Why not? she thought. "Okay."

"Well, a young fella from Colpoys saw a Mackinaw about six-fifteen a.m. on the day Thom died."

"A young fella?"

"Fine. My son. Doesn't matter which one."

For now, Naslund decided.

"My son saw one man onboard. He's sure it was Thom. Thom was like an uncle to him."

"That might not stand up in court."

"Court? This is anonymous, right?"

"Right," she said. "Completely anonymous. Pardon the line of questioning. Habit."

J.J. eyed her.

"You have my word." She told herself to get her head on straight. At this point in the investigation, court should be the last thing on her mind. She wasn't prosecuting a murderer, she was trying to find one. If court came later, and hopefully it would, she'd cross the disclosure bridge with J.J. then.

"All right," he said. "The youngster knows who he saw. I sat with him a long time. I believe him. He's a boat spotter, likes to use a pair of WW-Two binocs my father once owned. Anyway, that morning, he was camping on Hay Island with two kid brothers. There's a lookout on the east side. He was sitting there with the binocs when he saw Thom's Mackinaw."

"What exactly did he see?"

"Well, he saw a fishing boat moving fast, approaching the Mackinaw from the south."

"Did the boats meet?"

"He doesn't know. He had to get back to his campsite, to make breakfast for his brothers. You can't see the water from there. It's inland."

"Too bad."

J.J. nodded. "He identified the fishing boat as an Albin Tournament Express. There were two men aboard. He didn't think they were fishermen."

"Why?"

"According to him, they didn't look like fishermen. They were dressed like city guys: tank tops and tight shorts. They were young too. Under thirty, he figured. Most guys who fish are older."

"True."

"Coincidentally," J.J. added, "the Griffith Island Club has an Albin TE Thirty-Five. My cousin Marty Fox works over there as a guide. According to him, the club Albin was out that morning."

The club, a private fishing and hunting operation, owned the whole of Griffith Island. "Did you report any of this to the OPP tip line?" she asked. "Anything at all?"

"No. I'll be honest. I don't want your crew questioning my family."

"Understood," she said. "How about the *Wiarton Echo*'s tip line?"

"No. Didn't want anything interfering with my little investigation." He sounded apologetic. "But you can report it now. Just remember, no mention of Colpoys or my family."

"Absolutely," she said. "Another coffee?"

"No thanks."

"I'm going to jot down what you just told me. Are you okay with that?"

"Sure, Sarge. Scribble away."

"Here's my private number." She handed her personal card to MacKenzie. "Call me anytime."

☙❧☙

Having left the coffee shop, Naslund sat in her car and called MacKenzie's tip in to Moore. The inspector said he'd dispatch two officers to the Griffith club ASAP.

On the way home, she drove to the end of Bayview and walked to a lookout facing Colpoys Bay. Out toward Lake Huron, the water deepened, changing from turquoise to azure to navy. She gazed past the three islands at the mouth of the bay—White Cloud, Hay, and Griffith—to the larger waters of the lake, once called *La Mer Douce*, the Sweet Sea. On a map, the long finger of the Bruce Peninsula yearned toward the northern forests. She felt a yearning too. It felt like she'd been alone for years. She seemed to be slipping into spinsterhood. There were hardly any single men her age in the area. The ones that were didn't like cops. Lance Chu was nice—very nice—but she didn't want to date a cop. She'd learned that lesson in Toronto.

Leaning forward, she studied the bay. Two fishermen in a Lund drifted steadily offshore, trailing their lines. The wind had veered from northwest to southeast, a 180-degree turn. It was high time for her to make the same kind of turn. It was time to turn her home life around. She knew there were men in the city, yet she wanted to meet someone local, someone down-to-earth. There was a guy who worked at the *Echo*, Hal Bell, a journalist and writer. He wasn't a hipster, he wasn't a redneck. Two points already. He was exuberant and genuine. Two more. She liked his looks: tall, dark, the kind of hair she loved, longish in front, short at the back and sides. They'd chatted many times over the last few months. He seemed to like her.

She leaned farther forward. *Do it*, she told herself, *ask him if he wants to share a meal*. As it happened, he was running the *Echo*'s tip line for the Tyler investigation. She had a ready-made reason to eat with him—to ask if he'd share his tips more quickly with the OPP. The faster the team got tips, the better. She nodded to herself. *Call him.*

സ

Naslund sat at her kitchen table, checking her bank account on her phone. Hell! Two hundred and eighty-two dollars left for the month of July. She needed at least three-quarters of it to buy groceries.

Her money troubles were a recent development.

She'd let Pete talk her into buying a huge house. She'd also paid off his crushing grad school debt, which put her deep in the hole before the house came along. These days, after shelling out for an enormous mortgage, what was left of her decent pay packet barely covered utility and social club bills, work lunches, and groceries. Although she owned a century-old grange, it looked two centuries old. The paint was peeling. The roof sagged like spinach in an August drought. She'd sold her sailboat, a Jeanneau-27. She'd probably have to sell her house.

Being half-Scottish, she knew how to weather financial trouble. "Avoid" spending money. Always eat at home. But she couldn't invite Hal to her place. That was too forward. They'd have to eat out. Go Dutch. Eying her account balance again, she did an instant calculation. A buffet dinner plus half a liter of wine, maybe an aperitif. With the tip, over forty dollars.

What could she do? Over-extend her credit card again? No. She'd done too much of that.

She couldn't cancel her golf or curling memberships. The OPP brass expected their officers to be in the public eye. She wasn't going to quit her women's hockey team. She loved ice hockey.

She had no choice. She had to cut back on groceries. *Move it*, she told herself. *Call him now*. He'd hinted that he'd go out with her anytime.

I've been thinking, another voice said. *Why don't you cancel your life insurance? It makes no sense to insure your life if you're living half a life.*

Exactly, she thought. Pulling out her personal phone, she called the insurance company.

Despite languishing in on-hold hell for what felt like hours and repeating that yes, she wanted to suspend her plan—no, not add to it, or buy another one, or buy car insurance—she finally suspended her plan. Mission accomplished, she called Hal. After a nod to the weather and expressions of sadness about Thom Tyler's death, she broached the subject of discussing the tip line over dinner that evening.

"That would be wonderful," he replied. "We're lucky, you know."

That's good, she thought. "We are?" she kidded.

"Yes. The tips are flooding in."

"I knew it. Dinner will be all business. No time for fun."

"Damn it. I finally dine with the most beautiful woman in town, and she has to talk work."

"Only until nine p.m."

Hal chuckled. "Can you meet at seven-thirty?"

"That's fashionably late."

"As always, Sergeant."

"Eva."

Chapter 11

Naslund exited the shower and wrapped a towel around her hair. Catching sight of herself in the mirror, she smiled. *Good move, young lady.*

Well, she had to admit, that was half-true. Calling Hal was good, but she wasn't exactly young. Leaning closer to the mirror, she surveyed the wrinkles around her eyes. *Forget 'em*, she told herself. Wrinkles or not, she wasn't the worst catch around.

At five-feet-seven and 144 pounds, she wasn't as lithe as Carrie MacLean, but she was fit, and, as her father used to say, still full of mischief. In her mother's eyes, she was a Tomboy. In her father's, she'd been a paragon of Swedish womanhood, other than her unruly auburn hair, statuesque and strong.

As she styled her hair, taming the wildest waves, her duty phone rang. She walked to the bedroom and found the phone. "Sergeant Naslund, OPP."

"Hello, Sergeant," said a tentative voice. "Constable Derlago."

"Yes, Constable."

"I'm—I'm at the main CS, Tyler's boat. Someone stole some things from it."

Jesus. "Where's Sergeant Chu?"

"He had to go to Orillia. To a meeting. So did the other three. I—I was charged with keeping the site secure until twenty-two-hundred."

"What happened?"

"Well, I was at the MU and I spotted a man sneaking around the boat. I called out to him. He started running. He got away."

"Did you get a good look at him?"

"Not exactly. He was medium-build and bald, that's what stuck in my mind."

"Okay." Naslund decided to go easy on Derlago. He was the station rookie, still on probation.

"And he ran like a middle-aged man," Derlago said, gathering confidence. "You know, fast enough, but clumsy. He bolted and disappeared across Highway One. I tried to chase him down, eh, but he had a big head-start. He disappeared into the bush. I'm sorry."

"Okay," she said. "You did your best, Constable. So, what did the thief take?"

"I saw him carrying two lines. When I checked the boat, the bow mooring line was missing and the stern one too."

"Are you sure?"

"Yes. I did a once-over when I arrived. They were gone."

"And they were mooring lines?"

"Yes."

Well, at least the rookie knew boats. "Did you inform Sergeant Chu?"

"No. Not yet," Derlago added.

"I'll call him."

"Thank you. Seems like the thief didn't care," Derlago said. "Operating like that in broad daylight, eh. He must think he's untraceable."

"Likely." Naslund checked the time. An hour and a half before dinner with Hal. She better go to the scene. She better phone Moore as well. "Stay close to the boat, Constable. I'll be there in fifteen."

Signing off, she shook her head. Moore would probably blow a gasket. Too late for that. There was a bigger issue: why had someone burgled the skiff now? It didn't add up. The white coats had had plenty of time to lift any bio evidence. Perhaps the mooring lines held more than bio evidence?

She tried Moore's number. It was busy. She dried herself, pulled on a pair of tight jeans and a white camisole, and then tried again. Still busy. She left a message, telling the inspector about the theft and that everything was under control. Grabbing a lightweight blue jacket, she ran out of the house.

As she drove up Highway One, she phoned Chu on her hands-free set.

"Sergeant Chu, FID."

"Hello, Naslund here."

"Howdy."

"Bad news. Someone took two lines from Tyler's boat."

"You're kidding. What about that PC? He was guarding the scene."

"He was. But I don't think he was close enough to the boat. He was at the MU."

"Shit."

"Yeah."

Chu sighed. "What's done is done."

"The PC saw the thief," she said. "He can probably ID him in a lineup. If we get that far."

"Good for the PC, but we won't likely need him. The whole CS is under twenty-four/seven surveillance. Ross rigged up two cameras."

"Ah, that helps. I'll let DI Moore know that. I reported the theft to him."

"He'll hit the roof. Surveillance tape or not."

"I know. By the way, PC Derlago is on rookie probation. Let's go easy on him. I don't think he knew he should set up his station by the boat, not the MU."

"I didn't think to tell him. Thought he'd know." Chu sighed. "But you're right. Not totally his fault. I'm culpable too."

"Not really. I'll explain everything to Moore. Derlago would likely have used the MU toilet sometime during his shift. I'm guessing the thief was watching. He would have moved in then."

"I suppose."

"We can't guard all sites twenty-four/seven. Don't have the manpower."

"Personnel-power, you mean."

She chuckled. "Forget the political correctness. Okay, I'm heading to the CS now. I'm calling in Mitchell and Wolfe. We'll see if we can get any goods on the thief."

"All right."

"How was the meeting?"

"Bor-ing."

"Always are."

"See ya, Naslund."

Naslund called the ninjas, Mitchell and Wolfe, then drove to the scene, paying little attention to the speed limit. She had other things on her mind. There had to be a logical reason to burgle the skiff, for she was confident of one thing: Tyler's killers were logical. Crime scenes were generally organized or disorganized. Ditto for killers. A disorganized killer left multiple traces of their crime. But Tyler's killers didn't leave any weapons or bio markers. The skiff was tampered with and Tyler attacked, all within a tight time window. The killers used a boat, so they were mobile, which was another sign of organized perps. If, as appeared possible, one of the killers was the thief, he was not only organized, he was also daring. He hadn't waited until nightfall. Daring, or perhaps desperate.

Naslund concluded the mooring lines were important evidence. But why? She parked at the MU thinking why the mooring lines?

The afterglow of a long July day backlit the sky. The western horizon radiated streaks of red and orange. Jupiter dominated the southern sky. Despite the evening hour, the visibility was excellent. Naslund and the ninjas didn't need flashlights.

After conducting a slow, thorough search, they came up emptyhanded except for some crushed bushes and a partial shoeprint, too fragmented to be useful. She pulled out her phone and called Hal.

"Hal Bell." His voice was musical.

"Hello. Eva here. Sorry, I'm stuck at work. Busy day."

"I understand."

"How about we meet in half-an-hour?" She'd decided to leave the CS in fifteen minutes, regardless. The ninjas could finish the search. They were completely capable.

"Tonight?" Hal asked. "You're sure?"

"Yes. Eight-thirty."

"Very fashionable."

"I try."

She rejoined the ninjas, knowing that trying wasn't enough. She'd blown more than one relationship in the past.

During a major investigation, she usually had no home life—as her ex knew—until the investigation was closed. That was life as a detective. Work was first. And second. And third. She wondered if she could have a real relationship.

cℑℐcℑℐ

Sawyers Inn was hopping. Fool that she was, Naslund hadn't made a reservation. She and Hal were directed toward a small two-seater on the back wall by a youngster with a mammoth zit on his nose and what appeared to be week-old gravy on his tie. His moustache looked like a dead caterpillar. Naslund almost walked out. What was she doing? Sawyers Inn buffet was no place for a first date, albeit an unspoken one, especially with a man as handsome as Hal. With the twinkle in his eye, he looked like a contemporary Clark Gable. She chided herself for not dressing better. When a man like Hal was sailing offshore, approaching land, you didn't show a storm wall. No, you showed him how nice your harbor was. She discretely adjusted her camisole to show some cleavage.

Hal pointed toward a window table. "We'd like something with a view."

"I'm sorry," the dead caterpillar said, "it's reserved."

Naslund took a look around and pointed at a table with plenty of elbow room. "That one would be nice."

"I'm sorry, reserved."

She tried again. "How about that, then."

"Actually, ma'am, they're all reserved."

"All?"

"Not to worry," Hal said. "Go on, Eva." He nudged her good-naturedly. "We can make a mess anywhere."

The buffet was loaded with turkey and roast beef and glazed ham and home-made pickles and all the fixings, plus velvety-smooth mashed potatoes, honey-baked squash, fresh peas, and parsley carrots, not to mention date squares and pies—chocolate pecan and strawberry rhubarb—butter tarts, and shortbread. Up-country food, she thought of it, as unpretentious as a groundhog. Not exactly avant-garde, but she thoroughly enjoyed it. She could tell Hal was enjoying it as well—he hadn't stopped smiling.

Having relished a main-course plate and a dessert, she rose to get another dessert. This man, this Hal Bell, was rejuvenating her appetite.

"Can I bring you something?" she asked.

"Sure. Thanks. Anything with chocolate."

A man after my own heart, she thought.

After loading two plates with large slices of chocolate pecan pie, her eye lingered on the butter tarts. Why not? *Praise the lard!* She fit two tarts beside each slice.

Dinner over, Hal pushed his chair back, almost impaling the guest behind him, and asked Eva if she wanted a liqueur.

"Thanks, no, I'm already a bit tipsy." She smiled. "I shouldn't have told you that."

"No secrets here, my dear. A port maybe," he suggested, "or a cognac? I'll walk you home."

"No thanks, Hal, really."

Wine glass in hand, she felt ready to take the plunge. Many people used the *Echo*'s tip line because they didn't like talking to the police. Such lines often got better results than the OPP line. "Our Thom Tyler tip line has been pretty quiet," she began, then found she wasn't ready to ask Hal anything. "It's awful," she wavered. "Thom was a friend."

He nodded with sympathy. "Awful. A terrible loss."

She grimaced.

He placed a hand on her arm. "I know you want to ask me something." He smiled. "Ask away."

What a beautiful smile, she thought. She leaned across the table. Honesty was the best policy. "Could you share the leads that come in on your tip line more quickly, you know, as soon as you get them. As soon as possible, that is. It'd be a great help to our investigation." She stopped to gauge his reaction. He wasn't frowning. Maybe he would help.

"I can't, Eva, I'm sorry. I'd love to, but we have a protocol. We give people twenty-four hours to retract a tip."

She'd heard that. "Could you reduce the time?"

He shook his head. "I'm sorry."

"That's Okay." She felt deflated yet, at the same time, gratified. It seemed he'd be happy to help if it were possible.

"But we can do this again. I'll cook for you next time."

A man who could cook. Another point. She smiled. "What's on the menu?"

He laughed. "Beans and toast."

"With maple syrup?"

"Of course."

"You're on."

Chapter 12

As Naslund showered the next morning, her personal phone rang. She let it peal, its ring-tone crooning "Watching the detectives…"

Although her duty phone rang like a claxon, her personal phone crooned Elvis Costello. She'd set it to keep ringing, deeming it bad form to make callers leave a message.

"Watching the detectives," Costello sang.

She ignored the phone. The hell with her "form." Besides, she didn't feel like leaving the shower. She'd had a late night. Hal had invited her in for a coffee. They'd had a few glasses of wine and talked for hours.

"Watching the—"

She tried to shut out the phone. She closed her eyes, thinking of Hal. He was more down-to-earth than she'd imagined, and at the same time funnier. His place was like a fine hotel, white and clean and modern—the opposite of her own house. He'd kissed her goodnight. Twice.

"Watching the detectives."

All right, I'm on my way. Turning off the water, she grabbed a towel, left the bathroom, and found her phone.

"Eva here."

"Finally," J.J. MacKenzie said. "Are you that busy?"

"Always."

"You're the best cop ever." He chuckled. "Just a moment. Call on the other line."

She toweled herself dry. When he switched back to her, he sounded impatient. "I think you better get out here."

"Now?" She glanced at her phone screen: 0702.

"Yes. Marty Fox has some big news. I'll be busy after the funeral. Got a trawler on the fritz."

"Okay."

"One request. Disguise yourself. Wear old clothes. Put on a ball cap. Wear it backward."

"All right."

"Good. Marty'll pick you up. Be ready for hard work. We'll talk, have breakfast, talk more, have a few doughnuts. You know, like any crime fighter." J.J. guffawed. "Seriously, Marty'll have you back in town for the funeral."

"Sounds good."

"From now on, we keep a very low profile." His jocular tone was gone. "We'll use Marty's place. It's very private. I don't want anyone knowing about us putting our heads together. Some people have an Us and Them mentality. I don't trust them."

"Who are you referring to?"

He dismissed the question.

"Who?" Naslund pressed.

"Nobody in particular."

"C'mon J.J."

"Nobody," he repeated. "See you at Marty's place."

"Fine with me, as long as I can report what I need to. Anonymously, of course." She had no problem meeting J.J. privately, behind the barn, as it were. Sometimes you had to. She had the wherewithal. After years of undercover work, she knew how to avoid prying eyes.

"Agreed," J.J. said. "Okay, Sarge, Marty'll be at the marina in about twenty minutes. He'll be pretending to check out a C 'n C Twenty-Nine for sale. It's on Dock B."

Naslund hurried into a pink T-shirt and a pair of baggy knee-length shorts—red plaid—then pulled on dingy tennis shoes. Uber-ugly, but she didn't care. The team needed some leads. They still didn't have a clear picture of what had happened to Thom. He might have had a run-in with a fishing boat. Or with Larmer. Then there was MacTavish, although she'd verified that his boat hadn't been out since mid-June. Beyond that, there was the question of the mooring lines. Who burgled Thom's skiff, and why?

Slipping out her side door, she skirted a hedge and headed uphill, cut through two empty lots and then moseyed downhill. She'd pulled on one of her father's Tilley hats and a pair of his sunglasses. For a change, she wore lipstick and a wide circle of rouge. Effect: middle-aged bird-watcher or boater. Even though well after sunrise, Venus was still prominent in the east, twinkling brightly, hanging over the mouth of Colpoys Bay. She'd often used it to guide her Jeanneau home before sunup.

As she walked to the marina, deceptively rolling her gait, she considered the team's progress. To be honest, they hadn't made much. Although they'd processed over 250 exhibits, from blood and hair to anchor rollers and paintings, not one exhibit had been linked to a perpetrator. Late yesterday afternoon, they'd used J.J.'s tip about the Albin 35 to check out the Griffith Island Club but that lead had yet to pan out. Chandler and Weber had been dispatched to the club. The manager sheepishly admitted that someone took the club's Albin 35 for a "joyride" on the morning of Tyler's murder. However, Chandler and Weber didn't find anything to connect the incident to the murder. There was an APB out for the joyriders. At this time, they were still too inconclusive to count as suspects. So, who could the team count? MacLean. Larmer. Possibly MacTavish. That was their list of reasonable suspects.

Naslund felt frustrated. Walking on, she ordered herself to relax. They needed to adopt a long view. They'd have to dig into the past. While it was easy to murder someone in Wiarton, if a killer wanted to get away with it, he or she would have to plan. Naslund glanced at her watch. Better phone Moore. "Morning, Inspector. Naslund here. I'll be in a bit late today."

Moore remained silent.

"I'm pursuing a lead."

"Where?"

"Out Colpoys way." Enough information, she thought. Maybe too much.

"When will you be in?"

"After Tyler's funeral."

"*After*? We have a team meeting at oh eight hundred."

"Sorry," she said, "I won't make it. My case notes are up-to-date."

"I don't care about that. Well, I do. But meetings are sacrosanct."

Not to me, she thought.

"Don't miss another one."

"All right, sir."

"You're part of a team, Sergeant. Act like you are."

"Yes, sir."

Naslund ended the call, thinking that although the inspector was a good investigator, he was too combative, like her mother. Another old-school type who led with the sword. In Naslund's mind, murder cases and set meeting times didn't mix. Team members were far too busy to leave assignments and run to the murder room. As for actions, Moore could assign them by phone or email.

She ambled on, a nondescript, middle-aged woman taking a morning stroll. She liked working on her own. It had made her a good undercover cop. Now it seemed to be a liability. Apparently, she wasn't a team player. Although she liked teamwork—the banter, the give and take—she didn't like meetings. Admit it, she told herself. You're not good with meetings *or* authority.

As she reached the marina her personal phone rang.

For the second time that day, she decided to let it peal. It could wait. Hell, she realized with a fond smile, she was being un-Scottish. If all it took to make her mellower was a meal with Hal, she couldn't wait for another one.

The phone kept pealing.

"Watching the detectives…"

Damn it. Who was it? She yielded to her Scots side and answered the call. "Eva here."

"Were you still sleeping?" Hal kidded.

"Hey, I'm hard at work."

"You're a good woman."

"Sometimes."

He laughed. "So, Sergeant Naslund, I have good news."

"Wonderful, Mr. Bell. Pray tell."

"Well, I talked to my boss and the *Echo* board. They decided we can share tips with the police more quickly—" He paused. "—*if* we get permission from the tipper. I just received an interesting tip from someone willing to share their information immediately, but not their name."

"Understood. Thank you."

"You're welcome. A pair of kayakers reported seeing two sailboats in Colpoys Bay around six a.m. on July eighth. The smaller boat was a skiff with one man aboard. It was near the southern end of White Cloud Island. The other boat was northwest of the island and larger, over forty feet long, they guessed, with two or three crew aboard."

"Hmm." J.J.'s son hadn't mentioned a large sailboat.

"The wind kicked up, so the kayakers had to turn back. When they got in to shore, both boats were out of sight. From the course of the skiff, they assumed it went up the east side of White Cloud. As for the sailboat, they think it continued north, toward Cape Croker. That's it, Eva."

"That's great. Just to be sure, they said there were two boats?"

"Yes, two."

"Thank you very much. By the way, I had a great time last night." Why not tell him? Why hide her feelings? It had been a long time. Too long.

"Me too," Hal said. "Can I call you this evening?"

"Call away, sailor."

ℯↄℯↄ

The marina was quiet, not a boater in sight. Naslund strolled along a jetty, pausing to examine each boat. She missed her Jeanneau. Eventually, she approached the C&C 29 for sale and stood in front of the bow, evaluating the design. A fine hull, with the seaworthy lines of a larger craft. She knew the owner, who'd raked back the mast and reinforced the keel to enable aggressive sailing. Reinforcing the keel, that was a step she wouldn't have considered. Yet there was as much pressure on the keel as the mast and sails. If you had to beat hard to wind for hours, a weak keel could snap.

She studied the harbor. The wind trundled sacks of cloud across the bay. It was a good morning for sailing. Looking back to the jetty, she was distracted by a shaft of sunlight hitting the C&C's hull just above the keel. The keel. If your keel snapped, you were snookered. If your centerboard failed, ditto. She smiled. The sun had shown the way. Given what J.J. had said about centerboards, Thom's was likely disabled on purpose to throw off an investigation, to make it look like a damaged skiff contributed to his death. Another attempt at deception, like the blood planted on the boom. Coincidence? She didn't think so. Luckily, the storm hadn't sunk the skiff, but driven it ashore.

"Good looking C 'n C."

She turned and looked into the dark eyes of a man with sunburnt skin and black hair: Marty Fox. The lines across his forehead seemed to be sliced by a knife. She didn't know Marty, but she'd seen him around town. He wasn't fazed by her appearance.

He gestured with his head at the C&C and strolled its length, playing the charade of a prospective buyer. After returning, he pointed to the *For Sale* sign on the bow, which read *Twenty Thousand OBO*. "She's worth that. My truck's behind the main winter shed. A red F-One-Fifty. Side door's open. See you there in five."

Chapter 13

Sitting at Marty's kitchen table, Naslund surmised the man lived alone. Just as in her house, the counter tops were clear to appease the Scandal Brigade, but the sink was piled high with dirty dishes. Outside, the garden was a tangle of weeds and vegetables. Marty's F-150 reminded Naslund of her Mazda 3. The truck had seen better days.

J.J. sat across the table from her and grinned. "Nice war paint."

She winked.

"Nice shorts too. Who's the designer? Don Cherry?"

She raised her chin.

"Coffee?" Marty asked his two guests.

"Please," Naslund said.

J.J. declined.

"It'll help you think," Marty said.

"Like I need that." J.J. pointed to his head. "There's a herd of deer running around in there."

Marty nodded. "Milk and sugar, Sergeant?"

"Thanks. And call me Sarge."

J.J. pulled his chair into the table and eyed Naslund. "We can say whatever we want around Marty."

"Okay," she replied.

"Anything at all. Marty's sworn to secrecy. He won't talk about *anything* with anyone. Neither will I. That includes my wife. Everything in this room is confidential and anonymous."

"Good."

"Let's make sure we're on the same page, Sarge."

"Okay."

"I don't mind what you report, but anything you report is yours. Your words, your conclusions. Marty and I are never mentioned. Same for my son. Same for anybody from my family—extended family, that is."

"Exactly."

"We are never going to court. We are not standing as witnesses."

"As you wish." That could complicate things.

J.J. sat back.

"You folks hungry?" Marty asked. "I've got some home-made deer sausages. I'll fry 'em up with eggs."

J.J. smiled. "A little later. Let's tell Sarge what you know about the Albin Thirty-Five."

"Sure."

Naslund pulled out her duty phone. "Mind if I record our conversation?"

J.J. looked at Marty.

Marty shrugged.

"Why not?" J.J. said. He turned to Marty. "Let her rip."

"Okay." Marty settled into an old armchair near the table, his regular seat judging by the indentation made by his back. "I worked the Griffith Island Club this past weekend. I slept there Saturday and Sunday night. On Monday morning, July eighth, that is, the club Albin came in about seven a.m. I wasn't at the dock when she went out, but I heard her diesel start up just after six. Anyhow, when she came in there were two men aboard, mid-twenties I'd guess. Both of them were bruisers—white, big hulking bodies, and shaven heads. They were wearing sleeveless shirts, muscle shirts the kids call 'em. One guy was over six-feet-four, I'd say, and ran about two hundred thirty pounds, maybe two forty. The other guy was shorter but just as heavy—"

"Sorry to interrupt," J.J. said. "Sarge, I spoke with my son and asked him for a fuller description of the guys on the Albin. He described them as big, bald, and white."

"Thanks," Naslund said. "Just wondering, Marty, did they see you?"

"No. I was in the bunkhouse, looking through the blinds. They couldn't see in, but I got a good look out at them. Both were wearing soft shoes and gloves. Even at the time, I thought the gloves were strange. It was early, but early mornings in July aren't cold. One sounded foreign. Russian or something. I didn't know what to think. The Griffith usually caters to rich men. Some are loud, but most aren't, let's say, very physical."

"Marty didn't know either of them," J.J. said, "and he usually knows everybody over there and almost everything about them."

Marty shrugged. "Well, I know the important stuff, like do they go for salmon or whitefish, wild turkeys or ducks."

"C'mon, you know what they like for lunch, what they drink, when the wives call. Just for starters."

Naslund chuckled. She knew it was off-season at the club. Chandler had reported that there were five guests Sunday night. "Marty, do you think the bruisers saw any of the guests, or vice versa?"

"Not likely. The bruisers were gone just after seven. I know for a fact that the earliest guest got up at seven-thirty. They'd all had a late night, a poker night."

"Okay. Did you consider calling for help when you saw the bruisers? Two strange men like that?"

"No. I suppose I should have but, to tell the truth, there was no one to call. I was the only one on duty. The manager was in Owen Sound. The chef was up but what could he do? Run out waving a knife?"

"What about us, the OPP?"

"Didn't even think of you. Fact is, it'd be half an hour before your launch got out there. Besides, at the time, I had no notion the two did anything wrong."

"Understood," she said. "Well, there's an APB out for them."

"Good. For a change, I wish the OPP the best of luck."

"Me too," J.J. seconded.

"The way I see it," Naslund continued, "they hijacked the Albin. Can we be sure they took her toward White Cloud Island?"

"J.J.'s young fella saw an Albin east of the island," Marty replied, "which makes sense. When there's a heavy northwesterly, like there was on Monday, smart boaters get leeward of White Cloud, out of the wind. Leeward is the east side."

She nodded. If the hijackers knew what they were doing, they would have kept east of White Cloud. Or perhaps someone told them what to do. In either case, it still didn't verify where they'd been. The kayakers hadn't reported seeing an Albin. "Let me summarize things," she began. "We know two men hijacked the Albin. But we don't know where they took her. Is that fair to say?"

Marty glanced at J.J. "I know the engine hours were up by one. That's a trip to White Cloud and back. And the youngster saw the Albin east of the island, heading north."

"Could have been another Albin."

"Could have." Marty harrumphed.

"She's just sayin'," J.J. noted, smoothing things over. "Good points, Sarge."

"Don't mind me." She pointed to her nose. "I'm an inquisitive bugger."

Marty looked at J.J. They both laughed.

She joined them. She hadn't meant to be so direct. Fact-finding could do that to her, turn her into a machine. She'd have to watch it. Perhaps the kayakers hadn't seen the Albin because, from their vantage point, it was behind the island.

"You're okay," J.J. said.

"And you fellas too," she replied. "I have a few more questions. Okay?"

"Sure," J.J. said.

"Maybe the bruisers were poachers. Did they bring in any fish?"

Marty shook his head.

"How did they get into the Albin cabin and start the engine? I mean, did they break in and crank the diesel by hand?"

"They used her keys," Marty said. "All the club boat keys are hanging in the shed near the dock, with the spare engine parts and all. The shed door wasn't locked."

"Is that normal?" she asked.

"Yep. No reason to lock up out there. Well, there wasn't until Monday. The club changed that. You have to sign out a boat now to get her keys."

"Seems like the bruisers knew where the keys were. Like someone told them."

"Could be, but it wouldn't take much to guess that shed held the keys. It's right by the dock."

She nodded. Detective work tempted her to see connections everywhere, often where there were none. Pete used to call her a conspiracy bloodhound. "Okay, but I wonder, why would they go out to Griffith if they didn't know for sure they could use the Albin?"

"Good question. One of them had a kitbag. I heard it clanking, like there were tools inside. They probably had everything they needed to break in."

"How did they leave the island?"

"Used a little zodiac. I'd say it was a ten-footer. Had a small outboard, maybe a ten-horse. They headed to Big Bay. Closest spot to the island."

"Okay, but why use a zodiac to hijack another boat? Why not just use the zodiac to do what you want to do?"

"Probably not fast enough," Marty said.

"Those men were heavy," J.J. added. "A zodiac would be okay for a short run to Griffith, but a longer trip? Not on a windy day, and Monday was very windy."

"Right," Marty asserted. "The club Albin has twin diesels. She can do thirty, thirty-five knots and handle any seas."

"Would the two know that?"

"They might."

"If someone told them."

Marty shrugged. "Anyway, I took a good look around Big Bay after I finished work Monday."

"About what time was that?"

"Around one."

She nodded. Too bad. A lot of evidence could disappear in six hours. Regardless, she'd ask the ninjas to sweep the Big Bay parking area.

"From what I saw, the two left no trace of themselves after they returned to the mainland. I'm guessing they deflated the zodiac, rolled it up, and tossed it in the back of their vehicle along with the outboard. I doubt anyone was around that time of morning, which isn't strange on a Monday, even in summer. Colpoys Bay is usually quiet too. The young fella saw Thom's skiff, but no one else did."

Not true, she thought, not according to the tip Hal passed on. His tip confused things a bit. Besides a skiff, the kayakers saw a large sailboat west of White Cloud. So, Thom could have encountered the Albin or that sailboat. It seemed to her that J.J.'s son could have seen the sailboat. She eyed J.J. "Got another supposition. Pure supposition."

"Understood."

"If a sailboat was heading up the west side of White Cloud, would your son have seen it?"

J.J. shook his head. "His campsite had no sightlines to the water. When he spotted the Albin he was at a lookout on the east side of Hay. You can't see westward from there."

"Okay."

"Marty has more news. Do you want to pursue his lead?"

"Sure," she said.

J.J. motioned for Marty to continue.

"Well, whenever the Albin comes in, I always wash her down. Club orders. When the bruisers were gone, I set to work. I happened to find a smudge of blue-gray paint about two feet above the waterline, near the bow."

She sat straight up. Thom's skiff was dove-gray.

"The club Albin has a white hull. So, a little gray goes a long way. At least that's what my girlfriend says."

She chuckled.

"Now," Marty said, "what's the freeboard height of a Mackinaw?"

She let him answer.

"Two feet. So, this smudge on the Albin most likely came from an encounter with a boat hull painted blue-gray, a boat with its gunwale about two feet above the water. In other words, a boat with a freeboard similar to Thom's Mackinaw."

She leaned forward. "Did you, by chance, take a sample of the paint? Wipe a bit off onto a handkerchief or something?" There were a few cans of skiff paint in Thom's boatshed. The white coats could look for a match.

"No. I wasn't that suspicious at the time."

"Right." It had been a long shot, yet worth the question. "One more consideration. How do we know the gray smudge came from Thom's skiff? Maybe it was already—"

Marty raised a stop-sign hand. "Sorry, I should have mentioned. I washed the Albin when she came in Sunday evening. No gray marks. She didn't go out again until Monday morning."

"What about gray paint on the club wharf?"

Marty shook his head. "It's not painted."

"What about other wharfs around here? Maybe the Albin pulled into another dock that morning?"

"Could have," he allowed. "But I don't know any docks painted that color, not anywhere round here." He sat with his arms crossed, thinking. "Nowhere within a one-hour run at thirty-five knots."

Naslund nodded. Fair enough. "What about blood, Marty? Did you see any blood on the Albin?"

He shook his head.

"Just the gray paint," she prodded. She had to be sure.

He nodded patiently.

Thinking of Thom's blood, she cast her mind back to the Mackinaw CS. When Thom was assaulted, he fell or was knocked down. Before that occurred, his blood could have sprayed the attackers' boat. It was likely close enough. However, in the case of the Albin, there was no blood on it. Why? Her mind clicked. There was a possible answer. If the bruisers were the perps, they could have shielded the Albin from most of the spray. They were big enough. They could have washed off the rest. In that case, although there was no blood on the Albin, there'd be blood on them or their clothes. Perhaps they'd jumped in the lake to wash it off? She caught Marty's eye. "Did the bruisers look wet? I mean, were their clothes or skin wet?"

"They looked completely dry to me."

She nodded thoughtfully. Perhaps they changed out of their bloody clothes and sank them in the lake after attacking Thom. If they'd changed clothes, the clothes Marty saw might be different than those the youngster saw. "Do you remember what the two were wearing?"

"Yep. Muscle shirts and shorts. Long tight shorts."

"Both of them?"

"Yep."

The same kind of clothes the youngster saw, she reflected. But maybe the colors were different. "How about the colors?" she asked.

"Both guys had khaki shorts. One had a blue-and-yellow striped shirt. Vertical stripes. The other guy's shirt was red, all red with a small yellow insignia near the heart."

"Good eye," she said. She turned to J.J. "Can you call your son and ask him what colors he remembers? Don't mention the colors Marty saw."

J.J. pulled out his phone and walked outside. He returned almost immediately. "My son said they were both wearing red shorts and tank tops."

"Thanks." It seemed the bruisers had ditched their clothes, red clothes to boot—the better to hide blood. The ditching pointed to the Albin, not the sailboat. She'd have Chu's team check the Albin for blood. Even after powerful waves and frequent washings, there might be some residue left. As for the bruisers, they could have attacked Thom or accessed his anchor from the Albin, but couldn't have tampered with the centerboard mechanism. It was down near the Mackinaw's bilge, not accessible from the much higher Albin. One, or perhaps both of them, had boarded Thom's skiff.

Chapter 14

Naslund stared out Marty's kitchen window. The skiff boarding seemed to explain something else. When two boats rafted in mid-lake, they usually exchanged mooring lines. If the CS heist was connected to the murder, it accounted for the fact that the thief took the mooring lines—to remove two pieces of evidence. Sure, the man committed a crime but, to a murderer, crossing a police line was nothing.

She considered the other side. Wouldn't anyone who wanted to undermine the centerboard do it at Thom's boathouse? It'd be more stable working there than in mid-lake. Careful, she ordered herself, that supposition has holes. All a perp needed was some stability. The Albin would provide a stable raft. If the Albin wasn't involved, so would a large sailboat.

There was more to consider. Thom always did a full boat-check before he left a dock. Even if, for once, he hadn't, he would have detected a damaged centerboard within minutes and turned around. She was certain of that. So, someone messed with it in mid-bay. On the other hand, there was no proof someone boarded Thom's skiff. No DNA, no prints, no blood. No damned proof at all.

Hell, she thought, another *on the other hand.* She felt as if she were climbing a huge mast in a gale, the way she always did when she had to go by guesswork. Relax, she ordered herself, that's the way it is. She was torn from her thoughts by the sound of running water. Looking up, she saw Marty standing at the kitchen sink.

"You two ready for breakfast?"

"Sure thing," J.J. and Naslund replied, almost in unison.

As Marty fried up sausages and eggs, she looked at his book shelves: *Chapman's Piloting and Seamanship*, *The Ashley Book of Knots*, tomes on Great Lakes history, the Vikings, the Phoenicians, a complete collection of *The Seafarers*. The same books her father had owned. She'd read many of them as a girl.

"How about a doughnut?" Marty asked after they'd eaten breakfast.

J.J. shook his head.

"C'mon," Marty said. "Every meal deserves a dessert."

Naslund grinned. "I'll have two."

Having dunked a donut in her coffee, she pointed to Marty's books. "I see you have a nautical bent. What's your favorite?"

He didn't hesitate. "The *Ashley*. Most useful, anyway. Got four thousand knots in it, but these days I mostly use one."

"Oh? What's that?"

"A bowline. You can tie it tight as a nun's you-know-what, but undo it in a jiffy. If it's really tight, just stick an awl in the heart, or a screwdriver. Loosens it right away."

Naslund nodded. *A screwdriver.* Her mind hummed. *A Phillips screwdriver.* Thom's eye was speared with a Phillips screwdriver. His rode was attached with a bowline.

His centerboard system used Phillips screws. Screwdriver to eye. Screwdriver to bowline. Screwdriver to centerboard. Attack Thom, untie the rode and wrap it around his ankle, release the anchor, destabilize the centerboard. Get the hell out of there. Do it all in thirty seconds, for speed was of the essence when you were in plain view in the middle of a bay, even around dawn.

She exhaled noisily. One person, no matter how strong, couldn't overpower Thom, untie a rode, wrap it around his ankle, release the anchor, and disable the centerboard—not quickly. There had to be more than one. In the case of the Albin, there had been. Same with the sailboat. She nodded to herself. And yet it seemed too easy. The team had a few things to sort out. Why use a screwdriver and a hammer? Why not shoot Thom?

Well, she thought, that would attract too much attention.

Not with a silencer.

True. So why the bloody assault? The team would have to look into that. The two-assailant scenario only considered the how. It didn't answer the bigger questions: Who, exactly, and why?

"Something eating you?" J.J. asked.

She shrugged then took a searching look at him. "Can I ask you a few questions about Thom?"

He nodded.

"When did you become friends?"

"When we were kids. Some thought we were unlikely friends." He grinned. "Some still do. You know, him childless, me married with four kids. Him famous, me a mechanic. Despite what anyone says, we had a lot in common. I was into photography in high school. He was a great friend. Back then, I left a lot of bars in Owen Sound with blood on my face. Thom had bloodied knuckles after standing up for me. He was the better fighter by far."

Hmm, she thought, Thom was a fighter. She switched gears. "Do you know Ward Larmer?"

"Pretty well."

"What do you think of him?"

"He has an ego, no doubt about that. Doesn't mind being the center of attention. Not that there's anything inherently wrong with that."

"Anything else?"

"He's a bit of a hard-ass, likes people to think he's tough. And he is—" J.J. smiled. "—for an artist."

She grinned.

"Why do you ask?"

"History," she said. "There could have been bad blood between him and Thom. Do you know anything about that?"

"Well, I know Thom and Ward go back a bit. I was there when they met. Thom and I were working in Labrador when Ward showed up. We'd been there for two seasons. Saved a stack of money."

"When was that?"

"Twelve…no, thirteen years ago. Ward sat beside us in the mess hall one day." J.J. huffed. "A red-haired guy with a red face, sunburned to hell in half-a-day. But he didn't complain. His accent sounded British, mixed up—refined but also hard—as if he were both upper and lower class. Turned out he was from England. Birmingham."

"First impressions?"

"He was solidly built. Looked like he could handle himself."

"Did you like him?"

"He was okay. Other than his ego, but we all have them at that age."

She nodded.

"Something about his eyes said *I don't give a shit*. He

was always swiveling his head about, eying everyone, examining them for weaknesses. I couldn't quite read him. Still can't. Anyway, he was into art, like us." J.J. smiled fondly. "That was a helluva place up there. There was a bluff not far from the mine, above the Moisie River. You could watch the river charging through a canyon, rushing over rapids, swirling with tannins. On a clear day, the sky was turquoise, more like a sea than a sky. Thom was always sketching there."

She nodded. "Did you have much to do with Larmer?"

"You could say he insinuated himself into our company."

"Insinuated? Consciously, you mean?"

"I think so. Or maybe he was just lonely. He followed us around. I remember this hike Thom and I took. Great summer evening. We headed for a rock outcrop about five kilometers from camp, a hump of Canadian Shield that looked like a giant mushroom cap. When we reached it, we scrambled up and sat on the crown. The sun started sinking. Thom pulled out his sketching pad and charcoals. I had my camera. The outcrop beneath us seemed to be sending out signals. *Wait, wait*." J.J. shook his head. "Some days, some places, you never forget. Anyway, the sun sank and then sank some more. We kept waiting. Suddenly the sky began radiating reds, oranges, and purple golds. Amazing! We worked quickly. Thom still has that sketch. I didn't save any of my photos. Maybe I should have. For my kids."

She nodded and smiled. She wanted J.J. more focused on Larmer, but she didn't want to stop his story. "Please, go on."

"Well, as we were finishing our work, Ward climbed up and sat down beside us, as if he'd known us for years. We said nothing. I wanted to see if he could just sit. He could. The night sky slowly awakened. Hundreds of stars erased the blackness of space then thousands more appeared. The moon was full. The night seemed as bright as the day. I could see stones on the ground below. I thought of Colpoys on a clear, moon-lit night—the North Star, the Dippers, the Bear. I was homesick." J.J. shrugged. "Always the homesick one. Not Thom."

"And Larmer?"

"Right, Larmer. Well, he seemed to know Thom was an artist. Maybe it was instinct, or maybe he'd been through Thom's locker. Nobody locked their stuff there. Anyway, I think he figured Thom could help him, almost as if he knew Thom was a ticket to something big, which is how things turned out. The Gang of Eight and all. That night on the outcrop, he reached out and took Thom's sketch. 'What do we have here?' he said. I wanted to tell him to get lost but, really, he was just like us, struggling to make something of himself. He held the sketch up to the moon for a long look. 'Good lines. Not bad for a shaded piece.' I laughed. 'You a critic?' I said. He eyed me then winked at Thom. 'He's a wild man, Thom, an uncouth larrikin.' I almost clocked him. Thom got between us. Then Ward told us he was an artist too. Surprised the hell out of me. I hadn't figured him for the artsy sort. Told us his father was a commercial illustrator, that his mother was a right snob—a *Lady*—who hated anything created for the masses, not to mention the people who do it. Said it was a wonder she boinked his old boy." J.J. chuckled. "One minute you wanted to clock Ward, the next you were laughing with him. He said whatever popped into his head. Still does. Apparently, his mother sent him to Antwerp to study at the *Academie Royale des Beaux-arts*. 'Pillock of a name,' Ward used to say, 'but a great school.' He ran out of money after two years, and she wouldn't fork out. She sent him to a sister in Canada. That's how he ended up in

Labrador. He wanted to save forty grand. Enough brass, he claimed, for another year in Antwerp. Sounded like a lot of money to me." J.J. shook his head. "In those days, tuition might have been ten grand. You wouldn't need thirty G a year for living. But Ward liked his creature comforts. Still does."

"I can see that. Do you trust him?"

"Trust him?"

"Could he kill Thom?"

"Don't know. But I think the question would be why."

"You'd make a good detective."

"No thanks."

"What happened after Labrador? Did Thom see much of Larmer?"

"A lot. Thom went to OCAD, the art college in Toronto. Ward ended up there instead of Antwerp."

"Okay." She knew that Thom had moved back to Wiarton ten years ago. "Did Larmer come up here to visit Thom?"

"Yes. I'd say five or six times a year."

"Did you ever see Thom and Larmer fight? Physically, I mean."

"No."

"Argue?"

"Sure, plenty, but that was Ward. Considering Ward's ways, they got along well. Thom always cut him some slack. He was like that, Thom, a good friend." J.J. stopped. "Do you think Larmer had something to do with Thom's death?"

She shrugged. "We're all suspects. You better keep an eye on me."

"You're joking."

"I am. But, in a sense, I'm guilty. I'm a detective. I should have noticed Thom was in danger."

"Don't blame yourself, Sarge. I know how that feels. Don't go there."

She nodded. "Speaking of suspects, what do you think of Carrie MacLean?"

"Carrie MacLean? Huh. Well, I like what I see. What man wouldn't? Seriously, I think she's nice. Keeps herself to herself, but nothing wrong with that. Thom often told me she was good for him. Kept him grounded." J.J. tilted his head. "You think *she* had something to do with his death?"

"You never know with relationships, let alone marriages."

"True."

"You see it a lot. Someone goes wacko and pulls a gun. Who knows what couples are like when they're alone. The last few times I saw Thom with Carrie there seemed to be a fence between them. More than a fence. A huge emotional barrier."

Naslund was familiar with emotional barriers. She and Pete had built a few.

J.J. shrugged.

"All right. One last thing, and don't take offense, but I'm not sure the crazy act will help much, not to mention help your reputation."

"I don't care what small-minded townies think." He grinned. "By the way, I'm going to play a new role at the funeral today: Drunken Scotsman."

"Drunken Scotsman? Isn't that a bit—"

"Hell, what's the world coming to?" He shook his head in mock despair. "A Caledonian, a bonafide clansman, can't call himself a Scotsman."

She laughed. "It's the drun—"

"Screw them."

"You can call yourself whatever you like."

"Yep. And you know I will. People will start talking soon."

"I hope so."

Chapter 15

S itting in the back pew of the Baptist church, Naslund waited for the Tyler funeral to begin. The austere interior contained nothing but a plain wooden pulpit and dull oaken pews. The dark-paneled walls reminded her of the funeral parlor.

Glancing quickly about, she saw Larmer a few pews ahead, sitting with five members of the Gang of Eight. He was dressed appropriately for a change, in a low-key black suit. She turned her attention to the front pew. Her vantage point from the opposite side of the church and the back allowed her to observe the Tyler family in profile. Even from a distance, John Tyler appeared more defeated than on the day of the visitation. Her gaze shifted to Deirdre Tyler. She looked defeated as well.

Naslund felt an even greater urge to fulfill Deirdre's wish to get to the bottom of things. It wouldn't be easy for an outsider like Moore to dig into the past. It was often difficult for her, and she'd been in Wiarton over four years. Wiartonians could shut the door on outsiders. The team was lucky to have J.J. and Marty's help, anonymously or not.

Next on in the pew was Thom's half-brother Gordon Tyler. Zeroing in on him, Naslund studied Gordon's profile. He looked simultaneously pleased with himself and offended by everyone else. He considered himself a local pillar. His new hairpiece didn't soften the smug cast of his face. He'd been wearing it for about a month. The curve of his lips seemed to say *I don't care what you think, it looks good.* His sister Gillian sat next to him. She didn't look happy to be there. But maybe she wasn't happy to be with Gordon.

Naslund knew that Gordon Tyler was arrogant and abrupt at times. However, he was also hard-working and well-respected. He was thin, bordering on weak, definitely not physically capable of assaulting Thom. He seemed an unlikely murderer. Nonetheless, she made a mental note to debrief Conrad and Lowrie regarding Gordon Tyler's alibi.

Her eyes moved on. Carrie MacLean sat in the next pew back, wearing a tight black dress. She'd lived with Thom and yet she couldn't sit in the front pew. She wasn't part of the family. The snub didn't seem to bother her. She looked stoic. Her mother and grandmother, recently arrived from Prince Edward Island, sat beside her. Naslund examined them. The mother, quite the beauty herself, looked aloof and righteous. Naslund's intuition told her that the mother could be a dragon. Was her daughter secretly one too?

A moment later Naslund heard a loud stage whisper. "I'll shi, sit, where I wan."

J.J. She fought an impulse to spin around and observe him.

"Where I wan," J.J. said, more forcefully this time.

As he inched up the aisle, she saw he was with his wife Marie, but not his kids. Marie looked mortified. Naslund realized she wasn't in on his charade. He was putting on a good show, lurching occasionally and puffing out his cheeks. An usher hustled toward him.

J.J. stopped and swayed.

"Good morning, Mr. and Mrs. MacKenzie," the usher said in a hushed tone.

"*Gud*?" J.J. said. "I don't think so."

"Mr. MacKenzie, how about a seat here?"

J.J. blew out his cheeks. "We're goin to the frond."

"How about here?"

"Frond pew!"

"Sorry," the usher quietly said, "that's for family."

Naslund spotted another man coming toward J.J., Mr. Don Charon, the funeral home director. The director exhibited a pained expression, as if he'd swallowed a bee.

She switched to J.J. He looked truly angry. However, in a flash, he abruptly backed down. "'Kay," he contritely said.

The usher nodded. Mr. Charon veered off.

Naslund grinned to herself. J.J. had lit a bomb—the whole congregation had turned to see what was happening—then defused it at the last possible moment. People would be gabbing, all right. She still wasn't convinced it would help the cause, let alone J.J.'s reputation.

The service commenced. The pastor, a lanky bald man with long yellow hands, surveyed the congregation with false diffidence then launched into a sermon: "I say unto ye, God will forgive the endless iniquities of man..."

She studied her knees. What comfort would anyone get from that sermon? They didn't need to be forgiven. Thom certainly didn't. He was dead.

Celebrate Thom's life! she wanted to shout. Thom wasn't a sinner. He'd been a modest sort—the kind of man people liked from the moment they met him.

The pastor droned on, his arms assaulting the air as he sermonized, exhorting them to save their souls. She sagged in her pew. She had a better way to help people face death. "Death is unknowable," she'd tell them. "It might be coming for you tomorrow. One thing's for sure: it didn't come yesterday." That was all you needed to know. Seize the day, and the night too.

ℰↄℰↄ

Service finally over, Naslund filed out of church with the congregation. At Thom's gravesite the pastor beckoned someone forward. She craned her neck.

J.J. MacKenzie.

When J.J. faced the gathering, she saw his eyes in full: sad yet sober. The drunk charade was off. He was going to speak. Ho, she thought, that'll get people talking. She could hear them already. *Did you see that MacKenzie? Drunk as a skunk when he entered the church, but half an hour later he was sober. Don't know how those rabble-rousers do it.*

"Thank you for coming." J.J. began. "Thom, I know, would thank you too. He was a humble man. He was also a man who would want us to be outside." J.J. gestured toward the canopy of oak trees above them and the blue sky beyond. "So I asked Pastor Rutherford to let me deliver this outside. Thom Tyler was a son of the Bruce Peninsula. As a boy, he had everything he needed, but not a lot, certainly not by today's standards. Simplicity was a virtue. He hiked and fished all around Wiarton. He was good-hearted. Anything he had he shared with his siblings.

After high school, Thom travelled. The wide world only made him miss Wiarton more. He was quiet at times, but not shy. He liked to play practical jokes, keep people on their toes. He had the hidden confidence of a sailor. When he chose his path, that of the artist, he studied hard and worked hard. As a painter, he saw things no one else did. Yet he didn't talk about art theories. He talked about painting like a sailor discussing the wind, quietly considering the topic, thinking of what you saw, not what he painted.

"As I noted, Thom didn't need a lot. That was because he had his family, his friends, and his art. Thom Tyler was as good a man, as good a native son of the Bruce as there ever was, as honest and true as one of his favorite foods: a Wiarton whitefish. Thanks Thom, for everything. By the way, you painted as you lived. With no regrets."

There was a smattering of quiet applause. The pastor looked down his nose. Naslund joined the clapping. She had to hand it to J.J. The man had done an excellent job.

The pastor gave the final rites.

Ashes to ashes, dust to dust.

Clump. Clump.

Naslund's heart contracted each time a shovelful of earth hit the casket.

As she trod back alone from the interment, the finality of Thom's death sank in. No more sails or talks with her friend. Her step shortened with every footfall. She knew the larger world would miss Thom Tyler the painter. However, in her eyes, the smaller one—Wiarton and environs—would miss Thom the person more.

Chapter 16

The post-funeral reception gave Naslund the willies. The hall was as depressing as the church. She found no comfort amongst the circumscribed nods and sad faces. After paying her respects to Thom's parents, she headed for the door.

"Sergeant."

She turned to face the voice. "Mr. Larmer."

He looked contrite, almost meek, the opposite of the person she and Moore had interviewed.

"I'd like to apologize for my recent behavior," he said. "Let's forget our 'meeting' and start again."

She wanted to tell him to get lost but controlled herself. "Forgotten," she said. What game was he playing?

"We're having a little memorial lunch at Sawyers, a last-minute thing. Carrie, some of the Gang. I invited J.J. MacKenzie, but he's busy. Thom appreciated your friendship. I'd like you to join us."

Why not? she thought. The hell with Moore's schedule. "Thank you." She'd likely gather a few insights into Larmer, not to mention some of the Gang.

Larmer remotely unlocked his car, a sparkling new Mini Cooper with racing stripes.

She eyed it. "How long have you had this beauty?"

"Bought her a month ago. She's got legs. Speaking of legs, did you see the dress Carrie was wearing? Totally inappropriate."

Naslund said nothing. The dress *was* a little tight.

"I wonder about her, I do. On the phone Monday, I asked her how she was doing. Know what she said?"

Naslund smiled encouragement, not that she needed to. Larmer was in a talkative mood. He seemed to have a Jekyll-and-Hyde-type temperament, one day surly, the next day friendly.

He mimicked MacLean's voice. "'A trouble shared with you is not a trouble halved. It's a trouble multiplied. You think your nose belongs in everything.'" He shook his head. "If she shared things, people would help her. Friends do that—they share. But her?"

Naslund tsked in sympathy.

Larmer kept going. "She claimed she was being careful for Thom's sake, and the sake of his artistic reputation. *Careful*, I thought. How about purposefully evasive."

Even for a breezy bugger, Larmer was talking a lot. Why?

He let out a loud sigh. "Like I said, I wonder about her." He held Naslund's gaze. "I wonder if she had something to do with Thom's murder. Let me tell you something, Sergeant."

She nodded. The worst thing she could do was speak. When a POI wanted to talk, you zipped your lips.

"Any man can tell that she's a cracker in bed, but she makes you pay for it." He stopped. "Am I getting too personal?"

She shook her head. Keep going, sink yourself.

"After the biz...well, afterward...she talks your ear off. I know, you'd never guess. She hides it well. I don't know how Thom stood it. The nattering must have got to him. He liked his solitude." Larmer nodded emphatically. "The woman is an only child: self-centered, self-inflated. Thom probably lost his patience, told her to 'eff off' or worse. She wouldn't have stood for that, not Carrie. She might even have, you know, retaliated. To the hilt. It may sound dubious, but she can do anything she sets her mind to. She's super-efficient, deadly efficient."

"I see. Do you have something specific you'd like to tell me?"

"Well, no. Not yet," he added.

Naslund turned to her car. It seemed Larmer was trying to lead her down a cellblock path, one with Mac-Lean at the end. Was he trying to save his own skin, or did he have real evidence against Carrie MacLean?

၉၁၈၁၅

Inside Sawyers Inn, Naslund was directed to a U-shaped table with four chairs along each side and one at the top. Larmer sat at the top. She found herself seated next to three of the Gang: Raphael Barillo, Laura Newton, and Marnie Sass. Carrie MacLean was across the table, with two more of the Gang: Katherine Clarke and Brendan Liski. Only Emily Cardiff's chair was empty. She couldn't make it down from the Arctic.

Naslund glanced at MacLean. She felt a confused wind blowing off her, both antagonistic and sad.

The lunch did little to raise anyone's spirits. Larmer explained that in honor of Thom, who'd loved simple Greek food, and knowing that one of the cooks at the inn came from Athens, he'd ordered platters of moussaka and souvlaki. The moussaka was runny and the souvlaki dry.

After the dishes were cleared, short, burly Raphael stood. Originally from Florence, *Firenze* he still called it, Raphael had immigrated to Toronto ten years ago. He dressed like an Italian—tailored suits and hand-sewn shoes—and talked like one—with his hands.

"*Si, si*," he now said to the table, "let us remember the good. Tomaso was *ottimo* in every way, so very good. An excellent man and an excellent painter!"

As usual, handsome Brendan, a soulful Canadian of Irish-Ukrainian extraction, said nothing. He looked Raphael in the eye and nodded. Brendan didn't need to talk. With his Beethoven-like face and hair, everyone took him for a man of culture.

Katherine, a fifth-generation United Empire Loyalist, shook her head sorrowfully, reminding Naslund of a young Audrey Hepburn.

"Thom was so hospitable," Katherine said. "So wonderfully hospitable. I remember the first time he invited me to Mallory Beach. Carrie—" She stopped and bowed toward her. "—cooked a beautiful dinner the evening I arrived: a delicious whitefish! The next morning Thom drove me to Lion's Head. He helped carry all my equipment—my easel, painting box, and boards—out to a wonderful set of look-offs along the Bruce Trail and then he came back for me at sunset. For four days running. He did that every year, for nine years." She dabbed at her eyes. "Damn it! I told myself I wouldn't cry. He wouldn't want that." She dried her eyes and hung her head. "What will I do now?"

No one said anything.

Laura and Marnie looked like they wanted to leave. Naslund found it difficult to tell them apart. She knew they were lovers, but they seemed more like twins. The two always wore the same black stovepipe jeans and wide-shouldered jackets. With their shaggy hair and pouty lips, they looked like Carly Simon.

Larmer stood. "I'd like to share a memory." He drained his wineglass. "Back in the day, a fool arrived in

Toronto by bus, unannounced and with no money, which, as you know, was all the rage back then, especially amongst painters. The fool tramped from the bus station to a certain struggling artist's studio off King West near Bathurst. You might know the place." He smiled.

Naslund knew that they all did. Thom had kept it until two years ago.

"Well, the occupant of said studio wasn't home, so the fool slept outside the door. No occupant the next day either. The fool had enough cash for the odd coffee and plate of beans. After another night under the Studio Door, he was beginning to smell. Might have been his socks. Or the beans. Remember," Larmer said in mock disbelief, "none of us common folk had cellphones then. No one home meant no way in. Anyway, to cut a long smell short, I was about to head back to Montreal when Thom arrived. He took me in, fed me, got me on my feet and that was just for starters. He convinced me to paint again. I don't like to admit it, but back then I'd given up. I was beaten. Thom saved me."

Naslund's heart started thumping. Tears welled in her eyes. Larmer's story seemed earnest and warm. Maybe he was a true friend. She felt conflicted. She couldn't let her emotions come to the fore. She'd been trained to always be compassionate, yes, but, at the same time, dispassionate. It was the Holy Grail of policing. Not that she always managed to adhere to it. Cops weren't supposed to be grief-stricken or emotional. They were supposed to be focused. *No personal opinions,* she reminded herself. *Doubt a suspect at all times.*

Katherine nodded mournfully. "You know," she said to Larmer, "I remember how much you and Thom used to eat." Her face slowly became more cheerful. "Lord, you could shovel it in."

"We were a fine sight," Larmer joked.

Raphael smiled. "You remember that night Tomaso and I ate two pounds of spaghettini each, with olive oil only. *Due libbre!* Each!"

Katherine chuckled. "Ah, we were a parade of struggling waifs."

No one spoke. It seemed everyone was remembering the struggle.

A ringing phone broke the silence.

Larmer reached into his pocket. "Excuse me." Turning to one side, he answered the call.

As Naslund chatted with Raphael, she kept an eye on Larmer's face. The man didn't look pleased with his caller.

A minute or so later he hung up and exhaled noisily.

"What is it?" Katherine asked.

Larmer eyed Naslund. "Wiarton's Finest want to talk to me."

Naslund wasn't surprised. Inspector Moore, no doubt.

"*Chi?*" Raphael asked. "Who?"

"The police," Larmer explained. "At three o'clock. Looks like we'll be leaving for Toronto a little later. They'll probably torture me for an hour."

"Torture?" Raphael uttered in horror.

"Just joking."

Katherine looked disgusted. Her Hepburn eyes regarded Larmer with empathy. "Why are they bothering you? Don't they have anything better to do?"

He shrugged. "They think I killed Thom."

"That's ludicrous!" Katherine exclaimed. "Why in God's name would you do that?" She scowled at Naslund. "Why would anyone here?" Her gaze circled the table, stopping momentarily on each painter.

No one answered.

Finally Raphael replied. "The envy," he said. "*Invidia professionale.*"

"Really?" Katherine said. "Some of us, hell, all of us, may have wanted Thom's success, but did that turn us into monsters?" She turned to Raphael. "Did you really envy Thom?"

"I esteem him. Okay, I envy, but just a little." He held a thumb and index finger close together. "*Solo un po.* Always, it is this way."

She eyed Brendan. "You?"

He shook his head.

Laura and Marnie nodded without being asked. "A little," Laurie said.

Katherine pointed at Larmer. "You?"

"Well, to be honest, I did. But I didn't hate him. Christ, no." His eyes misted over.

Naslund wondered if he'd manufactured the tears, or if he was being genuine.

"I loved him," Larmer insisted. "Like a brother. He was my family in Ontario." He choked up. The room fell silent. Eventually he composed himself. "I remember my first sailing trip with him, up to Tobermory in May." His face brightened. "It was beautiful. The lake was midnight-blue, the maples had burst into leaf. The cliffs were entrancing. It was Thom's world. I loved it."

"Me too!" Katherine exclaimed. She dabbed her eyes. "The police are imbeciles." She glared at Naslund. "I'm leaving!"

The table followed her.

Naslund said nothing. Let them go. Soon the room was empty. In her mind's eye, she saw only Larmer. Was he genuinely upset? Concentrating on his mouth, she replayed his story about Thom, and then his claim that he loved Thom. She saw no dishonesty. She made a mental note.

As she left the inn, she saw Carrie MacLean standing near the parking lot, staring at the ground. The others were gone. MacLean seemed to be waiting for someone to pick her up.

Naslund thought about offering her a lift, but decided to observe her secretly, mindful of the detective's uncertainty principle: the closer you got to a suspect, the farther you got from the objective truth. She covertly searched MacLean's face. She'd caught her off-guard. She wanted her to stay that way. Carefully, she leaned a little closer.

MacLean looked like the same woman Naslund had met over four years ago, and yet she didn't. She was still beautiful—perhaps more beautiful; her face was definitely fuller—but Naslund saw a veil over her eyes. She was hiding something.

Naslund quickly turned away and walked to her car. Sitting inside, she called Moore. "Afternoon Inspector, Naslund here. I'm on my way."

"Where are you?"

"Close by."

"Where?"

"I'll be at the station in five minutes."

"Come to my office. Immediately." He hung up.

Chapter 17

Naslund knocked on her office door.

"Come in," Moore tersely said. "Sit down."

She sat.

The inspector had a pickle up his butt. "When did the funeral finish, Sergeant?"

"Around eleven-thirty."

He pointed at his watch. "It's thirteen-ten."

"Yes."

"Yes? Where were you?"

"At a memorial lunch. Getting leads."

"Hmm."

"Good leads, sir."

"I don't care how good they were. You said you'd be here after the funeral."

"Yes, sir. But then I was invited to the lunch, and I thought I should go. Six of Tyler's artist contacts were there, and MacLean as well."

"You're walking a thin line."

"Yes." No use arguing.

"I've been counting on you to help interview POIs. If you're ever unavailable, I'll use Lowrie. And keep using him. For other things too." Moore paused to let his displeasure sink in. "Do you understand what I'm saying?"

Naslund nodded. She didn't want to be shunted to the side. "It won't happen again."

"It better not."

"It won't, sir."

Moore uncorked a smile. "I like you, Sergeant. You have gumption."

Gumption? That was a word her mother used.

"Remember, though, there are rules, and we are a team."

"Yes, sir."

"Let's get on the same page. Chu's team didn't find any blood residue on the Albin thirty-five. The ninjas didn't find anything at Big Bay. It was too contaminated. So, we have no solid bio evidence on any perps. In such cases, you have to rely on...shall we say?...more traditional methods. You do what police forces have done through the ages. You observe. You dig into human nature. You use human psychology."

"Yes, sir."

"You might say you go old school."

"Exactly."

She sat back. That was an old-school scenario she agreed with. At least she and Moore were on the same page with something. At Central, dozens of detectives sat in fancy ergonomic chairs staring at screens. Gone were the days of the "gum shoes," the rubber-soled detectives, when everyone worked the streets, gathering intel in person. Ask. Listen. Read someone's complete body language. Hear 'em, see 'em, smell 'em. Which wasn't possible via the internet—not yet.

"That's why you're off the hook." Moore smiled again. "You don't spend all day in front of a computer. You get out there. You talk to people. Okay. Larmer's due at fifteen-hundred. Please meet him in the foyer."

"Yes, sir." *Please*, she noted. The inspector had

dumped the pickle. *Good*, she thought, one Bickell-pickle per station was enough.

"By the way, I canceled this morning's team meeting. We have a meeting at fourteen-hundred."

"I'll be there."

She walked to her hutch, removed her jacket, and began writing a report on what she'd learned from J.J. and Marty about the hijacking as well as what she learned at the memorial lunch, including Larmer's apparent attempt to frame MacLean.

As Naslund finished the report, the murder room began filling up. By 1355 the complete team was assembled, sixteen strong, including Bickell. No one was late. Even the MU squad was present, and they were shutting down that evening and returning to Central.

Moore kicked off the meeting by calling on Lowrie. The DC had five main points. Point One concerned Larmer's rap sheet. It was complete. It appeared he'd intuitively figured out the Slider. Point Two related that the salient details of Larmer's first interview had been cross-checked and verified. He'd called LaToya Austin, his city girlfriend, three times. He and Tyler had sailed together three days in a row. Point Three established that an in-depth trace of Larmer's phone calls to Carolyn Mac-Lean hadn't uncovered anything unusual. Until July tenth, he'd called her twice in ten months, nothing that would suggest a secret affair. In contrast, a trace of La Toya Austin's number revealed 322 calls. Point Four noted that the third set of FPs on Tyler's boat was Larmer's. The FPs were approximately a week old. However, Larmer admitted to sailing with Tyler a week ago. Point Five related that Larmer belonged to two gyms in Toronto. He was a karate brown-belt. He also knew how to swim. The lady next to his Hope Bay cottage reported that he went for a lengthy swim every day.

Chandler was next. The Senior PC projected a serious face. Naslund guessed he'd received a shellacking from Moore. *None of your shenanigans in my meetings.* Chandler hadn't learned of any stolen boats in the Bruce, nor could he link any recent boat rentals or purchases to Larmer. The suspect could have bought an inflatable craft with an outboard or a sailing rig. However, such equipment wouldn't fit inside his Mini and the car didn't have a roof-rack or a tow hitch.

Naslund wondered if they were jumping the gun with Larmer. While his martial arts prowess was suspicious, it was also circumstantial. The team could be wrong about him.

Moore gestured for Conrad to come forward. The DC still appeared to be cowed. He barely looked up as he spoke. His group had questioned fishermen and boaters about unusual activity on Colpoys Bay. They'd also questioned the five Griffith Island Club guests and all the White Cloud Island cottagers. They had no definite leads. Conrad looked up. He'd spoken to two cottagers from the east side of White Cloud who were there on Monday the eighth. About 0630 that day the cottagers heard a man yelling. They hadn't gotten out of bed to explore. The yelling only lasted a minute or so.

Conrad gathered steam. His group had questioned known local thieves, pot growers, and ex-pedophiles. Again, they had no leads. Mr. Tyler's family members and local acquaintances had been interviewed. They all had alibis. The alibis appeared to be solid.

Moore took over. He began by reminding the team they hadn't found the assault weapons or the cotton cloth. The three exhibits were still a top priority. Then there were common DNA carriers like hair, saliva, and cigarette butts. There had to be some out there. He chided everyone to work harder to find bio evidence.

Moore next reported that tip line activity had begun to ramp up. To date, they'd logged 267 calls and web leads, some claiming to have seen Tyler alive, as far afield as the Yukon. None of the tips had panned out. However, thanks to the *Wiarton Echo*, they were able to chase down one lead. A pair of Toronto kayakers who'd seen two boats in Colpoys Bay voluntarily released their contact info.

Moore had arranged for a Metro detective to show the couple photos of Tyler and his distinctive high-boomed Mackinaw. They identified it but reported that the man aboard was too far away to be verified as Thom Tyler. The couple weren't carrying binoculars. As for the other boat, they thought they saw two or three people aboard, but couldn't confirm the number or gender of the crew. Given the APB out for the Albin hijackers, Moore stated that the team would focus on tracking down the large sailboat. Its crew could be the perps or the last people to see Tyler alive.

Moore next reported that two Metro detectives had interviewed Tyler's artist contacts in Toronto. Without prompting, three of them said that Tyler's previous agent, Louise Hennigan, had been his lover fifteen years ago, when he was twenty-four and she was forty. There'd been a lot of acrimony when the affair ended. On Hennigan's side, it was apparently still simmering. Moore had arranged to interview her in Toronto.

Finally, he surveyed the room. "I trust you all remember what I said about lone wolves. I don't abide by them. We're in this together. We succeed or fail as a team. Understood?"

Everyone nodded, Naslund included. She believed in sharing all intel. However, she couldn't identify J.J. and Marty and thus lose them. She'd double-checked their whereabouts during the murder window. They were clean, and they had a lot to offer. Thanks to them, she rationalized, she was feeding important details into the case notes.

"I'd like to commend everyone," Moore continued. "I know the media hounds have been nipping at your heels, but they're not getting anything, not even a sniff. You're holding them at bay. Well done." He smiled. "I also know that I've been pushing you hard to find bio evidence. But you need to dig into human nature as well. I don't often say this, but let your inner psychologists loose. Think like a criminal. Think motivation. Keep hard at it! Your next actions are on the cork board."

He dismissed the team.

Meeting over, Naslund kept a close eye on the time. At exactly 1500, she strode to the foyer. No sign of Larmer. She stepped outside for some air. A wall of heat hit her. The afternoon sun looked like a ball of fire. The humidity had been building all day.

She turned around, walked back into the air-conditioned station, and waited for Larmer. Was the man playing games again? Upon reflection, it appeared the inspector had evaluated Larmer correctly. He was a me-first sort, a type difficult to trust.

A minute later, Moore hurried up to her. He looked irritated. "I had to cancel our fifteen hundred with Larmer. M and M didn't come through."

She nodded. M&M, the financial forensic section, aka the Money-n-Murder unit, was usually behind the eight ball.

"Can you join me in my office?"

My office, she thought then smiled. "Sure."

Once seated, Moore harrumphed. "I expected M and M to deliver some data to pin Larmer down." He pursed his lips. "We'll bring him back in a day or two. A few days might soften his shell."

"Exactly." She felt worn out. She'd thought of taking a short break and then working from home. Other than last evening with Hal, she hadn't had any time off. She'd been working seventeen or eighteen-hour days.

"Are you hungry?" Moore asked.

She wasn't but she nodded.

"How about a sandwich?" he suggested.

"Okay," she said. She wasn't going home. "I know a place near Bluewater Park."

๛๛

Sandwich finished, Moore proposed they sit outside. It was thirty-three Celsius, but the inspector didn't seem to be feeling the heat. He had his jacket on. They walked to the water and sat on a bench under a willow. Sunlight danced wildly on the bay. Naslund put on her shades and slid off her shoes. A gray jay abandoned the willow and buzzed Moore's head. He paid it no heed.

"Well," he said, "how do you think the case is progressing?"

She shrugged.

"We're a little stuck," he admitted. "Happens in every case. You go full-speed for three or four days and seem to get nowhere. The truth is, though, we're making some progress. But don't tell the team that. We have to keep a fire lit under them."

She said nothing.

"We're gathering details, sorting and re-sorting them, rejecting some, promoting others, building the big picture. It's like painting. You need to erase and re-brush. You need to apply hundreds, if not thousands, of brushstrokes to finish a canvas."

"Right. Are you a painter?"

"Amateur. Very amateur."

She decided to probe. "Is that why they assigned you to the case?"

He smiled perfunctorily. "I was the next one on the bench."

She didn't believe him. The Tyler case was a top priority. National icon killed in cold blood. Top-gun Moore would have been sent no matter who was next on the bench.

Moore clasped his hands behind his head. "Tyler's a master," he said. "But he wasn't a financial wizard. Not from what M and M says. Fortunately, I got a preliminary report from them."

"Good."

"Not bad. Short on ammo, but we have a start. Tyler had plenty of money coming in, yet he had more going out. A lot more. He had assets—boats, houses, a car—but didn't own much of it. The banks did. Well, they still do. There's a thirty-three-foot sailboat, refurbished and out-fitted for painting trips, a cottage in Mallory Beach with a double lot, a waterfront condo in Toronto with three bed-rooms and a full-length terrace, plus a 2012 Volvo station wagon. Apparently, the vehicle is paid for, but he has big loans on all the other items. His account showed red every month for the past three years. Blood-red. And what often goes with red money?" It was a rhetorical question. "Red murder." Moore stretched his stilt-like legs. "From what we know, Tyler didn't write a will. He died intestate."

Naslund nodded.

"M and M reported that none of his property is co-owned by MacLean. You'd think she'd be his benefi-ciary. In the eyes of the court, she's a civil partner. How-ever, as it happens, Tyler's father co-signed the sailboat loan. Ditto for the cottage and condo mortgages. The fa-ther was a joint owner of all three. He's now the sole owner. Given what he told Conrad yesterday, he's an un-likely suspect. Did you read the transcript?"

"Yes."

"Did you find his alibi solid?"

"Completely."

"Okay. As for MacLean?" Moore shrugged. "It looks like she'll inherit Tyler's vehicle. Might be worth twenty grand. I don't imagine she killed him for his car."

"Not likely," Naslund said. "She drives a new Subaru Forester."

Moore pursed his lips. "Maybe she stands to inherit some of his art, which, I can tell you, doesn't look promising either. As to property and money, it appears she was locked out of almost everything. She and Tyler had separate credit cards and bank accounts, with different banks, in fact. From what Tyler's bank records show, he only activated one bank card, his own. She may not have had any access to his money."

"Probably has enough of her own. She has an established business."

"Right. By the way, I ran a wider check on her. She's squeaky clean. Pays her taxes on time, charges HST, pays her staff above board. Not a hair out of place. Our Miss MacLean looks like a good girl. But the good-girl act could be a cover." He shook his head. "She's difficult to read. She might be an accomplice. At this juncture, she's still on the hook. If she colluded with someone, despite her apparent attempt to frame Larmer, it could be him."

Naslund shrugged. It could be, but she didn't see MacLean conspiring with Larmer. In fact, she didn't see MacLean conspiring with anyone. She was too independent.

Moore kept rolling. "Let's consider, for argument's sake, that Larmer used a boat. I know, Chandler didn't find any evidence of that, but we can't write it off yet. Larmer could have 'borrowed' one and returned it without anyone knowing it was used. MacLean could have done the set-up, compromised the skiff, that is. Are you confident the centerboard screws didn't pop out?"

Naslund nodded.

"Well, perhaps she compromised the skiff's centerboard at the boathouse and then Larmer assaulted Tyler in the bay."

"I don't think that's likely. I suspect someone compromised the centerboard out in the bay, and I think they came aboard the skiff to do it. The details are in my latest case notes."

"Summarize the salient points for me."

"Okay. Tyler always did a full boat check before he left a dock. Even if he hadn't, he would have realized the centerboard was damaged within minutes and turned around. That suggests someone compromised it after he left the boathouse."

"We don't know with certainty that Tyler did a boat check that morning. A defense lawyer would shoot holes in that."

Naslund didn't reply. A defense lawyer could shoot a lot of holes in their "evidence." So far, much of it was speculative or circumstantial.

Moore stood abruptly. "Excuse me. I need a little walk."

She watched him go. He looked aggravated. Was she being argumentative? Some old boys thought female detectives were too quarrelsome, not to mention too emotional, too invested in victims. And some were, she agreed. They believed you had to bond with victims, bring them back to life so that you could know their hearts. Method sleuthing, the old boys scoffed. Naslund went with them on that one. While she always felt for victims, she didn't need to know absolutely everything about them. Instead, she wanted to know everything about their potential killers.

Chapter 18

After mechanically pacing to the government wharf and back, Moore sat beside Naslund. Eventually he spoke. "Okay, Sergeant, here's what I see. Let's say MacLean didn't need money. However, maybe she was working with someone who did, someone like Larmer. M and M provided a cursory trace of Tyler and Larmer's fiscal connections. Over the last eight years, Tyler wired just over three hundred and eighty-eight thousand dollars to Larmer, usually in relatively small amounts, fifteen to twenty thousand dollars at a time."

"Ah."

"M and M found three wire transfers from Larmer to Tyler, to the tune of one hundred and twenty-six thousand dollars. Now, the two could have been buying each other's art, or something else, but I'd guess not."

She nodded. This was a side of the inspector she admired. The man was thorough.

"However, at this point, we have no proof. M and M is having a hard time digging up Larmer's financial history. Sketchy record of money in. Same for money out. Pays cash for his rent, ditto for major purchases like cars and air tickets. Other than the wire transfers, he flies off the radar or covers his tracks."

No surprise, she thought.

The inspector sat back.

She felt him thinking. She remained quiet.

"You know," he eventually said, "with more evidence, I think we'll have a good case against Larmer. But we need more evidence. On the other hand, I don't see a murder case against MacLean—even if she dropped some fingerprints on the skiff during the murder window. She doesn't benefit from his death. I don't see any deep motive for her. Do you?"

"I haven't seen one yet. However, from what I just saw at the memorial lunch, she's hiding something."

"What?"

"I don't know."

"So, it's a hunch?"

"Yes." In her view, hunches shouldn't be immediately discounted. Minor details, like a POI's body language and clothes, could generate big leads. She knew some people considered her too logical, too male. Admittedly, she didn't bring a bleeding heart to work, but she brought more than her head. She brought intuition, something men like Moore often seemed oblivious to.

"Do you think she's working with Larmer?" Moore asked.

"I wouldn't say it's impossible," Naslund replied. "But I'd say it's unlikely."

"Why?"

"I don't see her and Larmer as a team."

"Why not?"

"They're both very independent."

"Independent, eh?" Moore grinned. "I know people like that."

Naslund smiled. "Very independent. Beyond that, before lunch today, Larmer tried to frame her. The details are in my latest report. As for her, a few days ago, in her interview, she did her best to incriminate Larmer."

"True. However, that could be self-preservation. After the fact, as it were. Not too long ago, they worked together to murder Tyler, but now they're selling each other down the river."

"Maybe."

"It's a puzzle," Moore said. "She admitted to knowing about boats and anchors. Why would she do that if she's guilty? If I had blood on my hands, I'd keep my mouth shut. Most perps do."

"Maybe she wants us to think she's a straight-shooter. Maybe she's setting us up. The blood on the boom. The centerboard disabled to make it look like a damaged boat led to Tyler's death."

"Maybe."

"She's a planner. Caterers have to be planners. Banquets, functions, buffets. Can't serve them unless you're organized. She could have thought the whole thing through and acted as she did to throw us off."

"Could have," Moore said. "In any case, we'll finish with Larmer before we bring her back in. We'll dig into her connection to Larmer the next time we interview her."

"Okay."

"I've been working with a psychologist over at Central, a profiler. He ran data on Larmer and MacLean. Both are organized, both are strong-willed, both are no-nonsense, but that's where the similarities end. MacLean keeps things in. She's not emotionally demonstrative. On the other hand, Larmer lets things out. Rather than internalizing emotions like hurt or anger, he externalizes them. He's capable of aggression. Instead of feeling inferior to people, he feels superior to nearly everyone."

Naslund nodded. That fit the bill.

"Studies show that over seventy percent of killers are externalizers, like Larmer."

She'd read the research. In her opinion, the number was less than sixty. Pete used to say that she was no dumb-ass cop. He'd insisted she move into administration. Another strike against the marriage. As far as she was concerned, jockeying an office chair was hell.

"Then there's life-style," Moore went on. "Larmer may have a girlfriend, but he lives alone. He has no formal job, so he can do what he wants, when he wants. The psychologist said Larmer's emotional age is that of a fourteen-year-old. Larmer thinks he's a good communicator, but he isn't. He doesn't listen. He's two-faced. He has prior criminal activity, albeit minor. He has no feelings of remorse or guilt concerning said activity."

All true, she reflected. But nothing new. She shrugged.

Moore eyed her. "To know an artist, you study the paintings. Right?"

She nodded.

"To know a suspect, you study the data points."

"All right."

She had no problem with profiling per se. A detective had to view a crime from the suspect's perspective, not their own. However, in this case, the psychologist hadn't come up with anything new on either Larmer or MacLean.

"By the way," Moore continued, "I got a detective in Toronto to interview LaToya Austin. According to Austin, Larmer is very possessive. Very hot-headed. I realize much of what I just covered is speculative, but there's a lot of it. To cut a long story short, Larmer fits the profile of a killer. MacLean doesn't. Granted," Moore said, "she's not off the hook. As I noted, I see her as a possible accessory."

Naslund suspected MacLean could be more, but she had no proof.

"From what the bank records reveal, it's possible Larmer still owes Tyler over two hundred and sixty thousand dollars. He could have paid it off in cash, or other goods. Which brings us back to paintings. We have to comb through Tyler's possessions to see if he owns any of Larmer's art. Just in case Larmer paid him that way."

"Okay."

"I don't think MacLean will let us in the main cottage. We'll need a warrant to search it. How are the justices up here?"

"Reasonable. Let me do the paperwork."

"Thanks. I'll handle the city condo. Want to scour the cottage with me when we get the warrant?"

"Absolutely."

"We might uncover more than art. Larmer may have hidden the murder weapons inside to incriminate Mac-Lean. I see him as the type who'd turn on an accomplice."

"I'll give you that. But not MacLean as his accomplice."

Moore grinned. "We'll see. For now, we'll make paintings our main target. We need to determine if Tyler bequeathed his work to anyone outside of a will. Larmer might be an inheritor. He may have killed Tyler to get some of his art. Or all of it. As to work currently on sale, from what I've learned, there are sixteen Tyler canvases out there." Moore paused. "Their estimated market value is three-point-eight million."

Naslund raised an eyebrow. Three-point-eight mill. She had no idea.

"It looks like the Tyler estate will get about thirty percent of that. Ditto for the taxman. Tyler's art agent, Jock MacTavish, will get the rest. The man controls all sixteen canvases. I read your early case notes about him. You think he's suspicious. Why?"

"That's partially a personal opinion. Another hunch." She smiled. "However, Tyler once said that MacTavish could be cheating him."

"I see. How do you know MacTavish?"

"He knew my mother." That was all she needed to tell Moore.

"Okay. So, this MacTavish has a right to sell all sixteen canvases. I spoke with him a few hours ago. Tyler signed a contract with him for each canvas, with an agreed-upon amount being paid to Tyler when the painting sold. A fixed amount, not a percentage. That usually benefits the agent, especially after an artist dies. MacTavish got twelve months for each canvas. If a canvas wasn't sold in that time period, it reverted back to Tyler."

"What happened then?"

"Good question. We didn't get that far. MacTavish had to take a sales call. Like you noted, he seems suspicious. He sounded obliging and distrustful at the same time."

"That's MacTavish."

"So I arranged to meet him in Toronto tomorrow, before I interview Hennigan."

"Good."

"I'd like you to sit in on both interviews. MacTavish is slated for fifteen hundred, Hennigan for eighteen hundred. We'll stay overnight. I'll book us rooms at the Sheraton."

"Okay." A bit pricey, Naslund thought. The Holiday Inn would do.

"We'll drive down in my car. When we're there, we'll go to Metro HQ. They've assigned two Homicide detectives to help us. Did you finish the list of Tyler's non-artist contacts in the city?"

"Yes. It's shorter than I expected. Only fourteen names."

"Okay. How about we each interview seven tomorrow?"

"Sure."

"One more thing. I feel the case is getting a bit cold."

She did as well.

"You might think I'm trying to rush things." Moore glanced at her.

She shrugged. From what she'd seen, the inspector was inherently impatient. That's who he was. She knew he was frustrated. Two days ago, he'd told her that detection was usually a matter of logic plus a little luck. In most cases, you could build a solid POI list by organizing a set of facts and details, like moving beads on an abacus. Detection as addition. A smashed face plus opportunity plus a viable motive pointed the way to the potential murderers.

"Maybe I am," he admitted, "but I want access to Tyler's property. I don't know when we'll get a warrant. Besides, we won't likely get one to search the entire property."

"True."

"Even if we do, we can't afford to wait. We need to examine the lay of the land above Tyler's boathouse to determine if someone got to it from the road. I want to know that before we question Larmer again."

She nodded. Although she figured the Mackinaw was tampered with on the bay, she had to keep an open mind. The boathouse was a possibility.

"What if we search the property ourselves?" Moore paused. "Off the record, as it were. Do you see where I'm going?"

She did.

"I don't like to break the rules," he said, "but sometimes you have to."

"Sometimes." She figured he had friends in high places. His forensic requests were usually completed in a day or two. Her requests routinely took a week or more. In any case, the investigation was bogged down.

"I don't like asking you," he continued, "but I don't think we have any choice. Would you be willing to go in?"

Ah, she thought, *I go in. The inspector stays on the sideline.*

"I could go, but you'll do a better job. You're younger. You know Tyler's property." His gray eyes smiled. "Granted, it's not completely aboveboard. But no one will know. Don't enter the cottage, just examine the property. If anything happens, I'll take the heat." He looked her in the eye. "All of it."

She appraised him. His look implied that he could get away with most things. "You want *us* to fly off the radar?"

He shook his head. "No, Sergeant. Below it. There's a difference."

Off, she thought, *below*. A distinction without a difference.

Moore eyed her. "If the heat comes, *I'll* take it." He leaned closer to her. "I'm sure you know this. You can't always follow the letter of the law, not if you want to apprehend murderers. Follow the spirit of the law. Operate on the leading edge, but not the bleeding edge."

For the most part, she agreed. Nonetheless, she remained silent.

"Look, you can't succeed if both hands are tied behind your back. One hand, maybe, but not two. I know I told you to follow the rules, but you have to know when to break them."

"When's that?" she asked.

"When a case demands it." Moore held up a forefinger. "*And* when you won't harm anyone. I take my breaches seriously. Know this, Sergeant. I've never committed perjury or forced a confession, and I never will."

She nodded.

"You won't be collecting courtroom evidence or conducting an illegal search."

Okay, she reasoned, a little "private" investigation was a minor breach. In truth, she didn't want to wait either. Beyond that, her work with J.J. and Marty wasn't exactly aboveboard. She didn't mind occasionally "forgetting" the rules, temporarily. In fact, she did some of her best work when she forgot them. There were too many. Rules of hierarchy and method, of conduct and evidence. Rules about rules. "I'll go in," she said.

"Good." Moore paused. "How are you going to do it?"

"I have an idea." She'd overheard an interesting tidbit earlier that day, at the memorial lunch. MacLean and her family were going shopping in Owen Sound that afternoon and then eating supper there. Naslund consulted her watch. She had time. "We have a window now," she told Moore. "The cottage is empty and will be for a few more hours. I'll head home, change clothes, and then drive to Colpoys and hike in to the cottage via the Bruce Trail. Approach it through the woods."

"I'll get you a rental car. Keep everything off the record."

Chapter 19

Naslund parked well away from Highway Nine behind an abandoned barn. *Behind the barn again,* she thought. She wanted to check out the Tyler property, yet she felt apprehensive. As an undercover narc, she'd run a few private investigations that bit her in the butt. Think again, she told herself. You're not in Narcland. And this one is short and direct.

She grabbed her daypack, slunk along the edge of a field, then melted into the bush and found the Bruce Trail. The air hummed with crickets, the path smelled of baked clay. She was soon surrounded by towering beeches.

Within minutes, her T-shirt started sticking to her back. The air felt heavy in her throat. The sun beat down like a cudgel. She hiked onward, sweat rolling down her face. It felt good to be on a covert op again, no matter how ordinary. At least it was off the record. For once, she didn't have to feed a report to Bickell or update case notes.

Move it, she told herself. *You have a three-hour window—if that.* She picked up the pace. It was one of those sun-spiked afternoons when even the sky wanted somewhere to hide.

The tree cover didn't offer any relief. Nonetheless, she began jogging, heading for a ravine about two kilo-

meters away that led down to Mallory Beach near Thom's
cottage.

From what she knew, Thom's boathouse was only
accessible via a path that began outside the cottage's front
door. The previous owner closed off the double lot on both
sides, with fences down to the water. A walk-in intruder
could enter the lot from the road. However, in order to get
to the boathouse they'd have to use the path. The alterna-
tive was to fight through a thick band of cedars and pines
and scramble down a cliff. She mopped her face and
concentrated on her footwork, avoiding rocks and tree
roots, jogging on, shutting out the heat. The swelling humidity cast a haze over the sun, like a cataract coating an
eye. Reaching an east-facing lookout, she took a long
drink of water and studied the far shore. The Bruce Caves
were across the bay. She pulled out her personal phone.
Using Google maps, she verified it was almost time to
scramble down from the trail and sneak onto Thom's
property.

A hundred meters later she found the ravine. Braking
and skidding, she descended to the road, jolting her knees,
almost twisting an ankle. At the bottom, she paused to
check her position. There was Thom's driveway, ten meters to the north. The nearest neighbor was about thirty
meters farther on.

She scanned in the other direction. No people about,
no traffic on the road. She slunk across it and melted into
Thom's lot. Sneaking close to the cottage, she confirmed
MacLean's car wasn't there.

She crept southward, looking for a route down to the
boathouse. Although she'd visited Thom many times,
she'd never been more than twenty-five meters from the
cottage. A few minutes later, her way was blocked by an
extended east-west hedge, high and thick. She dropped to
the ground and hauled herself under the hedge comman-

do-style. She felt ten years younger. Up on her feet again, she picked her way forward to the southern fence, skirting a tangle of blackberry brambles and cedars, passing a band of crumbling shale. She found no access to the bay below.

Scrambling back to the cottage, she crossed the driveway and headed north. *Get a move on*, she ordered herself.

Five minutes later, having reached the northern fence, she dropped to her haunches. Same story: no bay access. She removed her pack and drank some water, confident an intruder didn't hack their way down to the water. However, it was possible that MacLean or someone she knew—an *insider*—could have taken the direct path to the boathouse.

Was that a car?

Yes, it was, and close. The car turned into Thom's driveway.

Naslund froze.

A moment later, she heard a woman call out, "Carrie, dear, is this your map?"

Naslund glanced at her watch: 1823. The women must have eaten an early dinner. She ducked behind some cedars and lay on her stomach. How could she explain her presence to MacLean? How could she explain it to anyone except Moore?

"Map?" Carrie asked.

"Yes, dear, I think it's for the trail above here. You know, the one you and Thom hike—hiked. I'm so sorry."

"It's okay, Gran."

"Really, dear, I'm not thinking."

"Come inside," a younger voice called, "Lord, this heat. It's enough to bake a ham."

"All right, Mother," Carrie said.

"Look," Gran exclaimed, "there's an X, like on a treasure map, and some letters and numbers."

"Hmm," Carrie said. "Strange: four-one-four. That's our place."

"I suppose Thom did it," Gran said.

"Thom didn't use maps."

"He should have," Carrie's mother said. "He got lost finding your wedding ring."

"Mother," Carrie warned.

"Completely lost."

"Mother."

"Lost."

"All right. Come, I'll make tea."

"Tea?" the mother huffed.

"Okay, a snort."

Naslund heard a scuffle of shoes. A moment later, she registered a door opening and then closing. She inhaled deeply and slowly exhaled. Almost immediately, she thought of the numbers. Who'd written Thom's street number on a map? Why? *Leave that for later*, she told herself. *Get out of here.*

After assuring herself the three women were settled, she headed off, keeping low, hugging the border fence. Skulking across the road, she melted into the bush and found the ravine. Tightening her pack straps, she started her ascent. It seemed steeper going up.

There, back on top of the world. She hiked toward Colpoys, cruising along, head in the clouds, thinking of calling Hal. Maybe she'd see him later this evening.

As she imagined his lips, her left foot caught on a root. Before she could stop herself, she stumbled over it and fell sideways. She heard a horrific wrench then felt it. The pain shot simultaneously down her foot and up her shin. She tried to stand and let out a loud gasp. *Quiet*, she ordered herself. She sank to the ground. Nearby, she spotted a dead branch on the ground and crawled toward it on her right side, protecting her injured ankle.

At last she reached the branch and picked it up. Using it as a staff, she tentatively stood, leaning on it for support. Good. The ankle didn't seem to be broken. She started to propel herself forward by numbers: *first lift the right thigh, extend the shin, place the foot. Now the left thigh. Not so bad. Shin. Foot. Damn! Easy now.* She gritted her teeth and kept moving. Thigh, shin, foot.

Five steps later, her ankle gave out.

Lying helplessly, she debated what to do. Should she call Moore? No. No way. She didn't want the inspector trying to rescue her. He could injure himself too. All the other officers on the case were bigger No's.

What about Hal? A further No. She didn't know him that well. In any case, she'd vowed never to mix work and pleasure. Another lesson learned in Toronto.

J.J.? Better. Of course, she'd have to lie. As Moore had suggested, sometimes you had to. You also had to pick your spots. This was one of them. She'd tell J.J. she took a hike to see how easy it was to get to Thom's place from the Bruce Trail. She wouldn't mention she'd gone onto Thom's property. In the scheme of things, a white lie.

She wriggled over to a tree, leaned against it, and shrugged off her pack. Reaching inside, she felt for her phone, pulled it out, and punched J.J.'s number.

No reply.

She tried again.

Nothing.

She called again and left a message. "It's Sergeant Naslund. I need your help. I'm on the Bruce Trail near Colpoys. I sprained my ankle."

She stretched out on the ground.

In what seemed another world, a crow cawed. A second answered. The breeze rustled a fir tree, ferrying a faintly medicinal elixir to her nostrils. She pulled her water bottle from her pack and took a short drink. Mouth refreshed, she closed her eyes and shut out the pain in her ankle.

⟢⟐⟣

"Watching the—"

What's that? Naslund opened her eyes. It was almost dark.

"Watching the detectives…"

Oh, her ring-tone. Her ring-tone!

She lifted the phone to her mouth and licked her lips. "Eva here."

"Is that you, Sarge?"

"Yes."

"What happened?"

"I tripped."

"Over what?"

"A tree root."

"Huh."

She tried to stand. Her left ankle screamed with pain. "Jesus!"

"Are you okay?"

"Sort of. I better not move."

"Do you have a GPS on that phone of yours?"

"Yep."

"Tell me your co-ords."

"Aren't you going to track me down?"

"Who do you think you're talking to? Davy Crockett?"

She chuckled then read out her position.

"Hold tight, Sarge."

⟢⟐⟣

Naslund sat on Marty's couch, sipping a brandy,

feeling no pain. The sprain was nothing. She chided herself for letting it happen. Her left ankle was wrapped, her leg propped up on a foot stool. J.J. had given her two tiny pills on the trail. Whatever they were, they'd worked like a charm. She felt light-bodied, as if she were flying. "You know," she said, "I should injure myself more often."

"Think again. Next time we send in the wolves." J.J. chuckled.

"Another brandy?" Marty asked.

"Thank you."

"Better hold off," J.J. advised Marty. "You'll knock the young lady out."

"What," she complained, "a lady can't have a drink?"

"Later."

"And I suppose you're abstaining."

"Yep. For now."

She shook her head. "For a man who's a drunk, you don't drink much."

"It's a talent." J.J. said.

"Truth be told," she admitted, "I do feel sleepy."

"No surprise, I gave you two of the best. I run the local volunteer ambulance. You're this close—" He held his thumb and forefinger a quarter-inch apart. "—from dozing off. I reckon you'll wake up around midnight. We'll talk then. I have some news for you."

"Good. Listen, I want to make a call. How about some privacy?"

J.J. winked at Marty. "I think she's calling Hal Bell."

Naslund tilted her head. So, J.J. knew about Hal already. Certain news traveled fast in Wiarton. She grinned. "I am. Now let us talk in peace."

"Marty has a bed ready for you in the guestroom. Lean on me, I'll take you there."

As J.J. closed the guestroom door, she pulled out her phone and connected to Hal. "Good evening, Mr. Bell."

"Eva?"

"I was hoping to see you this evening, but I'm a little…umm…a little indisposed."

"Ooh." He sounded disappointed.

Go on, tell him what happened.

"I sprained my ankle a few hours ago. Can't walk, as it happens. Well, shouldn't walk."

"Are you okay?" he worriedly asked.

"I'll be fine in a bit. I took a few pain killers. Just wanted to say hello."

"That's nice."

She smiled. "Listen, Inspector Moore has plans for me this weekend. Maybe we can get together Monday."

"Sure."

"Wonderful. See you soon."

"Sweet dreams, Eva."

She lay down on the bed and then remembered she hadn't called the inspector yet. She and Moore had set up a code. She punched his number. "Hi, sir," she said when he answered. "Just checking in. My day's finished." That was their code. *My day's finished* for no path hacked down to the water; *Got a new lead* if she'd found a path. No need to mention her injury. He'd see it tomorrow.

"All right," he said. "Let's leave for Toronto at oh-nine-thirty."

"See you then."

"There's a meeting at oh-eight-thirty."

"Oh. Right. Oh-eight-thirty then."

❧❧❧

Wiarton. July 13th:

"Sarge," J.J. called and opened the guestroom door. "Feeling better?"

"A bit," Naslund said. In truth, she felt lethargic. "You said we'd talk at midnight."

"I tried to wake you, but you were dead to the world."

"Huh."

"Shake a leg." J.J. chuckled. "Not your left one. Here's a cane. Use it for a few days."

"Okay." Her ankle wasn't throbbing. She dropped her left foot to the floor and tested it. Better, but not solid.

"Can you drive?"

She shook her head. She could—the rental was an automatic—but she didn't want him to see it. One lie always led to another, another reason why she rarely lied.

"No prob. After we talk, I'll drop you in town behind the marina shed. You can get a taxi from the main dock, if you want."

"Perfect."

"Coffee's on."

In the kitchen, she propped the cane against the table. She sat quietly, sipping her coffee.

"For someone who's just slept nine hours," J.J. said, "you look awful sleepy."

She raised her chin.

"How about some porridge?" Marty asked.

She perked up. Porridge! Exactly what she needed. "Please."

After preparing a pot of quick oats, Marty left for work.

Naslund devoured two large bowls. No cranberries, but the oats hit the spot. She felt rejuvenated.

"Well, Sarge," J.J. said, "let's get in gear. I've been thinking about the past. Thom had two long-time enemies here at Colpoys. He had an ongoing feud with the Murphy brothers, Jake and Willie."

"The Murphys?" She knew the brothers, a couple of local bikers. *Full-time fuck-ups*, Chandler called them.

Willie had recently been released from the slammer again after eighteen months for assault.

"Yep. Thom must have had ten run-ins with them. Nasty run-ins."

"Why?"

"Another long story."

She glanced at her watch: 0714. "Tell me."

"Well, it started about ten years ago. Thom and I were out in my Caledon Twenty-Five one night. We stayed out overnight, as we usually did. I remember that night too, Sarge. The bay almost still. The stars blazing. We didn't sleep. Sat in the cockpit talking about anything and everything. Unlike most men, Thom could listen."

She nodded.

"Anyway, at dawn we were near Hay Island. I asked Thom if he wanted to fish. He looked nervous. 'No way,' he said, 'not around here.' Years ago, the Murphy family used to have fishing rights off Hay. They act like they still do. Thom said he wanted to fish near White Cloud. He'd gotten dirty looks from the Murphy brothers when he'd parked at Colpoys wharf the previous day. I told him we'd fish right here, and that was that." J.J. nodded forcefully. "Those Irish blowhards won't ever stop me from fishing. Not a Loyalist like me."

She ignored the remark. The Bruce was sometimes as bad as Belfast. "And then?" she asked.

"We came in with a dozen whitefish. After we tied up the Caledon, I jumped in my truck to head home for an ice chest. In the rear-view mirror, I saw Thom ferrying a bucket of fish to the wharf." J.J. shook his head. "When I got back ten minutes later, he was sitting on the dock, his torso bleeding, his head in his hands. His left eye was swollen shut. The Murphys had attacked him. Willie pulled a knife. But Thom took care of them. Knocked Jake off the wharf into the bay and beat Willie to the ground."

"Did you call the police?"

J.J. looked at her.

"Okay. And that was the start of it?"

"Yep. Over the years, whenever I fished near Hay with Thom, the Murphys got their backs up. Just a week ago, they saw me give Thom four big splake. Willie lay in wait for him on Mallory Beach Road and ran his car off the road. When Thom jumped out, the guy ran at him too. Barely missed him then tore off yelling, 'Fuck off, Tyler! That's our fish!'"

"Can you see the Murphys murdering him?"

J.J. thought, then shook his head. "As much as I hate to admit, I don't see it."

"Why not?"

"They had a feud, I'll say that. But, Jesus, they had no reason to murder him."

"No motive?"

He nodded.

"You're a born detective."

"Cut the baloney. You're serving it with mustard." He chuckled then sighed. "You're making me think again. I don't trust those two."

"We'll look into them."

Chapter 20

Toronto. July 13th:

Naslund hadn't been in Toronto in months. She and Moore were driving along St. Clair, heading to MacTavish's Scollard Street gallery. The city seemed faster. Cars darted in and out of lanes like mad squirrels. Earlier that day, Moore had cancelled the 0830 team meeting, saying they didn't have any fresh information. He'd assigned his actions via email. Naslund had secretly applauded the new approach.

"Want a gelato?" Moore asked.

"No thanks."

They'd just finished lunch: all you can eat lasagna. She wondered how the man stayed so trim.

He stopped and blocked off an SUV.

She glanced at him. "Are you going to double-park?"

He smiled. "We're cops."

Waiting in the car, she watched him slide through the crowd. Instead of his usual gray suit, he wore a tailored hounds-tooth number with a blue shirt and a silver-striped tie. He'd told her he wanted MacTavish to see him as an art lover as much as a detective.

In her eyes, the inspector would never look arty. In

fact, he still looked like a cop. She knew that she did as well. Her blue shirt and wide-legged jeans said *country-girl with a badge*. She'd worn them on purpose. She wanted to look like someone from Wiarton, not Toronto.

∽∾∽∾

Naslund walked slowly across the street with her cane and followed Moore into the Gallery Canadiana. As the door closed, she thought *overkill*. The cleverly-lit interior reminded her of clubs she'd once staked out in the garment district. So did the young woman walking their way. Her blouse fit like a second skin; her blonde hair said top salon. You didn't see women like that in Wiarton—except for Carrie MacLean. But this one was younger.

Moore seemed annoyed by her appearance. "Good afternoon," he said brusquely. "We're here to see Mr. MacTavish."

"The boss, you mean." She smiled, revealing a set of dazzling teeth as flashy as her blouse.

Right, Naslund thought, *boss*. That smile didn't say junior sales associate.

MacTavish stepped from behind a showcase displaying Eskimo carvings and walked their way. "I see you've met Tatyana. Isn't she a treat?" He grinned. "A Russian doll, one surprise after another." He held out his hand to Moore. "Jock MacTavish. Let me guess, you're Inspector Morse."

"Moore." The inspector perfunctorily shook hands and gestured to Naslund. "This is my associate, Sergeant Naslund."

"I know the sergeant." He pointed at her bad leg. "Line of duty?"

She nodded. She'd looked up MacTavish's age. He was sixty-three, easily more than twice Tatyana's age. He was also shorter. But it could be her heels. With those spikes and her coltish legs, Tatyana looked six feet tall. A Claudia Schiffer clone.

"Come," MacTavish said brightly, "let's repair to my office. Coffee? Tea?" He quickly examined Moore from head to toe. "Oh, forgive me. From your casual attire, I assume you're off-duty. A brandy, per chance?"

Moore declined.

Casual attire, Naslund thought as she took in the agent's tie: burgundy silk embossed with golden stars. Stylish, she had to admit. Moore's snappiest clothes hadn't put him in MacTavish's league.

"Mineral water, perhaps?" MacTavish courteously asked.

Moore and Naslund nodded.

"A VSOP for me," MacTavish said to Tatyana, "and two San Pellegrinos. Thank you."

She turned smartly and sashayed away.

Moore kept his eyes forward. Gauging the height of his chin, Naslund suspected he'd written Tatyana off as a common tart.

"Tatyana's wonderful," MacTavish announced. "Speaks every tongue known to man. She can sell Eskimo art to an Eskimo."

"Where's she from?" Naslund asked. MacTavish had called her a Russian doll. Using a composite drawing based on Marty's description, Central had provisionally IDed one of the Albin hijackers as a Russian national.

"Etobicoke," MacTavish replied.

"Was she born there?"

"I never thought to ask her."

Naslund nodded. *Never thought, or don't want to say.* She decided to question Tatyana on the way out.

MacTavish bowed. "Onward, to my *sanctorum sancti.*"

Contrary to the gallery's sleek showrooms, Mac-Tavish's office was over-furnished. Taking in the disheveled appearance, Naslund recalled that he'd always seemed a man of two minds: orderly on the outside, unruly on the inside.

"Mr. MacTavish," Moore began then stopped as Tatyana entered with the drinks. He seemed aggravated by her presence.

Strange, Naslund thought. Despite being a seasoned detective, Moore didn't appear to think a woman like Tatyana was of any use. Naslund did. In her view, Tatyana could help them unpack MacTavish. As the doll leaned close to Moore, her skirt rode up her legs. Naslund wondered if he was offended by her appearance—which made little sense. A detective needed to keep an open mind.

Drinks served, Tatyana departed, her skirt swishing down the corridor.

"Mr. MacTavish," Moore began again, "as you know, we'd like to ask you a few questions about Thom Tyler. By the way, thank you for seeing us on short notice."

"You're most welcome. I'd like to help. It's awful, what happened to Thom. He was a wonderful man and a brilliant painter, with great years ahead of him."

"Absolutely," Moore said, "such a loss. I love his work."

MacTavish smiled.

"I'm a painter of sorts myself." Moore shrugged dismissively. "Well, a Sunday-dabbler. To me, Thom Tyler captured the essence of Canada. I see him as *the* Canadian painter: truthful yet inventive, controlled yet wild."

Naslund silently applauded Moore's patter.

"I agree," MacTavish enthused. "Thom was a brilliant man, a mysterious man. He lived like a rustic, the better to tend the fire in his soul."

A rustic? Naslund thought. Was Wiarton situated at the ends of the Earth?

"Mystery," MacTavish continued, "is what makes an artist. Not to be too commercially-minded, but it makes Thom's work more compelling."

"Indeed," Moore said.

"Perhaps you'd like to see my Tyler Room on the way out?"

Huh, Naslund thought, was MacTavish absolutely un-self-conscious? Didn't he know what he'd just done? Ten minutes ago, he'd denigrated Moore's clothes—in effect, his bank account. Now he'd invited him to buy expensive art.

"I'd like that," Moore said, apparently unfazed.

The agent sat back. "Well, Officers, how can I help you?"

"Mr. MacTavish," Moore began, "yesterday you related that you have sixteen Tyler canvases for sale."

"Yes, I do. I had a long business association with Thom. Seven years, in fact. We worked well together. I was a facilitator, you see." He smiled with attempted self-deprecation.

Naslund saw thinly-veiled hubris.

"I allowed Thom to focus on his art."

Moore nodded. "Please explain how your association worked, in simple terms."

"Of course. Let's look at the sales process for one painting. That's how we worked, one canvas at a time. Thom would entrust a painting to me for twelve months. I'd immediately begin my marketing campaign. Nothing crass, of course. I'd notify my best customers that I had a gem for sale, a new Tyler. I have an extensive network, not only in Canada, but around the world. If that failed to uncover a match, I—"

"Excuse me, Mr. MacTavish. I'd like to understand something before we continue."

"By all means."

"Would you say you had an exclusive right to sell the painting?"

"I suppose you could say that."

"So, no one else could sell it."

"Correct."

"Were there any restrictions?" Moore asked. "I mean, could you only sell it here at the gallery, or anywhere you wished?"

"Anywhere, to any buyer. My job was to sell. Thom didn't care who the buyers were or where they came from. He didn't interfere—unlike some. I had an excellent working relationship with him. Not that Thom was a promoter's dream." MacTavish smiled knowingly, as if to say *but what artists are*? "He didn't pander to buyers. He didn't do interviews." The agent shook his head. "But Thom got away with it. Even if he ignored buyers, they adored him. And bought his works, hand over fist. Just another Thom Tyler paradox. *Paradosso Tomaso*."

"I see," Moore said.

"Oh, yes, Thom was definitely a paradox. As a boy, he was bedridden for months with malignant pleurisy. When he recovered, he spent all his time hiking and fishing, alone in the woods. Solitude shaped him. A wonderful story. The autonomous child, haunted by color, fed by the power of nature. On the other hand, the adult Thom could switch from dedicated, driven artist to charming raconteur in a flash. *Paradosso Tomaso*."

"I see," Moore repeated. "Tell me, how did you pay him for his work?"

"I paid him when a painting was sold."

"How soon afterward?"

"It depended."

"On what?"

"I'm a business man, Inspector. On whether the buyer paid with cash or credit. I aimed for thirty days."

"Did you succeed?"

"I tried my best."

"What percentage did you take?"

"As I said yesterday, I didn't take a percentage. I paid Thom a fixed amount."

"How did you establish that?"

"Thom and I agreed upon a figure before we signed the contract."

"That must have been difficult. You know, to establish a fair value."

"No, it wasn't. We didn't squabble about money."

"Let me summarize things, Mr. MacTavish, if I may. The process began when Tyler signed a painting over to you."

"Not quite, sir. To be clear, he didn't sign anything over. He signed a contract which gave me permission to sell a work for a limited time period."

"Could he sell it himself during that period?"

The agent appeared flustered. "No," he admitted, "he couldn't."

"So, in one sense, you owned the painting for the period. No one else could sell it, not even Tyler."

"As I said, Thom didn't care about selling his art. That was my job."

"All right. To continue, Tyler contracted a painting to you, with a set sales price."

MacTavish shook his head. "Incorrect. Allow me to clarify that as well. The sales price was not set. We agreed upon a wholesale price, if I may call it that. The retail price was left to me."

"I see. You could charge what you wanted, but Tyler

got a set amount regardless of what you sold the painting for."

"Correct. Now, lest you consider that unfair, I should tell you that such contracts are quite common."

"In your world?"

MacTavish seemed about to speak, but merely nodded.

"What happened after the twelve-month period?"

"If I didn't sell the painting in that time, it reverted back to Thom.'

"Could he then use other agents to sell it?"

"Yes."

"Did he, Mr. MacTavish?"

"No. Of course, he was free to do whatever he wished. We had a wonderful partnership."

Sure, Naslund thought. Wonderful for you.

"So," Moore said, "would it be correct to assume that Tyler would contract an unsold painting to you again."

"That was the default. It was written in the contract."

"I see. Unless Tyler explicitly stated otherwise, the painting would be contracted to you again for another twelve-month period?"

"Yes."

"At the same wholesale amount?"

"Not always."

"But that was the default, I presume."

"Correct."

"Did your contracts with Tyler expire when he died?"

MacTavish shook his head.

"According to standard probate law, they would."

"Thom and I had a different kind of contract."

"Oh?"

"In the event of death, the end-date of each contract

was extended for a period of six months. All my contracts are," the agent hastened to add.

"I see. Well, Mr. MacTavish, thank you. We best be on our way."

"Would you like to see Thom's paintings?"

Naslund saw the flicker of a grimace cross Moore's face. However, he quickly nodded. "Please."

Good, she thought, keep the agent occupied.

"Would you like to join us?" MacTavish asked her.

"Thank you, another time. I'd like to look at the Eskimo art." As MacTavish and Moore left for the Tyler Room, she walked slowly to the front of the gallery, trying to muffle the sound of her cane. She stopped briefly at the Eskimo showcase then went in search of Tatyana. She smelled her as she approached the sales desk. The Russian doll seemed to have layered more perfume on.

"Hello, Tatyana." She'd definitely added more lipstick. Quite the lips, wide and red. A baited man-trap.

Tatyana smiled. "Hi, Sergeant."

"How do you like working here?"

"Here?"

"Yes."

"Is immaterial. I work anywhere. Is life."

Ah, a femme-fatale philosopher. "What's your last name, Tatyana?"

She smiled. "Last name?" Her eyes said *kitten*; her mouth, however, said *bulldog.* "Patronym, you mean."

Naslund nodded. The doll had a bite.

"Filipov."

"Where were you born, Tatyana Filipov?"

"St Petersburg."

"Leningrad?"

"No, St Petersburg. I never know Leningrad."

"I see. A pleasure to meet you."

"Likewise, Sergeant."

Naslund took a few steps then stopped. "One more thing," she said offhandedly, playing a Columbo card. "When did you arrive in Canada?"

"Seven...no, eight months ago."

"Are you a family-class immigrant?"

"Yes. I have uncle here."

"Is he a Canadian citizen?"

Tatyana shook her head. "Not yet."

"Thank you."

As Naslund carefully exited the gallery using her cane, the door closed noiselessly behind her.

She shuffled down the steps, making a quick calculation. Tatyana was born after 1991, when Leningrad was again named St Petersburg. That made her twenty-six at most.

Naslund returned to Moore's car and sat in the passenger seat. Waiting for him, she replayed her conversation with Tatyana. "Is immaterial...Patronym, you mean...I have uncle here."

She breathed slowly in and out, letting her thoughts cycle. Her mind clicked. There was something familiar about Tatyana's last name. *Filipov.* Yes. Nikolai Filipov was the Russian national on the boat. Uncle Nikolai? she wondered. Brother? Was the common patronym a coincidence? In any case, MacTavish and his doll were about to be looked into.

⁊⁊⁊

After checking into the Sheraton, Naslund and Moore walked to Metro HQ. Inside the building, the two went their separate ways, Moore to meet with homicide detectives, Naslund to see a former colleague, Jan Januski, now an inspector in Organized Crime. Compared to OPP Central, Metro HQ was harried and crowded. Januski met Naslund at the security desk and signed her in.

"Still tripping over men?" Januski gestured at her leg as they rode up the elevator.

She smiled.

"You look good," Januski said.

"You too," she replied, which wasn't true.

Januski had a twitch in his right eye and his lips were dry and cracked. She knew the signs. Her old friend was being overworked. She wouldn't keep him for long. She'd already run Jock MacTavish, Tatyana Filipov, and Nikolai Filipov through the usual databases—OPP and CPIC, Canadian Police Information Centre—but she wanted a wider net, with international scope.

Inside Januski's office, she cut to the chase. "Can you run three names for me?"

"Any time. I'll get Constable Marinca to do it. She's a wizard. Got a secure email?"

Naslund delivered it then gave Januski the particulars for Jock MacTavish and Tatyana and Nikolai Filipov.

Januski ordered two espressos from the commissary and swiveled his chair to face the window. His office overlooked Bay St. A fiery sun dominated the sky. A few blocks away, the slate roofs of the university shimmered in the heat. The espressos arrived almost instantly. A minor efficiency, Naslund thought, one of the hallmarks of the Metro machine. Sipping the coffees, she and Januski shot the breeze. Organized Crime was swamped. The usual gangs from Italy, Jamaica, the Philippines, Vietnam, Russia, Mexico. Newer ones from Somalia, Serbia, Romania. "An international piss-pot," Januski concluded. "And you, you swamped up there?"

"At the moment. Murder. High-profile."

"I think I read that. That painter, right?"

She nodded.

"There's no respite." Januski's phone buzzed. He picked up the handset. "Okay," he eventually said. "Thanks." He turned to her. "Marinca. Finished already. Nothing on little Miss F. Mr. F rang a few small bells. Your Mr. MacT had a trail, but a cold one. Check your email in five."

"Thanks," Naslund said. "I'd invite you for a pint." The Duke of Somerset was a block away. "But I know your answer."

Januski smiled. "Next time."

⦊ʘ⦋

Naslund exited Metro HQ and walked to the Duke of Somerset. She and Moore were interviewing Louise Hennigan nearby. Tyler's previous agent had agreed to come to Metro 52 Division. In the meantime, Naslund would have a pint for old times. The street was hot and hectic. Office workers jostled each other on the way to the subway. She kept to the inner sidewalk, prominently showing her cane.

Sitting on the Duke's patio, sipping a Scottish oat ale, she pulled out her phone and read the Marinca email. Jock MacTavish and Tatyana Filipov had Toronto addresses. Nikolai Filipov had a Laval, Quebec address. Tatyana had no familial connection to Nikolai. According to Interpol, Tatyana wasn't connected to organized crime. However, Nikolai was. He was twenty-seven, born in Volgograd, formerly Stalingrad. Currently a second-tier bratok, he was assumed to be part of a smuggling ring at the Port of Montreal. However, his Canadian sheet was clean. Mac-Tavish had a documented connection to mobsters. Three years previously, he'd been arraigned on fraud charges. He'd allegedly used Russian Mafia backing to seed a pyramid scheme which sold shares in a non-existent "art fund." Before that, he'd allegedly used the same backing to resell fraudulent European art. Both times, MacTavish's lawyers had gotten him off the hook. Currently, there was nothing on him.

For now, Naslund thought.

Chapter 21

Toronto. July 14th:

The next day, Naslund parked a borrowed Metro undercover car near the Gallery Canadiana and stepped into the street. It was a beautiful morning, bright and sunny. Her left ankle was still weak but the pain had completely subsided. She crossed the street with the cane, using it more as a fallback than a necessity.

Surprisingly, MacTavish had agreed to another interview without hesitation. Over breakfast that morning, she and Moore had admitted to being puzzled. They expected MacTavish to refuse or at least call in his lawyer. In Naslund's eyes, MacTavish was a prime suspect. First, there was his past; second, he was suspiciously accommodating. However, Inspector Moore didn't agree. He felt that Larmer was their man. During last evening's team teleconference, he exhorted them to dig deeper into Larmer's movements. Lowrie closed the teleconference by reporting on the Murphy brothers. Apparently, Jake and Willie had solid alibis. They'd been working during the murder window.

The Louise Hennigan interview had been short. She immediately admitted to being Tyler's lover. Naslund figured the woman was still in love, but kept her thoughts to herself. Moore was in no mood for hunches. He concluded Hennigan was clean. She had an ironclad alibi. She was at an art expo in Europe.

As for Tyler's non-artist contacts in Toronto, Naslund and Moore had been on the stump until midnight. They'd interviewed all fourteen contacts but had no leads. Moore had insisted on handling ten, to give his *gimpy partner* a break.

Naslund walked deliberately up the gallery steps. Per Moore's request, she entered the Canadiana at exactly 0900. Unknown to MacTavish, Moore had dropped by the agent's house to ask his wife and two sons about dad's recent movements. Moore had timed his arrival to follow MacTavish's departure for work.

As Naslund approached the sales desk, her nose registered a familiar scent: *femme-fatale* perfume. Passing the Eskimo art showcase, she slowed her pace. Given the swelling fragrance invading her nose, Tatyana was only a few meters away. She rounded the showcase.

There was Tatyana. Her man-trap lips looked wider than Naslund remembered.

"Sergeant." She smiled. "How nice."

Naslund nodded. Tatyana wore a skin-tight pantsuit with a tasseled cinch.

"Is Mr. MacTavish available?"

Tatyana smiled again. "Follow me, please." She looked back.

Naslund got the feeling that the doll was playing her.

Tatyana stopped outside MacTavish's office. "Would you like a coffee?"

Naslund shook her head.

"With cream," Tatyana proposed and licked her lips.

Naslund shook her head again. Was the doll gay? Or pretending to be.

"Come in," MacTavish called. "I'm waiting."

She strode into the office. She had no warrant to search the premises. However, at this point, all she wanted to do was uncover something on MacTavish.

"Well," he said as he rose and shook hands, "I see some detectives know how to dress."

Naslund was wearing her one decent suit, a sleek Italian indigo number. She sat, eying the disheveled office. It seemed more unkempt than yesterday.

"How can I help you, Eva?"

"Sergeant," Naslund said.

"Pardon me." MacTavish smiled wolfishly. "Sergeant."

"Mr. MacTavish, you related that when Thom Tyler died, your contracts with him were extended for six months."

"Correct. By the way, some agents insist on twelve months, minimum. We put a lot of effort into selling an artist's oeuvre."

Perhaps, she thought. "What is the procedure now when you sell a Tyler painting?"

"The wholesale price, as I referred to it, will go to the Tyler estate."

"When does the first of those contracts expire?"

"Just a moment, please." He consulted a rolodex. "September the thirtieth this year."

"How about the last of the contracts?"

He leafed through the rolodex. "March the thirty-first, next year."

"May I see the contracts?"

"Of course." The agent walked to a metal filing cabinet, unlocked it, opened a drawer, and pulled out a large file. Having returned to his desk chair, he shuffled an unruly stack of documents until he had them arranged as he wanted and then slid them across the desk. "You will find them ordered by expiry date."

She leafed through the contracts, noting the section headlines, occasionally skimming the text. They seemed to be valid legal documents. At the end of every document she found a section titled *Augmentation of Obligation*. In the event of Tyler's death, MacTavish was entitled to a six-month extension, with no further extension after that.

Well, she reasoned, so much for MacTavish holding on to the paintings for years, selling them when their value peaked—which, she had to admit, cast doubt on his guilt. Why would he kill Tyler? It would restrict his ability to sell extant paintings as well as prevent him from selling new ones. It was a double whammy. She straightened the documents. "I'd like photocopies of these."

"Of course."

Damn it, the man was cooperative. No delaying. No insistence he bring in his lawyer. The only black mark they had against him was the fact that he lied about paying Tyler within thirty days when a work sold. M&M had traced the date of all Tyler paintings sold by MacTavish over the past seven years and cross-referenced them to money transfers from MacTavish to Tyler. Although not definitive, the trace suggested the agent rarely paid the full amount within a month. "Mr. MacTavish, you lied to us. You didn't pay Mr. Tyler when you said you did."

"I don't know what you're talking about." MacTavish seemed truly perplexed.

"You said you paid him within thirty days."

"I can confidently say that nine times out of ten I paid Thom within a month."

"Can you prove that?"

"Of course. First, allow me to explain something. I advanced Thom a lot of money over the years—in cash. He always wanted cash. As it happens, he still owes me approximately one hundred and ninety thousand dollars. When I sold one of his paintings, he often asked me to apply a portion of the proceeds to his outstanding loan. Then I transferred the rest to his bank, which was sometimes less than half the wholesale price."

"I see."

"As I related previously, Thom and I had a wonderful partnership."

She stood. "Thank you for your time." Three steps later, she stopped in the office doorway and absent-mindedly turned back. "I'm curious, Mr. MacTavish. How long have you known Nikolai Filipov?"

"Who?"

"Nikolai Filipov, from Montreal. Originally, as you know, from Volgograd, Russia."

She saw that MacTavish had no idea who Filipov was. Or was pretending not to. "I'll ask you again. How long have you known Nikolai Filipov?"

"I don't know anyone of that name."

She casually retook her chair. "Are you sure?"

MacTavish nodded. "Hold on. Filipov? Is he related to Tatyana?"

"You tell me."

"How can I? I don't know him."

"We can check your phone records."

"Please do." The agent adopted an attitude of aggrieved silence.

She scrutinized him, holding his gaze.

He looked away.

"What can you tell me about your Russian connections?"

"Russian? Well, before Louise Hennigan, Thom had an agent from Russia, a Miss Vostokov, if I recall." He flipped through his rolodex. "Yes, Vostokov. I don't have a first name."

"Do you know her?"

"I never met her."

"But she's in the same business."

"Not really. She was on the edge. Street murals, art installations, that world."

"What else do you know about her?"

MacTavish raised his hands in a helpless gesture. "Nothing."

Naslund let it slide. She suspected MacTavish was leading her one way to cover up another. "Where were you on Sunday July seventh?"

"Toronto."

No hesitation. "Who were you with?"

"My family."

"The whole day?"

"Yes."

"I trust your wife will confirm that. Incidentally, Inspector Moore called on her," Naslund consulted her watch, "about an hour ago. He also talked to your sons."

"I'm not surprised."

"Oh?"

"You seem to think that because I had a satisfactory business arrangement with Thom Tyler I took advantage of him." MacTavish eyed her. "I didn't." He stood and handed her the bundle of contracts. "Don't forget these. You can ask Tatyana to photocopy them." He gestured toward the sales desk. "Why not invite her for a drink? She likes you." He grinned conspiratorially.

Naslund shook her head. Why was it that so many men assumed female officers were gay? Probably lack of imagination. Or brains.

He pointed at his watch. "*Tempus fugit*. I have an appointment. I wish you well, Sergeant. It's terrible what happened to Thom." He smiled. "If I can be of any further assistance."

"We'll call you." She turned away. That obsequious smile, it made her skin creep.

Leaving the office, she tried to solidify her opinion of MacTavish. Was the man simply a money-hungry art agent? Or was he trying to snow them? Was he hoping his Russian doll would deflect their attention? As Naslund walked down the corridor, she registered the scent of Tatyana's perfume. A few steps later she reached the sales desk.

"Oh, Sergeant." Tatyana raised a hand to her throat. "You surprised me."

"I'm sorry."

Tatyana bowed, showing Naslund the tops of her breasts. "Do you like," she smiled and then pointed at the contracts Naslund was carrying, "help with that?"

"This? Yes, please. Can we photocopy the whole bundle?"

Tatyana nodded. "Why you would want them?"

"Pardon?"

"Why take these?"

Naslund smiled politely. "Business, Tatyana."

"I am interested in law."

"Oh?" Naslund examined Tatyana's mouth. No apparent subterfuge there.

"I was pre-law student in St Petersburg. I study hard."

"Good."

"I see things."

"Yes?"

The set of her jaw seemed to say *Important things—things only I can see*. "Give me card," she said quietly.

Naslund handed Tatyana her OPP card.

"Can you meet in Etobicoke?" Tatyana asked.

"Yes."

"I finish at noon. I call you then."

తించి

Sitting in the undercover car, Naslund waited for Moore to phone her, as arranged. The car ahead had been parked in a ten-minute loading zone for at least forty minutes. Two old men shuffled across the street. She absentmindedly surveyed the rest of the street, wondering what Tatyana was up to. Was the doll playing her? Did she really see important things? If so, what kind of things? She seemed to be genuine. As Naslund reviewed the set of Tatyana's mouth—sincere—her duty phone rang.

"Sergeant Naslund," she slowly said, "OPP."

"You sound pensive," Moore said.

Did she? Maybe he was more attuned to her than she thought. "I was thinking about the case. Nothing important." She didn't want to mention Tatyana, given his apparent dismissal of her. "What's the news on MacTavish's family?" she asked.

"The man was at home all day on July seventh. And, according to his wife, all night too."

"That's what he told me," she said. "And it appears he was telling the truth about the Tyler contracts. As he said yesterday, they were extended for six months, that's it. I have copies."

"Good."

She sighed. MacTavish's words suggested he had no part in Thom's murder but she still wasn't sure. "I don't think we're finished with MacTavish."

"Don't get stuck on him. Homicides can make you too suspicious. Believe me, I know. You end up suspecting everybody."

"Well, it's just that…well, I can't put my finger on exactly why he's bothering me."

"Fair enough. He's a slippery sort. Run him to ground, but don't get overzealous."

Me overzealous? she thought.

"We're doing everything we can, Sergeant. All we can do is hunt down evidence, examine each piece, and take it forward or leave it aside. At the end, whatever we have makes the case."

"Yes. Absolutely."

"Remember, evidence isn't perfect. It's organic and messy, like life. It won't all fit. We'll have to drop what doesn't. If we don't, the final case won't work."

"Understood." *Spare me the speech, Inspector.*

"Don't forget, we have Larmer too."

Well, she thought, *you* have Larmer.

"A Metro detective is taking me to Tyler's condo now," Moore said. "We'll leave for Wiarton at noon. Can you meet me at the Sheraton?"

"Sure. But how about fourteen-thirty? I'm pursuing a lead."

Moore didn't hesitate. "Okay See you then."

ৎৡৎ

Just after noon Naslund sat on a park bench in Etobicoke overlooking Lake Ontario. Tatyana hadn't called her. Naslund leaned forward and cupped her chin in her hands. Although she hadn't sensed any ulterior motives in Tatyana's face or words, Naslund felt agitated. Did MacTavish have some way to benefit from Thom's death that wasn't yet evident?

Five meters away two swans took flight, their huge wings beating against the water. The explosive sound made her feel more agitated. She slowly inhaled and exhaled ten times. *Think things through*, she told herself. She was fully aware that Tatyana could be playing her. *What if she isn't?* an inner voice said. *If she isn't, she can help.*

Naslund nodded to herself. True. Tatyana might know things.

She certainly had an inside track. Beyond that, at this point, the team didn't have any other avenues into Mac-Tavish's world.

A boat raised its sails and skimmed away from shore. Naslund followed its passage until the couple onboard were invisible to the eye.

As she was about to stand and leave, her duty phone blared.

"Sergeant Naslund," she answered, "OPP."

"Sergeant?"

"Yes."

"Is Tatyana Filipov, from gallery."

She hadn't recognized her voice. "Hello, Tatyana."

"Can we meet for coffee?"

"Yes."

"I am on streetcar, soon coming to Lakeshore and Louisa in Etobicoke. There is coffee shop on corner."

"I know it," Naslund said. "Fifteen minutes?"

"Yes."

ᏋᏗᏋᏗ

"How long are you police?" Tatyana asked.

Quite a while, Naslund thought. "Sixteen years," she said.

"Only sixteen? You look more, what is word, established?"

Naslund nodded. Did she mean older?

"I think you are good police. Yes, I see that."

"Thank you." Naslund had decided to say as little as possible. She and Tatyana were sitting on a bench by the lake. Earlier, she'd purchased a few sandwiches which they ate in the coffee shop, chatting about the city and the weather. Tatyana had seemed formal, almost shy, definitely less flashy. Which was fine with Naslund.

"In my country, all is corrupt. All! Government, police, army. Russian system make me leave home."

"I'm sorry."

"Don't be." Tatyana's eyes hardened. "I want to be lawyer here."

Naslund nodded noncommittally. Was Tatyana stringing her along?

"I want to help system work. I told you, I see things." Tatyana stopped and examined Naslund's face. Apparently satisfied, she continued. "I will tell you interesting thing about Mister MacTavish." She paused. "Do you want?"

"Of course."

"I think he is dishonest."

"Oh?"

"But I am not sure. It is just feeling. I need to get evidence." She glanced at Naslund. "He doesn't know what I think of him. I am, what you say, all smiles at work," she said and smiled.

"I saw that."

"Yes, is good. I help in office. I file sometimes the sales invoices."

"Yes?"

"It looks like boss keeps changing them. He often has four or five versions for one thing. Like for same painting."

"I see."

"I think maybe he does same thing with contracts. Maybe Tyler contracts I photocopy for you were not most up-to-date ones. Boss might bring out other ones when those expire. I will, as they say, keep open eye."

"Thank you."

Tatyana smiled coquettishly and crossed her legs. She

was looking at Naslund as if she could be more than a confidant. The flash was back. Naslund checked her watch and stood. "Got a meeting. Thanks again."

Chapter 22

Wiarton. July 15th:

The next morning Naslund was in the shower when her personal phone crooned. "Watching the detectives…" She'd had a late night. Moore hadn't showed up at the Sheraton until 1700. He'd been in a miserable mood. His Metro contact had been called to a CS and left him hanging for three hours. She and Moore had pulled into Wiarton station at 2030 and then spent hours updating case notes.

Now, Naslund tried to shut out her phone. As usual, it didn't stop crooning. She gave in, turned off the shower, and found it. "Eva here."

"I have an idea," J.J. said. "Keep that thing next to you."

"I was in the shower."

"Again? Well, at least you're clean. Okay, Sarge, can you get dressed—your best plaid outfit—and get to the marina in fifteen?"

"Aye, laddie."

"Bless ya. Marty'll be waiting behind the main shed."

❧❧❧

"Good morning, Sarge," J.J. said. "Porridge or do-nuts?"

"How about both?"

"Can do. How's your time?"

Naslund glanced at her watch: 0746 and no 0830 meeting. "Good. We can have a few donuts, shoot the breeze, then have a few more, like you mechanics always do."

J.J. winked at Marty. "I think she's learning."

Marty smiled and turned to the stove.

"Okay, Sarge," J.J. said, "we'll move fast anyway. You know that feud between the Murphys and Thom? I used to think it was my fault."

She nodded.

"It wasn't. As it happens, the fish were just a fuse. One of my contacts told me the bomb was a woman. Jenny Murphy, Jake's older sister."

"Jenny Murphy?"

"Do you know her?"

Naslund nodded. "She got pulled in on a pot bust a few years back. Relax, J.J., growing, not personal use. I saw the plants out there." She smiled at Marty. "Nothing to worry about. Anyway, Jenny Murphy was innocent. Got caught up with the wrong crowd."

"That's Jenny."

"If I remember correctly, she went down to Toronto."

"Yep."

"Who told you she was the bomb?"

"A little birdie who wants to remain anonymous. I don't know why she's the bomb, but I know she's home now."

"I need to talk to her." Something told Naslund to move it. "ASAP. Thanks for the lead."

"No time for a donut?"

"How about a takeaway?"

❦

After Marty dropped Naslund off at the marina, she roared up Bruce Nine in her own car, foot to the floor. The hell with Bickell. She screamed past a slow-moving truck. She'd sensed Jenny Murphy wouldn't be in Colpoys for long. A minute later she pulled off the road and zipped up the lane leading to the Murphy house. The adjacent lots were unkempt. The land had an aura of decay. However, the property at the end of the lane blew the decay away. Mature fruit trees surrounded a quaint white house which resembled an English cottage.

As she reached the end of the lane, Jenny rushed out the front door with a suitcase and ran toward a blue Camry. Naslund parked tight to the Camry, cutting off Jenny's exit. Finally, she thought, a little luck.

Jenny shook her head in disgust.

Naslund stepped out of her car. "Hello, Jenny."

"You didn't have to do that."

"Maybe not."

Jenny shook her head again. She wore a white shirt with rolled-up sleeves and a pair of faded cut-offs. Her hair was much longer than the last time Naslund saw her, three years ago.

"You leaving?" Naslund asked.

Jennie eyed her as if she were stupid. "Brilliant, Sherlock."

"Why?"

"Because I want to." She faced the door. "Mother," she yelled, "you have a visitor."

"I'm not here to see your mother."

"My brothers aren't here."

"I know."

"You want to talk to me?"

Naslund nodded.

"I'm clean."

"Probably. Let's talk."

Jenny shrugged then gestured at Naslund's shorts. She hadn't had time to change. "New uniform?"

"You got it."

Jenny cracked a smile.

Naslund gestured at the Camry. "Where're you going?"

"Toronto."

Dawn Murphy scurried out of the house and bustled toward Naslund, eyes front, neck rigid, resolutely ignoring Jenny. In Naslund's mind, it was like watching a cartoon. Mother Hen pretending her chick wasn't there. Dawn waved Naslund to a wrought-iron table under a maple tree, chatting all the while. "Sergeant, you look prettier every time I see you. Tea? Yes, and scones."

She turned and curtly waved her daughter into the house. "Tea."

Jenny seemed about to say something then appeared to think better of it. Instead, she rolled her eyes.

Naslund watched her go, her gait now languid. After interviewing Jenny years ago, she'd opened up about her life. She'd told Naslund her mother infuriated her. Being an only daughter, she'd said, was like being a one-trick pony. Naslund knew the feeling. Refreshments served, Jenny lit a cigarette and whispered to her mother. Dawn huffed. Naslund surreptitiously examined Jenny. Her eyes were bright, as if she'd been on a purge. "So," Naslund said, "you came back. Why?"

"Well." Jenny waved her cigarette. "For a short visit." She looked at her mother. "Very short."

Dawn huffed again and marched into the house with a look that said *the shorter the better*.

Almost immediately, the air felt lighter. Jenny smiled openly. "Want a drink?"

Naslund pretended to consider it. "Better not. On duty."

"So?"

"Not today, thanks." So much for the purge.

Jenny crushed her cigarette into a full ashtray. "What brings you here?"

"The past."

"Huh."

Naslund took a bite of scone. She knew Jenny had once been crazy for Thom. She'd talked about him non-stop after the interview. Naslund put her scone down, seeing Jenny as she'd been three years ago. Her eyes had been like stars. Sitting across from her now, Naslund saw that much of their radiance was doused. She figured the bomb was connected to love. "Did you arrive too late for the funeral?"

Jenny stared at Naslund with wry amusement. *Don't bullshit me*, her eyes said.

Fair enough, Naslund admitted. However, she had no choice but to try again. "It was a long time ago. Carrie MacLean wouldn't have cared."

"Nothing to do with her."

Try again. "Did you want to marry him?"

"Hell no! Are you nuts?" Jenny pulled out a cigarette and lit it. She studied Naslund, seemingly deciding if she was still a good person to talk to. Eventually she nodded. Apparently, once a sympathetic listener, always a sympathetic listener. "Well, maybe. I was young, forever young. He was, well, beautiful. Only seven years older. Seven, and fifteen days. You don't forget those things."

There was more, Naslund saw. What? It came to her in a flash. A baby. Jenny Murphy had been pregnant. "How old is the child now?"

Jenny shook her head.

Naslund read her eyes. Jenny didn't want to divulge it, and yet she did. The collision of emotions in her face was unmistakable. Pain and pride warred with truth and acceptance. Naslund saw a sudden release, like a thunder storm in July. She saw Jenny's secret. She'd had an abortion. "So, he didn't want a child."

Jenny started running her hands through her hair. Her right leg bounced up and down. Only her gaze was steady. It was fixed on the ground. Suddenly, she became perfectly still and then looked up. "You're right. He told me that at the start. I tried to change his mind, but, well…" She stabbed out her cigarette. "I went to the city. I didn't come back much, not after he took up with Carrie."

"Ah."

"He didn't help me at all. Not one bit."

Naslund found that hard to believe.

"Didn't give me money, understanding, anything. Wiped his hands of me. I blame it on that friend of his, that J.J. MacKenzie."

Hmm, J.J. was in the mix. "Who did you confide in?"

Jenny didn't reply.

"No one?"

"No one here." She gestured toward the house. "Certainly not my mother."

"Your brothers?"

She looked away.

That was all Naslund needed to see. Jake and Willie knew the whole story.

Jenny looked back. "They didn't do anything."

Naslund remained silent.

"They didn't! Not my little brothers."

ഇരുന്നു

Naslund arrived at the station just after nine. The

Murphy brothers were back in play. Their alibis better be watertight. The staff parking lot was full. It was a beautiful day but no one was sitting outside with their morning coffee. Thanks to Inspector Moore, she figured. A cardinal darted from a tree, cleaving the air like a thick red arrow. Sitting in her car, with the sun on her face, she opened her laptop and made notes on Jenny Murphy, then updated the entries on the Murphy brothers as well as J.J. Go away for a few days and your note load doubled. Moore's Law of Case Notes. Not to be confused with Inspector Moore's Law, which said that if you don't do your notes every day, you're fired.

Having finally completed the casework, she left her car, took a last look at the summer sky, and entered the foyer. She got the impression someone had been watching her. And reported her activities, or lack thereof, to Moore. Maybe one of the ninjas. She hoped no one was onto her work with J.J. They shouldn't be. A background in undercover had its advantages.

As she walked down the corridor to the murder room, Moore called from her office. "Sergeant, join me for a moment."

She entered the office and sat.

"I reviewed your report on the hijacking," he said. "I'm going to revisit the manager of the Griffith Island Club with Chandler. I'd like you to follow-up on a lead we just got for a sailboat. Could be connected to the sailboat the kayakers saw." He referred to his notebook. "See Darrell Gundy. The end of Mallory Beach Road, number 744."

She jotted down the name and address.

"He'll be home after lunch. In the meantime, I want to run something by you. I've been thinking about Larmer and love triangles."

Still? she wondered. She figured she better mention

the Murphys before Moore got on a roll. "Sorry to interrupt, sir. I just got a lead about the Murphy brothers. We have potential motive. We need to review their movements during the murder window."

He nodded impatiently. "I'll assign Lowrie and Kraft to go back at them. Please update Lowrie on motive."

"Of course. With all due respect, sir, I think we should go after them this morning."

"We will. You can enlighten Lowrie in fifteen minutes. Now, on to Larmer. I examined all the case interviews again, both the ones conducted here and in the city. Do you know how many women said they loved Tyler or his painting? Without prodding. Almost ninety percent. I'm not saying they were all in love with him, but that they loved him or his work."

"He had a following."

"Sure did. As for the men? Some said they admired him. Others respected him. Others claimed they tried to live like him. In a sense, all three are male admissions of love." Moore held up a stop-sign hand. "I mean they loved Tyler as a person."

"Understood."

"I'd wager Larmer still loves MacLean."

She said nothing.

"Here's where things get interesting. I'd say he also loved Tyler. As a friend, I mean. A brother. An admiring yet jealous brother."

"Fair enough." From what she'd seen and heard, Larmer did love Thom like a brother.

"What's the opposite of love? Not indifference. That's academic BS. The opposite of love is hate."

"Okay."

"When I look at Larmer, I see someone who's trying to cover his guilt by lashing out at us, by acting angry and innocent. The more I consider his interview, the more I think so. He's hiding a lot of guilt."

She remained silent.

"M and M hasn't been able to confirm if he had any financial motives for murder. But he had at least two other motives. One, he acted to please MacLean. Two, he was envious of Tyler's success. As for opportunity, he rented a cottage in the Bruce this summer for the first time ever, which put him close to Tyler's cottage."

"True."

"They say envy is a monster. I'd wager Larmer hated Tyler enough to obliterate his eyes, the ultimate in artistic envy."

"Possible."

Moore shifted gears. "Do you remember the profiler I mentioned?"

"Yes."

"He's sure the killer was organized and an external-izer. That type of killer thoroughly assesses whether a planned action will be low risk or high risk. Such killers don't carry out high-risk acts." Moore stopped, waiting for Naslund to comment.

"All right."

"I see Colpoys Bay at dawn as relatively low risk. Large water surface. Few boats about, if any. Hence few people, if any. Poor light. What do you think?"

"Low risk," she mused. "Well, Colpoys Bay is usually quiet at dawn, that's true. But it was still light enough to see. For example, an unidentified witness saw an Albin and two kayakers saw a sailboat."

"Okay. But a self-possessed externalizer like Larmer wouldn't be worried about a possible witness or two around dawn. He knows the bay. He's comfortable and confident there. He knows how hard it is to ID people on the water at sunrise."

Naslund nodded. Moore wasn't about to drop his number-one suspect. But if Larmer was guilty, why had he killed Thom a week ago? He'd known Thom for years. If he wanted to kill his *best* friend—*his family in Ontario*—he would have had numerous opportunities. What made him snap now? She searched her mind. Did Larmer turn psychotic? He was two-faced, not to mention arrogant. It was easy to attach other labels to him. But was psychotic killer one of them?

Moore leaned forward. "From what we know, Larmer didn't use a boat. However, I think he could have walked out of his rental cottage and gone for a swim."

"Could have."

"We know he's a swimmer. Sunday July seventh was a very warm night, the kind you could hike in swim shorts and a T-shirt. If he swam up Hope Bay ten minutes, he'd reach the spot where the Bruce Trail veers inland. From there he could hike or jog to Tyler's cottage."

"That's a long way, especially at night." She'd measured the distance: almost fifteen kilometers.

"I know, but doable. Larmer's very fit. He could wear a head lamp. He may have stashed the lamp and a pair of hiking shoes nearby beforehand, but I doubt it. That would leave trace evidence. Earlier today I sent the ninjas to take a look. They didn't find anything. I suspect he brought his gear along for the swim in some kind of waterproof sack."

"Possible."

"Yesterday I determined there's no Larmer art at Tyler's condo. I want to verify that there's none at the Mallory Beach cottage. I have the warrant. Ready for a drive?"

"What about updating Lowrie on the Murphys?"

"Oh, right. See you in ten. Or less."

Or less. She shook her head inwardly. Always *his* schedule. Boss or not, it rankled.

Naslund knocked on Carrie MacLean's screen door. "Hello! Anybody home?"

"Yes?" Carrie called.

"It's Eva. Sergeant Naslund."

"Just a minute, Eva."

Carrie opened the door to find Moore standing next to her. "Oh," Carrie said.

"You remember Inspector Moore?"

She nodded curtly. Her eyes looked hollow. However, her face and body looked fuller. She wore pajama bottoms and a very tight top.

"We have a search warrant," Naslund said, "for the whole cottage."

"Why?"

Moore stepped forward. "Because, Miss MacLean, we need to conduct a search."

"Another search?"

"Correct." He showed her the warrant. "We request that you leave the cottage and wait outside. We'll inform you if we need any assistance."

"Assistance?"

"Yes. To access a closed area, for example."

"There are no closed areas."

"Good," he said. "Miss MacLean, you are excused."

"Hmmp." She spun on a heel and marched back into the cottage.

He opened his mouth then stepped forward.

Naslund tapped his arm. *Wait,* she motioned.

A minute later, Carrie returned to the door carrying a book and a tall glass of sparkling water with a slice of lemon.

"Water would be nice," Moore said.

"Try the tap." She strode off.

Naslund watched her go, chin up, back rigid. She tossed her hair as she dropped into a deck chair.

"You can hunt for the assault weapons," Moore said. "I'll take care of the art."

"Okay." In Naslund's eyes, Larmer's paintings were all heavy lines and empty spaces. To say Moore had a better handle on them was an understatement.

∽∾∽

Moore called off the search at noon. They hadn't found any hidden weapons or Larmer paintings. Naslund followed Moore to Carrie's deckchair.

"We're finished, Miss MacLean," the inspector said. "You're clean."

She raised her chin. "Of course I am."

The inspector tried to lighten the mood. "Didn't find any water in your basement."

"I don't have a basement." She eyed him. *Don't try to humor me.*

"Figuratively speaking, Miss MacLean."

Moore shook his head as they drove away from the cottage. "She's a piece of work. Okay, she might be beautiful, but other than that?" He shook his head again. "Would you do me a favor?"

"Sure."

"Open the windows and boot it."

Naslund obliged.

A few minutes later he called out, "Good! Thanks."

She closed the windows and turned the air-con back on.

"That cleared the cobwebs," he said. "Well," he continued, "no Larmer art. It looks like he still owes Tyler two hundred sixty G. Could be another motive for murder."

Chapter 23

Naslund drove slowly along Mallory Beach Road, past the Tyler cottage. A clutch of gray-white clouds clogged the western horizon. She felt the humidity building. She'd done a background check on Darrell Gundy. He was an eighty-seven-year-old widower with a clean sheet.

She turned off the road at Number 744, a one-story Pan-Abode. A white-haired man opened the front door. She immediately recognized him. She'd seen Gundy at the Legion calling bingo games. His back was ramrod straight and his body lean. Even in mid-summer, he wore a long-sleeved shirt.

"C'mon in," Gundy said. "I know you. You're the detective, right?" He spoke rapidly, his cadence influenced by decades of calling bingo.

She nodded.

Inside, Gundy directed her to the living room. Floor-to-ceiling windows overlooked the bay. "Have a seat." He pointed to a worn leather sofa. "How 'bout a tea, Detective?"

"Fine idea. Thanks."

"Milk? Sugar?"

"Just a little milk."

The tea came in a chipped mug. Gundy sat in a

straight-backed chair near the window. "My son Roy called last night," he said after sipping his tea. "He's my only child, an agricultural analyst in Chicago. He doesn't get home much. Anyway, I mentioned seeing a large sailboat in the bay on Monday morning. Early. Roy's been following the Tyler case on the internet, the web, he calls it. He thinks that sailboat could be important. He said I should call the police."

"I'm glad you called."

"I don't like the police much."

She understood the sentiment. There were cops she didn't like, usually cops who were bent, which was one reason why she'd left Metro and joined the OPP.

"I'll admit it, I was once a bit of a hell-raiser." His face broke into a mischievous grin. "Nothing serious, mind you. But my son said to forget all that and call you."

"Good."

"I'm not sure anyone will believe me." Gundy smiled apologetically. "I think my distance vision is fine, but Doc MacG just gave me a new prescription for reading. Anyhow, let's go out to the deck."

"Sure."

The deck extended to the water's edge. A moist breeze came off the bay.

"That's a fine view," she said. She could easily see across to White Cloud Island.

"Isn't it?" Gundy enthused. "Look at that flagpole, the one up from the island wharf. Do you see the one I mean?"

She gazed across to the wharf. "Yes."

"I'm not sure, what color is it?"

"Brown." She looked again. "Well, more light brown than brown."

"That's what I see. And now you say light brown. So did the neighbor."

She took another look and verified the color.

"Well," Gundy said, "I guess the eyes are okay."

"I'd say so."

After settling into a deck chair, he took up the thread. "As I mentioned, Roy thinks that sailboat could be important. Let me tell you what I saw. I'm a methodical man these days. I recorded the time."

"Good." She took out her duty phone. "I'm going to record you, okay?" Although she didn't need permission to record an interview, she often asked as a courtesy.

Gundy nodded. "It was Monday, July eighth, exactly eight minutes after the hour. Six-oh-eight a.m. A cutter-rigged sailboat was near the top end of White Cloud, heading north. You don't usually see boats that early on a Monday. So I took up my Bushnells." He pointed to a pair of binoculars hanging near the deck door. "When I got outside, I saw that the cutter was an old girl, a forty-footer, I'd say, with a dirty white hull and an orange cove stripe. She was tacking against the headwind."

"From the north, was it?" Naslund asked.

"Northwest."

She nodded. Correct for July eighth.

Gundy stared at the bay as if visualizing the sight. "There were three people on board."

"Are you sure?" His number sounded right. The kayakers saw two or three people.

"Yes. And I recognized two of them, a pair of young rascals from Colpoys. Always in trouble. The Murphy brothers, Jake and Willie."

The Murphys? "Not to be picky, Mr. Gundy, but I better ask you again. Are you absolutely sure?"

"Of course I'm sure." Gundy eyed her.

Naslund felt naked under his stare.

"I've seen them many times," he stated.

"Who was the other person?"

"I didn't recognize him. He was a white man, medium height, heavyset."

"Can you describe him a little more?"

"Well, he had gray hair, shorter than mine. He had a farmer's tan. He was wearing a blue singlet, and his arms where white above the elbows. His shoulders were white too."

"All right. Did he have any other distinguishing features?"

"Sorry, none that I can recall."

"Okay. Would you say he was friendly with the Murphy brothers?"

"I'd say so. Put it this way, he was smiling. Laughing too."

"Did you hear him?" she asked.

"No. But I saw his mouth."

"One more question: Did you see any other boats?"

"No."

"Nothing to the south?" By 0608 Thom's skiff was likely out of sight, blocked by White Cloud. However, the kayakers could have been in view.

"I only looked north, to follow the cutter."

"For how long?" she asked.

"Two or three minutes. Then I went inside for breakfast."

"Okay. Do you have anything else to report?"

"No, Detective."

"Thank you very much."

☙❧☙

Driving away from Gundy's place, Naslund considered the coastline from Mallory Beach to Hope Bay. Although there were no full-service marinas along that stretch, there were wharfs and anchorages. She turned off

Bruce Nine just past Adamsville and followed a series of narrow roads to the inlet at the top of Cape Croker. Nothing, as she'd expected. No boats or mooring buoys. The inlet was too exposed to be a good anchorage.

If the cutter was berthed anywhere local, she reckoned Sydney Bay was the spot. It was the only place with a decent-sized wharf. As she drove toward it, her heart began beating faster.

The closer she came to the wharf, the more agitated she got. *Rein it in*, she told herself. Looking westward, she saw that the gray-white clouds of an hour ago had become dark and ominous. There was a thunder storm on the way. She turned onto Sydney Bay Road. The sky darkened as she drove. The trees leaned eastward, bent by a strengthening wind. The road seemed to go on forever, as narrow roads in the Bruce often did.

She saw it before she saw the wharf—the distinctive sign of a cutter: two forestays. The boat's mast easily topped the cedars surrounding the wharf. Its height indicated a vessel well over thirty feet long. She drove up to the wharf and stopped five meters from the cutter. Bingo. Dirty white hull, orange cove stripe. The mystery sailboat.

The hairs on her forearms tingled. She opened her window. The air was damp. She felt strangely anxious but told herself it was just the impending squall. From what she could tell, the cutter wasn't occupied. The hatches were shut, as was the companionway door. She exited her car. Within two steps, the wind plastered her clothes against her body. She leaned forward, fighting a gust, slipping on the gravel underfoot. As she got closer, the cutter loomed larger. An air of surliness surrounded it.

She approached the bow. A cat balefully inspected her from the front deck and then scurried off. Nothing stirred inside the boat. She allowed herself to relax a bit. Pulling out her duty phone, she snapped a photo of the cutter's registration number. She'd search the boat reg database for the owner.

Pacing slowly, she examined the dockside hull from bow to stern looking for dove-gray paint marks.

Nothing.

She walked to the mid-ship boarding gate, opened the guardrail, and stepped aboard. The boat instantly rolled, swaying as if it had been hit by a wave. If anyone was onboard, that would bring them out. She stopped and waited, preparing her story: *Pardon my curiosity. Used to sail a cutter.*

No movement inside.

She walked to the bow as fast as she could, gripping the waterside guardrail. Although her left ankle was good, with the boat roll, the deck was treacherous. Holding the guardrail tightly with two hands, she leaned over the side and worked her way along the deck to the stern.

Again, no dove-gray marks. And definitely no sign of a recent wash.

As she disembarked, she solidified her findings. The cutter had no paint scuffs. From what she'd seen, it hadn't made contact with Thom's skiff. Which meant the Albin was still in play.

Back inside her car, she fished her personal phone out of the glove compartment and called J.J.

"Sarge here. Got a few minutes?"

"I can tell you have a bee in your bonnet. Get it out."

"Do you know who owns the old cutter at Sydney Bay wharf? The one with the orange cove stripe."

"Jake Murphy. Why?"

"Darrell Gundy saw a cutter go by his place—Seven-Forty-Four Mallory Beach—early on July eighth, heading north. I'm pretty sure it was Jake's cutter."

"Old Gundy?" J.J. said. "He's been around since God was a boy."

"Maybe, but I tell you, he has hawk's eyes."

"Okay. So why do you think it was Jake's?"

"Gundy saw Jake and Willie aboard. And he described the cutter as an old girl with a dirty white hull and an orange cove stripe."

"That's Jake's boat."

"Good. That's what I wanted to verify."

"Jake and Willie," J.J. muttered, as if to himself. "So, they were out that day. I should have known."

"We don't have—"

J.J. cut her off. "Bastards! They're like a north wind. They go through you instead of around you. I don't trust them, I tell you!"

"Relax, J.J. Let's not get ahead of ourselves. Our team checked their alibis. They were working. We're checking the alibis again. And Gundy saw another man with them. A white man, about fifty."

"Jake and Willie plus one. I don't care who he was. Any way you cut it, we have Jake and Willie Murphy. I don't like it!"

"Hold it." Naslund tried to project patience. "Let's review what we know. Your son saw an Albin heading for Thom's skiff, not a cutter. And Marty found dove-gray paint on the club's Albin. In case you're wondering, there are no dove-gray marks on the Murphys' cutter. I just took a good look at her. Another thing: she hasn't been washed in months, maybe years."

"I'm not surprised," J.J. said. "But I'm not convinced either. It doesn't mean she didn't raft with Thom's skiff. A good boatman uses fenders. He doesn't leave any paint marks when he rafts."

"Even in high seas?"

"Not if he's good."

"Is Jake Murphy that good? He's piloting a wonky old tub."

"I've seen him dock it cleanly in a storm."

"Okay." Despite J.J.'s explanation, objections swarmed in her mind. The Murphys' cutter wouldn't provide a stable platform to work from. It was the definition of wonky. And what about the two Albin hijackers? What were they doing out on the bay? One of them was carrying a kitbag full of tools, which could easily have included a Phillips screwdriver and a ballpeen hammer.

"Listen, Sarge, I'm not saying you drop the Albin line of inquiry. But can you look into this one too?"

She stilled her mind. J.J. had a point. The hijackers hadn't left a trail. As to the screwdriver and hammer attack, either Jake or Willie could have done it. Both were strong enough. Apparently both hated Thom. "Okay," she said, "I'm with you. I've got another question for you, on a different matter."

"Sure."

"Jenny Murphy said you turned Thom away from her. Is that right?"

"Pretty much. And I have no qualms about it. They didn't make a good pair. I was looking out for him."

"Couldn't he look out for himself?"

"Sure, he could, but not very well. Thom was an innocent in that regard. He got himself in some real binds. I was a wingman of sorts."

"Anti-wingman, I'd say."

"True."

ෙංෙ

Back at the OPP station, Naslund began writing up her report on Gundy's interview and the Murphys' cutter at Sydney Bay. Her personal phone crooned when she was halfway through. "Eva here."

"Hello Sarge," J.J. said. "Can you talk?"

"Call me in five."

She was outside when her phone pealed again. There was no one around.

"Safe?" J.J. asked.

"Yep."

"I have a thought. What if someone was hired to kill Thom? Someone like the Murphys."

"Or the two hijackers," she said.

"I know what you're thinking. Why would the Murphys need someone to hire them? They hated Thom."

"Right."

"Okay, they've wanted revenge for years, but here's the thing. It's possible someone turned up the heat by offering them a fresh incentive—like cash."

"Possibly," she said. "But who?"

"I don't know." J.J. sighed. "Gotta run. Working on a diesel."

"Thanks for the info."

"I'll call you later. I'm going to chase down Jake and Willie after work."

"I'm not sure that's wise."

"Just for a chat."

"A chat?"

"Yes."

"Okay, but don't do anything. Leave any action to us."

"I'm a big boy, Sarge."

Naslund held her tongue. She couldn't arrest the man to keep him safe.

Glancing at her watch, she saw that it was almost six. Hal had invited her to dinner at seven. She returned to her report and then sat back, considering the idea of a cash incentive. If someone hired Thom's murderers, who was it? Likely someone who wasn't strong enough to attack Thom themselves. Carrie MacLean? Someone else?

Maybe Gordon Tyler? DC Lowrie had re-evaluated Gordon's alibi. It hinged on his sister Gillian's corroboration, and the DC felt sure she would lie for him.

Who else? Naslund's thoughts were drawn to MacTavish. He was wealthy. He happened to be strong enough to attack Thom but he could keep his hands clean and hire someone. She stared at her computer screen. Was he the cash-incentive man? Of the suspects on the cash-incentive list, he seemed the best fit. Carrie MacLean was comfortable, but not rich, and while Gordon Tyler was wealthy by Wiarton standards, Jock MacTavish was far wealthier.

Naslund exhaled loudly. *Think it over.* She stood, walked to the staff room, and poured a coffee. Okay, MacTavish had the means, but why would he kill a goose that laid golden eggs? The more paintings Thom completed, the more money MacTavish made. It didn't make sense for him to kill Thom. No sense at all.

She trudged back to her hutch, feeling as confused as ever. Nothing added up. *Let it go*, she ordered herself. *Focus on what you know.* She pulled her chair into the hutch and resumed her report. The sooner she finished it, the better. Hal was at the end of the rainbow.

છ૭ે૭

Hal handed Eva a glass of Chablis. "You look tired." He smiled. "And famished."

"Guilty on both counts."

"What did you have for lunch?" he asked.

"Ah, a slice of pizza."

"You could eat healthier."

She nodded. Was Hal starting to pick at her already? Pete always criticized her eating habits.

"You could, but you don't have to." Hal laughed. "You should see the look on your face."

She chuckled. "I could eat better and I want to."

"How about a sprout salad?"

"Tonight?"

"Again, you should see your face. We have salmon, peppers, sweet potatoes, and asparagus. Grilled."

"Wow. What happened to those beans?"

"Dessert."

She laughed. "Right, the maple syrup." She strode forward and kissed him on the cheek. Her personal phone started crooning. Damn it! *Excuse me*, she motioned. "Eva here."

"Well," J.J. said, "a blue jay has come home to roost."

"A blue jay?"

"Some news you didn't expect to hear."

"Sorry, I'm about to eat dinner." She looked up at Hal. He mouthed *no prob*.

"This won't take long," J.J. said.

"Give me a moment." She walked to the sitting room. "Okay."

"My so-called 'crazy act' worked."

"It did?"

"Don't sound so surprised," J.J. said.

"Surprised is an understatement. Astounded is more like it."

"How about stunned?"

She chuckled. "Okay, fella. Out with it."

"I think the Murphy brothers are innocent. I owe you an apology," he graciously said. "I was wrong."

"No apology required."

"Well. In any case, here's the news. My niece Laurie works at Tim's. Part of her job is to wipe down the tables. As it happens, she overheard three farmers talking about that disgraceful J.J. MacKenzie, drunk at church." J.J. chortled. "I'm famous. So, Laurie hovered about. One guy said the Colpoys men he knew were hard workers. Just a week ago, he hired two to do an all-nighter to help clean his hog barn, an eight-thousand-square-footer. The two were Jake and Willie Murphy. And what night do you think it was?"

Eva could guess.

"Sunday July the seventh. The barn was being inspected on Monday the eighth. From Laurie's description of the farmer I found out who he was, a Carl Keppel from Shallow Lake. That's likely who Gundy saw with the brothers that morning."

"Good work."

DC Lowrie had recently reported that two witnesses saw the Murphys in Shallow Lake during the murder window, but he hadn't linked the brothers to Keppel.

"You're better than a movie detective."

J.J. laughed. "Better connected, maybe."

"I'll visit Carl Keppel tomorrow morning. Gotta go."

"What's for dinner?"

"Me to know," she said, "you to—."

"Say hi to Hal."

"Bye J.J." She grinned to herself and returned to the kitchen. Hal was serving dinner—a feast for the eyes. And the food looked great too.

"Pull up a chair," he said. "Your wine glass is full."

She smiled. The man was a mind reader as well.

☙❧☙

After watching a movie, Hal snuggled closer to Eva on the sofa. "Coffee, tea, or?"

Definitely *or*. However, she wondered about her "spinsterhood." She hadn't done the happy dance for over a year. *So what*, an inner voice said, *you haven't forgotten how*. She turned toward him.

Chapter 24

As Eva Naslund lay in bed the next morning—in Hal's bed, in happy-dance heaven—her personal phone crooned. "Watching the detectives…"

Hal had left for work. The bed still smelled of him: warm skin and Drakkar Noir. She'd come to bed naked, a sapphire pendant winking between her breasts like a tiger's eye.

"Watching the detectives…"

She ignored the phone. His bedroom was like the rest of his house—bright and modern.

"Watching the…"

Okay, I'm getting up. Rising to a seated position, she spotted her jacket then reluctantly left the bed and fished out her phone: 0636. "Good morning."

"Sarge?"

"Yes."

"Marty here. Marty Fox. J.J.—J.J.'s dead." Marty gulped then rushed on. "We found his body in the bay, off Hay Island. Close to his boat. I—I just pulled him out of the water." Marty drew in a sharp breath but didn't stop. "I know he went out alone in his Caledon last night, to stay overnight. You know, like he often does. He always heads back around dawn. You can count on it. Always, I tell you."

"Marty, slow down. Take a deep breath."

"Someone bashed his head in. Looks like with a hammer."

Jesus. "You sure?"

"Yes."

"Did you pull him out of the bay alone?"

"Yes."

"Don't touch him anymore, don't move him. Where's his Caledon?"

"Grounded on Hay, the west side."

"Leave it. Don't touch it. Is anyone with you?"

"I'm with a fishing client."

"Okay. You and your client, go back to the club. Have a coffee, have a brandy. I'll be there in about half an hour. I'll need to talk to both of you. Meantime, don't touch J.J. Don't let anyone touch him."

જ્જ્જ

On Griffith Island the meadows were dotted with white lady slippers. The wrens were singing. The previous night's rain had rinsed the sky clean. A gentle sun played on the water. Yet Naslund felt no peace. The OPP launch motored up to the club wharf. She immediately recognized the club fishing boat, the Albin 35, and directed Constable Chandler to pull the launch next to it. Marty caught their mooring lines and pointed to the Albin's back deck.

Naslund followed Moore aboard the Albin and knelt beside J.J.'s body. His hair was matted and bloody. He'd been hit on the top of the head. The left side of his forehead was caved in by multiple blows. A piece of his dura mater was hanging out. It was pinkish-gray and crinkled, like an old sausage. The frontal impact zone was bruised and livid. His lips were blue, his face, ashen. Death collapsed all faces, particularly the faces of heavy men, but J.J.'s face looked unusually gaunt, as if he'd lost a lot of blood.

Naslund inched closer. J.J.'s head smelled metallic, like dried blood. A few blowflies circled the dura mater. The wound imprints looked familiar. Very familiar. They appeared to be from the same ballpeen hammer that had bashed Thom. Her first thought was repeat murderer or copycat murderer? While the MO wasn't exactly the same—the assailant had only used a hammer, and not a hammer and screwdriver—seen via the naked eye, the weapon appeared to be exactly the same. Repeat, she thought. Forensics would provide the answer.

The inspector seemed unmoved. Naslund wasn't. She'd only worked with J.J. closely for a week but she felt shaken and immobilized. She could barely hear the gulls circling the fishing boat. Everything was muffled. She seemed to be underwater.

She turned slowly to Moore. "Mr. MacKenzie's boat grounded on Hay Island. I want to take a look at it."

"Okay. Then leave it to Chu's team."

Chu and company had been called back from Orillia, as well as Mitchell and Wolfe, the ninjas. They'd trace MacKenzie's last movements, starting at Colpoys wharf. Naslund rose. "I'm going to talk to the men who found MacKenzie, Marty Fox and his guest."

"Right. I'll question the rest of the staff and guests. Can you attend Dr. Kapanen?"

"Sure."

Disembarking from the Albin, Naslund held out her hand to Marty. "My deepest condolences." She wanted to say more but she couldn't. Her close association with J.J. was a secret matter.

"Thank you." Marty expelled a heavy sigh. "I don't

believe it. I don't believe he's gone." He hung his head. His shoulders started heaving.

She almost stepped forward to comfort him but forced herself to stop. Compassion with dispassion. Emotions in check, she walked down the pier with Marty ahead of her. Two murders in Wiarton in one week. Would there be more? Who was next? Marty? Not a chance, she said to herself, not if she could help it. Other than the investigation, Marty was her top priority. She had to keep him safe.

He stopped at a picnic table near the lodge and sat across from an older man with severe eyes and a military buzz-cut. The man was wearing a tan fishing vest.

Naslund sat beside him. "What's your name, sir?"

"Ralph Goderich."

"Mr. Goderich, was the deceased alive when you first saw him?"

"I don't think so. Marty yelled out to him, but he didn't answer. He didn't move."

"Did you help Marty bring the body aboard?"

"No. He told me to handle the wheel."

"Did you ever touch the body?"

"No."

"What's your profession, Mr. Goderich?"

"I'm a banker. In Toronto."

"Do you have ID on you? A driver's license, for example?"

"Yes." Goderich handed her his DL.

"Thank you." She took a photo with her duty phone. "What's your phone number?"

Goderich recited it.

She recorded the number. "Thank you, sir. Please wait in the lodge." The MU team would process Goderich for prints and DNA.

When Goderich left, she wanted to sit next to Marty, but remained across from him. His lips were clamped together. He was staring at the table. He needed as much comfort as she could give him.

"J.J. was a fine man," she said, trying to convey both steadiness and compassion. "A very fine man. He had time for everyone."

Marty eventually looked up and nodded.

She casually glanced around, verifying that the two of them were alone. She suspected Thom's killers had been watching J.J. and he'd gotten too close to the truth. "We won't meet any more. Stop your investigative work. Right now."

"All right."

"If you think of or hear anything you want me to know, call me. No matter how trivial it seems." She paused. "Can you answer a few questions now? We'll talk later if you want to."

"No. Now is good."

"All right. Do you know what time J.J. went out in his Caledon?"

"He called me around eleven. Said he was heading out at midnight."

"You saw those hammer marks. It looks like J.J. was murdered. Do you think he was killed because of what he was doing? Investigating. Stirring up talk."

"Yes. For sure."

"Do you think he was killed by the same person or persons who killed Thom?"

Marty nodded.

"Don't talk about that with anyone. I'm going to arrange for you to go away for a few weeks. I'll take care of the money side. You'll say you need to visit a sick relative."

He shook his head.

"You have no choice. There are killers at large. They may have noticed J.J. spending time at your place. Be vigilant, Marty. Constable Chandler will escort you home. You'll pack a bag and leave immediately."

"If I have to."

"You have to. There are two dead men. I don't want any more." Naslund stood. "Don't use your regular phone. Chandler will give you a burner, a throwaway cellphone. Just to be extra vigilant, turn it off when you're not using it." She leaned closer. "It can only be tracked when it's on. The number won't be linked to you, but people have been known to hack into cell carriers and execute their own searches. They throw a wide net but, given time, they can tighten it. Know what I mean?"

"Got it, Sarge."

"Okay. Call me anytime. For anything."

He nodded.

"Anything at all."

∽∾∽

Naslund requisitioned a runabout from the club and motored full speed toward Hay Island. The sun was almost blinding. The lake looked like the sky. Nothing seemed real; nothing seemed solid. As she drew near the Caledon 25, she cut the runabout engine and tossed the anchor overboard. After yanking off her shoes and socks, she rolled up her pant legs and slid into the bay. The water was warm, the bottom sandy.

The Caledon lay port side out, tilted at a thirty-degree angle, jammed against the shore. She approached to within half-a-meter of the stern and waded toward the bow through calf-deep water. Seven empty beer cans—Heineken tallboys—lay in the cockpit. Unusual, she thought. J.J. didn't drink much. Maybe he'd been boating with someone who did. Continuing to the bow, she saw that the hull wasn't damaged. There were four fenders out. She stopped. That didn't add up. J.J. was an experienced boater. Experienced boaters didn't leave their fenders out after they got underway. Perhaps he didn't motor to Hay. If not, how did he get there? She filed the question away.

Facing the stern, she waded the whole length of the boat a second time. No blood, scuffs, scratches or chipped paint. No evidence of an assault or a struggle. It didn't look like he'd been attacked on the boat. She moved closer to shore and waded a thirty-meter stretch south of the boat, visually sweeping the shore and scanning inland as far as she could see. Nothing. No prints, no blood, no cans, no obvious DNA carriers. She waded back to the boat and searched thirty meters north. Again, nothing. She considered searching farther inland, but waded toward the runabout. Although she had CS gloves on, she wasn't wearing protective gear. Besides, Chu's team would take care of Hay, plus the beer cans and any other evidence on the Caledon.

Motoring back to Griffith Island, she throttled up to full speed, letting her mind cycle. The beer cans suggested someone else had been present. J.J.'s body had been found close to the Caledon, but there was no blood on it.

Perhaps J.J. was killed on another boat, the assailant's boat? Lured or forced there, killed, and then pushed overboard. Which suggested something else. He could have been intercepted shortly after leaving Colpoys wharf, ordered to motor to Hay Island, and killed near there. Had the perps forgotten to remove the cans? Were they inept, or just pretending to be? If so, why?

კ•ᲔᲔ

Having returned to the club wharf, Naslund called Moore. "Naslund here."

"Yes, Sergeant."

"It appears MacKenzie was attacked on land or another boat. His Caledon Twenty-five displays no evidence of an assault." She paused. "Just a hunch, but he could have been forced over to Hay Island and killed there. It's possible his assailants had a boat and he was killed on it. I took a quick look at Hay. I didn't find any signs of a CS on or near the shoreline. If Chu's team and the ninjas do rule out a land assault, that boat will likely be the CS."

"Possibly. I'll tell Chu to search all of Hay Island, starting near the Caledon. When you're done with Kapanen, return to the mainland and interview the Murphy brothers again. Judging by your case notes, they had a beef with both Tyler and MacKenzie, as did their sister. Even if they weren't involved in Tyler's murder, they need to be questioned regarding MacKenzie's. By the way, I don't think we need a coroner to tell us he was murdered."

"Right. I'd like to interview that pig farmer as well, Keppel's his name." She wanted to verify J.J.'s assumption that the Murphys were innocent of Thom's murder. If so, it was less likely that they'd murdered J.J.

"Fine," Moore said. "Report back to me when you're done."

"Yes, sir."

"By the way, your staff sergeant volunteered to notify MacKenzie's family."

"That's good of him," she said. She owed Bickell again.

As she waited for Kapanen, her mind circled back to the killers. Were they inept or pretending to be inept? She didn't know which way to lean. They could be poorly-organized greenhorns. However, from what she'd seen of Thom's skiff and J.J.'s Caledon, the killers were well organized. They hadn't left any bio evidence on the skiff and there was no blood on the Caledon. It appeared they'd been strategic enough to kill J.J. on land or on their own boat. So, she speculated, they could be organized killers who wanted the OPP to think they were inept. However, that didn't make sense either. If they were organized, they'd know pretending wouldn't help them for long. The staging of the Mackinaw CS hadn't set the team on a wild goose chase. On the other hand, maybe a "boss" hired the actual killers. Maybe the boss was organized, but the killers were less organized and partially inept. Or some of the killers were organized, and the others weren't.

Naslund shook her head. Confusion upon confusion. Looking up, she saw Kapanen arriving in a water taxi. If anything, the coroner's face was redder than the last time she'd seen him. As usual, he wore a tight suit. He was steady on his feet, which she was happy to see. It was just after 0800.

"I need a helicopter to serve you people," Kapanen grumbled. "Are you alone, Detective?"

She nodded and led Kapanen to the Albin's back deck.

"Don't people die on land anymore?" Kapanen shook his head. "Another body on a boat." He pulled on gloves, knelt down, and examined the body. "Doesn't look like a drowning," he finally said. "Why do I say that?"

She pointed at J.J.'s mouth. "No blood or mucus. No foam."

"Correct. I don't see any evidence of drowning, either wet or dry. There is no trace of vomit, which indicates a victim became submerged while alive." Kapanen pointed to J.J.'s eyes. "Consider the horizontal line bisecting the sclera or white of each eye. Those lines are consistent with death on land. Of course, a pathologist will examine the victim's lungs and organs. He may rule differently. From what I can now tell, the victim was dead when he entered the water. As I've noted in the past—" Kapanen stopped and eyed her as if to say *many times in the past*. "—an autopsy will confirm or overrule my findings."

She nodded. *I know*.

"All right," Kapanen said, "to the head wounds." A few minutes later, he looked up. "Regard the top of the head, the crown. I detect two heavy blows by a blunt force instrument with a rounded impact surface. Now consider the left side of the temple and the left frontal region. I detect three heavy blows by the same instrument. The skull has been breached. There is a large open wound and an approximately seven-centimeter length of protruding meninges." Kapanen paused. "I can't say for sure, but the blunt force instrument looks very similar to the one used a week ago. Most likely metal. As a week ago, I don't see any wood splinters."

"Okay. What's the—"

"Don't even ask. I know what you want. PMI. And I'll do my best."

"Good," she said.

"Good? Of course it'll be good."

"Yes, sir. I mean, yes, Doctor. Of course."

Kapanen eyed her. "Georgian Bay complicates matters. However, unlike last week, it appears the victim's life vest worked. Was he found floating on the surface of the bay?"

"Yes."

"Do you know the depth of the water where he was found?"

"Not the exact depth. But I do know it was less than two meters."

"What is the surface temperature today, Detective?"

Naslund had anticipated the question. On the way to Griffith, she'd dropped a marine thermometer into the bay. "Eighteen Celsius in shallow water near shore," she reported. "We can assume a degree or two colder overnight.

According to the victim's friend, the body likely entered the bay sometime after midnight."

"Very good. Let's look at lividity. Help me here. What do you see?"

J.J. wore a short-sleeved shirt and long shorts. "Well," she said, "I see some blood pooling in the back of the neck. Given the victim was wearing a life vest, he was likely floating face up, which caused pooling in the neck."

"Valid assumption. Would algor be reliable in this case?"

"No. Well, not very."

"Why?"

"There are multiple factors at play," she ventured. "For example, there are various air temperatures, ranging from readings at midnight to eight a.m., as well as variable water temperatures, depending on depth."

"True. Let's consider rigor." Kapanen eyed the body. "The victim appears to weigh well over two hundred pounds. Hence, I'd estimate that in the overnight conditions, considering both air and water temperature, full rigor would be slightly delayed. It would take roughly thirteen to fourteen hours. The victim has not yet reached full rigor. How do I know that?"

She pointed to J.J.'s legs. "The quadriceps aren't stiff. As rigor sets in, it progresses from the body's smaller muscles to the larger ones."

"Excellent, Detective. Given that rigor has not yet affected the larger muscles, we can deduce the victim has been dead for eight to ten hours. Approximately."

"Thank you."

"As for my final findings, the victim suffered severe head trauma and was dead when he entered the water. The wounds he sustained were not self-inflicted. He was attacked. Cause: Blunt force injury. Means: Homicide." Kapanen sighed. "Sounds distressingly familiar."

She nodded.

"I wish you the best."

"Thank you, Doctor."

Chapter 25

Upon returning to Wiarton Marina, Naslund jumped in her car and headed to Keppel's farm. She reached it just as a stocky, gray-haired man was climbing aboard an old tractor. She stepped out of her car. "Carl Keppel?"

"Yes."

"Detective Sergeant Naslund, OPP. Do you have a few minutes?"

"Yes, Sergeant."

"I understand your hog barn was inspected on Monday the eighth."

"It was."

"Can you show me the barn?"

Keppel looked puzzled. "Sure, but what's this about?"

"Part of another investigation. Do you want me to get a warrant, Mr. Keppel?"

"Oh, no."

She nodded. "Just a quick look." In part, it was a decoy. She needed to examine the barn's exit points, to see if the Murphys might have been able to sneak out, kill Tyler, and then return to complete their cleaning work. However, she also wanted to evaluate Keppel's responses before mentioning the Murphys.

As she approached the barn, the air thickened. It smelled of dry grass and ammonia: bedding straw and pig shit. Keppel stopped outside the barn office door. "What exactly did you want to see?"

"The back and side doors."

"There's only one, a back door."

"Please show it to me."

"Sure. It's always locked. We use the main door, the big sliding one."

Naslund established that there was only one exit other than the office door and the sliding door. From the amount of rust around the back-door lock, it hadn't been opened in years. She also saw that while there were many windows, they were too small for anyone to use as escape hatches. Having left the barn, she walked towards the tractor with Keppel. "You have a fine operation here. Sorry to inconvenience you."

"No trouble at all."

She started to turn away then stopped. "Just curious. Did you do a bit of a clean-up before the inspection?"

Keppel nodded.

"Did you get anyone to help you?"

"Yes. Two men."

"What time did they start?"

"They arrived around eight p.m. on Sunday."

"When did you finish?" she asked.

"Just after five a.m."

"On Monday the eighth?"

"Yes."

"How did you pay them?"

He looked nervous. "I paid them well. Above minimum wage."

She knew he was avoiding her question. He'd probably paid them under-the-table, no tax. But she let it go. It wasn't her bailiwick. "Were the men working the whole time?"

"Yes. Except for a break we took around one a.m."

"Did they go anywhere?"

He shook his head. "The three of us sat in the office. My wife had made sandwiches. I made a fresh pot of coffee."

"Were the two with you the whole time you were cleaning?"

"Yes. That and more. After we finished the job, they invited me for a sail, a cool-downer after the all-nighter. They owned a big sailboat."

Naslund smiled. "Good to get out on the water. Where did you sail from?"

"Sydney Bay."

"Nice. Where did you go?"

"Down to the top of White Cloud Island and then back."

"About what time did you turn around and head back?"

"I can't say for sure." He looked skyward as if he were thinking. "I'd say the sun had been up for at least twenty minutes. So I'd estimate it was just after six."

"Thank you." Keppel's estimate came close to Gundy's time of 0608. "Did you see any other boats?"

"There was a kayak out there. Way south of White Cloud."

"Okay. Would you hire the two workers again?"

"Sure would. One fella, Jake was his name, was real friendly. The other fella, his brother—Willie, he was called—was quiet but a fast worker. They were good, hard workers."

"Were they ever out of your sight?"

"Let me think…Just once. Willie went to the can, which is in the office. Jake went after him."

"How long were they gone?"

"A few minutes each."

"Do you recall their last name?"

"Murphy."

"Thank you, Mr. Keppel. I appreciate your time."

∽∾∽

Walking to her car, Naslund decided to interview the Murphy brothers at the station, rather than at Colpoys. She pulled out her duty phone and called DC Lowrie. He answered on the first ring.

"Morning, Constable. Naslund here. I want you to get Jake and Willie Murphy into the station ASAP."

"Yes, Sergeant."

"Their numbers are in the Tyler Case directory, under POI. Call them. If they give you any trouble at all, call me immediately." If she had to, she'd arrest them for obstructing a police investigation. It wouldn't stick, and Justice O'Reilly would give her hell, but she didn't care. She didn't want any delays.

∽∾∽

Naslund reached the station ten minutes later. As she sat at her hutch, Lowrie walked up to her.

"The Murphys will be here at ten hundred."

She glanced at her watch. Twenty minutes. "Thank you."

"I'll take them to the interview room. I've added another Slider."

"Excellent. I want you in the shadow room."

"Certainly, Sergeant."

She booted up her laptop and began writing a requisition to handle Marty's protection. At 0957, Lowrie informed her that the Murphys were entering the station. She opened her laptop's security-cameras feed. Jake looked unconcerned, Willie, less so. Jake wore a blue T-shirt and jeans, Willie, an army-fatigue tank top and neon-red shorts. While Willie was good-looking, Jake was movie-star handsome: tall, dark and chiseled. She followed the brothers as Lowrie led them to the interview room. They might be Jenny's *little* brothers, but they were certainly big enough to attack Tyler or MacKenzie. With every step, Willie looked less comfortable. Lowrie directed Jake to one Slider; Willie, to the other. After Lowrie left the brothers said nothing. They knew they were being watched.

Naslund let the two hang on the hook a few minutes before entering the interview room. *Curing the carcasses*, Chandler called it.

"Good morning," she said. "Good of you to come in on short notice."

"Glad to." Jake prodded his brother.

"Glad to," Willie echoed.

"Are you men working full-time?"

Jake shook his head. Willie followed.

"Part-time?"

"Yes," Jake said.

She waited for Willie to answer.

"My brother's a bit nervous," Jake said. "He doesn't like cop shops—stations, I mean."

She buzzed Lowrie. "Detective, please escort Jake Murphy to another room."

As Jake was led out, Willie's anxious look intensified. She eyeballed him before proceeding. "What kind of work are you doing?"

Willie shrugged. "This and that. You know, construction work, temp work."

"What was your last job?"

"We dry-walled a basement."

"Who?"

"Me and my brother. Me and Jake."

"Before that?" she asked.

"We cleaned out a pig barn."

"When was that?"

"Ah, ah. Last week. Last week, *Sergeant.*"

"When last week?" she asked.

"Last Sunday night, Sergeant."

"When did you finish the job?"

"Monday morning, about five. Sergeant."

"What did you do then?"

Willie seemed confused.

"What did you do after you finished work?"

"We invited the barn guy for a sail. The owner, I mean. He treated us good."

"What was his name?"

"Carl Keppel," Willie said.

"Let's move ahead, to this morning. To Hay Island." Naslund stopped to observe Willie. No apparent sign of unease or guilt. "Where were you today from midnight until seven a.m.?"

"In bed. Sergeant," he added.

"You can skip the *sergeant*." She eyed him. "Do you have someone who can verify that?"

"Yes, Sergeant. I mean, yes."

"Who?"

"A girl. A young woman, I mean."

"J.J. MacKenzie's body was found off Hay this morning." Naslund scrutinized Willie's face. Again, no apparent sign of guilt or agitation. "When was the last time you saw him?"

"Yesterday evening."

"When?"

"Around eight."

"Where?"

"I was at Jake's place. MacKenzie dropped by to ask if we'd been out on the water July eighth."

"*Dropped by*, did he? Sounds like a tea party."

Willie shrugged.

"And what did you tell MacKenzie?"

"We told him we had been."

"When?"

"Early. Around five-thirty. We went for a sail with that barn guy, Carl."

"Did you argue with MacKenzie that evening?"

"No."

"Did you mention your sister Jenny?"

"No."

"You're here voluntarily, Willie, but let me remind you. Although we're not in court, our conversation is on tape. If you change your mind later, it won't look good. Did you do or say anything to stand up for Jenny, anything to 'get even' for her?"

"Hell, no. I mean, no. Jenny can look after herself."

True, Naslund thought. "Did you know MacKenzie well?"

"Not real well," Willie said.

"Did you like him?" she asked.

"Ah."

"Did you like him?"

"Not real well."

"Did you like Thom Tyler?"

"No."

"Same as MacKenzie?"

"No, less than MacKenzie. Much less. But that's history."

"History?"

"Yep. History. May he rest in peace. MacKenzie too."

She evaluated Willie. He looked sincere. "Do you have any idea who might have wanted MacKenzie dead?"

"No. Most people around here respected him. If not, they tolerated him."

"What about you?"

"I didn't think about him."

"You must have thought something. Did you respect him, or did you tolerate him?"

"Tolerate."

"Do you know anyone who, let's say, disagreed with his politics? His *independents* stance?"

"No. Not much."

"Explain."

"Well, a few people thought he was too pushy. Sometimes. But he was honest. No BS."

"Okay. You'll remain here while I talk to your brother."

Willie let out a huge sigh.

Fifteen minutes later, DC Lowrie escorted the brothers from the station. Jake's interview had corroborated Willie's statements. Jake had cleaned out Keppel's barn and sailed with Keppel. MacKenzie had dropped by Jake's place, but Jake hadn't touched him or confronted him verbally about Jenny. As for Jake's whereabouts during the MacKenzie murder window, he claimed he'd been in bed with his wife.

ભળ

After the Murphys left, Lowrie joined Naslund for a debriefing session. He thought the brothers had told the truth. Although Willie was a bit tense, the DC put that down to his time in court rooms and jails. Pending confirmation of the brothers' alibis for MacKenzie, Lowrie figured the two were clean. Naslund agreed.

Eating a sandwich, she wrote up her case notes on Keppel and the Murphys then completed the requisition for Marty and flagged it high-priority. She put Inspector Moore's name in the Requestor section. She'd found that any request with his name got quick results. After submitting the requisition, she called him.

"Naslund here. Got an update on Keppel and the Murphys."

"Go ahead."

"The Murphys were working for Keppel during the Tyler murder window. They had no opportunity to commit Tyler's murder. As for MacKenzie's murder, Lowrie is checking their alibis. They could have hired someone, but I doubt they have the money. Furthermore, if they wanted either Tyler or MacKenzie dead, they could do it themselves."

"Okay. I have some news on MacKenzie. It appears he was attacked at Colpoys wharf. I'm there now, with the ninjas. They're re-creating the scene. The evidence points to MacKenzie being assaulted at the dock and then thrown into the water. Looks like his boat was set adrift to make it appear he was assaulted near Hay Island. From what we can tell, the wind took his boat and his body across to Hay."

"Sounds plausible," she said. So much for her hunch about the assailants' boat.

"There's multi-blow blood splatter on the dock, plus three blood lines leading to the dock's edge. No other DNA yet. Nothing except blood. Call me a pessimist, but it's probably all the victim's."

She suspected Moore was right.

"He had a lifejacket on so he was likely just about to cast off. From what we can piece together, his attacker surprised him. That's understandable. It was likely around midnight. There's only one light near the wharf, about ten meters inland. There are no signs of a fight. He was a big man, but it seems he didn't fight back. However, we were able to establish where he fell. There are signs—partial prints and the blood lines—that his body was then lifted, carried a few feet, and thrown off the wharf."

"Ah."

"I dispatched Conrad to canvass the Colpoys area with two PCs. With any luck, someone will have seen or heard something. Afterward, he's going to conduct a digital canvass, looking into murders anywhere in North America by ballpeen hammer." Moore kept rolling. "Chu's team will be here in a few hours. So far, except for seven beer cans, they haven't found anything on the boat or Hay. They're going to run the cans through the lab. Might be some FPs or saliva on them."

"Did they check the mooring lines?" she asked. "The perps likely handled the lines if they set the boat adrift." She kept going. "Take a good look at the lines. There might be FPs or bio matter on them."

"All right, Sergeant. I'll call Chu. By the way, I spoke with Dr. Kapanen. He noted that MacKenzie was attacked with a blunt force instrument, likely the same one used on Tyler. Not the same MO, but very close. If we solve Tyler's case, we'll likely solve MacKenzie's. And vice-versa."

"Agreed."

Moore rolled on. "Given the second murder, Tyler's murder was not likely a mistake, a confrontation that got out of hand. He was targeted, and then MacKenzie was targeted. The evidence points to two premeditated first degrees. I had doubts about premeditation with Tyler, but none now. What about you?"

"None."

"Okay, Sergeant, I'll be there in fifteen minutes. Central is pulling out all the stops. Dr. Leonard is doing the autopsy today at fourteen hundred. I'd like you to join me."

Chapter 26

As Naslund walked into Central's forensic department, she felt a jolt of optimism. Dr. DeVeon Leonard was waiting at the morgue door.

"Good afternoon, Detectives. As per the norm, we're audio- and videotaping this, but please stop me if you miss something or have any questions."

Moore and Naslund nodded.

Leonard looked subdued. He led them to the top of the autopsy table. "I believe Dr. Kapanen covered virtually everything. We'll begin with the head wounds. As Dr. Kapanen noted, the top of the head was impacted by two blows from a blunt force instrument with a rounded surface. The focal point was zero-point-eight centimeters anterior of the crown." Leonard indicated it with his pointer. "The blows punctured the crown, resulting in a series of secondary skull fractures. Both blows left indentations almost two centimeters deep. Very deep." Leonard paused. "You have a strong assailant. The instrument was a metal ball-peen hammer. The hammer head had a fifteen-centimeter circumference and deposited three tiny gunmetal gray paint chips—the same circumference and the same kind of paint chips found during the Tyler autopsy."

Leonard moved down the table. "Consider the left temple and left frontal region. They were impacted by three blows from the same blunt force instrument. It deposited four gunmetal gray paint chips. Again, the same kind of paint chips found during the Tyler autopsy. The chemical composition matched the Tyler chips precisely. I'm confident the same instrument was used in both assaults." Leonard paused. "Any questions?"

Both detectives shook their heads.

Leonard traced the five blows with his pointer. "Blood has leached from all the wounds, but they are clearly antemortem. The victim was alive when they occurred." The doctor indicated the large open fracture above the left eye. "Two blows landed on or near the nexus of this fracture. One or both of them breached the skull and fissured multiple cranial bones. That, in turn, resulted in a protruding meninges and triggered massive subdural and subarachnoid hemorrhaging." Leonard stopped. "I can't be certain how long he lived after the blows. We took a CAT Scan. It suggests the hemorrhaging was extensive enough to generate herniation, which means it could have caused enough intracranial pressure to trigger brain death. That is, death within minutes."

The two detectives remained silent.

"It's likely the assailant knew what he, or possibly she, was doing," Leonard said. "The cranial bone plates are thinner in the frontal region than elsewhere. If you want to kill someone with a blunt force attack to the head, that area is optimal."

The detectives nodded.

"Regardless of gender, the assailant was strong. As I noted previously, the wound indentations are very deep. It appears the assailant approached the victim from behind.

As to the sequence of events, we might assume that the two blows to the crown knocked him down. It looks like he broke his own fall. There are no indications of a free-fall. No knee or facial abrasions, no broken teeth. When he was down, the assailant rolled him over and attacked the vulnerable frontal region and temple. From the angle of the blows, they came from directly above. There is a high probability that one or two frontal blows would have been enough to kill him, yet the assailant delivered three. Five heavy blows in total. A vicious attack."

Naslund's chest tightened with anger. She breathed deeply, trying to control it. *Relax*, she ordered herself, *don't make this personal.*

"As with the Tyler case, it appears the assailant was right-handed. I stress, *appears.* The victim's left temple and frontal region were attacked, which suggests the ballpeen hammer was held in the assailant's right hand. However, due to the fact that the victim was then on his back, we can't conclude that the assailant's dominant arm was the right one. It's possible the assailant perpetrated the attack from the victim's left side. According to the impact angle of the frontal indentations—straight down from above—either arm could have been used." Leonard shrugged apologetically. "I'm sorry I can't be more definitive."

"Understood," Moore said.

"There is another matter to consider. The indentations left by the two crown blows indicate they came from a vector angle of seventy-six degrees. That is—given a hammer with a handle, even a short handle—almost from above. Which suggests the assailant was likely as tall as the victim, perhaps taller. The victim was six-foot-three, so we're looking at a tall assailant." Leonard raised a cautionary hand. "*Unless* the assailant was wearing high heels or shoe lifts or standing on a portable platform of some kind. I don't recall the CS report mentioning evidence of a platform." He looked at Moore. "Do you?"

Moore shook his head.

"As for high heels?" Leonard shrugged. "I wouldn't count it out, but unlikely. Not very stable. A five-ten or -eleven person wearing four-inch heels? Might work for a pole dancer, but a killer?" He grinned. "I'm trying to see it, but I can't."

Moore harrumphed.

"However," Leonard continued, "shoe lifts are possible, although typically they don't add over two inches. Regarding defensive wounds, I detect no marks on the victim's arms or hands." He moved down the body. "And none on the shins and no indication that the victim struck out with his feet. I do not see any evidence he put up a fight. I assume that he was unable to—despite his obvious size. He probably lost consciousness soon after falling. It appears he was quickly overpowered."

"Seemingly," Moore said.

"All right, Officers, next step."

Leonard selected a scalpel and made a Y-incision in MacKenzie's chest. Naslund's stomach churned. Her lunch—a tuna fish sandwich—rose in her throat. The doctor sawed through the rib-cage, excised the chest plate and extracted the inner organs. After dissecting the heart and lungs, he looked up at the detectives. "There is no evidence of water ingress. Nonetheless, we'll analyze the lung tissues for microscopic lake algae. Consistent with Dr. Kapanen's findings," he concluded, "I do not detect any evidence of drowning. I surmise the victim was dead when he entered the water, which is what Dr. Kapanen reported. I concur with his PMI estimate. The victim likely died somewhere between ten PM last night and midnight."

Moore nodded.

"The toxicology screen results will be back in three to

four days. I'll release the body tomorrow at eleven a.m."

"Thank you," Moore said.

"As with Mr. Tyler, I'm ordering burial rather than cremation. Any questions?"

Moore shook his head.

Naslund remained silent. She felt deflated. As usual, Dr. Leonard was excellent and yet they hadn't learned anything new—other than that the assailant could be either right or left-handed. No forensic dots, no lab magic. The team didn't have much to go on.

☙❧

Outside Central, Naslund waited for Moore. The inspector had excused himself to make a call. Ten minutes later, he reappeared. "I called Justice O'Reilly," he said. "I floated the idea of a warrant to search Larmer's Hope Bay cottage. I gave O'Reilly probable cause. I emphasized we have two murders on our hands, with almost the same MO, and that one of the assault weapons, a ballpeen hammer, was used in both murders." Moore smiled in triumph. "The justice will grant a warrant provided we focus on the weapons. However, any other evidence will be inadmissible. We'll file the paperwork at the station."

Naslund nodded.

"I ordered a squad car to check on Larmer. He's home. They'll make sure he stays there." Moore began striding toward the parking lot. "Central wants some progress. The politicos are breathing down their necks. The news hounds are hungry."

"Always are," she said. In her eyes, Moore had done a good job of feeding them yet controlling their access. "But we can't make a murderer out of a POI."

"Larmer's more than a POI."

She remained silent.

"Can you call Wiarton as I drive?"

"Yes, sir."

"We'll go in with Lowrie, Chandler, and the four junior PCs. I want everyone wearing Kevlar and fully armed. At the very least, it'll be a photo op for the hounds. We leave for Larmer's cottage at eighteen-thirty. No advance notice."

☙☙☙

Naslund drove quietly along Hope Bay Road, eyes forward, mind uneasy. Although the road was perfectly level, she felt her car rushing downhill, spinning out-of-control. Moore sat silently in the passenger seat beside her. She could smell the inspector's sweat through his aftershave, the sharp ketones of a man who seemed to be running on empty.

Chandler and Lowrie manned the squad car behind them, followed by Kraft and Weber in a third car, and Singh and Derlago in a fourth. The team was badgered by a media posse as they left the station. The second murder in Wiarton in a week had whipped reporters into a frenzy. Moore had sent them packing, allowing only photos.

Naslund drove on. In her mind, Larmer was no saint. He'd kick you when you were down. However, that didn't make him a murderer. She hadn't been able to convince Moore to hold off on him. The team hadn't heard anything from Tatyana Filipov so MacTavish was on the back burner.

Moore had slotted MacLean farther back, after MacTavish and Gordon Tyler.

Naslund pulled into Larmer's driveway and braked quietly. Moore jumped out. Weber and Derlago fanned out to secure the property's perimeter. Lowrie and Singh headed for the front door. The team knew their way around. They'd studied the cottage floorplan and lot survey.

"Up here," Larmer called. "I'm on the deck."

A line of tall cedars hid the deck. Naslund couldn't see Larmer. The man didn't sound concerned or dangerous. Nevertheless, Moore stormed up the deck stairs, followed by Naslund, SIG Sauers cocked and raised. Chandler and Kraft trailed, Remington 870 shotguns primed. They emerged onto a large deck to find Larmer alone, lounging in a pool-chair wearing swim shorts. He seemed amused, apparently entertained that they were treating him like a dangerous felon. Naslund hadn't seen him for almost a week. He looked as if he didn't have a care in the world. He gestured the inspector to a patio chair. "Have a seat."

Moore shook his head irritably.

Chandler moved to cover the sliding door into the house. Kraft entered the house under Chandler's cover. Chandler followed his partner.

Larmer chuckled. *Watch out,* his expression seemed to say. *It's dangerous in there*.

Well, Naslund thought, Larmer might have fewer cares, but he still seemed to want a fight. From the stiffness of Moore's back, the inspector was going to give him one.

Within a minute, DC Lowrie appeared at the sliding door and nodded. The circle was complete. The cottage was secure.

Moore stepped forward. "We have a warrant to search this property, Mr. Larmer. First, we'll have a little chat. Let's go inside."

Larmer didn't move. "I like fresh air."

"Good for you," Moore said, "but we're going inside." He lifted his chin as if to say *Don't fuck with me* and marched Larmer into the kitchen.

Chapter 27

Naslund dropped into the chair at the end of the kitchen table.

Chandler and Kraft closed off the room, shotguns still primed. Lowrie and Singh were already on their way to the garage.

The inspector sat across from Larmer. "Let's establish a few facts. First, Mr. Thom Tyler was murdered, and now Mr. John MacKenzie. They were both friends of yours."

Larmer remained silent, but his face said *So? What are you saying?*

"I'll take that as an affirmative. We'll start with the first victim. A forensic pathologist determined that Mr. Tyler drowned. He inhaled water into his lungs. When a man drowns in such a manner, he experiences severe chest pain. He suffers simultaneous circulatory and respiratory failure. The victim usually succumbs within four to eight minutes of immersion. Four to eight minutes."

A flicker of gray eyes. Larmer sat motionless.

"Four to eight minutes of hell, wouldn't you say so?"

Naslund sighed inwardly. Did Moore have to play his script from the top?

The suspect nodded. *Of course it was*, his expression said. *Don't ask me stupid questions.*

Moore rapped the table. "Don't you have anything to say?"

"Yes, Inspector, I do."

Moore waited.

Larmer stared at the table, as if considering a momentous confession.

Naslund could hear Moore breathing in and out. Larmer examined his hands, fingernail by fingernail. He eventually looked up. "On second thought, I have nothing to say."

Moore exhaled loudly then pulled his chair in to the table, scraping the legs across the hardwood floor. They wailed like a cornered cat. He slowly leaned closer. "Is that right?"

Larmer didn't look at him.

"You're contradicting yourself."

The suspect mimicked him. "Is that right?"

Moore ignored the barb. "You better get your story straight. A week ago," he said with a false smile, "you told us that you'd be happy to give a formal statement. Do you want a lawyer?"

"I don't need a lawyer. I'm innocent."

Moore harrumphed. He rose, walked toward Larmer, and bent to his ear. "We know exactly how Thom Tyler died."

"Good. Then find his killer. You're wasting your time on me."

"Oh? Do you know what I do when someone tells me that? I dig deeper. For starters, there's your friendship with Carolyn MacLean and Thom Tyler. Given your friendship, pardon me, your *relationship*—" He lingered over the word. "—I wonder why you didn't visit them last weekend."

"Those two had their life," Larmer replied. "Thom and I had another one."

"It looks like you were caught in the middle. I'd say you were part of a love triangle."

"A love triangle?" Larmer snorted as if to say *The mindlessness of cops*. "Let me explain something. Carrie and I slept together. Carrie fell for Thom. Carrie and Thom slept together. Carrie and I didn't." Larmer smiled insincerely. "No overlap, Inspector, no triangle. No mindless jealousy."

"That sounds rather cut and dry."

"Perhaps. But that's the way it was."

"Is that right?" Moore said.

Larmer remained silent.

"When three people love each other," Moore continued, "there is often another feeling present. What feeling would that be?"

The suspect shrugged, as if to say *You tell me*.

"Jealousy, Mr. Larmer. Envy. Hate."

"That's three, Inspector."

Naslund sensed Moore about to jump out of his chair and grab Larmer's throat. The inspector's face reddened. The vein in the middle of his forehead started throbbing. His mouth clenched. The jaw muscles near his ears bulged.

The suspect smiled.

Smug snot. Naslund wanted to give him a piece of her mind but sat back and breathed slowly in and out. *Let it slide*, she ordered herself.

Almost immediately, Moore controlled himself. His jaw muscles relaxed. He eyeballed Larmer. "Do you know one of the tenets of homicide investigations?"

The suspect shook his head.

"People rarely murder people they don't know."

Moore held up a forefinger. "Here's another one. They often murder people they love. Or once loved."

The suspect remained silent.

"What often happens in love triangles?"

"I have no idea. I've never been in one."

"One person kills another. That's what happens."

"Huh."

"You think you know everything, don't you?"

No reply.

"Tell me this then: how did Mr. Tyler 'fall' overboard?"

"I don't know."

"Ah," Moore said. "For once Mr. Larmer is stumped." He smiled with contempt then leaned forward. "But I don't suppose you would. Because he didn't 'fall' overboard, did he?" He shook his head. "No, he didn't. Our forensic team reported the boom didn't make contact with Mr. Tyler's body. But other things did." He stopped.

The suspect said nothing.

Moore leaned right across the table. "Do you know what other things?"

Larmer shook his head.

I think you do, Moore's expression said.

Larmer eyed him with distaste.

"No idea? Well, let me tell you. The right side of Mr, Tyler's head was impacted by three blows from a ballpeen hammer. They smashed the orbital bones and destroyed his right eye."

Larmer blinked.

"But whoever wielded the hammer wasn't satisfied with that, were they Mr. Larmer?"

He said nothing.

"The assailant then deployed a pointed instrument. Pointed, but not particularly sharp. It made a bloody mess.

You see, the instrument was driven into Mr. Tyler's left eye."

Larmer stared at Moore.

"The instrument, a Phillips screwdriver, to be precise, went right through the victim's pupil. Right through. Are you familiar with screwdriver types?"

The suspect shook his head, apparently in shock.

Naslund couldn't tell if he was truly distressed or play-acting.

"I think you are," Moore said. "The forensic pathologist reported that Mr. Tyler's left pupil exhibited a star-like perforation consistent with a puncture generated by a Phillips screwdriver approximately eleven millimeters wide." He paused to emphasize the details. *See,* his look said, *we know exactly what you did.* "Given the hammer blows that destroyed his right eye, his vision was immediately impaired. He likely tried to save himself like someone fumbling in the dark. Must have been awful, especially for a visual person like Mr. Tyler."

The suspect sat motionless. The blood had drained from his face, as if he were in shock.

"Mr. Tyler was thrown from his boat. We know you're a strong person, Mr. Larmer."

The suspect's eyes said *Fuck off.*

"I'll ask you again, where were you on the night of July seventh, from nine onward?"

"At my cottage."

"Unfortunately—unfortunately for you, that is—you have no proof." Moore smiled. "By the way, we found three different sets of fingerprints on Mr. Tyler's skiff. I believe you know who they belong to."

"How would I know?"

"You seem defensive."

"You've worn me out."

"Three, Mr. Larmer. Mr. Tyler's, Miss Mac-

Lean's—and yours. We found your prints on the center-board mechanism."

"Yes?" Larmer seemed genuinely perplexed.

"Don't play stupid. It doesn't suit you." Moore pursed his lips. "After assaulting the victim, you untied the anchor rode and released the anchor when the rode was wrapped around the victim's ankle."

Larmer regarded him with disdain. *I did?*

"Then you loosened the screws that held the center-board tight, Phillips screws," the inspector added and stopped to study Larmer's face. "Did you think that would fool anybody? I thought you were smarter."

Larmer ignored him.

"You wanted to render Mr. Tyler sightless and voiceless. You bashed in his right eye and stabbed his left—with merciless intent." Moore paused. "Who would be able to get close enough to do that? To attack Mr. Tyler without raising suspicion? Someone who knew him. Someone like you, Mr. Larmer. Where are the clothes you were wearing? I assume they're soaked in blood—Mr. Tyler's blood. Aren't they?"

Larmer stared straight ahead.

"As for taking his voice," Moore continued, "a full-immersion drowning is soundless. When Mr. Tyler could no longer hold his breath, water rushed down his throat, blocking his airways. He soon lost consciousness and died."

Larmer didn't react.

"Don't you have anything to say for yourself? Nothing? Are you dumb, Mr. Larmer?"

Larmer took the bait. "Of course my prints are on the centerboard. I sailed with Thom. I told you that."

"So, you tampered with the centerboard mechanism. You confess to the murder of Thom Tyler."

"I do not. I did not *tamper* with the centerboard. I used

it. I adjusted it. You do that when you sail, Inspector. But one can't expect you to know that." He shook his head in disgust then pointed to Naslund. "Ask your colleague."

"Confess, Mr. Larmer. It will be better for you."

"I have nothing to confess. I'm innocent."

"I don't believe you. In fact, I believe you were involved in a second murder, Mr. John MacKenzie's."

"I was?"

"Don't play stupid. Where were you today from midnight until seven a.m.?"

"Are you asking me for another alibi?"

"Call it what you want."

"Bullshit. You think I'm a murderer. I'm not, but you don't believe me."

Moore harrumphed. "I'm not in the habit of believing everything people say. Certainly not you. I repeat, where were you today from midnight until seven a.m.?"

"I was in Toronto."

"Can someone corroborate that?"

"Yes. LaToya Austin."

"When did you arrive in Hope Bay?"

"Just before noon."

Moore glanced at Chandler. "PC Chandler looks tired," Moore said. "I think he wants to go home. I think you better tell the truth."

"I told you the truth. I was in Toronto."

"PC Chandler looks cranky."

"Are you threatening me?"

"Threatening you?" Moore said with fake indignation. "Not a chance. We just want to get everything settled, get you back to painting and swimming. Whatever your heart desires." He smiled. "But we need to know the truth. Tell us whatever you know about the murders of Tyler and MacKenzie."

"I don't know anything."

"It will be better for you if you tell us."

"I don't know anything."

Moore rose. "We'll see." He strode to the door, beckoning for the two PCs and Naslund to follow him.

"Sergeant Naslund?" Larmer called.

She turned around. "Yes?"

"I'd like to talk to you."

In the corner of her eye, she saw the inspector stop.

"But not to him." Larmer gestured toward Moore. "Or them." He pointed at the two PCs.

As Moore and the PCs left, Naslund retook her seat at the table. "Go ahead, Mr. Larmer."

"LaToya can verify where I was today," he said, "but she can't prove I was here on July eighth. No one can. But that's where I was." He looked like he was going to cry. "I loved Thom, I did." Suddenly, his eyes were wet. He swiped at his tears. "He was like a brother, you know that."

She said nothing.

"We argued, we yelled, we dug in and battled, but he was my brother." Larmer stopped to dry his eyes. His face hardened. "And you lot think that I killed him. Well, your inspector thinks I did."

"Yes?"

Larmer didn't reply. He rose and fetched a bottle of whiskey from a kitchen cabinet and returned to the table with two shot glasses. "Glenfiddich?" he asked her.

"No thanks."

"Your loss. Me? I love whiskey. There are two kinds: good and very good."

She started to shake her head then nodded. "True. I love beer. Imports. Tuborg, Heineken." *As in Heineken tallboys.*

"Never touch the stuff. Piss-water and swill." He

poured a shot of whiskey and downed it. "It's been a hard week."

She nodded. "What do you want to tell me?"

"I'm sick of Inspector Moore. *Detective Inspector Moore*," Larmer mimicked. "*Homicide*. You won't find a more bloodless twat. Less is Moore, indeed." He reached for the whiskey bottle then put it down. "He's frantic as hell. Stop or go, no middle gears. So I gave him the treatment." Larmer nodded with satisfaction. "Gave him exactly what he deserved." He chuckled. "Anyway, I have to admit—" He stopped in mid-sentence then carried on. "—well, I've been thinking about things." He nodded twice and looked up. His animosity had dissolved.

"Go on," Naslund said.

He straightened in his chair. "I'm not proud of this, but I owed Thom money." He paused. "A lot of money. I didn't pay it all back. I, umm, I took advantage. I owe it to Thom's parents now. I'll pay them."

She remained silent.

"Well, I think I should tell you what I know about Carrie. It's not a smoking gun, but it should help."

"Go ahead."

"She's pregnant. And she told Thom she was pregnant. Let me put it this way: He wasn't pleased."

"How do you know that?"

"She told me last week. Two days before Thom's funeral. She also said she asked Thom to marry her, but he wouldn't. He wouldn't show her 'that decency.' Her words."

"And does this information somehow clear you of murder and implicate her?"

"You'll soon learn the truth. I'll tell you about Thom and Carrie and kids. It'll set you on the right path."

Naslund shrugged.

"Fine, doubt me. Presume I'm guilty. You don't have to believe I'm innocent. But believe me about Carrie. Go and ask her about her unborn child and her unmarried state. See what she says."

"Go ahead, Mr. Larmer."

Larmer poured a shot of whiskey and then ignored it. "About ten years ago, I joined Thom at the site of his first big commission, a portrait of the Lonsdale 'cottage' on Lake Rosseau—a baronial mansion in reality, with vast wine cellars and cathedral ceilings. It was post-Thanksgiving, the perfect Canadian scene. The granite house, itself perched on a granite outcrop, the mirror-like lake vibrating with brilliant fall colors. Perfect!" Larmer raised his whiskey and downed it. "Thom pulled out his oils and etched the lines of the house, mixing burnt umber and green umber to render the gray granite, adding ivory black to portray the roof and the darker, shaded areas. Lastly, he depicted his favorite elements: trees. Within minutes his sumacs dripped dragon's blood, his maples fluttered with Venetian red, his tamaracks glinted Naples gold." Larmer smiled. "It was good work. Very good. He'd deviated from 'the truth.' He'd added a dozen trees and rounded the angular granite outcrop. The house was much more of a departure. It didn't even look like a house. He'd elongated it and tilted it forward, making it appear human, like an avuncular guardian protecting the water. In fact, the whole composition was tilted forward. It appeared to embrace the viewer." Larmer beamed from ear to ear. "I loved it! He'd captured the core of the place. Not the reality, but the essence."

Naslund nodded and glanced at her watch.

"Okay, okay. You know you can't rush a painting or a story."

"All right."

"Well, this is where Carrie comes in. Back then,

Thom and I could barely afford to paint, let alone raise children. That day I told him Carrie didn't want to be a childless concubine. You might wonder how I knew that. Carrie fell for Thom but she also split up with me because I didn't want kids. She's older than Thom and me. She's been thinking about the clock for years."

Naslund knew that story. She'd danced a similar jig with Pete. Maybe next year, he'd say, then renege when next year came.

Larmer rolled on. "I told him if he wanted to be an artist, he had to put art first. Ahead of everything, including marriage and kids. Did he listen? Did he understand?" Larmer shook his head. "'I'm looking out for you,' I told him. 'Some men—' I pointed to myself. '—should never get married. Others don't have to. You're one of them.' I told him why. He didn't need marriage. He had a home. Most of what he wanted to paint was here in Ontario. He needed to be free to paint it. 'Don't be a Thom-fool,' I told him. 'Don't get married.'" Larmer shrugged. "Last week when we were sailing, he talked a lot about Carrie. 'She's going to push you now,' I warned him. He didn't reply, but I could tell she was already pushing him. Hard. She hated introducing him as her boyfriend or partner or better half. She hates being called *Miss* or *Ms*. She really hates it. Then, when we spoke before Thom's funeral, she said she'd asked him to marry her. She was pregnant. She wanted a father for her child and a husband for herself. I'm guessing Thom pushed back. She'd reached her limit. She retaliated."

Naslund scrutinized Larmer. "So, she killed Thom because he wouldn't marry her?"

"I know, I understand that sounds far-fetched. But maybe she finally got fed up." He sighed. "I've told you what I know. You're the cops, you're the professionals. Question her. See how she reacts."

ɛɔɛɔ

The moon had just risen above the hills ringing Hope Bay when Moore and Naslund drove away from Larmer's cottage. The last lees of daylight were all that remained. The team hadn't found the assault weapons or any incriminating evidence. Naslund wasn't surprised. As they rolled along Hope Bay Road, Moore asked about her conversation with Larmer. She delivered the details. "Larmer looks clean," she concluded. "And MacLean doesn't. I think we should go after her."

"We will," the inspector replied. "First thing tomorrow. But we're not finished with Larmer. It sounds like he's trying to sell her out."

"I don't think so, sir. I think he's innocent."

Moore harrumphed. "He'll crack," the inspector insisted. "It's just a matter of time."

She didn't reply.

"I went at him hard, maybe too hard. I might have caused him to clam up. Sometimes you play the wrong card." Moore sat back. "Larmer's a stubborn snake. We'll check out LaToya Austin."

"I think she'll verify his recent alibi. I think it's solid."

Moore harrumphed again.

Naslund couldn't keep her mouth shut. "We seem to be putting two and two together and coming up with five."

"Better than coming up with three."

She gripped the steering wheel. The inspector was like a heavily-laden laker. He couldn't pivot quickly, he couldn't change course. She exhaled as quietly as she could. No suspects would be cleared until the killers were found, but she was confident the Murphys and Larmer were clean. Three down, yet no closer to the truth. And now there wasn't just one victim, but two.

Chapter 28

Wiarton. July 17th:

Naslund hadn't slept well. Toward dawn she hadn't slept at all. She'd been turning over Larmer's story in her mind, particularly the part about Carrie MacLean. She pulled into her parking spot at 0700. Walking by her office, she saw the inspector already at work. He called out to her.

"Morning, Sergeant. Can you join me?"

She entered the office and took a seat. "Morning, sir."

The inspector was wearing what she thought of as his original gray suit. It looked like he'd slept in it.

"A lot on the boil," he said.

She nodded.

"Just got some bad news. Nikolai Filipov was sighted in Northern Quebec and then he fell off the grid."

"Where?"

"North of Val-d'Or. Land of mines and missing POIs."

She shook her head. Another possible lead down the drain, one she'd had hopes for.

"I want to discuss the MacKenzie CS as well as Gordon Tyler. First, we'll get MacLean in. I'm calling her now."

Naslund raised an eyebrow.

"I don't care if I interrupt her beauty sleep. She's a caterer. Most days, I'm sure she gets up well before seven. Besides, I'm doing her a favor. She's too beautiful."

Naslund grinned.

Moore switched on the speaker phone and punched her number.

"Hello?"

"*Miss* Carolyn MacLean?" the inspector asked.

"Yes."

"Detective Inspector Moore, OPP."

"Yes."

A very unfriendly "Yes," Naslund observed.

"We need to see you this morning at ten."

"Not possible, Inspector."

"Not negotiable," he replied. "Be at the station at ten."

"I'm on site until two."

"We can visit you there then."

"That won't work."

"Then we'll see you here."

"But—"

"Here," he interrupted. "Ten o'clock. Not a minute later. Do you have a lawyer?"

"No."

"Mr. John Clay can be here at ten."

"I don't need a lawyer."

"As you wish. Ten, Miss MacLean."

The inspector ended the call and turned to Naslund. "Okay, Sergeant, on to Colpoys wharf. I checked the wind yesterday. At oh-one-hundred it was southwest, fifteen knots. I spoke to Chandler. He said a wind like that would likely get MacKenzie's body and boat over to Hay Island in three or four hours, possibly less."

She agreed.

"The ninjas said the wharf grounds are riddled with

boot prints and tire prints. Totally contaminated. No luck on that front. Furthermore, they didn't find any bio matter. Chu's team didn't find anything on the Caledon's mooring lines. The lab worked on the wharf blood overnight. It all belongs to the victim. I'm not surprised." Moore shook his head. "You remember those beer cans?"

She nodded.

"No FPs, but Chu's team found traces of the victim's saliva on all seven. However, they determined it was planted, like the blood on Tyler's boom. Someone is trying to play us again. I assume they want us to think MacKenzie was drunk and fell from his boat. Yet the wharf CS is loaded with his blood. They must think we're a bunch of country bumpkins. They're trying to waste our time, disperse our resources. I've seen it before. It didn't work in the past, and it won't work now." Moore pursed his lips. "By the way, Conrad and the PCs didn't get a sniff. Nobody saw or heard anything or, if they did, they're not talking."

Unfortunate, she thought, but not unusual.

"We'll redouble our efforts. Somebody must know something. I assigned Lowrie to establish a list of MacKenzie's family and friends. He'll assemble a team to interview them. Please check in with him before noon. Go over his list."

"Yes, sir."

"As with the Tyler murder, we have no bio evidence. No forensics. These days, it seems that all juries want is forensics. CSI this, CSI that. In my experience, solving a murder often has more to do with finding motives than DNA. If you don't have forensics, what do you need?" It was a rhetorical question. "A confession. That's where we are. We have to get a confession."

Naslund couldn't agree more. In that sense, she was as old-school as the inspector.

"That's why I went at Larmer so hard," he said.

"Understood." On the other hand, there was more than one way to trap a rat. You often had as good a chance of getting a confession if you didn't belittle a suspect. Next time, given a narcissist like Larmer, it might be better to appeal to his ego. Make him look smart, make him think he was in control.

"I'll be going at MacLean in the same way."

Naslund nodded. *Of course you will.*

"On another note, Gordon Tyler is bothering me, and not only his alibi for July eighth. You remember that mooring-line theft from Tyler's skiff?"

"Yes."

"Last night, I reviewed the surveillance footage. The thief was bald and not very athletic. Remove Gordon Tyler's hairpiece and he'd be bald. And still not athletic."

She chuckled. "Very true."

"We need to find out where he was on Wednesday July tenth, between fifteen hundred and nineteen hundred and also confirm his July eighth alibi. According to Lowrie's notes, he gets up at oh-seven-thirty every day." Moore glanced at his watch. "We'll get him in ASAP."

The inspector called Gordon Tyler. The man didn't hesitate or play games. He agreed to come in to the station at 0830.

❧❦❧

After ushering Gordon Tyler into the interview room, Naslund took a post in the shadow room. Thom's half-brother looked the picture of propriety. He wore a dark brown suit and a muted brown tie. His hairpiece seemed buttoned down, as if permanently glued in place.

"Good morning, Mr. Tyler," Moore said. "Thank you for coming in."

"It's my duty. I always support the police."

Huh, Naslund thought, a civic paragon.

"First, my condolences," Moore said with apparent conviction. "It's difficult to lose a brother."

"Half-brother," Tyler said. "But, yes, it is difficult, more for the family than for me."

"Oh?"

"I wasn't that close to Thom."

"I see."

"I don't mind telling you that. I have nothing to hide. I know why I'm here. I'll tell you what I know directly, once and for all."

"Good."

"Thom and I weren't the best of friends. However, I wished him well. I wanted him to succeed. I helped him with money in the past, and I was going to do so again."

"How so?"

"He asked me to lend him three hundred thousand dollars."

"Three-hundred thousand?"

"Correct."

"When was that?"

"Three weeks ago yesterday."

"Did you?"

Tyler shook his head. "We were close to a satisfactory arrangement, but Thom died. Was murdered, I should say."

"What makes you say he was murdered?"

Tyler eyed the inspector. "*Everyone* says he was murdered. Let me be direct again. I don't know what happened to Thom. As I told your Detective Lowrie twice, I wasn't part of Thom's social circle or his daily life. I don't know anything about his skiff, or his fishing habits, or his painting routine." Tyler sat back. "I wish I could help you more, but I can't."

"I think you can. What kind of arrangement were you discussing?"

"I was going to lend Thom three hundred thousand dollars at fifteen percent. However, we couldn't agree on the loan collateral. Hence the arrangement didn't come to fruition."

"That sounds like a blow to you," Moore said. "Losing a deal like that."

"It's not. I'll put that capital to use elsewhere."

"At fifteen percent?"

"Possibly. Possibly not. In either case, I'll put it to use."

"Did Thom Tyler owe you any money?"

"No."

"None? What about his earlier loans?"

"He paid them back."

"With interest?'

"Yes."

"So, you disagreed on the collateral for the new loan. What was the disagreement?"

"I asked Thom to sign over his complete list of paintings to me as security for the loan. He offered this year's list. It wasn't enough. I know he's part of the family, but when I loan money, it doesn't matter to whom, it has to make fiscal sense."

"And this loan didn't make sense?"

"To Thom, maybe, but not to me. In the past, Thom took years to pay back his loans. I didn't want that to occur again. In the event that it did, I needed to secure my money."

"With his complete list?"

"Yes."

"Sounds excessive."

"Perhaps. But it was a strong incentive for Thom to repay me, the kind he needed."

"I'll take your word for it. Where were you on the night of Sunday, July seventh, after eight p.m.?"

"At home, watching a baseball game on TV."

"Who was playing?"

"The Blue Jays and the Yankees."

Naslund knew Gordon Tyler's alibi had been checked twice—he'd said he was home with his sister Gillian, who was his live-in housekeeper—but Naslund liked the inspector's angle. One more prod might trip the wire. Lies often took time to surface.

"Where were they playing?" Moore asked.

"Toronto."

"Did you watch the whole game?"

"Yes."

"What Blue Jay stole third?"

"You mean which two Blue Jays. Josh Donaldson and Kevin Pillar."

"What was the final score?"

"The Blue Jays won, six-to-three."

All correct, Naslund knew. And no hesitation.

"Was anyone there with you?" Moore asked.

"My sister Gillian."

"Thom Tyler's half-sister?"

Gordon Tyler nodded.

"What time did you get up the next morning?"

"At seven-thirty."

As usual, Naslund thought. According to Gillian, correct as well.

"Where were you last Wednesday afternoon, July tenth, between three and seven p.m.?"

"I was at my office until five-thirty. Then I went home to eat supper."

"What time did you get home?"

"About ten minutes later. Gillian can verify that. I walked. I live five blocks away."

Naslund nodded to herself. Tyler didn't seem aggravated by the new line of questioning.

"What time did you eat?" Moore asked.

"Six. Gillian can verify that too."

"Did you go out afterward?"

"No."

"Can someone verify you were at the office from three to five-thirty?"

"I was with Mr. James Kinch between three and four, and Mrs. Janice Mendelsohn between four and five."

"And five to five-thirty?"

"I was wrapping up the day's business."

"Was anyone there with you?"

"No."

Naslund considered Gordon Tyler's movements. He couldn't have gotten to Cape Commodore and back and burgled the skiff in half-an-hour, or even forty minutes. Derlago reported that the thief bolted and disappeared into the bush. Presuming he eventually resurfaced and drove off in a vehicle, that in itself would have eaten up half-an-hour, if not far more.

"Where were you yesterday from midnight until six-thirty a.m.?" Moore asked.

Again, Tyler didn't appear aggravated by the question. From the look on his face, he knew Moore was alluding to MacKenzie's murder. "I know you're busy, Inspector. So I'll be direct again. I was at home. Gillian was there. She can verify that."

"What were you doing?"

"Sleeping. I got up at seven-thirty, as I always do."

"Thank you, Mr. Tyler. May I ask you a personal question?"

"Yes?"

"What do you think of Carolyn MacLean?"

"I don't know her very well."

"You're a direct person, Mr. Tyler. Please be direct in this regard. I repeat, 'What do you think of Carolyn MacLean?'"

"What do I think? Well, over time, I've made some observations." Tyler paused, as if to marshal his thoughts. "I can tell you this. I found it strange that she wouldn't marry Thom. Or perhaps Thom wouldn't marry her. But I don't know why. As you can see, I don't know much."

Moore smiled. "But you do. Please continue."

"Fine. In my opinion, she was after his money. But I don't know that. Not for sure."

"Continue."

"Here's another observation. She was always cozying up to my father. I think she wanted something from him. She was trying to use him."

"How?"

"I don't know." Tyler looked frustrated. "I just don't know."

Moore nodded. "Do you have any other observations?"

Tyler shook his head.

"Thank you, Mr. Tyler. We appreciate your help."

❧❧❧

After escorting the POI from the station, Naslund joined the inspector in his office.

"What's your read on Gordon Tyler?" he asked.

She hadn't detected any suspicious behavior or contradictory statements. "He looks clean."

Moore nodded. "Christ. Is everyone clean?"

She had no reply. The Murphy brothers' alibis for MacKenzie had checked out.

The inspector sighed. "The ninjas just submitted an update on the Colpoys CS. According to their ground study, it looks like two people carried the victim to the wharf's edge and threw him into the water. There is no evidence the body was dragged. Dr. Leonard didn't note any either. I thought we might only have one perp, someone strong enough to carry MacKenzie without dragging him. That changes things."

Not for me, she thought.

"I think we also have to consider two perps for the Tyler murder. Maybe more."

She nodded. Exactly. "I have a suggestion. On a different matter."

"Yes?"

"Given what Gordon Tyler said about MacLean and John Tyler, I'd like to visit John Tyler now. Gordon said MacLean was always cozying up to Tyler Senior, trying to use him. I want to hear what he says."

Moore glanced at his watch.

"I'll be back before MacLean arrives," she said.

Chapter 29

As Naslund entered the Tyler house, Deirdre Tyler searched her eyes hopefully.

"Sorry, Mrs. Tyler," Naslund said, "nothing to report."

Deirdre nodded with resignation.

"I'd like to ask your husband a few questions."

She called John Tyler. "Coffee, Sergeant?"

"No thanks."

"I have a big pot on the go." She pointed to the kitchen counter. "Muffins too."

"Oh. Okay. Thank you very much."

John Tyler hurried into the kitchen. "Good morning, Sergeant."

"Morning. Can we sit in the front room?"

"Sure."

As Naslund expected, the front room was empty. Thom's younger siblings had gone back to Toronto. She sat across from Tyler Senior in an old leather armchair. After eating a bite of muffin, she got straight to the point. "I want to ask you about Carrie MacLean. Do you think she was trying to use you?"

"Use me? For what?"

"Anything."

"Use me?" Tyler Senior said again. "That's a strange question."

"Take your time. Cast your mind back."

He gazed out the window. Eventually he turned to face her. "I can only think of one thing. And I'm not sure of that. I wouldn't call what she did trying to use me."

"Please continue."

"Well, she hinted the cottage should be in her name as well as Thom's. She asked me to bring the matter up with Thom, but I never did." Tyler Senior shook his head. "She didn't press the issue. Was that using me?"

"When was that?"

He thought. "About a month ago."

"Thank you. Sorry to barge in like this."

"No problem at all."

Naslund stood. "I'll see myself out."

"Sergeant, do you think Carrie was involved in Thom's death?"

"We don't know, Mr. Tyler." Naslund suspected MacLean, but wanted to keep it quiet. "What you and I just spoke of is private. Keep the matter to yourself. Completely. Don't even mention it to your wife."

༉༇༉

Back at the station, Naslund went directly to Moore's office.

"Come in, Sergeant."

Naslund sat. "I have some potential ammo for Mac-Lean's interview."

"Good."

"John Tyler wasn't sure if she was using him, but she hinted the cottage should be in her name as well as Thom

Tyler's. A suspicious mind might think she wanted to get co-ownership of the property before she killed him."

Moore nodded.

"Add that to Larmer's words yesterday, and we're beginning to get motive for MacLean."

"Right." He glanced at his watch. "Can you meet her in the foyer?"

"Of course."

"Please sit in the shadow room."

"Yes, sir."

Naslund waited near the front door. At 1005 she strode into Moore's office. The inspector's lips were pursed. Having switched on the speakerphone, he punched MacLean's cell number.

"Hello," her hurried voice answered.

"Inspector Moore speaking. You're late."

"I know."

"So do I. And I don't like it." He hung up.

⟅⟐⟐

"Coffee, Miss MacLean?" Moore politely asked.

Naslund watched from her post in the shadow room. Good move. The inspector was starting soft. It'd rankle MacLean more when he switched gears.

The suspect shook her head forcefully. "Tea," she said.

Naslund focused on her mouth. Her lips were curled in a churlish manner.

"Milk? Sugar?" Moore asked.

"Milk," she curtly ordered. "No sugar."

He switched on the intercom to the shadow room. "Sergeant Naslund, can you please deliver a tea with milk?"

"Of course, sir."

Naslund fetched the tea from the staff room, moving slowly, letting MacLean ripen a bit. It was time to turn the tables—to keep the suspect waiting.

A few minutes later, she entered the interview room and placed the tea on the table. She didn't look at MacLean. Moore sat in the lead chair, reading a report, ignoring the suspect. Naslund returned to the shadow room. She felt her optimism building. Perps were often right under your nose. She sensed the team closing in. The cottage ownership was a gate. If it opened, MacLean would likely fall.

"How are you today?" Moore asked MacLean after she sipped some tea.

She stared at him. *How am I?*

"I don't expect you're well," he said with false concern.

She tilted her chin.

"How could you be, with two murders on your mind? Perhaps I should rephrase that. On your conscience."

She eyed him as if to say *What are you implying*?

"As you no doubt know, Mr. Tyler's best friend was murdered yesterday. Another murder, Miss MacLean. Another blood bath. Very bloody. As you no doubt know."

"What are you saying?"

"I'm saying two men were murdered, two men you knew well. Both of them were attacked with the same instrument, a ballpeen hammer. An instrument you could handle with ease. You're a strong woman. You manhandle huge pots, you lug around large bags of flour and sugar."

"I lift, Inspector, I carry. I don't *manhandle*."

"You're a strong woman, a match for any man."

"I doubt it."

"Don't belittle yourself. You're a very accomplished woman. Very capable."

"Spare me the theatrics."

"Murder is not theater," the inspector snapped. "It is real. All too real."

"You think I don't know that?" Her eyes flashed. "My Thom is dead! Gone!"

Moore ignored her. "Where were you from midnight Sunday July fourteenth until seven a.m. Monday July fifteenth?"

"Owen Sound." Contrary to her reasonable tone, her eyes were still angry.

"Where?"

"With my friend Terry and her family." She pulled herself back in the Slider. "She's a chef. I stay with them when I work late. I worked until two a.m. Monday morning."

"Where?"

"The Cobble Beach Golf Club."

"What's your friend's full name and address?"

"Terry Kincardine. Ninety-Two Eighth Avenue West."

"Were you there between two a.m. and seven a.m.?"

"Yes. Until nine a.m., to be precise."

"I'll take your word for it."

"Please don't. Check my information. Terry and her husband were still up when I arrived. I slept in the same room as their two kids."

"All right, Miss MacLean, it appears you have an alibi. Congratulations." Moore smiled insincerely. "But that doesn't mean you're innocent. You could have paid someone to murder Mr. Tyler. And then Mr. MacKenzie."

She stared at him in disbelief. "I'd never bring harm to Thom. Or J.J."

"We have reason to think you would. We know you and Mr. Tyler were at loggerheads. You weren't spending time together."

"I admit, we were going through a bad patch, but who doesn't? I'd never hurt him. Never!"

"You didn't have to. You paid someone."

"Paid someone? Why? Even if I wanted to, how would I know who to pay? Who? Why?"

"Enough. *I'll* ask the questions." Moore leaned forward. "You wonder why? Because Mr. Tyler drove you to it. Are you pregnant, Miss MacLean?"

She appeared to be taken aback. "Yes."

"It may not be showing yet," he said, "but we have our sources. A Mr. Ward Larmer, to be precise."

She shrugged as if she wasn't surprised.

"He also told us that you asked Mr. Tyler to marry you and that Mr. Tyler refused."

"Thom didn't refuse. He said we had to wait."

"Wait?"

"Yes, until he got some debts paid off."

"What debts? To whom?"

"I don't know."

"Come, Miss MacLean, you lived with him for ten years."

"We kept our finances separate."

That rang true, Naslund thought.

"So," Moore said, "you didn't covet his money?"

Covet, Naslund said to herself. *That's old-school to the core.*

"Of course not," MacLean replied. "I make more than enough money."

"I'll take your word for it. Nonetheless, you asked John Tyler to help put your name on the cottage. Why?"

"For the baby."

Moore acted as if he hadn't heard her. "From where I sit, you wanted the cottage. If you murdered Mr. Tyler, it'd become yours."

"It was for the baby."

"It was for *you*, Miss MacLean."

"Me? Are you serious? Think, Inspector. If I was after Thom's property, why didn't I put my name on everything? The cottage, the condo, his boats, his art. Listen, listen carefully. The cottage was for the baby." She glared at him. "It would have helped the baby. *His* baby. Are you deaf?"

"That's enough! I'll ask the questions."

"Thom's dead!" she cried. "What else do you want to know?"

"The truth, Miss MacLean."

"I've told you the truth. Let me state it bluntly. I didn't kill Thom or have him killed."

Moore eyed her. "All right, you didn't murder Mr. Tyler. But your associate did. Your *partner*, I should say, in more ways than one."

"My partner?"

"Your lover."

"Lover? What lover?"

"Ward Larmer."

"Are you crazy?"

"You aided and abetted Ward Larmer in the murder of Thomas Tyler. Miss MacLean, you're an accomplice to first-degree murder."

She stared at him.

"Confess. It will be better for you. You colluded with Ward Larmer. You gave him access to your Mallory Beach boathouse and dock. You informed him of Mr. Tyler's movements."

"I did nothing of the kind."

"Confess, Miss MacLean."

"I have nothing to confess."

"Confess. It will be better for you."

"I'm innocent."

"It's no use lying. We'll uncover the truth."

"Please do. And please find out who murdered Thom."

"We will." Moore eyed her then strode confidently from the room.

⁂

A few minutes later, Naslund joined Moore in his office. The inspector waved her to a chair. "She's as slippery as Larmer," he began. "I don't believe either of them."

Naslund remained silent.

"From what I've seen and heard, MacLean is different things to different people. She's all over the place. She's the long-suffering saint, the supportive partner, the fair-minded boss." He shook his head. "I don't buy it. I don't trust her."

Fair enough, Naslund thought, but distrust didn't translate to guilt. She sat back. From what she'd just seen, MacLean was clean. So much for the cottage being a gate. So much for her optimism.

"What's the best way to crack a liar?" Moore asked. "Let them think you believe them. Then go back at them. Again and again. They'll eventually muddle their stories." He nodded with assurance. "In the meantime, we have a team meeting at eleven hundred."

⁂

Sitting at her hutch, Naslund updated the case notes on John Tyler. As she completed them, the team filed into the murder room. No one was absent. No one was late.

Moore called the meeting to order and asked FID Constable Wolfe to address the room. The ninja rose and told the team that he and Mitchell hadn't found any useful bio matter or workable prints at Colpoys wharf. However, they'd collected soil samples. If the perps used a vehicle, it might have deposited floral or mineral features that could be linked to a specific location, leading to the perps themselves. On the flip side, someone not residing in the Bruce might own a vehicle that presented floral or mineral features unique to the Bruce, thus indicating they'd been in the region.

Moore interrupted Wolfe. "A soil analysis operation can take weeks. Nonetheless, we need to give it top priority. I've also assigned Detective Chahoud to the operation. I may assign other officers next week." Moore waved Wolfe on.

"It's possible," Wolfe continued, "that the perps parked far away from the wharf and walked to it, perhaps using the Bruce Trail, which has numerous access points."

Wolfe went on to report that he, Chahoud, and Mitchell had begun collecting samples from the closest access points. The lab would zero in on floral and mineral matter from distinctive bio-regions. Such bio-regions were generally small, making a match manageable, if not timely.

"Time is our enemy," Wolfe concluded.

Moore broke in. "If a match is there, the lab will find it. Even high-powered carwashes don't rinse all trace matter off."

Naslund silently agreed. She wondered why criminals ever used a car. If they knew what forensics could pin on them, they'd ditch all cars, or severely limit their use. Ditto for firearms. Which, she concluded, was what the Tyler-Mackenzie perps seemed to have done.

Wolfe went on to relate that a ground study of the wharf suggested two people carried the victim to the wharf's edge and threw him in the water. He and Mitchell found three lines of blood leading from the spot where the victim went down to the wharf's edge. They also found partial prints indicating two sets of large shoes, both provisionally identified as size thirteen, moving in tandem at an average of .82 meters apart, starting at the victim-down position and ending at the edge. Although the prints were not complete enough to yield a match, they reconstructed the scene. Two people moved in the same direction at a steady distance apart using short steps—consistent with the steps used to carry a load about .60 meters wide, the width of the victim's shoulders. Wolfe made a final point. He and Mitchell had found no evidence the victim was dragged.

As Wolfe sat, Moore stood. "Thank you, Detective." He addressed the room. "Detective Wolfe just delivered important information. There were likely two perps. Although the reconstruction is not conclusive, it is highly suggestive. What do courts need to convict? Not absolutely conclusive evidence, but evidence beyond reasonable doubt. What Detectives Wolfe and Mitchell reconstructed appears to be beyond reasonable doubt." Moore nodded gravely. "Going forward, I want everyone to be on the same page. In the MacKenzie case, we are likely dealing with at least two perps. Ditto for the Tyler case. Both murders appear to have been committed by the same perps. If we solve one case, we'll likely solve the other. Sergeant Chu will now update you on the blood at Colpoys wharf and the bio matter found on MacKenzie's boat."

Chu rose and explained that the blood at Colpoys wharf was all the victim's, just as the blood at the main Tyler CS was all the victim's. There was no ancillary blood. However, the team had some solid evidence. The same weapon was used to perpetrate both murders: a gray metal ballpeen hammer. Chu went on to note that his team hadn't found any useful DNA carriers on Hay Island. As for MacKenzie's boat, all they'd discovered was saliva on seven beer cans, saliva with the same DNA profile. It was the victim's saliva. However, it was planted.

"Constable Chahoud—" Chu pointed to his MU associate. "—detected minute cotton fibers in the saliva itself as well as directly on three of the seven beer cans. He concluded a cotton cloth was used to transfer saliva from the victim's mouth to the mouths of the cans. Unfortunately for us, the saliva cloth did not match the cloth used to plant blood on Mr. Tyler's boat. Any questions?"

There were none.

Moore stood. "Thank you. As Sergeant Chu reported, the saliva was planted, like the blood on Tyler's boom. It was no doubt planted in an attempt to deceive us, to mislead our investigation." He held up a finger. "It didn't work. We're on track. Keep focused!" He pointed to the cork board. "I've posted new actions. Attend to them."

Having dismissed the team, Moore beckoned Naslund to his office.

"I have a task for you, Sergeant," he said after she sat. "First, did you check in with Lowrie on that MacKenzie list?"

"Yes. It looks good."

"Okay. I realize you want to go after MacTavish. I can read you. Sometimes." Moore grinned. "Go down to the city and pay him a surprise visit. Interview him re the MacKenzie murder. By virtue of the Tyler case, he's a prime suspect. Hook him if you can."

"Yes, sir." In Naslund's eyes, with the two Murphys, Larmer, Gordon Tyler, and Carrie MacLean seemingly clean, Jock MacTavish loomed large. A small forensic detail—the likely height of the killer—supported her supposition. All five of the "clean" POIs were under six-feet tall, the tallest being five-ten. MacTavish was six-two.

"One more thing." Moore paused. "This is off-the-record. Use all the rope you need. Don't worry about the letter of the law. Walk the edge."

"Right."

"Best of luck. I have absolute confidence in you. I've been watching you." He smiled sincerely. "You'll go places. You have the recording eye of a real detective."

Naslund wasn't sure what to say. In her father's view, a detective's eye wasn't good enough; you also needed a detective's mind. Well, at least Moore figured she was half-way there. Glass half full. "Thank you," she replied.

"You're welcome, and thank *you*. You know, Sergeant, it's easy to see everything through your own eyes, your own bigotries and assumptions. It's a bad habit, one I need to break. You've helped me start." He smiled again. "Stay safe. Call for back-up if you need to shake any big trees."

Chapter 30

Toronto. July 17th:

Naslund entered the Gallery Canadiana at 1700. Moore had arranged for a city detective to shadow MacTavish and let her know if he left the gallery. He hadn't. He'd been inside for the last three hours.

As she stepped forward, a wall of perfume hit her nose. Tatyana was nearby. Her eyes lit up as Naslund approached. Per usual, her lips were wide and red, her hair said top salon. But there was something different about her blouse. It had three open buttons, not two. Her bra was visible. It was skimpy and sheer.

"Sergeant, you are back." Tatyana smiled. "I see you park in street."

Naslund wondered if that triggered the three-button opening. It seemed the doll was still playing. "I'd like to see Mr. MacTavish."

"Of course. Your leg, is good now?"

"Yes, thank you."

"Very good." Tatyana looked quickly behind her. The room was empty. "You catch boss. Ask to see sales invoices. I find no multi-contracts."

Naslund nodded. Too bad, but she wasn't surprised. Not having heard from Tatyana, she assumed her search hadn't succeeded.

"Follow me." Tatyana smiled again. "This way, Sergeant."

Her hips swayed; her hair bounced. Her flash factor was over-the-top.

She glanced back at Naslund, who was looking ahead, down the corridor. The doll seemed disappointed. Her sway increased. Her skirt snapped with each step.

"Coffee?" she asked as they reached the office door. "With lots of cream? I know you like."

Naslund shook her head.

"Water?"

"No thanks."

Tatyana pivoted on the ball of one high heel, like a stage dancer.

"Come in, Sergeant," MacTavish called. "Don't dally."

Naslund entered the office. It was as disheveled as on her previous visits. "Good afternoon, Mr. MacTavish."

"What brings you to the Canadiana?"

"Business." She sat. "I'd like to see the invoices for all your Tyler sales."

"All of them? That's seven years."

"So you say."

"Give me a moment."

Forty minutes later, she leaned back. She'd counted 168 invoices and quickly scanned them. Although MacTavish had sold thirty-two canvases in seven years, he'd prepared 168 invoices. Just as Tatyana had said, there were multiple invoices for the same painting, all with different prices. Was MacTavish scamming the taxman? Was he scamming Thom? "Explain something for me.

Why are there four, five, or sometimes six invoices for one Tyler sale?"

"It's simple, Sergeant. When I put a Tyler canvas up for sale, I prepared multiple invoices beforehand."

"Why?"

"To facilitate a sale. Let me explain. Everything was the same—the artist, the name of the work, the date of the work, etcetera—except for three entries. I left the sales date and sold-to name blank. I then printed numerous invoices with different prices, according to the price range I determined I could get."

"The price range? Don't you have a set price?" She knew he didn't, but wanted to irritate him.

"No. As I told you and the inspector, there is a set wholesale price, not a set sales price."

"Why did you print a range of prices?"

"To ensure that I could immediately close a sale. It was a step saved. A seemingly minor, but very important step." MacTavish smiled with attempted modesty. "Over the years, I've learned it's important to have a number of invoices pre-printed, with a range of prices. That way, when the price is set, I can get the client to immediately sign on the dotted line."

"What happens if you agree to a price that is not pre-printed?"

"That rarely happens."

"Oh? Why?"

"Experience. I know my inventory and I know my prices."

"Why not just write in the agreed-upon sales price, as you do with the sales date and sold-to name?"

"Security, Sergeant, which is closely linked to provenance. You want the price set in stone. You don't just write in an amount. I use a special printer font and ink, unique to my business. It is far easier to change a hand-written price than to alter a uniquely printed price."

Spoken like someone who'd done it, Naslund thought. "What about the sales date and sold-to name? Why don't you print them?"

"Some agents do, but I don't."

"Please elaborate."

"By all means. I write the sale-to name in ink and immediately hand the pen to the buyer for his or her signature. Regarding the date, although I am experienced, I am not clairvoyant." He grinned as if he'd just told a brilliant joke. "As you might appreciate, it's very difficult to forecast a sales date."

"I suppose. But isn't the name as important as the price?"

"No." He rolled his eyes as if to say *I live in a world of Philistines*. "What is the main function of provenance?"

She shrugged.

"Establishing the value of a work of art. Which is why I focus on the price. Consider both the date and the sale-to name. While the two elements are indeed important, the main element is the price paid. Price is the single most important factor in determining value, which, in turn, dictates what a future buyer will pay." MacTavish paused. "Most of my buyers don't care about the sold-to name, unless, of course, the previous owners were famous, in which case the work's value usually increases. For example," he said, "if the queen owned a Thom Tyler, it would make it much more valuable than if you did."

"Of course." *Snide bugger.*

"By the way, what I just told you applies to all my paintings, not just the Tyler paintings. Would you like to see my other invoices?"

"No thanks." Time to switch gears. She smiled. "I wonder if you can help me on a personal matter."

"Of course."

"I'd like to invest in an art fund. Can you recommend one?"

MacTavish's face fell. "That was the past, Sergeant. I got out when I saw what was happening. Are you going to arrest me for bad judgement?"

"Tell me what happened."

"I got out, that's all I care about now."

"Why did you get in?"

"I needed help. In short, loans. Do you have any idea how hard it is to get ahead in the art market when you're competing against Sotheby's and Christie's?"

"Where were you yesterday from midnight until six-thirty a.m.?"

"At home."

"Doing what?"

"Sleeping. Probably snoring. My wife can verify that." He smiled. "Both things."

"When did you get up?"

"Seven."

"What's your wife's cell number?"

MacTavish told her.

She punched the number into her duty phone. A soft-spoken woman answered.

"Mrs. MacTavish?"

"Yes?"

"Detective Sergeant Naslund, OPP. I have a quick question to ask you. When did your husband go to bed the night before last? Sunday night, that is."

"Ah. About eleven-thirty."

"When did he get up yesterday?

"Seven. Why are you asking?" She sounded worried.

"Did he snore?"

"Why yes, he did. Why do you ask?"

"Part of an investigation. Thank you, Mrs. Mac-Tavish."

Naslund disconnected and pocketed her phone.

MacTavish was nodding. "See, you can believe me. Give me some credit."

"Do you offer unverified credit, Mr. MacTavish?"

"I give credit where credit is due."

"So do I."

He waved a hand. "Enough. We may disagree, but we both have jobs to do. And you're doing yours very well. I commend you."

She remained silent.

"Tatyana gets off at six," he said suggestively and glanced at his watch. "Five minutes. I'm sure you can wait." He winked. "Why don't you take her for a drink? There's a nice bar across the street."

Naslund shook her head wryly. MacTavish's innuendo didn't surprise her. However, his blithe certainty did. "I have plans. In fact, they include you."

"Oh?"

"I'm going to escort you home."

"That's not necessary."

"I know, but I'll be following you home."

"I could be half an hour."

"No problem."

"Why don't you have a drink with Tatyana?"

"I have some reading to do."

"She won't bite." MacTavish grinned. "Unless you want her to. Not that I know," he quickly added.

"I have some reading to do," Naslund repeated. "Please show me all of your invoices for the last three years."

He pointed to a filing cabinet. "Be my guest. Top shelf for the past two years. Middle shelf for three years back. Would you like a beverage? Tatyana can bring you one."

"No thanks."

⁂

Naslund left the Gallery Canadiana at 1840, following MacTavish's Audi. She pulled into his driveway twenty minutes later. The agent owned an older brick ranch off Oriole Park Way. The hedges lining the property were overgrown; the flowers, drooping.

He stood waiting by his Audi. Naslund walked up to him.

"Thank you for your escort, Sergeant."

"My pleasure. Now I'd like to take a look at your toolshed."

"My toolshed?" He seemed amused. "I don't have one, but there's a workbench in the garage."

"We'll start there."

"I suppose you have a warrant."

She shook her head. No time for that. She was riding the edge.

He smiled magnanimously. "A woman with a job to do. That's fine. Follow me. I'm not a handyman," he said as they walked. "You can ask my wife. And my boys are sportsmen, not builders."

Naslund nodded.

Having reached the garage, he pointed to the workbench. "Whatever tools we have are there."

"Do you own a ballpeen hammer?"

"A what?"

She scrutinized his mouth. The man had no idea what a ballpeen hammer was.

Hours later, after MacTavish amicably left the garage and allowed her to search the complete building as well as the yard and basement, she thanked him and nodded goodbye. No Phillips screwdrivers, no ballpeen hammers, no hammers at all other than an old one with a very loose head. Barely enough tools to build a doghouse. As for MacTavish's office, she hadn't found any incriminating invoices or contracts. In the end, she hadn't found anything. Not a hair out of place, as the inspector would say. MacTavish was clean.

Wrong, she thought as she started her car. *Every* POI was clean.

Chapter 31

Ten weeks later, Naslund was sitting in her own office. Inspector Moore had been recalled to Central in mid-September. His soil analysis initiative had been shelved. He'd grilled Ward Larmer and Carrie MacLean again and dropped in on Jock MacTavish, to no avail. All POIs and contacts had been checked and rechecked. No new leads had emerged. The Tyler and MacKenzie cases had gone cold. The murder room was once again Bickell's boardroom.

Recently, whenever Naslund could—she'd taken to shunting other work to the side—she pored over interview tapes, transcripts, and notes from the Tyler and MacKenzie murders. She'd started working chronologically. That morning, she reached July twelfth. She cast her mind back. What had happened on July twelfth? She sipped her coffee. It was the day of her first meeting with J.J. and Marty at Marty Fox's place. The day of Tyler's funeral. The memorial lunch at Sawyers Inn. The M&M discussion with Moore. The afternoon of the "visit" to Tyler's cottage. The ankle injury. The night she stayed at Marty's.

Memory refreshed, she opened the case database. The

July twelfth material ended with the M&M discussion. Why? She scoured the database then combed through four boxes of papers and printouts. Nothing anywhere on the visit to Tyler's cottage. She stood, circled the office, and circled it again. Just as she was about to go outside for a walk, the answer came to her. The "visit" was off-the-record. Her mind kicked into gear. There was something she was supposed to remember. What was it? A little thing.

Step back, she told herself. *Recreate the details*. She searched the Tyler property, the MacLean women returned early, she hid behind a hedge, she heard them talking. Right! An X on a map. The grandmother found a map with letters and numbers and an X written on it. Naslund pulled out her personal phone.

"Morning, Carrie. Eva here."

"Hello."

A suspicious *hello*. "Do you have a moment?" Naslund asked.

"For what?"

"A quick question about some evidence. Just me, no Inspector Moore."

"Good."

"Can I drop by?"

"Well. Okay."

"See you in fifteen."

છ૭૯૭

"Pull up a chair," Carrie said to Naslund. "Coffee?"

Naslund shook her head. "No thanks." Carrie looked tired. Her baby bump was huge. Naslund had heard she was carrying a son, due in eight weeks. "Don't want to keep you long."

"That's okay," Carrie said.

"I know your grandmother found a map with an X on it."

Carrie eyed her. "How do you know that?"

"Can't say."

"You're right," Carrie eventually said.

"Can you show me the map?" Naslund asked.

"I'd have to find it. You sure about that coffee?"

"Yes. Thanks anyway."

Naslund settled in to wait. Intuition told her the map was important. And they had no record of it. That's what happened when you went behind the barn. You could broaden an investigation, but you could also weaken the evidence pool.

Ten minutes later, Carrie returned with a small folded map. To Naslund, it seemed like hours later. She donned a pair of CS gloves. Her heart started thumping. Her fingers tingled. With a focused effort, she controlled her breathing, opened the map, and revealed a local publication featuring the Bruce Trail. A small blue *X* marked the Tyler cottage. In the bottom right quadrant she noticed two inconspicuous lines handwritten in blue ink:

414 MB

JY8 5.30

The handwriting was small and neat, yet deeply etched. The letters and numbers slanted forward. They were tightly spaced. *Humm,* she pondered, *414 MB.* Four-hundred-plus megabytes? No. She reconsidered. It could be the cottage address, 414 Mallory Beach Road. As for *JY8 5.30*? Possibly July eight, five-thirty a.m. The date and approximate time of Thom's last departure from his boathouse. One potential hook, she thought.

She put the map down and looked up at Carrie. "I have a few questions."

Carrie nodded.

"Is this your map?"

"No."

"Was it Thom's?"

"No."

"Why did you keep it?"

Carrie shrugged. "My grandmother found it."

"Did anyone ask to see it or borrow it?"

"No."

"Where was it?"

"Under a pile of books in the guest room."

Naslund nodded. Her fault again. She'd searched the guest room when she and Moore executed the warrant. "Is this your handwriting?"

"No."

"Do you recognize it?"

"I don't know. Maybe." Carrie looked closer. "Sort of."

"Go on."

"I'm not sure. It looks like the writing of Thom's first agent. It's been a while. Almost ten years."

"The agent before Louise Hennigan?"

"Yes. Elina Bayeux."

The name didn't ring a bell. Naslund remembered a *Vost*-something. "Please confirm that name."

"Elina Bayeux. Thom didn't talk about her. Not often. She didn't help him much. Point of fact, she was a hindrance, not a help. Actually, more than a hindrance."

"How so?"

"Well, she borrowed a lot of money and didn't pay it back. She didn't sell any of Thom's art. Not one piece. She was useless." Carrie sniffed. "Always flitting around in knee-high boots. Even in August."

"Please continue."

"She screwed him. Figuratively, and literally too." Carrie smiled tightly. "Elina Bayeux was a slut. An art groupie. She used to come around here. Until I made Thom kick her out."

"When was that?"

"About five years ago."

Before my time, Naslund thought. "Have you seen her since then?"

"No."

"How about Thom? Did he see her?"

"I don't know. Does it matter now? Women liked him. He sent quite a few packing. I had to watch that spectacle more than once. Some had no shame. Screaming, crying, saying they'd keep house for him if that's all he wanted. Begging, pleading."

"Were they angry?"

"Sometimes."

"Was Elina Bayeux angry?"

Carrie nodded. "She went ballistic. Said she'd given him her best years." Carrie harrumphed. "Maybe she did. I know how that feels."

Two hooks, Naslund decided. Possible timeline fit and potential motive. "Do you happen to have any examples of Elina Bayeux's writing?"

"Let me look in Thom's studio."

"I'll join you. Can I do the actual searching?"

"Sure."

Naslund followed Carrie to the studio, where she unlocked a large cabinet and pointed to the top shelf. "Try in there."

Naslund soon uncovered what appeared to be two samples of Elina Bayeux's penmanship, an envelope addressed to Thom and a birthday card. She placed the samples next to the map. To her eye, all three documents exhibited the same handwriting. Neat, tight, forward-slanting. She pulled out her phone, took photos of all three, and turned to Carrie. "I need to impound these."

"Of course." Carrie swept a lock of hair off her forehead. "There's something I've been thinking about. A small thing." She hesitated. "I'm not sure it means anything."

"Please, tell me."

"Back in the last week of June, I saw Louise Hennigan on Mallory Beach Road very early in the morning—twice. I know her car, a powder-blue Mustang. I didn't think anything of it at the time. I was leaving for work around five-thirty and there she was, driving back toward Wiarton. Then I saw her again the next day, and her lights were off. Seemed a little strange then, seems stranger now. The early hour, no lights. Like she was skulking around."

"Did she stop or wave?"

"Oh no. She didn't see me."

"Okay. I'll look into that."

※※※

On the way to her car, Naslund called Orillia.

"Forensic Documents. Constable Jack Harding."

"Morning, Harding. Detective Sergeant Naslund, Bruce Peninsula."

"Yes, Sergeant."

"Got some handwriting. Three documents. I need to know if there's a match." She didn't mention the connection to the Tyler-MacKenzie cases. Officially, she was no longer assigned to them.

"Sure."

"I'll send the originals by secure courier. Express. Meantime, I'll email photos you can blow up."

"Sounds good."

"Can you get back to me ASAP?" She paused. Why not push things? Moore would. "Today, if possible."

"Possible. Later in the day. How's eighteen hundred?"

"Thank you."

Back at the station, Naslund looked up Louise Hennigan's number and phoned her. The call went to voicemail, the greeting saying Hennigan was on holiday. Naslund didn't leave a message. She'd keep trying until Hennigan answered.

Switching focus, she dug up the particulars on Elina Bayeux. *Elina Marlena Bayeux, née Vostokov; DOB 3/25/72; birthplace Volgograd, Russia.* Naslund stopped. *Volgograd.* Nikolai Filipov was from Volgograd. As for *Vostokov*, she thought MacTavish had mentioned the name. She reviewed the case notes. Right. On July fourteenth, he'd mentioned a Miss Vostokov, the agent before Hennigan. Convergence. Possibly double convergence: Volgograd and Vostokov.

Naslund continued her Bayeux née Vostokov search—12 Iris Road, Etobicoke, Ontario; D/L M3458-10402-12735. Divorced. She had a record: three counts of Disturbance of the Peace, all at 14 Iris Road. Apparently, she didn't like the neighbors. Or vice versa.

Naslund saved the details to her laptop. Sometimes you got lucky. Not only had she managed to recover a "lost" exhibit, it might lead somewhere. She didn't care about Elina Bayeux's record. She was a POI, regardless. She'd known Thom Tyler—and she'd fallen through the cracks. Even if the handwriting on the map wasn't hers, Naslund still had to interview her. For now, though, she had to wait for Harding.

She tried to concentrate on two open B&Es. The hours dragged on. Her concentration waned. By late afternoon, she couldn't concentrate anymore. She left the station, drove to the end of Bayview, and walked to a water-side lookout. The autumn air was cool but Colpoys

Bay was still warm. Swirls of mist rose off the water. The sun cut through them. Her mind was drawn to Hal. He was a good man, in more ways than one. He was three years younger, which she liked. Younger men were usually more open, more accepting. She'd checked him out. No sheet. He'd been working at city newspapers in Ottawa and Sudbury. She'd have to ask him why he'd come to Wiarton. Some day. For now, there'd be no questions. She didn't want to come across as a cop on a case. She'd done that before. Tonight they'd eat and laugh. And then, yes, then they'd enter the white room.

She glanced at her watch—1811. Where was Harding?

Her thoughts segued to the cold cases. With Moore's relentless pace, the investigations should have succeeded. She shook her head. Maybe they were snake-bitten.

As she was about to walk to her car, her radiophone receiver buzzed. It had to be Bickell. No one else called her by radiophone. "Sergeant Naslund."

"Bickell here," the chief hurriedly said. "Get to 414 Mallory Beach Road immediately. Suspicious death. Carrie MacLean."

Jesus. Carrie. "Copy."

"Reported by John Tyler."

"Copy." Naslund ran to her car.

Chapter 32

Siren shrieking, Naslund roared up to the Tyler cottage to find two cars in the driveway. She recognized both: MacLean's Subaru and John Tyler's Toyota. Bickell had just informed her that Kapanen and Chandler were en route. She parked on the roadside; hastily dug out a clean suit, shoe covers, and gloves; and hauled them on. Stepping quickly yet lightly, she skirted the cottage driveway and front path, calling out to Tyler Senior.

He answered on the third call. "Down here! The boathouse!"

"Stay there!" she called back. "Don't touch anything!"

She walked carefully down the stone staircase to the boathouse, avoiding the middle of each step, examining the stones and adjacent shrubs. No blood or noticeable prints. Nothing caught on the shrubs. Reaching the bottom, she saw Tyler Senior sitting on a rock ledge, staring at the bay.

He didn't move as she approached. "Mr. Tyler, you reported a death."

He turned to face her. "Yes."

"How did you know Carrie MacLean was dead?"

"Her forehead's completely caved in." He stopped. "Sorry, I'm feeling a bit off."

Naslund waited.

Eventually Tyler recovered his equanimity. "Her stomach is crisscrossed with stabs."

"Where is she?"

"At the end of the dock."

"When did you arrive at the cottage?"

"About half-an-hour ago."

She glanced at her watch. "About six o'clock?"

"After six. I was a bit late."

"For what?"

"Dinner at six. She'd invited me." Tyler sighed. "We were going to talk about the cottage. I'd decided to hand it over to her. For her son. She was going to have a son, you know."

Naslund nodded. "When did you find the body?"

"About ten after, I'd say. I didn't look. I called nine-one-one right away."

That fit, Naslund thought. Bickell's suspicious-death call came in just after 1811.

"She wasn't in the kitchen," Tyler said. "She wasn't anywhere in the cottage or studio. That's why I walked down to the boathouse." He stopped and shook his head.

"All right, Mr. Tyler. Please remain exactly where you are. Don't walk around. Protocol. We'll be taking you to the station. We need a formal statement."

"Of course."

"One more thing. When I arrived, you were staring out at Colpoys Bay. Why?"

"I thought I saw something."

"What?"

"Well, about ten minutes ago, I thought I spotted a small boat on the other side of the bay, far from here, heading toward Big Bay. Low in the water. One person aboard. But I'm not sure. With the sun going down, the bay was murky. At that distance, everything was murky."

"Did you see anyone on Mallory Beach Road half-an-hour ago? Any cars parked on the roadside?"

"No."

"Thank you."

Eyeing the sun, Naslund calculated the amount of daylight left. Less than thirty minutes. She strode toward the wooden dock. No blood. Within ten seconds, she saw the body.

Carrie MacLean lay on her back, her long frame limp, head rotated to the left. Naslund knew what that implied: the victim died on land. She approached the body, knelt, and placed a finger on the right hand. The skin was warm. Rigor hadn't begun. MacLean's bowels had loosened. The corpse smelled of feces.

Naslund shut out the stench and inventoried the scene. Multi-blow blood splatter discolored the dock. Blunt force splatter. She turned her gaze to the forehead. Almost unrecognizable. Shattered bone, blood, and brain matter, one eye swollen shut. MacLean's face bore no resemblance to the face Naslund had seen barely six hours ago. She bent closer. Four deep wounds, already hosting flesh flies. Almost immediately, she recognized the weapon imprints. She'd seen them twice already. The same ballpeen hammer used to attack Tyler and MacKenzie. The same MO. The same killer?

Her eyes moved down the body. The lower abdomen had been slashed multiple times. No blood flowing, not even oozing, specifying wounds sustained after death, when the heart had stopped. It appeared someone had killed MacLean with a hammer and then stabbed her.

Naslund quickly surveyed the puncture wounds. Over half-a-dozen slash lines, delivered by a wide blade, each slash about fifteen centimeters long, presenting an almost star-like pattern. Why the knife attack? Why the pattern? Almost instantly, an answer came to her.

The baby.

The killer had purposefully attacked MacLean's unborn child, purposefully made sure her son was dead. The star-like pattern told a story. The slash lines radiated out from the navel like spokes on a wheel, penetrating the whole lower abdomen, the home of the womb.

Naslund exhaled and stood. Someone had just removed two of Thom Tyler's potential heirs, not that MacLean had made an official claim on his estate. In time, her son—Thom's direct blood line—may have. Now he was dead.

In the corner of her eye, Naslund noticed Chandler approaching and turned. She was relieved to see him wearing CS shoe covers and gloves.

"Evening, Sergeant."

"Evening. I'd like you to go back up top, Constable, and guard the property. Don't allow anyone on it, not even the driveway. That includes the coroner. Please send him down as soon as he arrives. I want him clean. Get him in a whitesuit and shoe covers."

"Yes, Sergeant."

"Do you have a spare flashlight in your squad car?"

"Yes."

"Please send it down with him."

"Roger."

"Take John Tyler with you," she quietly said. "Lock him in your car for now."

"Do you think he's the perp?"

"There's no blood on him," Naslund said, then shrugged. She wouldn't bet against it, not this time.

Chandler nodded. "Better in S-S than B-S."

"Exactly." *Better in small shit than big shit.* "Tread gently. Don't walk on the path or driveway." With no more POIs to question, the best she could do was preserve evidence.

As Chandler and Tyler ascended the stairs, the sun sank below the beach cliffs. Almost instantly, the light level dropped. She phoned Bickell on her cell, reported the apparent murder, and asked for two PCs to canvass the neighborhood, one working south, the other north.

Standing by the corpse, she took in the darkening bay. Three dead. In a sense, four. Tyler, MacKenzie, MacLean, Tyler-MacLean's unborn son. There had to be a link. What was it? As she sought the connection, Kapanen arrived, short of breath, as usual.

"A dock," he announced. "Again."

She nodded.

He gestured at his clean suit. "Did you have to gift-wrap me?"

"You're welcome."

He snorted, handed her a flashlight, and pulled on gloves.

Naslund directed two beams at MacLean's head. Kapanen knelt down. "Not a drowning," he quickly said. "Look at the forehead. I detect four substantial blows by a blunt force instrument with a rounded impact surface." He stopped. "I'd say the same instrument used a few months ago." He moved closer. "Unless toxicology tests establish otherwise, the victim was killed by blunt-force blows. Please direct the light down the body, to the abdomen." Eventually Kapanen looked up. "I'd conjecture the victim was over six months pregnant. As you no doubt know, Detective, assaults on females are frequently associated with sexual interference. However, in this case, I see no evidence of sexual predation. On the other hand, there is ample evidence of post-mortem assault." He pointed at MacLean's stomach. "Look at those slashes. I detect nine, delivered by a wide-bladed knife. Extensive and deep slashes but relatively little bleeding. The victim was dead when the knife assault occurred."

Naslund nodded. As she thought.

"I won't hypothesize as to why the victim was assaulted in such a manner. That's your job." Kapanen jutted out his chin. *Get with it*, his pose seemed to say. He eyed her. "I hope you have more luck with this case than the last two."

"I hope so."

"In fact, from what I hear around town, you better. You're letting your side down."

She said nothing.

"Right. I thought so. Nothing to say."

She held her tongue. What could she say? She'd heard the same rumors, and she felt awful. She *was* letting the Bruce down.

"Now, on to what you really want. Actually, the only thing you detectives seem to care about. Which is?"

She shrugged then thought the hell with it. Play along. "PMI."

"Brilliant deduction."

She couldn't be bothered telling him off. And that she cared about justice, not PMI numbers.

He turned to the corpse. "No fully established rigor," he announced. "Which suggests the victim died less than four to six hours ago. As for lividity, no sign of it, not to the naked eye. Which only tells us the victim has been dead less than three hours. We'll have to rely on algor." The coroner carefully pulled up MacLean's blouse and pierced her right side with a liver thermometer. "Thirty-four-point-eight Celsius," he read. "I'd conjecture the victim died approximately two hours ago, possibly two-and-a-half. Definitely less than three."

"Thank you." She turned her back to Kapanen and

called Bickell. "Murder confirmed. Two to three hours ago. Perps might still be close."

"Roger that. I'll road-check the base and top of the peninsula, as well as Highways Twenty-Six and Ten. We'll cover the airports and marinas too."

At this point, Naslund knew that apprehending MacLean's murderers was possible, but a long shot. "Look for a ballpeen hammer and a wide-bladed knife and perp clothes with blood."

"Roger. By the way, I called Central. DI Moore has been summoned."

She caught Bickell's snideness. "Better get his murder room ready," she joked.

"I'll leave that to you, Detective."

"I thought you would."

"They're due first thing tomorrow."

"I'll set it up tonight."

She signed off and faced Kapanen.

"Are you ready for my final findings?" he asked.

"I have enough information. Detection One-Oh-One."

He huffed.

"I'll read your report later," she said. "Be careful going up the stairs."

"You care, Detective?"

"Of course." She smiled over-sweetly. "Be careful not to damage any evidence." Her duty phone blared. "Sergeant Naslund, OPP."

"Harding here."

"Yes Constable?"

"We have a match. All three documents."

"Thank you. Appreciate your work."

She pocketed her phone, thinking, *Yes, a match.* Considering the handwriting on the map, it seemed Elina Bayeux had been tailing Thom Tyler, or she'd sent someone to tail him. Intuition told Naslund it could be

Louise Hennigan. In any case, she had three hooks: possible timeline and motive, plus a forensic hit. She'd get to that later. For now, her hands were full.

Waiting for the morgue transport, she went over the MacLean CS in her mind. Given the head wounds, there should be blood on the dock leading to the stone stairs, and possibly on the stairs themselves and the property above. But there was none. No prints either, no evidence of perps going up or down the stairs. Had the perps used a boat, the boat Tyler Senior might have seen? Perps? Think again, she told herself. Tyler Senior mentioned seeing one person. There might only be one perp. On the other hand, considering the hammer attack, there seemed to be a connection to the Tyler and MacKenzie murders, and they'd been committed by two or more perps. She shook her head. No definite connection.

As she kept her vigil, searching for connections, the sky began filling with stars. A half-moon rose above the dock, its red face eerily similar to the one she'd seen months ago, sitting by Thom Tyler's body. She turned away. She'd seen enough red moons. Waves lapped against the dock. The sound brought her back to the bay. If Tyler Senior was right, he'd seen a boat low in water—which implied a heavy load, possibly a large man—heading toward Big Bay. The Albin hijackers had used Big Bay. Was the heavily-loaded boat manned by one of the hijackers? Nikolai Filipov had fallen off the grid, but it could be the other bruiser. Maybe she had more than a hammer connection to the Tyler-MacKenzie cases.

Chapter 33

Wiarton. October 1st:

Naslund arrived at the station at 0600. She'd already heard from Bickell. So far, the road checks, still ongoing, hadn't produced any leads. Ditto for the airport and marina checks and the canvassing of Mallory Beach. Chu's MU team had processed the cottage property and found no blood other than the splatter by MacLean's head and two smears nearby, on the water side of the dock. Their work suggested the killer or killers had come and gone by water.

Unfortunately, Tyler Senior's statement didn't corroborate that. He'd mentioned a very vague sighting of a boat. The team had no verifiable connection to a boat-based murderer, let alone an Albin hijacker. As Naslund entered the foyer, Inspector Moore strode toward her.

"Well, well, Sergeant." The inspector was all smiles.

"Good to see you, sir." And it was.

"Can you join me in the murder room?"

"Why don't we use my office?" She grinned. "Your office."

"The murder room is fine."

"I insist, sir." She'd cleared her desk last night.

"All right. Thank you, Sergeant."

Inside the office, Naslund sat in the guest chair.

"I'd like you to get me up to speed," Moore said. "I read the coroner's report. Homicide by hammer blows. Do you agree?"

"Yes."

"And the knife assault? Post-mortem?"

"Yes. By the way, I have a theory on that. A hunch, I should say." She'd seen over twenty dead bodies in her four-plus years in the Bruce, mostly traffic fatalities, except for three murders—two domestics and a botched B&E—and now three murders in three months. She figured greed was the key. A sign of the times. "I think MacLean's murderer knifed her unborn child. A son. The murderer wanted to eliminate him as an heir. You read about the nine slash lines?"

He nodded.

"They radiate out from MacLean's navel like spokes on a wheel, covering the whole lower abdomen. The womb."

He nodded again. "I see where you're going. Two possible heirs with one stone."

"Yes. Eliminate blood lines. Given the excessive force—hammering and knifing—I'd say hate's a motive, but greed too. Money may be the main motive."

"I agree. Any obvious perps?"

She shook her head.

"Perhaps Larmer?"

She didn't see it, or MacTavish either. "I don't think MacLean's death will enrich any of the previous suspects."

Moore nodded. "I'll get M and M on that."

"Another thing, sir. I have a new lead on the Tyler case."

"You do? What's new?"

"Looks like a former art agent, an Elina Bayeux, tailed Tyler or she sent someone to tail him. Possibly Louise Hennigan."

"Hennigan?"

"Yes. That's another hunch. Yesterday MacLean told me she saw Hennigan skulking around Mallory Beach Road about a week before the Tyler murder. Early in the morning, twice. I tried to reach Hennigan a few times. She's on holiday. Last night, I tried to find her whereabouts but didn't succeed." Naslund paused. "But we could go after Bayeux. She lives in the city. Etobicoke. Her maiden name is Vostokov. It appears she's the art agent before Hennigan. MacTavish mentioned her on July fourteenth."

"Is your Bayeux lead solid?"

"Not ironclad, but solid. Possible timeline and motive plus a handwriting match. I know we have a new investigation on our plate, but I'd like to interview her ASAP." Naslund pressed on. "Maybe this evening?" She'd almost let the map slip through the cracks. She didn't want to lose Bayeux.

Moore sat back and pursed his lips. "Okay," he eventually said, "here's a plan. How about you debrief the ninjas and Lowrie this morning, and then work on POI lists, one personal, one professional. MacLean may have made some business enemies. I've been told to expect her autopsy early this afternoon, but Lowrie and I can attend it. You can leave for the city around sixteen hundred."

"Good. I'll email you Bayeux's particulars and my notes on that lead."

He nodded.

"Do you think you can call in a favor at Metro? Get Bayeux into a station this evening? Any station," she added.

"Glad to. By the way, I'd like to be there. In the shadow room."

"Of course."

දැංග

Toronto. October 1st:

In the late evening light, Metro 22 Division looked almost deserted. As Naslund pulled into the parking lot, she spotted Moore's black Ford Explorer. Having cleared security, she was directed to a basement interview room she'd used a decade ago. It looked the same: faded gray, not a lick of fresh paint. Bayeux was due in ten minutes. Naslund took off her coat and walked to the shadow room. Before she could knock on the door, Moore opened it.

"Good trip, Sergeant?"

"Fine. And yours?"

"Not bad. I read your notes. Bayeux-Vostokov looks promising."

Promising, Naslund thought. She hoped so, and more. "Any suggestions?"

He shook his head then pursed his lips. "Oh, one. M and M got her tax records. She shows zero employment income for the last three years. Ask her what she's working at."

"Right."

"And impound her car. Might get a soil analysis match. But I bet you already thought of that."

Naslund nodded. She had.

"Got some possible leads. The MU team established that the blood smears on the dock were made by a gloved hand. Lends some credence to the water access theory. I also have news from MacLean's autopsy. The fetus was stabbed multiple times. Dr. Leonard reported that its heart was ruptured. It was likely targeted."

She nodded, unable to reply. Her job sometimes pierced her heart. She turned away and walked slowly to the interview room, inhaling deeply and slowly exhaling. Opening the door, she ordered herself to focus.

As she sat in her chair, the POI was led in, flanked by two Metro Homicide detectives, Shiffman and Tilley. Naslund recognized the names from the case notes. So, Moore had pulled more than one string. Metro Homicide was in their corner, not just Div 22.

Naslund gestured Bayeux to the Slider. The two detectives left. The POI looked younger than her age, early-thirties rather than mid-forties. Her dark brown hair was pulled back in a bun. Her eyes were lively and intelligent. She wore faded skin-tight jeans and a tight-fitting denim shirt. The clothes were a bit déclassé. Or maybe just old. Despite them, she projected youth and refinement.

"Good evening, Miss Bayeux. I'm Detective Sergeant Naslund, OPP." Neither the words *detective* nor *OPP* seemed to bother Bayeux. She now knew she wasn't in on a local disturbance charge. "We appreciate you coming in to the station," Naslund began.

"I had no choice."

No sign of an accent, Naslund noted. "Miss Bayeux," she paused, "do you prefer to be called Miss or Ms.?"

"Ms."

"Would you like a drink?" Naslund asked. "Coffee? Tea?"

"Tea would be nice. No milk, three sugars."

Having returned with the tea, Naslund scrutinized Bayeux as she sipped it. Not thrilled to be there, Naslund concluded, but at ease. "What's your maiden name, Ms. Bayeux?"

"Vostokov."

"Where were you born?"

"Russia."

"Where in Russia?"

"Volgograd."

Step One, Naslund thought. "Ms. Bayeux, I understand you were an art agent for Thom Tyler. How long did you work as Mr. Tyler's agent?"

"Depends on who you ask."

"Please elaborate."

"He never fired me."

"When did you start?"

"Ten years ago."

"But he had other agents after you. Two, according to our records."

"Your records." Bayeux waved dismissively, then shrugged. "Okay, he had other agents. However, I was more than an agent. I was his muse." She smiled with pride. "But I don't expect you to understand that."

"Why not?"

"You're not an artist."

Naslund ignored the gibe. The majority of people thought cops were one-dimensional—or, as MacTavish might say, Philistines. She rarely tried to change their minds. "Did you know Tyler's other agents?"

"One of them."

"Name?" Naslund asked.

"Louise Hennigan."

Step Two. "Are you friends?"

"Not really. She used to come around to my place a lot, but stopped about five years ago."

"When was the last time you saw her?"

"About five years ago."

"When was the last time you spoke to her?"

"The same, Detective."

"But you work in the same world."

"No, we don't. I represent the avant-garde. She's mainstream."

Naslund decided to move on. Perhaps there was no current connection between Bayeux and Hennigan. "How long did you know Mr. Tyler?"

"Twenty-three years."

Twenty-three, Naslund thought. Well before Larmer. Well before MacLean.

"I was twenty-two when we met." Bayeux raised her chin. "I don't mind revealing my age. But you know it already."

Of course we do. And more. "Ms. Bayeux, what's your profession?"

"Artist and art agent."

"Current profession, Ms. Bayeux."

"Artist and art agent."

"You reported zero income the last three years from art or art sales."

She shrugged.

"How do you make a living?"

"I have property."

"Where?"

"Russia. And payments from my ex-husband."

"We'll be verifying that." Naslund eyed her. "Why didn't you reassume your maiden name after you got divorced?"

"I like Bayeux."

Naslund pulled her chair closer to the table. "Are you aware that Mr. Tyler was murdered?"

"Yes."

"Why didn't you go to his funeral?"

"I wouldn't have been welcome."

"Why not?"

"His current woman is a *harpy*." Bayeux spat the word out. "No, beyond a harpy. She's a gold digger."

Tit for tat, Naslund thought. One's a gold digger; the other's a slut. "Did you visit the Bruce Peninsula this past summer?"

"No."

"No trip to Mallory Beach?"

"No. I wasn't in the Bruce, as I said. In fact, I didn't leave Toronto this summer."

"Can someone verify that?"

Bayeux nodded. "My partner."

"What kind? Business or romantic?"

"Romantic."

"Name?"

"Max Carling."

"Address and phone number?"

Naslund wrote them on a pad. "So, Ms. Bayeux, you weren't in the Bruce recently. Nonetheless, we have a Bruce Peninsula map with your handwriting on it. Why would that be?"

"I don't know." She shrugged. "I used to go up there a lot."

"Used to?"

"Yes. Until about five years ago."

"Why did you stop?"

"The Harpy."

"Her name?"

"MacLean. *MacDirty*, more like it."

More bad-mouthing, Naslund reflected. Was there malicious jealousy at play? Possible murderous jealousy? "Have you seen Mr. Tyler in the last five years?"

Bayeux shook her head.

"You never met for a drink or a meal?"

"Never."

"For a coffee?"

"Never."

"Did you have any contact with Mr. Tyler? Phone? Email?"

Bayeux nodded. "I sent him a birthday card every year."

"How?"

"By post."

Naslund drew out a copy of the map. "Is this your handwriting?"

She glanced at the writing. "Yes. Where did you get that?" She reached for the map.

Naslund withdrew it.

"That's a copy," Bayeux said. "Where's the original?"

"We'll get to that later."

"Where is it?"

"I assure you, the original is safe. It hasn't been harmed."

Bayeux seemed mollified.

"What does *Four-One-Four MB* mean?" Naslund asked.

"It refers to Four-One-Four Mallory Beach Road. Thom's address."

"And the *X*?"

"It marks the address."

"The *JY8 five-thirty*?"

"Johan's Year Eight. He—he's my son."

"The *five-thirty*?"

"His birthday. The thirtieth day of the fifth month. By the way, that's his map. Where did you get the original?"

"From a friend."

"Where? What friend?"

"Steady now, Ms. Bayeux. When did you write that information on the map?"

"Years ago. Johan was eight."

"How old is he now?"

"Twenty-one."

"What's his birth date?"

"May thirtieth, 1996."

No delay, Naslund saw. "Why did he have a Bruce Peninsula map?"

Bayeux hesitated, as if considering her whole future, and that of her son. "He used to go up there."

"When?"

Bayeux stared at her hands. Naslund suspected she was deciding how much to tell her. Finally she looked up. "When I did. I wanted him to meet Thom." She hesitated again. "To know Thom."

Bingo, Naslund thought. *To know Thom.* There was more to Bayeux's words than *knowing* Thom. Something about her eyes—defiant, yet wounded—reminded Naslund of Jenny Murphy. Had Elina Bayeux been pregnant—pregnant by Thom Tyler? Naslund sensed a common thread. Elina Bayeux, Jenny Murphy, Carrie MacLean. More than a thread, a workable connection. "Was Thom Tyler his father?"

Bayeux wavered then nodded. "How did you know?"

"A guess, Ms. Bayeux." Naslund's head started roaring. The case was cracking open. She ordered herself to calm down. "Did Johan know that?"

"No."

"Are you sure?"

"Yes."

"What's your son's full name?"

"Johan Ivanovich Bayeux."

"Where is he?"

"Laval. I haven't seen him for three years. He's been living near my ex since he was eighteen."

"What's your ex's full name?"

"Jean Claude Bayeux."

"Those three public disturbances at Fourteen Iris Road, were they Johan's?"

Bayeux hesitated. "Yes." She bowed her head and stared at her hands again. Eventually she looked up. "He was a handful as a boy. Alternately depressed then fuming with rage. Always in trouble at school. He went off the rails when he was fourteen."

"The charges are on your sheet, not your son's. Were you trying to protect him?"

"Yes." Her eyes misted over. "I tried, Sergeant. I tried. I really did."

Naslund stood, turned toward the door, and then stopped. "Where were you on Monday July eighth?"

"Toronto. I told you, I was in Toronto all summer."

Naslund said nothing. She left the POI and walked directly to the shadow room, wondering if Elina Bayeux had told her the whole truth.

Inspector Moore looked antsy. "I set the wheels in motion on Johan Bayeux," he said. "The Sûreté du Québec is on the case, as well as the Laval police. His mother may have set him up to murder Tyler. Then MacKenzie and MacLean."

"Exactly."

"I got prelims on him. He works as a bartender at a nightclub near the Port de Montréal. He's got a hefty sheet for a twenty-one-year-old: two counts of cocaine possession, one of assault, one of aggravated assault."

Naslund nodded.

"I asked Shiffman to check out the Max Carling alibi." Moore rolled on. "We should go after the son ASAP."

"Right."

"I booked us a twenty-three-hundred flight to Montreal. Billy Bishop to Pierre Trudeau. First, I want to question the mother." He glanced at his watch. "We have two hours, enough time. Normally, I'd let her hang for a bit, but not this time. Are you okay with that?"

"Absolutely."

He smiled. "How did you know Tyler was the father?"

"Intuition," she said, "and luck."

He shook his head. "Women's intuition." He grinned. "We need more of it."

℘ℑ℘

Sitting in the shadow room, Naslund watched Bayeux stand and shake Moore's hand. "Detective Inspector Moore, OPP. Homicide," he added. "Have a seat, Miss Bayeux."

"Ms."

"A seat, *Miss* Bayeux. I'm going to ask you a few more questions."

She shrugged then sat. In the space of a few minutes, she looked dejected.

Moore remained standing. "You said you met Thom Tyler twenty-three years ago. Where?"

"Toronto."

"Elaborate, Miss Bayeux. Exactly where."

Bayeux rolled her eyes.

Moore stared at her. She stared back.

Naslund glanced at her watch.

Eventually Bayeux looked down. From the slump of her shoulders, it appeared she couldn't be bothered to resist Moore anymore. "At an art gallery opening," she said, "at Calhoun's, to be *exact,* on Queen West. It's gone now."

"Miss Bayeux, where were you on the night of July seventh from nine p.m. onward?"

"As I told the other officer, I was at home. That's Twelve Iris Road, Etobicoke. Max Carling can confirm that. He was there."

Moore sat. "How did you contact your son in July?"

"I didn't."

"Throwaway cellphone? Letter? Private courier?"

"I didn't contact him."

"Where were you yesterday, September thirtieth?"

"Home, in Toronto."

"All day?"

"Yes, other than a walk I took with Max."

"Can someone prove that, other than Max?"

"Yes, his mother. She was with us all day. Her friend as well, Eleanor Crawley."

Moore shuffled through a pile of papers and pulled out a copy of the Bruce map. "Is this your handwriting?"

"You know it is."

"Why is it on this map?"

"I wrote that thirteen years ago, as I already said. The map was for Johan. A memory of his father. Biological father, that is. Thom Tyler abandoned him at birth. Thirteen years ago, the two of them went for a hike on the Bruce Trail. A short one. Very short." Bayeux shook her head in disgust. "Thom Tyler. The famous Thom Tyler."

Naslund evaluated Bayeux's eyes. *I gave Thom everything*, they seemed to say, *everything, and he gave nothing back.*

Bayeux shook her head again. "Johan was cheated, short-changed, abandoned—call it what you want. His real father may be a prick but at least he was there for Johan."

"Is that why your son killed Thom Tyler?" Moore asked.

"What do you mean?"

"Johan killed Mr. Tyler because he was abandoned."

"Johan didn't know he was abandoned."

"We think he did. He knew he was adopted."

"Pardon?"

"Johan knew he was adopted. Jean Bayeux told him."

"You're lying!"

Exactly, Naslund thought.

"No, Miss Bayeux. I'm not."

"You're lying."

Moore quietly shook his head. "We just spoke to your ex," he softly said.

Bayeux seemed to believe him. "I told Jean to bury that. Forever! Fool! The boy has a mean streak, a vengeful mean streak."

"Vengeful enough to kill?"

Bayeux didn't reply.

"Miss Bayeux, I'm going to leave you with Detectives Shiffman and Tilley. You'll remain at the station until we find your son. You'll be kept isolated. No visitors, no cellphone, no electronics. Do you understand?"

She nodded. Her eyes welled with tears.

Chapter 34

Naslund and Moore exited the Arrivals Hall of Pierre Elliott Trudeau airport at 0030. In a matter of seconds, a tall young man in a black leather jacket strode up to them. Introductions over and IDs verified, the young Sûreté detective hustled next to Naslund.

"Aucun bagage?" he asked.

She shook her head. He was a good-looking guy.

"Rien?"

"Rien. Nothing, thank you."

Moore stepped up and started rattling off questions in rapid-fire French. To Naslund's ear, he sounded like a real Quebecer, not a Parisian. *Quelle surprise.*

As Detective "Leather" answered Moore, his eyes strayed to Naslund, checking her out on the way to his car. With a flourish, he opened the front passenger door for her. She ducked in the back, looking him in the eye and pointing to her ring finger. She'd worked in Quebec before. If you didn't want to play, it was best to let the boys know right away. On the plane, she'd pulled on her old wedding band. It had its uses.

Leaving the airport, Leather angled his rear mirror to

put her in view. She shook her head. He winked. The ring didn't seem to deter him. She slid to the far right so that he couldn't see her. On the way to the Laval Police HQ, she opened her window. The breeze was sharp and clean. She felt invigorated.

Leather dropped them at Laval HQ in short order, winking again at Naslund as he drove off. *I'll try you later*, his grin said.

In the HQ foyer, she and Moore were greeted by two Laval homicide detectives, who, thankfully, paid little attention to her. They immediately began debriefing Moore in Quebecois. Naslund picked up the gist of the conversation. Johan Bayeux was in a holding cell on a phony charge, suspected possession of cocaine for trafficking. He hadn't been in the local drug game for months. Apparently, he'd gone straight. The detectives figured he was preparing to move on to something bigger, maybe something international. Naslund agreed. She'd seen it before. The underworld career ladder beckoned. Bayeux had come in willingly, seemingly without a care. However, they'd cuffed his hands behind his back. He'd snapped once in the past. Playing it safe, the older detective said in Joual.

Moore turned to her. "Why don't you start Bayeux? He speaks English. I'll sit in the backroom."

"Okay."

"I'll likely jump in."

She nodded.

"You know, good cop, bad cop. Got any suggestions for me?"

She smiled quizzically.

"Seriously," he said.

"Can't think of any."

He shrugged. "Next time. See, I can ask for directions."

"Heard and noted."

ⅇⅇⅇ

The interview room looked like any other Naslund had used. Same worn paint, same metal table, same glaring lights. She tested the Slider. It went the other way, tilting POIs backward. Not bad, she thought. Although it didn't force POIs into the hands of a questioner, it would force them to sit up straight more often. Less hiding of facial tells. Always a bonus.

As she arranged a sham accordion file on the table—stuffed with bogus reports—two big Laval officers led Johan Bayeux in, sat him in the Slider, and arranged his cuffs behind the chair-back. The POI looked unruffled. He was far bigger than the officers, close to two meters tall, muscular, with a cleanly-shaven face, and thick wavy black hair. He wore a sleeveless black T-shirt and sleek black track pants. His biceps were huge. Definitely strong enough to attack Tyler and MacKenzie, she saw, not to mention MacLean. And tall enough to hammer MacKenzie on the top of the head. Incongruously, his face said *bon vivant*, not raging muscleman.

"Good morning, Mr. Bayeux," she began. "I'm Detective Sergeant Naslund, OPP."

"Morning, Detective," he replied pleasantly.

With his size, hair, and urbane demeanor, he reminded her of Mario Lemieux, one of her favorite hockey players. "You were brought in on a suspected drug offense, but it seems there was a mistake."

"Ah. I thought so. Well," he said forgivingly, "mistakes happen."

"So, I expect you're wondering why you're still here."

He grinned. "Exactly."

"As I mentioned, I'm an OPP officer. That means I'm from Ontario. But I'm sure you know that."

"I do. It's my home province," he said with apparent fondness.

Bayeux might be young, Naslund thought, but he knew how to dissemble. Well-spoken. No hint of a temper. Not what she expected, given the shackles and his sheet. Regardless, they had some seemingly damning intel on him. Back at Div 22, Moore had contacted Central to request a rush three-month Ontario trace of Bayeux's license number. The results had come in as they'd landed in Montreal. Bayeux's plate was photographed three times on Highway 401, the main corridor between Ontario and Quebec, on July seventh and fifteenth, and then on September thirtieth. The plate was also photographed on July eighth at 0724 on Highway 6, just south of Wiarton. Moore had already requested a soil analysis of the car. July seventh, eighth, fourteenth, and fifteenth were the windows for the Tyler and MacKenzie murders; September thirtieth, for the MacLean murder. The Laval detectives had determined that Bayeux was off work on all five days. Even if he could prove he hadn't been in his car, he had some questions to answer.

Naslund smiled disarmingly. "I hope you can help us. We have evidence that a Quebec car registered to your name was in Ontario on four different days recently. Specifically, July seventh and eighth as well as July fifteenth. And then September thirtieth."

A barely perceptible cloud passed over Bayeux's face.

"Were you in your car in Ontario on those days?" She gave him another friendly smile. "Take your time. Think about it."

He held her gaze. However, she couldn't help seeing his shoulders rolling. Intimidating shoulders. "Yes," he agreeably said, "I was there the first week in July. I'm sorry, I don't remember the exact dates. Possibly the seventh and eighth. Then a week later. I don't remember exactly."

"What about two days ago, September thirtieth?"

"No." He rolled his shoulders again. "I had the flu. I was stuck at home."

A lie, Naslund thought. If she knew Moore, he was already asking for local help to check that alibi. "Did you enjoy your Ontario trips?" she asked.

"Very much."

"What were you doing?"

"I was on holiday."

"That's a lot of coming and going, Mr. Bayeux. Anything to do with drugs?"

"Oh, no. Nothing."

Likely correct, given that he was currently out of the game. But she was after something else. "You're sure?" she asked.

"Yes, Sergeant. Absolutely."

"Good." Enough of the fake drug line. She now had a read on Bayeux. Moore probably had one too. Whenever Bayeux told the truth, the corners of his lips curled up a fraction of an inch. It'd now be easier to catch him at a lie. "Did you happen to visit the Bruce Peninsula in July?"

"No."

Another lie, she suspected. His car had been there. However, someone else could have been driving it. "Are you sure?"

"Why are you asking?"

She regarded him with forbearance. Answering a question with a question. A classic evasion tactic. And a sign of guilt. "Did you travel on Highway Six in July?"

"No."

She scrutinized his mouth. His lips were straight. She

saw no up-curl. That suggested a lie. However, his shoulders and legs were quiet. No facial cloud. No other tells. "What about Owen Sound," she asked, "were you there?"

"No," he said. However, his lips said otherwise.

"Mallory Beach?"

"No."

A tiny hesitation plus straight lips. She'd bet he'd been in both places. Live by the car, die by the car—by soil analysis, by license scanning, or both.

Bayeux smiled, but it was definitely forced. "Why the third degree?"

She said nothing but smiled back, thinking it would be a good time to start a bad cop routine.

As if on cue, Inspector Moore stepped into the room. He nodded curtly at Bayeux and gave his usual greeting. "Detective Inspector Moore, OPP. Homicide," he added with a knowing sneer.

Naslund enjoyed the greeting. Maybe she was getting used to Moore's shtick.

He sat next to her and tilted his head back. "Mr. Bayeux," he began, "you said you weren't in the Bruce Peninsula in either July or September of this year."

"That's right."

"Would you take a lie detector test?"

"Why would I do that?"

"For your benefit. I repeat, would you take a lie detector test?"

"Yes—yes, of course."

Naslund noted the evasion and the double *yes*. As for the polygraph reference, she knew Moore was simply trying to unsettle Bayeux. Polygraph evidence was inadmissible. "All right, Mr. Bayeux, let's assume you weren't there. Then perhaps you can tell us why your car was?"

Bayeux didn't skip a beat. "I lent it to someone."

"Is that right?"

"Yes." Bayeux's eyes hardened. He flexed his shoulders. Apparently, he didn't like to be challenged.

"So," Moore said, "you lent it to someone to drive from Montreal to the Bruce Peninsula?"

"No, from Toronto to the Bruce."

Straight lips, Naslund saw, plus *the Bruce*. Bayeux had used the local term, which implied familiarity.

"Who?" Moore asked.

"A friend of a friend."

Moore smiled patiently. "Who?"

"A guy visiting Canada."

"What's his name?"

"I don't remember." Bayeux's eyes flashed. *Don't ride me*, they warned.

Moore seemed unperturbed. "I asked you, who?"

Naslund had to hand it to Moore. He was tenacious, more a terrier than a bulldog. Bayeux could break him in half like a twig. And her too. No doubt at the same time.

Bayeux didn't reply.

Moore pressed on. "Who? I'm going to keep asking. Who?"

Bayeux clenched his jaw. His demeanor shifted. *Back off!* his eyes shouted.

Moore grinned. "Mr. Bayeux, our conversation is just beginning. For starters, you can tell me who borrowed your car."

"A friend of a friend."

"Who?" Moore's look said he could play a waiting game far longer than Bayeux.

Bayeux glared at him. "I don't remember."

Straight lips again, Naslund saw.

"I don't like liars," Moore said and turned to her. "Do you, Sergeant?"

"No." *Play the good cop, stay on Bayeux's side.* She

shook her head sadly. "We'd like to help, Mr. Bayeux, but lies torpedo your cause."

Moore faced the suspect. "You may as well tell us. We'll find out."

Bayeux shrugged insouciantly, but his face betrayed him. He looked anything but carefree. His cheeks were two shades darker.

A snap's coming, Naslund thought.

"Tell us," Moore repeated.

"Tell *you*?" Bayeux snorted. "I want a lawyer."

Moore gestured for Naslund to leave, and then stopped at the door. "*Bon nuit,* Mr. Bayeux*.*"

"Fuck you."

"What's your read?" Moore asked Naslund in the corridor.

"Bayeux's the killer," she said with certainty.

"Women's intuition?"

"Something like that."

"We'll wait him out," Moore said. "He'll crack eventually."

For a change, she agreed.

⁓⁓⁓

Next morning, as Moore and Naslund tucked into pancakes drenched in pure maple syrup, his phone rang. When he put it down, he smiled broadly. "Guess who just turned up at Dorval Airport en route to Moscow?"

"Who?"

"Nikolai Filipov. The man's fake passport was good, but his fake beard failed him."

She grinned. "By the hair of his chinny-chin-chin."

Moore chuckled. "The Sûreté is bringing him to Laval HQ. He admitted to knowing Bayeux. Said his buddy was in Ontario four days in July. And apparently Saint Nik has more to say."

"No luck for three months," she said, "and then the dam breaks."

"Finally."

☙❧

Late that evening, Moore and Naslund were sitting in a bar near the Laval Holiday Inn. Naslund had conducted two long interviews with Bayeux, his arms and legs shackled. She'd stroked his ego, playing up his abandonment at the hands of Tyler. He'd said that when he was a boy Tyler had promised him many things, many times, but never delivered. The genius was always too busy. He was scum. By the end of the second interview, Bayeux had rescinded his alibi for September thirtieth and admitted to being in Wiarton during all three murder windows. Then his lawyer advised him to clam up and later tried to make a plea bargain. As for Filipov, he hadn't clammed up. He'd spilled the beans, trading intel in exchange for leniency.

Just after noon, in a Laval HQ interview room, Filipov had confessed to aiding and abetting Bayeux in the murders of Tyler and MacKenzie, but not MacLean. He'd been hiding in Northern Quebec when MacLean was killed. When Naslund asked him why he helped Bayeux, he said he owed money. Bayeux had paid him thirty grand. After his arrest at Dorval, he figured it wasn't enough, so he sold out Bayeux.

Filipov's confession filled in a lot of blanks. While he handled the Albin 35, unscrewed the Mackinaw centerboard, and wiped blood on the boat's boom, Bayeux killed Tyler. During the MacKenzie murder, Filipov wiped the saliva on the beer cans and helped Bayeux throw MacKenzie off the wharf. Both men shaved their heads a week before Tyler's murder, and then let their hair grow back. There was another person involved, someone Filipov had never met. A woman named Louise, who'd once been Tyler's art agent, had pre-scouted the Wiarton area. She'd let Bayeux know Tyler's routine. She'd also carried out the July eleventh theft of the two mooring lines. She'd worn a bald-man's disguise.

Moore issued an all-ports international APB for Louise Hennigan. Five hours later she was apprehended in a cottage near Kingston, Ontario. She admitted to aiding Johan Bayeux in the Tyler murder, but claimed she had nothing to do with the others. Naslund and Moore would interview her themselves. They figured Bayeux had been close to her as a teenager. Maybe more than close.

Now, sipping a scotch, Moore glanced at Naslund. "I get Filipov's game: money. What about Hennigan's?"

"Probably money and revenge."

Moore nodded. "Sounds right. Just like Bayeux. Assuming DNA proved he was Tyler's son, with MacLean and her son dead, he'd get a big piece of Tyler's estate. If he played his cards right, he'd be the main heir."

"Exactly," Naslund said. "The front of the blood line."

Chapter 35

Colpoys Bay. July 8th:

Thom Tyler closed in on his favorite fishing shoal. The closer he got to the shoal, the stronger he felt it Something was waiting for him. "Show yourself," he said under his breath, "make yourself known."

He scanned the bay. No vessels in sight.

A few minutes later, he looked up from uncoiling his first fishing line and saw a boat at the southern end of White Cloud. It looked like the Griffith Island Albin. The boat started steaming north.

ભ૭ભ૭

"Hello," a big man called. "You are named Tie-lar?"

Thom nodded. The man was younger than him, bald, with wide shoulders. He didn't look like a local. He had ice-blue eyes. His skin was as pale as a peeled potato. Another young man appeared, bigger than the first. The new youngster looked familiar. Was it Johan Bayeux? Young Johan? Thom hadn't seen him for years. He was tall and heavily muscled. He had the same nose and lips as Johan but his eyes looked decades older.

The youngster waved his associate to the wheel, leaped out of the Albin cockpit, surged forward using the handrail and hung two fenders off the bow. "Grab the rope," he said and tossed Thom a line.

For some reason, Thom didn't question him.

"Tie the boats together," the youngster said.

Again Thom complied. Was it Johan? "Johan, how are you?"

The youngster didn't reply. He stepped aboard the Mackinaw. "You're going down." He pulled out a hammer. "What's yours will be mine."

What's this? Thom thought. "Who are you?"

The youngster lunged forward with the hammer. "Your son. Johan."

Thom screamed and pawed at his right eye.

"You're dead!" Johan grunted. "Dead! You did nothing for me. Not a fucking thing." He raised the hammer.

Thom dodged to the left and held up his arms. The hammer glanced off them. Then it hit his head, again and again. In his good eye he saw a screwdriver.

He blacked out. He came to his senses underwater. He felt a weight around his ankle. He kicked up, fighting the weight, cresting the surface. Then the weight dragged him under.

Even in July, the deep water was shockingly cold. He struggled to keep his legs and arms moving. He couldn't see anything. His hearing seemed magnified. The bay was alive with whooshes and whirrs.

The cold drove spikes into his body. His heartbeat faded. The bay took over.

Whoosh.

Whirr.

ACKNOWLEDGMENTS

My deepest thanks to the staff of Black Opal Books for their enthusiasm and support, especially to Lauri Wellington, Faith C., and Jack Jackson. Over the years, many writers, Arts Councils, friends, and family members have helped me on the writing road, among them Lesley Choyce, Guy Vanderhaeghe, Jane Nicholls, Ken Haigh, Ontario Arts Council, Canada Council, J.R. Harrison, Bill Gries, Fraser Mann, Mike Potter, John Potter, and, of course, Ninety-Nine.

About the Author

A.M. Potter grew up in Nova Scotia and Boston. He's traveled the world, working dozens of jobs, from sommelier to art salesman to IT analyst. Like any good detective, he knows both sides of the thin blue line. He's used numerous aliases (for non-nefarious purposes, of course). You'll have to take his word on that. *Bay of Blood* is the first book in the Detective Eva Naslund series. Potter writes North Noir, aka Canuck Noir.

CPSIA information can be obtained
at www.ICGtesting.com
Printed in the USA
FSHW021006030120
65696FS